Barry Wilson

Fires
of
Time

EPOCH
PRESS

Salt Lake City, Utah

Epoch Press
Salt Lake City, Utah

Copyright © 1999 by Barry Wilson

All rights reserved. No part of this book may be reproduced in any form or by any electronic or mechanical means, including information storage and retrieval systems, without permission in writing from the author.

This is a work of fiction. The events and characters portrayed are imaginary. Their resemblance, if any, to real-life counterparts is entirely coincidental.

Library of Congress Catalog Card Number:
99-63289
Wilson, Barry
Fires of Time / by Barry Wilson

ISBN 0-9725615-0-1

Printed in the United States of America

First Edition
10 9 8 7 6 5 4 3 2 1

EPOCH PRESS
Visit our World Wide Web page at:
www.firesoftime.net

Acknowledgments

I'm grateful to all the people who gave me encouragement and support while writing this book. The firehouse crews who made me feel like I had some writing ability and the helicopter crews who left me alone when I locked myself away for hours on end. And my family who indulged me through it all.

Jeff and Tom Zirbes: Friends. Thank you for providing me the surface to write upon.

Dave and Mary Bailey: Friends. Your ideas and criticism helped me immensely and your enthusiastic encouragement was invaluable. Thanks.

David Nielson: Battalion Chief and friend whose home library rivals that of Scott McLean. Thank you for all your help. Whenever I needed facts about fire history, you came through with flying colors.

Sonny Hendricks: Helicopter pilot and friend. I valued your ideas and reinforcement. Thank you for spending so much of your valuable free time between flights reading for me.

Alana Olsen: Author and friend. Your encouragement and advice meant the world to me. Thank you for everything.

Jennifer: My oldest daughter. Your faith in me helped me through the hardest parts. Thank you for believing in me.

Jerry Smith: The man! You kept my original antiquated computer running for me. Thanks.

My wife: You gave me the original idea, then supported me all along. Thank you so much.

To all my other family and friends who supported me and cheered me on ... you know who you are. Thank you all.

Dedication

There are various people and organizations I feel I should dedicate this to, like all the firefighters, paramedics, dispatchers, etc. who shared my life and experiences for all these years. Also, all the doctors, nurses and other medical personnel I worked with throughout my career.

I feel compelled, in light of the events of 9/11, to include all those who gave their lives that day, doing what we all have done countless times on the job ... risking their lives so that others might live.

I watched in horror that morning as those towers fell, knowing full well that a lot of my brother and sister firefighters were in those buildings. Even as a writer with a pretty decent command of the written word, I still can't find the words to describe the shock I felt then. And still feel today. I extend my heartfelt condolences to their families and to all the firefighters who lost their friends in the tragedy of that day.

Barry Wilson

Foreword

During my twenty-six years as a firefighter paramedic, about a third of my life has been spent in firehouses with an extraordinary and unique group of people. To "ordinary" (or perhaps I should say, "normal") people, they are oftentimes considered bigger-than-life heroes. To each other they are engine and truck companies, rescue crews, partners, friends, and family. Brother and sister firefighters. They share their lives with one another. They share in the tragic, and sacred, last moments of the lives of complete strangers. They also share in the exhilarating, and precious, saving of strangers' lives. As they live through all these events together, on a regular basis, an unbreakable bond is formed.

The firefighter bond is not restricted to immediate partners, crews or departments. It's a worldwide brotherhood unlike any other. Attending conferences and visiting firehouses around the country, I've always found the same thing; as a firefighter, I have family in every firehouse. It seems the firefighters are all the same, only the names have changed.

At one point in this story, firefighter Scott McLean, talking with a firefighter from the past, points out to him, "You different firefighters are all alike."

There's a good reason for that ... it's true.

Chapter One

Susan Caufield truly believed nothing could happen to spoil such a perfect day. She stood at the kitchen sink slicing apples for the pies she was making. Her pies were known throughout the neighborhood for being incredibly delicious.

An elementary school principal, she smiled as she thought about the great day she'd spent working with her teachers in preparation for the next day's parent-teacher conference. Miraculously, everything went smooth, so all Susan had left to do was shake hands and smile pretty at the conference.

Thinking her 6-year-old daughter was napping in her upstairs bedroom, she called out, "Natalie, are you on your bed?"

"Yes, Mommy," Natalie's sleepy voice said from her daybed.

"Okay, honey. Close your eyes, and when you wake up, we'll have pie."

No answer, suggesting Natalie was already drifting off.

Susan's husband Dan, a systems troubleshooter for a large computer corporation in the area, was due home from work within the hour. Jason had come home from school and gone next door to play with Nate Morgan. Since the age of four, 9-year-old Jason and Nate had been "best friends for life."

Susan laid the strips of pie dough crust in a criss-cross pattern on the tops of the two pies and pushed her dark bangs back from her sweaty brow. She reached into the cupboard for cinnamon, the finishing touch.

"Oh, shoot. No cinnamon. I wonder if Esther has some," she said to herself while picking up the phone to call her friend.

Esther Adamson and her husband, Blaine, the retired couple across the street, were like parents to Susan and Dan and grandparents to the kids. While the phone rang, Susan took off her apron.

"Hello," Esther said when she picked up the phone.

"Esther, this is Susan. Do you have a little cinnamon I can borrow? I'm just finishing some pies and I need only a—"

"Of course I have some, hon," she interrupted. "Come right over and I'll get it for you. Did you say pies?"

Susan smiled because she knew how much Esther craved her apple pie. "I'll bring one over later on. Be there in a minute."

Susan set the oven temperature and went upstairs to check on Natalie, finding the little girl sleeping soundly. *She should be all right for a few minutes,* Susan thought as she went across the street.

The front door was just swinging shut when Jason and Nate opened the back door and walked into the kitchen. "This is gonna be so cool," Nate said. "Tim showed me how to do it last night." Tim was Nate's 13-year-old brother.

The two boys ran into the living room and down the seven stairs to the basement of the four-level split, then hurried into Jason's bedroom next to the family room.

Jason closed the door and Nate, holding a can of hair spray in his hand, said, "You got the lighter?"

"Right here," Jason said, pulling a red Bic lighter from the pocket of his 501s.

"Okay, hold the lighter about there." Nate raised his hand to Jason's chest level and Jason held the lighter out at arm's length.

Nate sprayed a little hair spray to make sure it was working properly, getting some on his hand. He wiped it off on the faded orange front of his too-small Mickey Mouse T-shirt.

Nate's brown eyes opened wide. "Ready?"

"Yep."

"You sure?"

"I'm *ready*, already!" Jason gave him an exasperated glare.

"All right, light it."

Jason flicked the little wheel on the Bic, spinning it three or four times before finally producing a flame. "It's lit. Hurry up."

"Hold it real still." Nate turned the can around in his hand to make sure it was aimed in the right direction.

"I am! Do it!"

"Okay, here we go," Nate said, holding the hair spray can up to the flame and depressing the button.

A huge, three foot ball of flame shot out and up, creating a surprising amount of heat that startled both boys. Jason jumped back, sat down hard and dropped the lighter while Nate stumbled and fell on the carpeted floor, dropping the spray can. The surprised boys sat and looked wide-eyed at each other for a few seconds, like young boys do, then they both burst out laughing.

"That was so cool!" Nate said.

"Rad!"

"Now you do the can and let me do the lighter."

After tucking his white T-shirt into his Levi's, Jason picked the can up off the floor. Nate snatched up the Bic and stood back up, holding the lighter at arm's length.

Jason held the hair spray can up to the lighter. "All ready?"

"Go for it, dude." Nate ran his hand across his dark, short hair, then flicked the wheel on the lighter, producing a flame on the first try.

Jason held the nozzle of the spray can closer to the small flame, but didn't notice the direction of the tiny arrow on the top. He pushed the button and another fireball ballooned out from the little flame.

An enormous ball of fire enveloped Nate's slender upper torso, igniting his shirt. Nate stiffened and dropped the lighter to the floor, standing paralyzed

FIRES OF TIME * 5

in mute, mortal agony, his mouth open wide in a silent scream. The Mickey Mouse on the front of his shirt curled up, then was consumed by the rapidly expanding torch as the fireball climbed his body.

Jason stood frozen in place, his small hand in a deathgrip on the spray can while his index finger firmly held the nozzle in the open position. The innocent looking can operated with the smooth effectiveness of a military flame thrower, delivering a jet stream of fuel directly into the fire. Watching in wide-eyed horror, the anguish in Nate's terrified eyes penetrating to the heart of Jason's soul, his best friend was turned into a roiling inferno.

Nate tried in terrifying desperation to breathe, inhaling only super heated gases that seared the tissues inside his lungs. He reeled around and charged blindly for the bedroom door. But in his confusion, he stumbled through the door of Jason's closet, falling headlong over the clutter of dirty clothes, shoes, and assorted sports equipment. The boy's lifeless body collapsed in flames against the back wall of the closet, igniting the clothing that hung in the small, fiery tomb.

Jason stood paralyzed, the hair spray can dangling from his hand at his side, with dreadful fear etched into the features of his face as he gazed at the raging blaze. The words he tried to say were frozen in his throat, *Stop ... drop ... and roll ... Nate.*

The phrase never came out.

As he stood alone in the middle of his room and watched, the fire engulfed the closet, then rolled out the closet door and across the bedroom ceiling in search of more oxygen. Jason knew he should do something, like call 9-1-1, but his thinking was numbed. An eternity of seconds passed before he was able to react. He dropped the spray can to the floor and opened the bedroom door, then stepped through it and calmly pulled it closed behind him.

Jason stood alone in the family room with a million thoughts racing through his head: *Mom will be really mad. I'll be grounded for life. I hope Nate's all right.*

He instinctively headed for his usual hiding place behind the sofa and crawled into it. As he lay on the floor between the sofa and the wall with the image of his best friend's eyes indelibly imbedded in his mind, Jason began to cry.

The only evidence of Jason's presence in the room was his left foot. A size five and a half, black and white Nike extended just beyond the end of the sofa.

Little Natalie was still sleeping peacefully on her beautiful white daybed right upstairs, directly above her big brother's blazing bedroom.

The fire, still confined to the one room, was devouring oxygen from every available source and searching for more while the heat grew more and more intense, causing the basement window to weaken.

* * *

Standing beneath an unmerciful sun in the ninety degree heat, Scott McLean felt a rivulet of sweat tickle its way down between his shoulder blades to the small of his back, creating an irritating itch he couldn't scratch. The temperature inside his heavy fire turnout coat had already exceeded the century mark and continued to climb. Simply standing in the sun was nearly unbearable while wearing full turnout gear. The mid-thirties, 6' 2" firefighter waited in the starting position to begin the annual torture known as the "Combat Challenge" course.

The course measures a firefighter's ability to perform the most strenuous tasks involved in the job. The course designer incorporated a group of five job related tasks, performed consecutively in seven minutes or less. A few *Ironman* types thought it was the greatest thing since spandex workout shorts. The *nearly normal* people knew it was conceived by the same person responsible for the Bataan Death March.

This is nuts, McLean thought as he watched his captain, Josh Evans, emerge from the training tower and continue on with the course, completing it a few minutes later.

At forty-two, Evans was one of the most experienced firefighters in the department, with twenty-one years under his belt. He was only the third black firefighter to ever be hired by the department, and the first to advance to the rank of captain. Respected as an officer and a gentleman, and well liked by his peers, Josh was the first choice of most of the other firefighters for the upcoming promotion to battalion chief.

After crossing the finish line, the lean, six-foot captain immediately tore off his facepiece and helmet. The waiting firefighters removed the airpack harness and turnout coat from his broad shoulders in one easy motion. Evans slid his wide red suspenders off and attempted to remove his turnout pants and boots, but his wrists and fingers were so weak that he couldn't even manage to open the one buckle.

"Let us do that," one of the firefighters offered, opening the velcro fly and buckle and dropping the pants down around Evans's ankles.

Two other men grabbed him under the arms and lifted him right up and out of his boots. He doubled over and held on to the legs of his dark blue workout shorts, trying desperately to suck more oxygen into his searing lungs.

"Way to go!" the firefighters yelled to him as paramedics supported him on each side and walked him over into the shade.

They sat him down on the grass next to an EMT who was tearing open an oxygen mask and hooking it to an O_2 bottle. In his late twenties and with black thin hair, paramedic Tom Buttram clipped an oxygen saturation monitor to Josh's right index finger while a fellow paramedic, Tony Escobedo, began taking a blood pressure on his left arm.

"Pulse is 174 and sats are only 88%," Buttram said to EMT Keith Ryan, a 21-year-old firefighter. "Let's get some O's on him. He has the pulse rate of a hummingbird and the O_2 percentage of a houseplant."

"B/P is two-sixty over one-fourteen," Tony said, removing the B/P cuff from the captain's left arm. Looking at Evans, the second-generation Mexican-American paramedic added, "High enough to blow the top of your head off, Josh buddy."

"No kidding!" Evans said sarcastically, gasping for air. He drew his left forearm across his forehead in an attempt to wipe the sweat from his brow with an arm already dripping with sweat.

Buttram checked the red, digital readout of the sat monitor. "Pulse is down to one-forty and the sats are moving up. Kinda slow, though, why don't you crank up the O's, Keith, and see if we can pink him up a bit."

Tony tossed a dry towel to Evans, who caught it as he turned and cocked his head, giving Tom a quizzical look. "Pink me up? Nice choice of words, Buttram."

"Already flooding it in boss." Ryan held the oxygen mask closer to his captain's face. "You look a little pale there, Cap. Maybe you're ready to go for a job in Fire Prevention."

Evans gave him a look of disgust. "Don't *you* start with me, rookie. You'd be wise to just do your job there. I think I've still got a few good years left in me. Besides, I'd rather retire, or die, than work with the lame, lazy and crazy bunch in that office."

Tony interrupted the firefighters. "Okay. You certainly seem to be improving nicely, old fella. How 'bout we move on to the next one, Tom? Looks like we saved another one here."

"Thanks a lot, boys," Evans said sincerely. "I feel a lot better."

Keith folded his hands under his chin and swooned melodramatically. "Those guys are my hee-roes."

The captain smiled.

"Go ahead, abuse us, everyone else does," Buttram said, removing the pulse oximeter from the captain's finger. "Man, we fuss over you, yank your butts from the clutches of death and what do we get? Abuse. Nothin' but abuse."

The two paramedics stood up to leave as Evans and Ryan looked at each other with feigned expressions of self-righteous indignation.

"What?" Captain Evans said, acting innocently surprised.

Ryan put his hand to his cheek. "Oh, those guys are just so, how you say? Oh, yeah. Sensitive. I heard they teach 'em that in medic school right after they learn how to walk on water."

As the two medics were walking away, Tom held his hand up behind his back and flipped them off.

* * *

Susan stood on Esther's front porch holding a can of Schilling cinnamon. Esther had insisted on Susan seeing the quilt she was making for the church bazaar.

"That will be a beautiful quilt, Esther," she said as a white pickup truck roared past on the street in front of the house going at least fifty miles-an-hour.

"Oh, those Jones Construction people," Esther said, fidgeting with her permed white hair. "I've called their company and the police to complain about them, but nobody seems to care enough to make them slow down. It'll probably take someone getting hit before anything gets done about it."

"I know," Susan said, watching the truck disappear from her view. "I've called the company too, with the same results."

The two ladies talked on the porch for a few more minutes until Susan became worried about Natalie waking up alone in the house. Turning to leave, Susan added, "I've got to hurry home and check on my little girl."

Esther crinkled up her nose and stopped Susan. "Do you smell something burning?"

Susan sniffed the air. "You know, it does smell like smoke out here. I wonder what it could be?"

Suddenly, she remembered leaving the oven on and felt a chill shoot through her entire body. She whirled around and bolted in the direction of her home. When Susan reached the walk in front of the house, she saw wisps of smoke curling up from the basement window beside the small front porch. Jason's bedroom window.

In denial of what her own eyes were seeing, she thought, *Jason isn't in his room, he's over at the Morgan's house.*

Susan heard a scream, then turned and saw Nate's mother, Kathy Morgan, running across the lawn toward her with a horrified look on her face. Instantly, both mothers were filled with a terrible feeling of dread. Not knowing, but knowing, the reason why.

"The boys are in the house!" Kathy screamed at her.

The two panicked mothers raced up the sidewalk, reaching the bottom of the stairs together. But before they could climb the steps, the basement window beside the small porch exploded, belching black smoke and a very hungry flame.

"My babies!" Susan screamed.

Nate's mother cried out at the same time. "Oh, my God!"

Chapter Two

Scott McLean started up the eight flights of stairs carrying a fifty foot length of inch-and-a-half hose line on his left shoulder with Dennis Graham close behind him.

"Pace yourself Scott," the muscular, 38-year-old, 240-pound engineer said.

Scott wasn't listening to Graham. He was busy listening to the sound of his own breathing as he trudged up the stairs. The sound of the air moving in and out of his air pressure regulator reminded him of Darth Vader in the movie Star Wars. He thought, *in full turnout gear, we even look like Darth Vader to a child who sees us through the smoke of a burning room. It's no wonder kids hide from us, they think we're some kind of high-tech boogeymen coming to get 'em.*

Navigating the stairs in the building was made difficult by the stiffness and bulk of his turnout pants and bunker boots. *One time I wish they could make a pair of these boots that fit halfway decent,* was one of the many thoughts running through Scott's head.

He could already feel the air hunger intensifying and hear his respiratory rate increasing as he tried to rein in his thoughts. He kept his eyes trained on whatever step was at his eye level, letting them rise up the eight flights at the same pace as his feet. On reaching each landing, he grabbed the railing with his right hand and let his momentum carry him around to face the next set, never varying his pace.

"Looking good," Graham said.

Yeah, right, Scott thought.

Reaching the fifth floor of the training building, he drooped his shoulder down to allow the fifty pounds of inch-and-a-half to slide off and drop to the cement floor, the aluminum couplings clanking against the concrete.

"Take it slow and easy, McLean," Dennis said in his ear.

Scott leaned out over the railing and looked down at the ground. Forty-five feet below lay a fifty foot roll of two-and-a-half-inch hose, weighing about sixty pounds. The hose was tied to a rope that extended from the ground to the fifth floor. The rope was tied off to the fifth floor railing, waiting for him to grab hold and hoist it up.

He laced his left leg through the railing and wrapped it around the middle bar, bracing his other foot against the four inch concrete lip in which the railing was anchored. Leaning out as far as he could, Scott started hauling the hose load up, hand over hand, sapping pretty much all of the strength from his hands and arms and using nearly all of the upper body strength he could marshal.

"Hey, Traci is at the starting line," Dennis said. "I heard she's gonna be staying the rest of the shift for

Buttram. Cap said she'll be here for the next few shifts while he's on vacation, too."

Scott brightened a bit at the news. A 28-year-old firefighter paramedic, Traci was one of Scott's former partners. They worked together for two years, and she was one of his favorites. When together, Scott and Traci seemed to share a sort of telepathy on calls. Other firefighters noticed how they always knew what the other was thinking, a beneficial thing when working stressful incidents. The common saying was that they shared the same brain.

Give 'em hell Trace, he thought, hoping for the 5'5" redhead to do well on the test. She flashed him a smile and a thumbs up and mouthed the word "thanks."

We've still got it, Scott thought, as he tried to smile back. Traci continued to watch him pull the rope, looking out through her facepiece with her blithe, green eyes. Her freckles were visible through the facepiece plexiglass from Scott's vantage point five floors up.

I really hate this, Scott thought as the hose roll neared the fifth floor. He couldn't grip it tight enough to keep it from slipping, so for every foot he lifted, it slipped back down six inches through his nearly useless hands. He moved faster, hand over hand, increasing the fatigue in his forearms and biceps. When he finally got the load to the outer top of the railing, he had to take a break to find a little bit of hidden strength in his hands.

Then, with all the strength he could muster, Scott hoisted the bundle over the rail and dropped it on the landing. He turned around and started down the stairs, feeling the air hunger intensify. The sensation of total fatigue in his forearms and hands rendered them numb and useless for the time being.

"Lookin' good, McLean. Two minutes exactly," Graham said. Trying to sound encouraging he added, "No hurry, man."

You don't have to worry about that one ol' buddy, he thought. *I just may turn in my slowest time ever, 'cause it's way too hot to be breaking any speed records today.*

He plodded down the steps at a slow, methodical pace, giving himself a chance to try to catch his breath, clenching and unclenching his hands in an effort to get some feeling and strength back into them. When he reached the bottom of the stairs, Scott stepped back out into the bright sunlight and walked over to the steel sled. He picked up the orange sledgehammer.

I hate this thing, too, he thought. The hammer wasn't even a real sledgehammer, but a bright orange colored, plastic coated thing that looked like it was made by Fisher Price. It was very lightweight and mostly ineffective for the job it needed to perform, which was to pound on a steel I-beam until it slid about five feet. Not as easy as it looked. Wearing full turnout gear, air pack and facepiece, helmet and gloves, and breathing from an air tank was a trying effort in itself. In addition, bending over and beating a heavy piece of steel several feet with a toy sledgehammer made it quite strenuous. Tack on the ninety degree heat and the whole thing escalated to true suffering.

"Go for it, Scotty," Dennis said.

Swinging the hammer, he struck the end of the beam. Again and again, pounding away on the piece of steel and moving it only three or four inches with each swing.

After sixteen swings, Graham yelled out, "You made it! Go!"

FIRES OF TIME * 17

Scott turned and let the sledgehammer slide from his nearly lifeless hands and fall to the ground right at the feet of his proctor. He staggered off the sled, gasping for air, and stood right in front of Graham, facepiece to nose. Staring him in the eye for several seconds, he yelled into his facepiece, "There! Up yours!"

Dennis smiled and pointed toward the next area.

Of course, Scott wasn't mad at Graham, but when he was in the middle of the test, he had no friends. He hated everybody.

He turned to follow the pathway that was marked by yellow lines on the asphalt of the training facility. The color of the paint reminded McLean of the yellow crayon the police use to mark the outlines around dead bodies and he thought, *I hope they have enough left to paint a line around* my *body in a few minutes.*

"Three minutes and fifteen seconds!" Graham yelled out as Scott walked an even pace along the pathway.

Suddenly, they were interrupted by the dispatch alert tones.

Dispatch: "*Station Five, Station Three, Battalion One, respond code three, structure fire, 8765 South Hempstead Drive. Smoke and flame visible. Time out: 1652.*"

Jeez, what a bummer, Scott thought. *Now I'll have to start this stupid thing all over again next shift.*

* * *

As Engine Five turned onto Hempstead Drive from 8700, the fire crew could see the header of thick, black smoke billowing up from the middle of the block.

Engineer Graham yelled over the noise of the siren. "Looks like a burner, Cap."

"Right on," Captain Evans said. "Looks like we're first in, too. Better find out if there's anyone still—"

The captain was interrupted by radio traffic.

Dispatch: "Engine Five and Engine Three. Reporting party states there are three children still in the structure, break ... hydrant locations: 87th and Hempstead, northeast corner ... 88th and Hempstead, northwest corner."

Evans reached for the mike as Graham pulled the engine to a stop, positioning it in the street in front of the Caufield home. The captain quickly sized up the situation and keyed the microphone.

Captain Evans: "Engine Five and Rescue Five at scene. We have a two story, wood frame and masonry structure with smoke and flame showing."

Dispatch: "Copy Engine Five and Rescue Five at scene at 1658."

Captain Evans jumped down from the engine and hurried around the front of it to get a better look at the fire. At the same time, the two tailboard men, Ryan and Escobedo, emerged from the jump seats of the engine and McLean and Kingston stepped from the squad. The tailboarders were already wearing their airpacks and the two paramedics started putting on their own airpack harnesses.

Evans yelled orders to his crew.

"Tony and Keith, pull an inch-and-a-half and stretch it to the front door. Scott, Trace, I want you two on primary search and rescue."

At that moment, an hysterical woman grabbed Evans's coat sleeve and tried to drag him toward the house. "My babies! Please, my babies!" Susan

FIRES OF TIME * 19

Caufield screamed. "My children are still in the house! Do something! Oh, God!"

Evans took her firmly by both shoulders, holding her steady to get her full attention. "Try to slow down, ma'am," he said evenly. "Where in the house are they?"

Talking very fast and running her sentences together, she yelled in the captain's face, "Natalie's in her bedroom ... upstairs ... I don't know where Jason is, maybe in his room downstairs ... Kathy, Nate's mom, said they're in the house somewhere!"

"Where is Natalie's bedroom, in the front or the back?" Evans said calmly, keeping eye contact with her.

"Upstairs, I told you! Oh, in front. In the front!"

"The boy's room?"

She screamed frantically, "In the front, downstairs, please, save my children!"

Susan pulled away from the captain, then stood up on her toes and jerked her head from side to side in an attempt to see around him.

"How old are they?"

"Nat's six. Jason's nine. Hurry, please ... dear God!"

"Is there another child in the house?"

"Yes. Yes! Nate, Jason's best friend. Please?" the frantic mother pleaded, not understanding why Josh didn't simply run in and rescue her kids from the burning house instead of standing there quizzing her.

Susan Caufield had no way of divining the captain's reasons for asking the locations and ages of the children. Josh knew the importance of knowing where to look and knowing what size persons they were looking for. Identifying the ages also gave them a clue as to how the kids might react in the situation. The captain wasn't being mean to her; in fact, his number one goal was to find the children and get them out alive as soon as possible. His number one priority in accomplishing that goal was to get his crew back out of the house alive. When the rescuer dies, no one gets rescued.

He keyed the mike on his portable radio.

Captain Evans: "Captain Three. Captain Five."

Captain Three: "Captain Three, go ahead."

Captain Evans: "Lay a line on your way in. We have three kids still in the house. I need your truck crew for a primary search and ventilation."

Captain Three: "Ten-four, break ... Dispatch, Station Three at scene."

Dispatch: "Dispatch copies Station Three at scene at 1701."

Dennis Graham held up an airpack harness and helped the captain put it on.

Evans then turned and yelled to the paramedics as he was hurrying up the sidewalk. "The 6-year-old girl is in the bedroom, upstairs front. Get in there and we'll bring in a line."

McLean signaled okay to the captain as he and Kingston started up the steps to the house, then disappeared into the surging smoke cloud.

Battalion One: "Battalion One at scene," was heard over the radio. *"I'll be Incident Commander and this will be the Hempstead incident."* Battalion Chief Matt Johnson hurried over and talked briefly with Captain Evans as a dispatcher acknowledged his arrival.

Dispatch: "Chief one at scene at 1702."

Lieutenant Three: *"I.C., Truck Three, Lt. Hendrix. Where do you want us?"*

Using his hand held portable radio, Chief Johnson, the 44-year-old incident commander responded, *"Truck Three. I.C. I need you at the scene for primary."*

Chief Johnson had a difficult time getting through all the radio traffic, so he keyed his radio and ordered, *"Dispatch and all traffic this incident, go to tack two."* Tactical two was just one of the other radio channels used at incident scenes to leave the primary channel for the rest of the fire department. It also kept non-emergency traffic from interrupting the incident.

The battalion chief talked briefly with Captain Evans, then set about the business of running the incident.

Battalion One: *"Battalion One,"* he said into the handheld.

Dispatch: *"Battalion One."*

Battalion One: *"I need two more ambulances and one more paramedic rescue, code three. And I need traffic control here. Have the police block 87th and 88th on Hempstead, break... Lieutenant Three, get a crew into the basement on a primary and another to open up that roof, break... Ambulance Three, stage in front of Engine Five."*

Matt Johnson, a battalion chief with eighteen years on the job, had a knack for feeding all of the information, verbal and visual, into his head and then getting the right people exactly where they needed to be. He always knew where every crew from every unit was located and what they were doing, and he made the right decisions. Johnson was "the man."

"Natalie!" Susan Caufield shouted.

Paramedic Kingston appeared through the clouds of smoke billowing from the front door of the house. She was holding her facepiece over the face of the little girl while carrying her down the steps. She handed her to the EMTs from Ambulance Three, then donned her facepiece and turned to re-enter the burning house.

Natalie was coughing violently and had a black, sooty face. She was also very much alive. The EMTs started giving her oxygen as they took the 6-year-old and her mother to their ambulance. Two more ambulances arrived at the scene, staging in the front.

On the front porch, Traci joined Scott so they could work their way into the basement. Two firefighters from Truck Three joined them.

"You take the wall left and I'll go right!" McLean yelled to Kingston, motioning for one firefighter to join each of them. "Go with Kingston, Joe. And you come with me, Greenhaul."

Crawling into the family room, Scott recognized all the familiar sounds of working in a good burner. He heard the roaring noise of the fire itself and the distinctive sound of objects popping, probably glass, as things falling from the ceiling crashed to the floor. He could hear the muffled resonance of the hose crew as they worked their way to the seat of the fire. His Darth Vader respirations were a constant reminder of his own vulnerability to the power of the fire. All he could see through the smoke was the faint orange glow of the flame ahead.

"Looks like a lot of fire," Greenhaul yelled out to Scott.

Scott didn't hear a thing through Greenhaul's facepiece.

Eerie, would best describe Scott's feeling as he crawled through the burning building, with the visibility hitting his helmet and his shoulder on its way to the floor.

He stopped, turned his head and yelled, "You still with me, Greenhaul?"

Greenhaul tapped him on the back. "Right behind you."

Moving further along the wall, Scott bumped up against another obstacle, and putting his facepiece right against the object, he saw it was a television. He worked his way around to the front of the TV and his knee came down on something hard.

"Ow! Damn!" he groaned. Getting right against the object, he saw that it was a Playstation. Shaking his head, he said, "I hope we find you kids in time to need a new one."

Moving back to the wall, he crawled up and over a bean bag chair, slipping off of it forward onto his face and knocking his helmet off center. "Come on, Scotty," he chided himself as he pushed his body back up. "You're the rescuer here, don't become the victim."

Suddenly, Greenhaul was beside him, pulling him back to his knees and yelling in his ear. "Are you okay?"

Scott nodded and yelled back, "Fine. Let's keep moving."

Greenhaul nodded, moving in behind as Scott made his way around another corner and bumped into the arm of a sofa. He felt down behind the sofa and across the top of the cushions, working his way across the length of it, then was startled when something suddenly loomed up in front of him and someone grabbed him by the side of his helmet. Traci held McLean's facepiece right in front of her own with her flashlight shining up eerily at their faces from below.

at absolutely zero and the heat intense. The constant, dull roaring of the fire, along with all the other sounds, were muffled by the thick, hot, atmosphere. The feeling never differed, no matter what type of building.

"Same fire, different day," Scott said to himself, thinking about one of the old firefighters he worked with when he was a rookie.

Pieces of the ceiling fell onto McLean as he felt his way around the perimeter of the room. He worked quickly along the wall to his right, bumping into a table and knocking it over. A lamp fell from the table and glanced off his helmet as he flailed his arms in a feeble attempt to catch it. His left hand came across and backhanded the lamp, sending it across the room to crash to the floor somewhere out in the smoke.

Coming to a corner, he made the turn and felt his way along the next wall. He heard the sound of water being put on the fire and within seconds, the hot, humid steam added to the already stifling heat. The super heated steam and gases sought out and found the only exposed skin on his body. It suddenly felt like the back of his neck was on fire. Scott knew his neck wasn't burning. He'd learned about it many years before in his very first fire.

Man, I wish I could remember to wear that Nomex hood, instead of just carrying it in my coat pocket, he thought. The hood protects the ears and neck from being burned, but being a relatively new thing, most of the older firefighters forgot to wear it into fires.

McLean could tell by the way the debris was falling that the fire had moved into the ceiling of the room he was in. "Keep moving, Scotty," he told himself as a large chunk of something fell from above,

She yelled through her facepiece, "I'll double check down your side. You do mine. We'll meet back at the stairs and do another room."

Scott nodded. "See you there."

Traci and firefighter Joe Pace moved on past while Scott continued working his way in the other direction, rounding the sofa and reaching for the wall. He stuck his hand behind the sofa and felt around, but didn't feel anything. As he moved on and made the turn, his knee bumped against something. He put his facepiece down against the object, shining his flashlight on it. It was only a shoe. As he unconsciously picked up the shoe, he realized there was a foot in it. He grabbed the ankle and pulled an unconscious boy from behind the sofa, lacing one arm under the child's arms. Encircling Jason's chest with his arm, and with Greenhaul helping, Scott dragged him toward the stairs.

Pace noticed them as Scott brushed by, and took one of the boy's arms to assist with the rescue. When they reached the bottom of the stairs, he helped Greenhaul lift Jason into Scott's arms and they started up the stairs.

McLean walked out the door, through the smoke, and into the sunshine, carrying the small, limp, unconscious body.

Jason Caufield wasn't breathing.

One of the waiting EMTs took the boy from Scott's arms and laid him on the grass in the front yard. He turned to make sure the others had made it out of the house just as Traci ripped off her helmet and facepiece and ran down the porch steps toward the young fire victim.

Scott then turned and saw the EMT performing mouth-to-mouth on Jason. He tore off his facepiece and helmet and dropped them to the ground.

Traci shouted orders to the firefighters and EMTs. "I need an airway kit, heart monitor and drug box. Strip me two IVs Ringers with blood sets and get a stretcher over here." She cut off Jason's shirt as she gave orders.

Scott kneeled down on the grass opposite her. "Whaddaya need, Trace?" He already knew, but out of courtesy, asked anyway.

"See if you can tube him and I'll get a line going."

As Traci answered, Scott was already taking the airway kit from an EMT. Another firefighter put the drug box and heart monitor on the ground and set them up.

Kingston hooked up the EKG leads. "He's in a sinus rhythm with a heart rate of 182. It's a bit tachycardic, but it might be effective. His blood pressure's low, 60 over nothing, and he shows 100 percent oxygen saturation on the pulse ox."

Hearing her, Joe Pace said, "Can that be right?"

Tracy didn't look up or miss a beat in her treatment while she answered. "That's normal for smoke inhalation. The sat monitor can't tell the difference between carbon monoxide and oxygen saturation in the blood, so it reads CO as O_2. This boy is clear full of carbon monoxide. He needs to be in the hyperbaric chamber at Mercy Hospital ASAP."

Scott managed to get the boy intubated and hooked up a bag-valve and oxygen. Traci got one IV in and Scott plugged a second one in the other arm. With bilateral IVs running, and bagging the non-breathing boy, the firefighter crew of EMTs and paramedics loaded him onto a stretcher and wheeled him to the ambulance.

Traci talked on the radio to the trauma center.

> *Kingston:* "Mercy Center. Rescue five."
> *Mercy Hospital:* "Mercy, R.N. Calder."
> *Kingston:* "This is Rescue Five, paramedics Kingston and McLean. How do you copy?"
> *Mercy Hospital:* "You're 10-2, loud and clear, Rescue Five. Go ahead."
> *Kingston:* "Mercy, we're en route with a 9-year-old male fire victim. Patient is unconscious and non-breathing. Unknown how long patient was down before our arrival. Vitals are: pulse 182, BP 60 over zero by palpation, sats at 100 percent with heavy smoke inhalation, monitor shows sinus tachycardia. Patient is intubated and on high flow O_2, bilateral large bore IVs with Ringers Lactate, all monitors are on. Did you copy, Mercy?"
> *Mercy Hospital:* "Copy that, Rescue Five. Is this from the same fire as the little girl Ambulance Three just brought in?"
> *Kingston:* "Ten-four, Mercy. I think this is her brother. Our ETA is about eight minutes. Any other questions or orders?"
> *Mercy Hospital:* "Yes, Rescue Five. Any visible burns?"
> *Kingston:* "Negative, Mercy."
> *Mercy Hospital:* "Copy that, Rescue Five. We'll see you in about eight. Mercy Center clear."
> *Kingston:* "Ten-four. Rescue Five clear."

She replaced the telemetry radio handset and Scott yelled to the firefighter driving the ambulance. "Better take us in code-three."

The ambulance pulled away from the fire scene, lights and siren, heading for the hospital with Susan Caufield's precious cargo on board.

As the ambulance turned the first corner, they passed a police roadblock where a man was getting out of his stopped car. The officer told him something and then pointed down the street.

Dan Caufield raced down the sidewalk toward his house.

* * *

Rescue Five backed into the station at 2015 hours after working two additional medical calls since the Caufield fire. McLean and Kingston got out of the squad and walked to the kitchen where the rest of the station's crew was sitting around the table.

Captain Evans spoke first. "Hey, it's our long lost medics, 'bout time you came home. What've you been doing?"

"Oh, same-o, same-o. Out saving lives and property," Scott said.

"You check on the kids?" Dennis asked Scott.

His face lit up. "Yes. The little girl is great and she's been released. You should have seen it, her mom and dad were holding on to her like she was made of solid gold."

"The boy, Jason, is in the pediatric ICU and they say he's looking pretty good. He took in a lot of smoke, so they'll probably keep him a day or two for observation. All in all, we done pretty good."

Tony spoke up. "Took in a lot of smoke, eh? That doesn't sound too good. He'll probably grow up wanting to be a firefighter."

"Bite your tongue," Evans said sternly.

"Poor kid," Tony said. "Maybe we should warn him."

Keith Ryan added, "Hey, I like being a firefighter."

FIRES OF TIME * 29

Dennis stared menacingly at Keith. "Put a sock in it, probie. Nobody cares what you like."

Captain Evans smiled as the rookie sank dejectedly in his chair. He knew Graham liked the kid, but couldn't let the rookie know that. After all, there were traditions to uphold.

The back door of station five opened and Matt Johnson walked in carrying a box from Krispy Kreme. "I thought you folks could use a treat after the way you worked your guts out on that little fire. You all did a great job out there today. I heard we had two good, solid saves." Looking at McLean and Kingston, he added, "Way to go, you two. You guys need a medal or anything?"

"No thanks, Matt," Traci said. "But you *could* bring us a box of Krispy Kremes every shift."

The dark-haired battalion chief smiled. "I'll see what I can do." Out of nowhere a concerned look appeared on Matt's face. "I wanted to give you people the bad news face to face."

He stammered a bit and seemed to be searching for the right words. Everyone at the table turned silent, knowing they weren't going to like what he had to say.

"When the Engine Three crew was overhauling the fire scene, they found the other boy in a basement bedroom closet." The veteran chief firefighter paused, his eyes watering, then continued. "The boy you guys pulled out, Jason? It was his best friend, named Nathan Morgan, nine-years-old. He lived next door."

Nobody said a word, but the chief knew exactly what they were thinking. He'd been there before. They were all wondering what they did wrong, what they could have done to save the child.

He knew those tough firefighters with their bigger-than-life images took it personally when they lost someone, especially a child. Not because they want to look like heroes, but because that was "their fire" and those three kids were "their kids." They were responsible for those three lives and they somehow failed one of them.

Matt broke the silence. "Nothing you could have done. Trust me."

Most firefighters are emotional, but manage to hide it pretty well, which could be the reason they entered the profession to begin with, or maybe it's just the result of doing the job. Either way, they feel good about the job they do when it goes right. But when it goes wrong, for whatever reason, it always hurts.

Tony spoke up. "How do you know, Matt? If we'd gotten to him before the fire did?"

"The fire didn't get to him. He *was* the fire."

Chief Johnson explained what they'd figured out about the fire.

"We found a cigarette lighter and a hairspray can. The can exploded somewhere along the line. The victim's 13-year-old brother told me that he showed his little brother how to make a hairspray blowtorch." Matt paused to swallow and compose himself. "The poor kid started sobbing and then collapsed on the lawn. His mother heard the whole confession, got down on her knees beside him and hugged him. She forced herself to be strong because she could see he was the one that needed her most, then she told him she still loved him." Matt shook his head and continued. "I admire her courage and her compassion. She's really an impressive person."

Tony spoke again. "Sounds like it. That's the kind of woman I need, compassionate and forgiving. Is she married?"

"You're a sicko, Escobedo," Graham said, throwing his doughnut at Tony.

It skimmed Tony's ear and hit the wall behind him, the raspberry filling squirting out, then oozing down the wall.

"Oh, man!" Evans wailed. "That was a jelly! You just wasted a jelly!"

Chief Johnson smiled and shook his head as he headed for the door. "You folks will be just fine. See you later."

"Adios," somebody called after him. As Matt walked out the door, he heard Tony trying to defend himself, so he paused to listen.

"Sicko? What's so sick about me wanting a forgiving woman in my life?"

"For one thing, your timing stinks," Graham said. "And the woman hasn't been born that's forgiving enough to put up with you."

Josh Evans interrupted. "I think she may have been, Den, but it could be a while before another Mother Teresa comes along."

Grinning to himself, the battalion chief closed the door, got in his vehicle and drove away.

Chapter Three

George McLean looked at his 7-year-old brother. "Come on, Packy. We have to meet Dad when he gets off work to walk home with him."

"Okay," John Patrick McLean Jr. said, pulling his fishing line in and wrapping it around the bamboo pole.

George picked up their worm can, laid his pole across his shoulder, and the two boys set out for the Lull and Holmes Planing Mill to meet their father.

The day was Saturday, October 7, 1871, and the McLean boys had been fishing on the Chicago river all day. They usually stayed on the river until their dad finished work so he could walk home in the dark with them. The three of them were always famished by the time they got home and Mom, Maggie McLean, always had a nice hot supper waiting for them.

After all of her boys had been fed, Maggie wanted the two young ones to take a bath, being it was Saturday night. Maggie and John carried the big washtub into the house and set it down in the middle of the kitchen floor.

"I'll get the water boiling if you'll get the boys out of those clothes," the 34-year-old mother said.

John Patrick McLean, Sr. stepped into the living room and yelled for the boys. "Come on, you two. There's no sense delaying the inevitable. Saturday night and bath, go together like fishing and bait."

He was just starting to pull Packy's shirt up over his head when they heard a clamor outside.

Packy told the story about that night in the journal he started when he was only six. Until he was ten or eleven, Packy drew pictures in the margins of the journal depicting the events of each day. When he finally began to write on the pages of the diary, he went back to the beginning and filled in the early years, little by little, using the pictures to jog his memory.

The journal was handed down from one generation to the next, father to son, ending up in the possession of Scott. The story had been faithfully told and embellished by parents and grandparents for five generations.

From Packy's own writing in his journal:

After supper Mom and Dad drug in the big washtub and put it on the floor in the middle of the floor. In the kitchen. Dad said the same thing to us that he always said every week to us that we had to take a bath on Saturday night whether we need it or not. Mom put water on the stove to get it hot as Dad started to get me and George out of our dirty clothes. Mom told him that only a father with a bad old factory could stand the stench from us two boys.

Before we got clear undressed, we heard the bells from a fire wagon. Me and George ran to the front door to see it go past and when we got out on the porch we saw a steamer wagon with three horses go flying by in front of our house. I never saw a real steamer run right down Jackson street before. There was cinders and clinkers that was still red hot flying out of the smoke stack and they looked real neat when they flew through the dark. They made ribbons of orange lights that exploded when they hit the street like bright orange snowballs. Big clouds of black smoke rolled out of the smoke stack too with the clinkers. It was so much smoke it looked like the steamer wagon was burning. It was so great. There wasn't ever anything greater than that.

Packy was so excited, he started jumping up and down and tugging on his father's muscular arm, pleading with him to take them to the fire scene.

"Come on, Dad, you have to take us," Packy said while pulling his dad off the front porch. "This looks like the biggest one yet."

And it *was* the biggest in Chicago's history — to that day. Chicago had been having big fires every day for a week, with multiple fires on most days. Packy had seen some of them with his brother and dad, and the two boys were even allowed to help the firemen on one of the fires. They didn't actually help to put water on the fire, but they did get to help drag fire hose to the plug. One of the firemen even lifted

George and Packy up onto the top of their hose wagon where they sat and watched a fire. Packy was elated. He was in little boy heaven.

"Bye!" the boys yelled after kissing their mother goodbye.

They ran out of the yard in the direction of the fire. As they neared the fire scene, John Senior stopped dead in his tracks and stared in the direction of the burning structure.

"Oh my," John muttered, seeing his planing mill engulfed in flames.

John and George were stunned at the sight of their family's livelihood going up in smoke, but Packy was oblivious to their feelings as he continued running to the fire. The shock his father felt was in no way felt by his youngest son, in fact, Packy was probably the happiest kid in all of Chicago at that moment.

"What's takin' you guys so long?" Packy yelled, running ahead of them. "This is great!"

The fire spread to cover four city blocks, destroying many buildings and businesses. The firemen fought the blaze until three-thirty in the morning before finally stopping it by using every operable piece of fire apparatus and half the Chicago Fire Department. Many civilians and firemen were injured during the blaze and fully half of the available firemen were completely exhausted.

The McLean troupe returned home just after midnight amid the protests of the youngest boy, and after the entire family had gone to bed, Packy stood at his bedroom window watching the orange glow in the sky. Exhaustion finally overtook him and he fell asleep curled up on the floor under the window where he slept the night.

The next morning, Packy was up bright and early to see if the fire was still burning. He threw open his window to look out and could still smell the smoke in the air, but there was no longer a big header of smoke rising from the direction of Canal Street.

He ran into the kitchen to have breakfast and found his parents at the kitchen table talking quietly with sad looks on their faces.

"What's wrong?" He couldn't imagine how anyone could possibly be unhappy after the glorious night they'd just experienced. "Can we go see what the fire looks like today, Dad?"

Maggie brushed her shoulder length hair from her eyes, then took Packy's arm and pulled him over close to her. "Son, your father's mill burned down in last night's fire. He no longer has a job and we're concerned about what to do next."

Packy thought it over, but his young mind figured his dad should be happy about it. "I'd be happy if the school house burned down, Dad. Isn't that kind of the same thing?"

His dad smiled at him, then at his mother. "Not exactly, Packy, but you may have the right attitude. There's nothing we can do about anything until Monday, so let's go see the damage. Eat your breakfast and I'll get George out of bed."

Walking around the rubble of what, until the night before had been his source of income, John McLean talked with his son about the importance of getting a good education.

"This was my only source of income. I only went to the eighth grade in school, so I don't have anything to fall back on. These ashes represent what is left of my career."

Packy glanced at his father's rugged face and strong body. "But Dad, you can do anything."

John laughed. "To you, it seems like I can do anything. In reality—" He paused and squatted down in front of his son. "I want you to have so much more than me, and the best way to do that is for you to stay in school and learn as much as you possibly can. Be a doctor or lawyer or teacher. Heck, be the president for that matter, just prepare yourself first."

"But Dad. I already know what I want to be."

"You do?"

"Yeah. I'm gonna be a fireman."

"A fireman?"

"Yep. There isn't anything in the world I ever want to be except a fireman. Wouldn't that be all right?"

John thought it over for a few minutes before he answered.

"You know, being a fireman wouldn't be half bad. It's an honorable thing to do and they always have jobs. In fact, if I were a few years younger, I just might try it myself."

Later that evening, after eating supper, Packy and George were swinging on the glider out on the big front porch of their Jackson street home. At that same moment, over on De Koven Street, a cow was allegedly kicking over a lantern in Mrs. O'Leary's stable.

Packy saw the bright orange glow shimmering in the billowing smoke just as George heard the clanging of the fire wagon bells. "Look George!" Packy yelled. "Look how big it is!"

He got excited and ran to the middle of the street to get a better look at the column of smoke rising high into the sky. Just then a horse drawn steamer wagon careened around the corner behind him. George saw what was happening and ran after his brother, yelling at him.

"Look out, Packy! Don't run out there!"

He wasn't fast enough to reach him or loud enough to be heard over the noise of the speeding fire wagon. George caught a glimpse of the third horse over when it was only inches from Packy's back.

"Packy!" the frenzied boy yelled again. "Packy's been run over by the fire wagon!" George called out in the direction of the house as he ran toward the edge of the yard.

In the darkness, he saw nothing but the side of the steamer and heard only the sound of the powerful horses' hooves on the street as the fire engine raced past his face and continued down the street toward the fire.

"Packy, where are you? Packy!"

George was terrified by what he expected to find as his head swept frantically from side to side and his eyes searched the night for the body of his young brother.

Packy came running abruptly out of the darkness and into the yard, more exuberant than before, if that was possible. "Did you see it? Did you?"

Seeing Packy alive and uninjured both relieved and infuriated 11-year-old George so much that he started yelling at him. "You almost got run over by that steamer! I thought you were dead!"

Packy didn't pay any attention to him as he ran back into the street, picked something up, then ran back to the front steps of the house. He was sitting on one of the steps trying to put his misshapen shoe on his foot. "My shoe got knocked off, but I think I can get it back on."

George went and stood over him, only to start yelling again. "It got run over by the steamer! Look at it, that coulda been you! What're ya, nuts?"

"Boy, that was a close one," Packy said as he finished putting on the deformed shoe.

George glared at him. "You were lucky to get outta the way. You coulda been killed."

Packy ignored what he was saying as he jumped up and grabbed his brother by the hand, pulling him in the direction of the fire. "Come on! We have to get there before they put it out!"

John Patrick McLean got there long before they put it out. The conflagration lasted nearly two days, destroying 17,000 buildings in a three and one half square mile area of the city. Watching the courageous firemen work on that fire so inspired him that from then on, more than ever, he wanted nothing more in his life than to be one of those brave and fearless men.

That lean boy with the shaggy shock of light brown hair and the green Irish eyes that sparkled whenever he smiled grew up to become a smoke-eating, leather-helmeted Chicago fireman.

He never regretted his decision.

Thus began the long and honorable tradition of McLeans in the fire service. The family's involvement in fire departments spanned just over one hundred years and included three cities.

Chapter Four

Scott McLean was born in the state of Wisconsin as the only son of Harry McLean, a captain in the Milwaukee Fire Department. Harry was the fourth generation of McLeans to serve in the fire service, leaving Scott to keep the tradition alive in the fifth.

Scott moved from Wisconsin at the age of fourteen when his mother was offered a job as a chemist at the copper smelter. Rosalyn had earned a degree in chemistry from the University of Wisconsin, but she only used it sparingly, usually teaching part time, until Scott's father was killed in an explosion while working a silo fire. She accepted the chemist's job shortly after that.

Scott was in the eighth grade when the family moved to their new home where Scott met Patricia Davis during the first year in his new school. They dated only each other all through high school, and a year after graduating, at age nineteen, Scott McLean and Patty Davis were married.

Scott worked in the laundry business for a few years for a man named Jelesnik. Old man Jelesnik loved Scott like a son and taught him everything he knew about the cleaning and laundromat business. So when the old man died suddenly, Mrs. Jelesnik offered the business to Scott. She didn't think her late husband would have wanted anybody else to have it. And since old man Jelesnik left her in a comfortable financial condition, she made Scott and Patty an incredible deal on the laundromat and dry cleaners. They kept her on to manage it for them.

Scott and Patty improved the business, and within two years, acquired a second laundromat. The McLeans were on their way to becoming veritable laundromat magnates before Scott finally buckled under to the strong personal desire, not to mention the long family tradition, to become a firefighter.

He'd been a firefighter for eleven years, nine of those years as a firefighter paramedic. Scott, a seasoned veteran, was well liked and respected by his peers, acquiring a reputation as one of the best field paramedics in the fire department.

He earned a degree in Fire Science, and because of his family background and a keen interest in history, extensively studied the annals of the fire service. Few people anywhere knew more about the great fires in American history than Scott McLean. He assembled an extensive collection of fire service memorabilia dating back to a leather fire helmet worn by his great, great grandfather, and a small, leather-bound journal the same man kept from the age of six.

Scott would have given almost anything for the opportunity to be on the scene of many of those historical fires, or to race to the scene driving a team of two or three high spirited horses pulling a steam powered pumper wagon. Steamer wagons, they were called, and being the steamer driver was the prestige position in every engine company. As an adult, he occasionally slipped into the same daydream.

Casey, their first child, was born soon after Patty received her degree in Organizational Communications. She had planned to use her degree in the work force, but it didn't pan out that way for her. She worked full time running the household and the laundromat/dry cleaners. Using her innate business sense, along with the business training she had received in her college courses, Patty was responsible for turning the family business into a thriving enterprise. All of the growth was a direct result of her wise decision making and management skills.

* * *

At the end of his 24-hour shift, Scott pulled into his driveway. He stepped from his Chevy pickup and was attacked by two small children. Missy threw her little arms around his neck and tried to squeeze the life out of him, saying, "I luzyou, Daddy."

Scott looked into her big eyes and told her he loved her too. She was giggling, which always made him laugh. She had the infectious kind of giggle that made everyone smile. With tiny dimples that appeared whenever she smiled and those laughing, sky-blue eyes, her entire face seemed to smile. She had straight blonde hair that was always on the fly, giving her the look that inspired Patty to sometimes call her the *Wild Child*.

Scott walked across the driveway carrying Missy, with 7-year-old Casey hanging onto his leg, making him step with one leg and drag the other. He looked like Dr. Frankenstein's "Igor" limping up the step to the back door of the house. He opened the door and saw Patty in the kitchen. Hunching his back, he said in his best Igor imitation, "Can you helllp me doctor? I seem to have this grrowwth on my leg."

Casey let go, then punched his dad's leg. "Dad, it's only me on your leg."

Patty laughed as Scott told Casey, "Oh, yeah, I forgot."

Still in his arms, 3-year-old Missy squeezed Scott around the neck again and giggled, "Daddy, you're so funny."

When he finally stepped into the kitchen, Patty threw her arms around Scott and hugged them both tightly.

"I saw you on the news last night. I'm sorry. That must have been awful for you. Those poor kids. How do you do it, hon?"

"Y'know, somebody's gotta do it, and it *is* in my blood."

She stepped back, folded her arms and stared at him with a stern look, which meant she didn't want to hear any of that "in my blood" talk.

"Wrong answer, huh?"

She nodded, her lips drawn in a tight line which was neither a smile nor a frown. "Uh-huh."

Scott put Missy down. "It's really difficult sometimes. When I brought that little boy out all I could think about was Casey. And the other boy we weren't able to save. Oh man, Pat. What if that was our son? I don't know what I'd do."

She put her arms around him again and hugged him tighter. "I don't know, but I do know one thing."

"What's that?"

She leaned her head back to look into his face, her shining blue eyes darting around it, taking in every feature. "Somebody had to go in and rescue those kids. They needed you. I'm proud that it was you."

He was embarrassed by the praise. "You always say that 'proud' thing."

"That's because I always am."

Scott jerked and gently pushed away from Patricia with a look of sudden acknowledgment on his face. "You saw me on the news?"

Patty knew what he was thinking. "'Fraid so, dear. Ice cream for the crew, huh?"

"Looks that way."

"How did that tradition get started?"

"I don't have the faintest idea, but with the amount of news coverage we get, it seems like somebody brings treats almost every shift. It's surprising we all don't weigh three hundred pounds."

"Do they do the same thing in all departments?"

"I don't believe so. Some have different traditions like cooking dinner the next shift. I know in some departments they buy everyone on the crew a beer after they get off shift. There are a lot of different ways of paying off, but one thing is pretty certain."

"What's that?"

"No matter where you work, you're gonna get nailed for your moment of fleeting fame. It's tradition, you know."

"Don't I ever, dear. In a profession filled with tradition."

"Right on."

* * *

The next morning, Patty sat at the breakfast table, lost in thought as she gazed out the window at the movement of the clouds in the bright blue sky. She smiled and said to Scott, "Missy was so cute riding that elephant at the zoo."

Patty and Scott spent Friday taking the kids to the zoo, something they tried to do two or three times a year.

Scott started to laugh. "Really, that terrified look on her face when we first put her on the elephant's back. And then that giggle, what a little sweetheart."

Patty grinned at him. "And how about when Casey asked me what those monkeys were doing to themselves?"

Scott furrowed his forehead. "And you told him to ask me, because I'd know a lot more about that kind of thing than you? Thanks a lot."

"No problem."

They both laughed.

Patty thought about how much Scott adored those children, ever grateful that her kids were given such a devoted father. She stared lovingly across the table at her husband.

"What's that look about?"

Patty smiled, her eyes sparkling. "Wanna go upstairs?"

Scott looked into the TV room and saw Melissa and Casey engrossed in Saturday morning cartoons. "Hmm, I don't know. How fast can you get there?"

"Watch this." She jumped from her chair and ran for the stairs with Scott right behind her.

FIRES OF TIME * 47

Later, Scott and Patty were lying together on their bed with only a sheet pulled up over them.

Patty ran her finger over Scott's mustache. "What do you have planned today?"

"Brian wants me to come over and give him a hand with his project."

Brian and Joellen Daniels were neighbors and had been best friends for years. Patty remembered Brian's last project: the popcorn ball machine he made out of Jo's largest stainless steel mixing bowl, her steam iron, her blow dryer, and various other items he found lying around. The contraption actually made a real caramel popcorn ball from start to finish, which would have been great if people wanted popcorn balls the size of basketballs. Brian had said that it just needed a few adjustments, then set it aside and went back to work on some old project.

"What's he building this time?"

"I'm not sure." He paused, then continued. "No, that's not entirely true. He did tell me something about an invention he's been trying to perfect for years, but he asked me to keep it a secret and I promised I would." Scott looked puzzled, then added, "Come to think of it, he never did tell me what I was keeping secret."

"That man is a real study." Patty put her arm across Scott's chest to snuggle, laying her head beside her arm with her eyes closed.

"Big understatement," Scott remarked.

When she slowly opened her eyes, the chair in the corner of the bedroom came into view. Her eyes sprung open and she jerked her head up at seeing Missy sitting in the chair watching them.

"Hi, Mommy. Hi, Daddy."

Scott spun his head around and saw her sitting there, did a double take, then looked at Patty, who was smiling at Missy.

"How long have you been in here?"

"I don't know, Mommy." She giggled, "You guys are funny."

Patty gasped, rolled onto her stomach and pulled the sheet up over her head, then started quietly laughing.

"Oh, Scott," she whispered, still laughing. "She was watching us."

Scott stared at Melissa, smiled and nodded his head. "I know why little children are so cute. You can get away with just about anything if you're cute enough."

Patty, still hiding under the sheet, shook the bed with her laughter.

Missy sat smiling back at her daddy, wearing a Winnie the Pooh shirt and holding onto her stuffed Pooh Bear. "Am I cute 'nuff, Daddy?"

"Uh ... Scott?" Patty tapped him on the arm. He was busy smiling and nodding his head at his little daughter, so Patty tapped his arm again. "Scott?"

"I hear you, babe." He was still smiling at Missy as she looked at him with her sparkling eyes.

"Scott, honey, Missy is learning to tell time, you know."

He lifted the sheet and peered under at his wife, noticing her long, blonde hair spilling down over her tanned back.

"That's nice. Did you want me to teach her something right now?"

She poked her head out from under the sheet and looked up at him, smiling coyly. "What I meant was that I was planning on giving her a watch for her birthday, but it looks like we already gave her one."

He gave his giggling wife a disgusted look, then shook his head and said, "I've got to keep you away from the fire department."

Scott asked Missy to go down and watch TV for a little bit and close the door on her way out. After the door closed, he scooted down in the bed and pulled the sheet up over their heads.

"Now," he said. "Where were we?"

Chapter Five

Walking toward his best friend's house, Scott started thinking about Brian and his many experiments. Brian Daniels had been his closest friend since they met in the eighth grade when Scott first moved from Wisconsin.

That was right after Dad died, he thought. *I've known Brian over twenty years and he's exactly the same today as the day I met him.*

Brian was a geeky kid with long, brown hair that always needed combing. He always wore John Lennon glasses because he thought they made him look kind of cool, but he didn't have to look cool to be Scott's friend. Scott wouldn't have wanted anyone else for his best friend.

A physics genius with two doctorate degrees, Brian became a scientist in the space technology industry. There was never reason for Brian to feel inadequate next to him. In fact, it should have been the other way around.

Reaching Brian's garage, Scott stepped through the door of the shop and saw his friend hunched down beside his project, wearing blue coveralls and dirty white deck shoes.

"Hey, what's cookin', Bri?"

Brian peered around the large, cylindrical object and greeted him. "Scotty. Glad you're here."

Staring at the large object, Scott said, "Holy cow! What have you done to that thing?"

Brian stopped what he was doing, stood up and took one step toward his small bar fridge and asked, "You want a beer before we get started?"

"I just finished breakfast, Bri. Maybe later."

"Okay then, let's get on with it. Now, I hope you're ready for this, 'cause you probably won't believe me. At first anyway. And you'll likely think I've gone completely nuts, but what else is new?"

Scott only shrugged his shoulders in response. The thing he had referred to was taking up a good sized chunk of space in the middle of the floor. It had originally been a huge commercial clothes dryer. A couple of years earlier, Brian had asked Scott if he, being in the laundry business, could locate a big dryer drum for him. Scott was getting ready to replace all four of the dryers in the store so he gave one of the old ones to Brian.

When Brian convinced Scott that the drum's diameter of nearly five feet and depth of about four and a half feet made the dryer perfect for his project, Scott had the whole works, motor, gears, pulleys and drum, delivered to Brian's garage — gratis. Brian had been overly excited about receiving it. So much so that he talked Scott into giving him the other three. At the time, Scott didn't have any idea what he was so excited about, but he'd learned long before not to worry about the workings inside Brian's head.

The single drum sat on its back on an 18-inch high platform. It didn't look much like it had before, except for the basic shape. It had been painted a glossy, hunter green color. There were tanks, wires and tubing mounted to the frame of the platform, along with an interesting looking group of gears and shafts. Several other familiar looking items, like electric motors and insulators were also mounted to the frame. Large diameter glass tubing encircled the outer circumference of the drum several times. The glass tubing was connected to an adaptor which was attached to a curved pipe made of a different material.

Brian walked around the large gizmo and waved his hand over the top of it. "Well, what do you think?"

"I don't know. What should I think?"

Gently caressing it as he walked around the invention, Brian said, "My good man, this is my time machine."

Scott stared emotionless at the machine, knowing Brian had been known to say and do some pretty outrageous things.

"No, really. It truly works."

"Right," Scott smirked. "It's a clothes dryer."

Brian stopped with his back to Scott. "You don't believe me, do you?"

"Brian, I know you."

"What's that supposed to mean?"

"It means I know you, Brian."

He turned around to face his friend. Brian looked hurt. "You're looking at me like I'm weird or something."

Scott hesitated and smiled. "You *are* weird or something."

"What makes you say that?"

"What makes me say that? Brian, look at me." He leaned forward and tapped his chest with both hands. "This is Scott, your best friend. I've seen almost every experiment you've ever done. You've got to admit that you've done a lot of very strange things."

"Maybe a couple," he said timidly.

"Maybe a couple hundred."

"Aw, get real, Scotty," Brian said in defense as he turned away.

"I could name a few."

"I doubt it." He turned back around and held up one finger to challenge Scott. "Name one."

"All right, let me see." He looked up toward the ceiling and thought it over, then looked back at Brian. "Remember that time you put your cat in your mom's washing machine and set it on the spin cycle? What was up with that? You nearly killed the poor thing."

"Right, but I didn't, did I? Old Schrodinger lived another twelve years."

"What about the limp she always had afterward. And I know she was brain damaged."

"Possibly." He pointed to his black cat with the white paws and face that was sleeping in the sunlight on the windowsill. "But she did manage to produce some fine offspring after that. I present proof. Schrodinger II, Son of Schrodinger. She still lives on in her son."

"Yeah, I guess she does. What did you learn from that washing machine experiment, anyway?"

Brian scratched his chin in true mad scientist style and thought for a moment. Looking baffled, he shrugged his shoulders. "That I needed a lot more speed?"

Scott burst out laughing and Brian joined him.

Following that, Brian got serious again. "Honest. This really is a time machine and it really does work."

Scott nodded, doing his best to look and sound sincere. "Okay. I'll try to keep an open mind. Show me how it works."

Brian put his arm around Scott's shoulders and said quietly, "Step into my office."

Brian began the tour of the time machine, pointing out the various components as he described the operation of the time travel vehicle.

Touching a very small electric motor, he said, "As you can see, this is the motor, a 12-amp electric I took from a commercial vacuum cleaner."

"It hardly looks powerful enough to move that big thing."

"Stay with me, I'll get to that later. I've used a series of reduction gears and the automatic transmission from my old BMW motorcycle to get the revolutions per minute that are required. As you see here, the interior — wall, seats, etcetera — is firmly attached to the frame of the platform and holding the cockpit stationary."

Scott gave him a funny look.

"I know it's a commercial clothes dryer drum, but cockpit sounds better, okay?" Brian got down on his hands and knees to point under the machine. Reaching up and taking hold of Scott's shirttail, he pulled him down to the floor. With Scott down on his hands and knees, he continued. "The cockpit, like

I said, is attached to the stand in a fixed position while the outer shell is set up to move. The hatch, or escape portal opens into the cockpit."

Scott held his hand up. "Escape portal? It's getting deeper."

Brian continued without missing a beat. "This allows the entire outer shell to rotate independently of the interior." He glanced at Scott. "Still with me?"

Scott nodded his head.

"I've used a motorcycle battery to power the electric motor, utilizing this group of power converters to boost the power and prolong the life of the battery. I've also attached a spare battery right under one of the seats inside. You never know when you could use a spare."

"I understand completely. The first one could go dead. And if you've traveled to someplace — some time — like say, the seventeenth century, it might be a challenge to find someone with a good running Chevy to give you a jump."

"Right," Brian said, ignoring Scott's little scenario. "Now, you see this air tank?" He pointed to the small air cylinder and Scott nodded. "It is an aluminum, high pressure Survivair SCBA tank, connected to the same gear system as the motor, adding a pneumatic drive to the design. The pneumatic setup has two purposes. The high pressure air provides sufficient power to initially turn the drum. Then, on reaching enough rpm's, the electric motor takes over to steadily increase the speed. Then, when the rpm's reach the right speed, the computer kicks the pneumatic system back in to give a very powerful burst of speed. Kind of like the way a dentist's drill works." Brian stood back up.

FIRES OF TIME * 57

"I'll run through that in a minute. Now, let's look inside."

Scott stood up to join him. Brian opened the hatch on top of the machine, in reality, a standard commercial dryer door, complete with a round window in it. Looking inside, Scott could see two bucket seats facing each other on opposite sides of the interior.

"The cockpit?"

"Precisely."

"So how do you start it?"

"What do you mean? Oh, how does it work? Let me explain. It all has to do with some of the laws of quantum physics and a few of the basic laws of nature." Brian stooped down beside the machine and pointed to an object underneath. "That is a generator, shafted directly to the outer shell. When I get the rpm's high enough on the shell, the onboard computer engages the generator." Brian paused for a moment, pointing to some converters. "Now, you can see here where the generator feeds into another series of power converters to boost the electrical output higher."

"How high?"

"Way."

"That high, huh?"

Raising his eyebrows and rolling his eyes, Brian grinned, "You wouldn't believe how high."

He pointed to another object. "The electricity is sent from the generator to this capacitor, where it builds to even higher levels. Then, when the energy reaches the maximum level, the capacitor releases it in one huge charge out through this big wiring harness to the reactor."

"Huge charge?"

"Humongous."

"Sounds pretty scary."

"I'm shivering just telling you about it."

"Whoa. Wait a minute. Back up," Scott said, signaling time out. "Reactor? What do you mean, reactor?"

"Oh, that," Brian answered calmly, pointing to a shiny, brushed stainless steel canister about the size of a football. "You see this here?"

"Yeah."

"Well, this is where the atom smashing takes place."

Scott grimaced. "You mean kind of like a nuclear reaction?"

"No, I mean exactly like a nuclear reaction."

"Isn't that dangerous?"

"This is a controlled reaction, Scotty," Brian said smoothly. "I'm achieving speed here, not mushroom clouds."

Scott wasn't completely convinced. "Okay, let's go on. Does that mean you've got some radioactive material in there?"

"You could say that. Yes, yes I do." Brian hesitated. "Plutonium."

Scott was shocked. "Plutonium? Plutonium? He stepped away from the machine and stared at Brian. "Where in the hell did you get that?"

"Don't ask. Just don't ask." Brian lowered his head and shook it. "I didn't steal it. Honest."

Scott looked puzzled. "But, plutonium. Isn't it illegal to have that in your possession?"

Brian rationalized to Scott. "It's all right. I got it legally and nobody will ever miss it. Trust me, I know how to use it."

Scott looked shell shocked and said "I think I'm ready for that beer now."

Brian walked over to the small refrigerator, removed two cans of beer and tossed one to Scott. He popped open his beer.

"Please continue, you have my attention."

"Listen, if I ever have a heart attack or something, I'd trust you with my very life because you're the best there is, in that field. Trust me here. I do know what I'm doing."

"I do trust you. It's just. Plutonium. Maybe it sounds more ominous to someone like me."

Brian tried to assure his friend. "It is pretty heavy material. But in the right hands it's relatively safe."

"You know I'd trust you with something as serious as that. You're the smartest person I've ever met. I was just surprised."

"Cool," Brian said. "You want to hear the rest?"

"Go."

Brian stood back from the machine and motioned toward it. "In a nutshell, this is how it works. The computer is set with the proper trip data: time, date, place and return information. When it leaves from here, I activate it by transmitting from the home base computer. Anywhere else, it can be activated by turning the two keys simultaneously and punching the enter key. The onboard computer regulates everything from that point on, including the return trip."

Scott ran his hand over his light brown hair and took a deep breath, while Brian fiddled with the zipper on his coveralls before he went on.

"On activation, the whole system is powered up, putting every component on a ready status. The computer signals the air pressure valve to open and the outer drum begins to turn. When the rpm's reach the proper speed, the electric motor powers up, increasing the speed. At the same time, the valve closes on the pneumatics as the motor increases to its maximum speed, causing the computer to engage the generator." Brian stopped, looking concerned. "You still with me?"

Scott scratched his chin. "I think so. Go on."

"Okay, here's where it starts getting really good. When enough energy is built up in the capacitor, the charge is released into the reactor, starting the reaction. That gives us the huge amount of energy required to start the photon race."

Scott looked confused. "The what?"

"Photon race."

"Do you want to tell me what a photon is?" Scott said.

"You don't even know basics like that?"

He took a long draw on his beer. "Maybe basics to you, but I never understood any of that physics stuff. You know that."

"Okay, sorry. A photon is a quantum of light, does that make sense?"

Scott gave him a totally disgusted look, threw up his one empty hand, then turned around and took a couple of steps away. He stopped and turned back around to face Brian. "You win. Just leave out all the techno-junk and tell me what happens next."

"Sorry." Brian began to pace around the shop as he talked, splashing beer from the can as he waved his arms around in the air for emphasis. "Basically the energy from the reaction creates a tremendous

FIRES OF TIME * 61

amount of photons, light, shooting them through this short, curved, lead covered pipe and out to the glass tubing around the outside of the machine's shell. I'm talking light here, so dense that it could almost be classified a solid. This creates a photon field that completely surrounds the machine, and of course, the field is traveling at the speed of light."

"Of course," Scott said, staring and listening intently to everything Brian said. He understood, but was still unmoved. Taking another drink of his beer, he waited for Brian to continue.

Brian was getting excited, waving his hands around even more and motioning to the machine while demonstrating the movement of the photons. "Don't you see it? I've created an inner core, the cockpit, that sits inside a field of photons traveling at the speed of— "

Scott interrupted. "Wait a second. If these photons are made of light, why don't they just leak ... or shine ... out through the clear, glass tubing?"

"Oh, that. Some does, but the light is very dense, and it's shot through a curved lead pipe. The curve of the pipe starts it off in just the right direction to follow the curvature of the tubing. And I had the tubing specially made of a type of flint glass, so it contains the light better than the normal composition of silica glass. The lead oxide gives the light a bit of a greenish tinge, in fact, it makes it look kinda cool."

"Flint glass?"

"That's right. Flint glass is made with a percentage of lead oxide, so it does a good job of holding the photons in check. At least long enough for our purposes here, which is to create a light-speed field around the inner core for a few seconds, tops. You see, the theory is if you can travel faster than the speed of light, you can move in time. I have proven that theory."

"You said it travels the speed of light."

Brian looked around, first to the left, then to the right, as if to make sure nobody else was listening, then looked back at Scott.

"Oh, yeah, I didn't finish. The outer shell is traveling at the speed of light because of the photon race. But..." He paused to hold one finger up, trying to emphasize his point. Scott just stared blankly. "...the shell, to which the photon piping is attached, is spinning by the power of the electric motor. So any additional positive rotation of the outer piping advances the speed of the photon race, thereby increasing the rpm's past light speed. At this point, the computer kicks off the generator and allows the motor to reach its maximum rpm's."

Scott grunted. "So, now it's going faster than the speed of light, does it take off or something?"

"No. And that's one of the problems I ran into in the early going. For some reason, I need a really good burst of speed to get the machine to jump into the continuum. But once it's there, the electric motor controls the travel speed more accurately." Brian paused and looked at the time machine, caressing it lovingly, then turned his attention back to Scott.

"That's where the pneumatics come back into play. The final step begins when the high pressure pneumatics kick back in and give a quick burst of speed to the outer shell. That puts the space in the cockpit inside a field traveling at a speed greater than 186,000 miles-per-second," he said triumphantly.

"Is that the speed of light?"

FIRES OF TIME * 63

Brian hesitated a moment to give his friend a look of pity. "You really are intellectually challenged, aren't you my friend?"

"Forgive me." Scott hung his head in shame.

Brian clapped his hands and declared, "Well, that's about it."

"What happens then? Does the thing explode and blow you into the past?"

"I'm afraid nothing quite that exciting happens," Brian said without even pausing his narration. "The photons, racing around the outside faster than the speed of light, cause the entire machine to leave the present and travel to the past. As their speed increases, the machine's speed increases into the past. When the destination is reached, the computer stops the process and deposits my time machine at the pre-set coordinates."

"Do you de-materialize or anything like that?"

"Nope, and Scotty doesn't beam you aboard, either. You will simply be traveling, time traveling."

"You? You said you. What's up with that?"

"Oh, yeah. There was one more thing."

Scott glared at Brian. "In your dreams, bud."

"Just listen for a minute. Trust me."

With a mock look of disgust, Scott said, "Brian, Brian, Brian. I trusted you when you told me you could make my hamster disappear. Remember?"

"Yeah, so? I made it disappear, didn't I?"

Scott exhaled hard, "You flushed Skippy down the *toilet*!"

"I said I was sorry. Besides, it was the last part of a science project. I needed to see if a hamster could swim in a whirlpool." He poignantly paused. "I felt really bad afterward."

"Really? You never said anything about a science project, and you certainly never told me you felt bad about it, either."

"You didn't speak to me for two weeks!" Brian said, raising his voice. "By that time, I guess I just forgot to tell you!"

Trying to soothe his friend, Scott said, "Chill, Bri. I didn't mean to open an old wound. That was a long time ago and I'm not mad anymore, so tell me about that science project."

Scott sat down on the time machine's platform. Brian polished off his beer, then put the can on the work bench and took off his glasses. He took a red shop rag from the back pocket of his blue coveralls and started cleaning the lenses.

"I did a project studying eight different small animals. In the study, I showed how each one of them could or couldn't swim in various types of currents and or substances."

"What was the point?"

"What do you mean, point?" Brian said, putting his John Lennon glasses back on.

"The swimming animal thing. What was the reason for the experiment?"

"Reason? We're talking science here. In science, you don't really need a reason."

"I guess I just don't understand," Scott remarked, walking over to the window and looking out at a dryer drum in the back yard. "How did you decide on that particular subject for your project?"

"Oh, that. My zoology teacher required us to complete a project involving the study of any group of animals of our choice, comparing them to one another in some kind of experiment. I was having a difficult time coming up with something. Then, I was walking home from school through the alley behind Johnny's Auto Repair one day. Do you remember that alley?"

Scott nodded and turned to face his old friend.

"Well, there was a 55-gallon oil drum sitting behind the shop, about three-fourths full. I looked in and saw a grasshopper that had managed to hop up into the drum and was trying to swim out of the oil. That's what gave me the idea. Pretty simple. And pretty stupid, really."

Watching Schrodinger jump down from the windowsill and stroll across the floor of the garage, Scott said, "So why did you decide to turn it into a study involving small animals instead of insects?"

"I'd already done my insect project for the year and I needed to do one that involved some kind of larger animals."

Scott had a pained expression on his face. "But you've been an animal rights activist every since I can remember. How could you do that kind of thing? Didn't you feel bad?"

Brian bent down and picked a screwdriver up from the floor, tossing it into one of the drawers in his big red toolbox. His cat walked between his feet and rubbed against his leg.

"Bad? I felt terrible. Why do you think I got involved with my animal rights group in the first place? I wanted to be a scientist. A physicist, not an animal torturer. I know I did some mean things to my cat before that, but I was just a kid. Once I matured enough to realize that those animals had feelings, and—"

He stopped talking and stooped down to pick up his cat, then stood back up and scratched

Schrodinger behind the ears, while Scott watched in silence. Finally, he went on.

"I couldn't go back and change anything I'd done, but I could try to help in the future. That's when I joined up with the ASPCA and started helping out at the Humane Society's shelter."

Scott turned away from the window and let his eyes adjust to the dimmer light in the shop. "So, what did you prove with the results of your study?"

Brian cocked his head to the right and gazed at the computer monitor, thinking it over. "Jeez," he said, looking back at Scott. "I don't know. I guess about the only thing it really proved was that I could get an 'A' in zoology." Slowly, a cheesy smile spread across his face.

Scott smiled at his friend, shaking his head. "Ya know, I'm glad you finally saw the ills of your ways, 'cause you were a real sicko back then. I'm also real happy I didn't have any other small animals."

Brian glanced at Scott with a guilty look and swallowed hard. Then, as his cheesy grin changed into a sly smile, he turned to walk over to the workbench. Scott barely heard him say, quietly and quickly, "You had a turtle."

Scott's jaw dropped open in disbelief as he stared after his friend. "My turtle?" He just stood and stared at Brian's back.

Brian gently put his cat on the workbench, picked up a small notepad and moved back toward the time machine. "Like you said, that was a long time ago." Trying to change the subject, he added, "Let me show you what I've already done. Come over here."

Still looking mildly stunned, Scott walked slowly toward the machine while mumbling to himself, "T-Rex. I looked for that turtle for *years*. What happened to him?"

"You don't wanna know."

Scott looked blankly at him. Brian handed the notepad to his shocked friend and waited for him to get over his post-amphibian trauma syndrome.

"I've logged all the trips on that notepad."

Scott looked in the book and saw notes detailing six trips. In each entry, Brian had recorded geographical locations, places in time, and return data. "These were actual time travel trips?"

"Yes sir, actual."

"You went back in time?"

"Oh, no. I can't go. Somebody has to be at the home console to keep it operational during every trip."

Scott looked at Brian's cat. "You sent—"

"Yep. I sent Schrodinger and he seemed to like it"

"Six times?"

"Actually, only four, so far."

Scott perused the notebook. "What about the other two?"

"Oh, those. Just experiments."

"Experiments? All those other drums. I saw one in the back yard, but where are the others?"

"Well, one of them is sitting out in the back yard, like you said. The other two, well, I kind of lost them."

"Lost them?"

"Don't worry. There weren't any living organisms on either one. Honest. I had to do some experimenting to work out the bugs, so I used the empty ships with monitoring equipment on board. I had to find out if it was going to be safe before I put Schrode on board a ship, didn't I?"

"Ship?" Scott tipped his head back and rolled his eyes. "Now it's a ship?"

"Gimme a break, here. It makes me feel good. In control, like a captain or something. Okay?"

Scott fought hard to keep the impertinent smirk off his face. "I'm sorry, I didn't know you had this ... captain fetish." He quickly changed horses and added, "You mean you lost two other machines somewhere in time?"

"That's right, two. I really hope they didn't cause any harm."

"Why didn't they come back? Do you have any idea?"

"One of them didn't have the improved system, so it had no way of returning. The other one, though. I don't know, Scott. I just can't figure that one out. It had to be something mechanical, like a leaking air hose or a loose battery cable. I'm very careful now to inspect every part before and after each trip. I made up a thorough checklist so I'll never miss a thing."

"Stop for just a second, Brian," Scott said. "I have to admit that I haven't been taking this very seriously up to now." He grabbed the back of his neck and massaged it with his left hand, then glanced over at the time machine. "But is this time machine really for real?"

"As real as the nose on your face."

Scott paled a bit. "Okay, prove it"

"Piece of cake." Brian lifted his cat off the workbench, put him in a kennel carrier and took it over to the time machine. He stepped onto the platform and set it on one of the seats in the cockpit. After strapping the kennel in, he closed the hatch and stepped down. He motioned for Scott to follow him over to the computer terminal. "I hope you're ready for this 'cause I think you're really gonna like it."

Reaching the computer terminal on the workbench, Brian began typing times, dates and coordinates. "Come and see this. What I'm doing is putting in the facts and figures for trip number seven. I'm sending Schrodinger on a trip that I already experimented with once before. To demonstrate to you that the machine really works, I'm going to send him one minute ahead in time. I'm also designating a different spot, right over there." Brian pointed to the large empty space in another part of the garage.

"You can designate places as well as times?"

"Oh, yeah. Once you're traveling the space-time continuum, you can travel in both realms."

Scott was getting a bit frazzled from the information overload. "There, you said it again ... continuum. I thought that was something somebody made up for the movies. Do you mean to say that there really *is* a space-time continuum?"

"Space-time is very real, Scotty. It includes the three dimensions of space and the one dimension of time. The point where the four dimensions meet is where an actual event took place in time. Does that make any sense to you?"

"Not a bit," Scott said with absolute honesty. "Should it?"

"Probably not. But what it means is, not only can we travel in time, but we can move geographically as well. I'm not really positive how the geographical part works. I kind of lucked into that one. Luck plays a big part in the scientific community, you know."

Scott nodded as if he actually knew.

"Anyway," Brian said, pointing to the other side of the shop. "I'm going to set ol' Schrodinger down right over there, one minute ahead in time. I've set the time coordinates to bring him back in three minutes, so we'll see him over there for that long before my machine brings him back. Just stand right here and get ready to be amazed, Scotty boy." He looked at Scott and smiled, then winked and added, "You're gonna love this. It's *damn* exciting stuff."

Brian typed GO on the computer keyboard and pressed ENTER. The time machine came to life and made an ear piercing hissing noise as the outer shell began to turn. After it gained momentum, the small electric motor started up and the loud hissing of the compressed air ceased.

Scott watched in astonishment as the electric motor bogged down slightly, then quickly regained its momentum. A crackling sound, like power lines crossing and arcing in a windstorm, filled the shop. The outer shell of the ship was spinning very fast when an electrical, humming sound started out low, building to a crescendo. Suddenly, there was a tremendous crack, like lightning striking, then the ear splitting sound of the pneumatics kicking back in.

The ship's shell became a blur of hunter green and a brilliant flash of light consumed the entire shop. Scott was momentarily blinded and had to close his eyes to gain back his vision. On opening his eyes, he could see only a bright yellow flash image. By the time the image faded, the time machine was no longer sitting on the original spot.

Fact was, the machine and the cat had vanished completely.

Chapter Six

Scott McLean stared into the empty space created by the disappearance of the time machine. "No way!" He shook his head. "No possible way!"

"Way," Brian said, glancing nervously back and forth between Scott and his watch. He'd been counting on a profound response from his best friend and he certainly wasn't disappointed. In fact, he couldn't have been more delighted if Scott had passed right out.

Scott started to say something, but was momentarily speechless.

"It's okay, man. Take some deep breaths."

"I don't understand ... how?" Scott said.

"You breath in and out slowly and deeply, then— "

Scott interrupted. "I know how to take deep breaths! What happened to the ship? And Schrodinger?"

"Ship? You called my machine a ship."

"Sorry."

"No, it's great. Your first thought was ship instead of dryer drum. You were impressed."

"That's an understate— "

"No time for that now," Brian said, looking intently at his watch. "You ain't seen nothin' yet. Watch this."

Still looking at his watch and reminding Scott more and more of a mad scientist, Brian started counting, "Four ... three ... two ... one."

What appeared at first to be a small, fist-sized cloud of very dense, deep-gray matter, materialized in mid-air over the bare floor on the other side of the garage. As quickly as it appeared, it expanded from the ceiling to the floor. With the center opening like a camera shutter, it resembled a large doughnut. A large cloudy doughnut.

Suddenly, a brilliant flash of light illuminated the entire cloud and the doughnut hole aperture expanded to a diameter of over five feet.

Scott watched intently and saw the side of the time machine move into view in the center of the hole. He kept his eyes glued to the cloud and saw the entire machine emerge from the smoky gray. When the air cleared, he knew he had witnessed a momentous event. His friend had really gone and done it this time. Scott wasn't yet sure exactly what he'd done, but Brian had definitely gotten into some tremendously heavy scientific stuff.

The time machine rested gently on the floor of the shop, perfectly intact, and Scott was once again speechless.

Finally, Brian broke the silence. "We don't have much time, less than three minutes now."

"For what?"

Brian grabbed him by the elbow and pulled him toward the ship. "I want you to see and touch it before it comes back home."

Checking out the ship and its equipment, the two of them walked all the way around the outside before stepping onto the platform to look through the porthole in the hatch. Peering into the cockpit, they saw the kennel cage, still strapped to the seat with Schrodinger staring peacefully back at them. Scott couldn't believe what he was seeing, even though he knew he was seeing what he was seeing.

"I don't get it," he stammered. "What exactly happened here?"

Brian paused and looked at the ceiling. "Hmm. Let me explain this to you in its simplest form."

"Please."

"I sent ol' Shrode one minute into the future. When he left our time, he disappeared from our presence. One minute later, we caught up to him and were re-united in time, which is why we're able to see and feel the ship. At the end of three minutes, the ship will leave the time it's now in and return immediately to our current time. Clear?"

"Clear as flint glass."

"Clever," Brian said, smiling as he glanced at his watch. "Never mind. Let's get out of the way."

Again, Brian took Scott's elbow and led him back across the shop, counting, "three ... two ... one."

The machine started up again with its hissing, humming, and spinning.

"Look away and close your eyes this time."

Scott closed his eyes and turned his head just seconds before another dazzling flash of light filled the shop.

"Now look."

Turning back and opening his eyes, Scott could just barely see the fading shadow of the ship as it disappeared from its spot on the other side of the shop.

Instantaneously, another fist of gray cloud appeared in the air above the original time machine resting spot, expanding from floor to ceiling. The small aperture appeared, followed by a flash of light. Then, the opening enlarged and deposited the time ship gently back on the floor of the shop.

Brian opened the hatch and extracted the kennel, then placed it on the floor and opened the small wire door. When he removed Schrodinger from the kennel and held him in his arms, the old cat was purring loudly. Brian smiled at Scott and said, "He seems to really enjoy the ride. The old boy's been contented like this after every trip."

"Yeah, it must be quite a rush. Brian?" Scott said, scratching his head and squinting his eyes. "I don't know what to say, man. I mean, I feel pretty weird, actually talking seriously about this, you know? I think I just witnessed time travel. Time travel! I saw it! I know I saw it, but I'm having trouble believing it. I did see it, didn't I?"

"You saw it and it is real. You'll get used to the idea, honest."

"Okay. I think I understand what you did, as unreal as it seems, but I have another question. Why did you have to send it to another spot in the shop? Couldn't it have, like vanished from one time and re-appeared in another time in the same spot? Or does that violate some kind of physics law or something?"

"No, it wouldn't violate anything I'm aware of, unless maybe the times overlapped. But I figured that as long as I could make it move in space, I would. Quite honestly, I did it for your benefit. I thought maybe it would have a greater effect on you if it moved to another location. You know, make a bigger impact on you."

"Good call, Bri. It worked."

Brian put the cat on the floor and hopped up to sit on the work bench. He thought for a moment, then said, "You know the incident with the cat in the washing machine?"

Scott nodded.

"That was one of my first time travel experiments. I was working on this clear back then. We were only fourteen, you know."

"I know."

"I've been convinced all along that traveling in time was possible, but it just took a while to work out all of the problems. Maybe I'm not as flabbergasted as you are by all of this because I've had a little longer to get used to the idea."

"It did come as a bit of a shocker. That's quite a nugget of scientific breakthrough to lay on me so suddenly."

Brian cleared his throat and grinned. "You don't know how excited I've been, knowing I was finally going to share this with my closest friend. I appreciate your sticking with me and letting me demonstrate it for you."

Scott walked around in circles, shaking his head in disbelief. "You have got to be kidding. You just finished showing me, before anyone else in the world, the most incredible scientific breakthrough in history, and you appreciate my listening? I've always admired you, Brian. You've performed some impressive experiments in the past. But, holy cow, man. This really takes the cake. You've more than outdone yourself this time. I bow to the master." He performed a low bow.

"Thanks." Brian humbly lowered his eyes toward the floor. "You're too kind."

The two men were silent for several minutes, both of them staring numbly at the time machine.

Scott broke the silence. "Why did you decide to trust me with this? I mean, why me?"

Brian laughed and stared at Scott like he was completely stupid. "You're kidding."

"No, not really."

"Scotty," Brian said, still not believing his friend had asked him such a dumb question. "I've got twenty years worth of reasons to trust you. In all that time, you never once gave me reason to think I couldn't trust you with my life." He paused and looked at Scott. "You want an example? Okay. How about the infamous graduation night. Have you forgotten about graduation night?"

A smile appeared on Scott's face at the thought of the celebration following their high school graduation ceremony.

Brian was never much of a drinker, but he did decide to get drunk on that night like most of the other kids in their class and Scott was going to join him. Since Scott was delayed at the school for about an hour after the ceremony, Brian agreed to pick him up there. He showed up in the parking lot driving his dad's truck, a taxi-cab yellow, 1968 Dodge Power Wagon with huge wheels. The cab sat almost three feet off the ground, which made it like riding in an eighteen wheeler.

Brian was already drunk when he got there, having downed a pint of Black Velvet and gotten a good start on a bottle of apricot brandy. When Scott offered to drive, Brian agreed. But he had one small thing to do first.

He told Scott he was going to repay Mr. Potts, one of his chemistry teachers, for being such a dick. He drove around the school to the chemistry lab, put the Power Wagon into four wheel drive, and drove the big truck right through the windowed wall. The truck high-centered on a big lab table sitting in the middle of the room, so Brian rocked it forward and backward, destroying the table and much of the lab.

They got out of the truck, leaving it parked in the chemistry lab, and were sitting out on the lawn looking at the damage when the police arrived. Scott told Brian to shut up and follow his lead and everything would be all right, then proceeded to take the blame for the "accident" because he hadn't been drinking. Nobody ever doubted the story of the star athlete, senior class president, and his best friend, the sterling scholar honor student.

"Did you ever tell anyone the truth about the accident, Scott?"

"I may have told Patty after we got married."

"You know, I could have lost my scholarship over that. Mr. Potts was the teacher that sponsored me." They both burst out laughing.

"Then why did you want to destroy his lab?"

"Because he was such a dick!" Brian shouted. "He sponsored my scholarship because he was ordered to do so by the head of his department. He hated me because I didn't want to be a chemist, 'wasting all of that genius,' he said. I couldn't stand him, either, because he was such an academic snob. But I had a great scholastic record, so they had to help me get a scholarship. And they could have certainly ruined it if they'd known what really happened." Brian looked pensively at Scott and continued. "You saved my butt that night."

"It worked out all right. I didn't get in too much trouble, but what does that have to do with your telling me about the time machine?"

"It isn't about the time machine. It's about trust. And friendship. You took the blame that night and saved my bacon, and you never did give me away. I know I can trust you with anything, Scotty."

"You would have done the same for me."

"I like to think I would, but you've never done anything stupid enough to give me the opportunity."

"I'll see what I can do." They both smiled, thinking about the long friendship they enjoyed. Changing the subject back to the time machine, Scott added, "Brian, have you seriously considered the ramifications of this? I'd ask if you know what you've got here, but I think you realize what you've got. But, let me ask you one thing. Do you know what you've got here?"

"Yeah, I know what I've got here."

Scott surveyed the entire shop, scanning all of the equipment. He saw the various tool boxes, welding equipment, and bits and pieces of assorted small appliances. There sat the old BMW, cannibalized as it was.

Suddenly, Scott remembered the day when Brian bought it and dragged it home. The motorcycle was at least fifteen years old at the time, and so was Brian. It was a pile of junk, but Brian spotted some inner beauty that no one else was able to see. He completely rebuilt the old relic. At one point, every last nut and bolt was laid out neatly on his father's garage floor. Then, on his sixteenth birthday, the day he got his driver's license, he wheeled his pride and joy out of the garage onto the driveway. It was absolutely beautiful with its eight coats of new black, hand-rubbed paint, and the two distinctive horizontal manifolds. When Brian started it up, it was the quietest motorcycle Scott had ever heard. It literally purred like a kitten.

"Get on. Let's go for a ride."

Scott did.

"You're gonna love this. This is a BMW, the Cadillac of motorcycles."

It seemed strange at first, seeing the tall, geeky Brian riding on a fine road machine like that, but before long the BMW was just an extension of its rider, and vice versa. He soon became known as the guy that rode the cool, black bike.

Maybe that's why he was able to date a fox like Joellen, Scott thought. He remembered how good they looked when they rode together on it, with Brian's long brown hair blowing in the breeze. Jo's short, dark hair offset his as she rode behind with her arms around his middle.

Maybe Brian wasn't such a geek after all. At least Jo didn't think so. And they were both very fortunate they lived through those unhelmeted years. Now, all of a sudden, the automatic transmission from that bike has become an integral part of a time machine. Quite a concept.

Of course, the focal point in the shop was the time ship. Scott pondered the strange looking piece of equipment and then looked back at Brian. "Hey, do you remember making the statement that going faster than the speed of light takes you into the past?"

"I do."

"Then, how is it you sent the cat into the future?"

Brian sat for a few seconds, trying to come up with a way to describe it so Scott would understand. "You know the automatic motorcycle transmission on the machine?"

"Yeah," Scott said warily.

With a straight face, Brian replied, "Well, I just put 'er in reverse."

Scott stared blankly at him.

"What?"

"Is it that far over my head?" Scott asked.

"I'll be honest with you. This stuff is over my own head. In fact, it might even be over Steven Hawking's own head."

"Whoa," Scott said. "You dare say something like that about your greatest hero?"

"I said *might* be over his head, not *is*," Brian said reverently, bowing his head.

They both turned and looked at the picture of Steven Hawking on the shop wall above the computer console.

After a moment of silence, Brian went on with his explanation. "This reversibility stuff gets deep. It's what took me so many years to figure out, and as I proved with two of my prototype ships, if I sent it into the past, I needed to find a way to bring it back home. Two of them didn't come back."

"So how do you put it in reverse? I rode that bike a lot, and I know for a fact that there was never an 'R' on the gear shift."

Brian pondered the problem for a couple of minutes. "Do you know anything about anti-matter?"

Shaking his head and pulling over an old, retired kitchen chair, Scott straddled it, facing Brian. He folded his arms on the top of the seat back and rested his chin on his arms.

"Negative."

"Clever answer."

"Really? I didn't mean it to be clever," Scott said truthfully. "What about anti-matter?"

"To get the opposite effects of photons ... it's very difficult to explain, the process involved in putting the time machine into reverse. Do you want me to give it a try?"

Scott gazed at Brian and slowly moved his head from side to side. "It's cool. I can wait, but I do have another question for you. Do you have any plans for sharing this with the rest of the world, or at the very least, with the scientific community?"

"No," Brian said firmly.

Scott was taken aback by his answer. "No?" He bolted upright on the chair. "Brian, you just spent twenty years of your life designing and building the impossible. It has to be worth a fortune and the notoriety would be unbelievable, so how can you keep it from the rest of the world?"

"I have to. For now, at least. Do you realize what the world could do with this technology? Think about what most governments would do with the ability to travel in time. Just imagine if they were handed the capability to alter events in time to enhance their own advantage." Brian took a deep breath and then continued. "And what if it found its way into the hands of some bad guys, like *Oil Can Harry* or *Snidely Whiplash!* You know, *villains*."

Scott grinned.

Brian paused for a few seconds, then went on. "I can't let that happen. I do have to admit, though, I was so intent on completing this thing that I didn't even think about the consequences until it was finished. But now it is, finished that is, I'm quite concerned about the power it could come to represent. In fact, my machine may be too dangerous to ever reveal to the world, I'm not sure."

Scott shook his head. "Bummer."

"I hear that."

"You could be filthy rich."

"It's okay. What would I do with a lot of money, build a bigger time machine? Maybe a four-seater. Or how about this? A time bus. Maybe I could even open a time travel agency. No, I don't think the folks in other times would appreciate a bunch of time tourists nosing around in their business. It would likely piss off a lot of people."

Scott laughed.

"Really. Think about it. Imagine you live in a small, quiet town in the year, say, 1855. You're happily working away in the big doorway of your blacksmith shop, when out of nowhere, a group of people suddenly appears. Weird looking people wearing very strange clothing like flowery Hawaiian shirts and Dockers shorts. Maybe even brown socks with sandals. And carrying small video recorders and large plastic coffee cups that say 7-11 COFFEE BRAKE CLUB on the sides."

Scott leaned on the back of the chair again and gazed at his friend, thoroughly amazed.

"There would probably be a tour guide dressed to the nines, but wearing running shoes or cross trainers for comfort. She'd be pointing things out to the group while she spouted out her canned narration."

Brian spoke in a high, hotsy-totsy voice. *"Please ... everyone. Try to stay together as a group. Now if you look to your left, you'll see a real blacksmith shop with a real blacksmith doing real, live blacksmith things. These poor, backward people don't have electricity. Or running water. They don't even have television or the Internet. Can you kids imagine what that would be like? Yet they manage to survive in this primitive environment."*

Brian paused and stared at Scott. "Can you see my point?"

"You still have quite an imagination," Scott smiled.

Brian hopped down from the workbench and stood facing Scott. "I suppose most people think scientists are nothing but brains filled with facts and figures, but quite the opposite is really true. It takes a tremendous amount of imagination to come up with most scientific advances ... and inventions." Brian was getting worked up. "Think of the imagination of Thomas Edison or the Wright brothers. I'll tell you what, those were some very active imaginations."

Scott stooped down and opened the door on the fridge. He took out a couple more beers, then stood back up and walked over near the time machine. Handing a beer to his friend, he said, "Am I to suppose that I'm already sworn to secrecy?"

Accepting the beer, Brian answered, "There's no one in this world I trust more than you. I'm not even a little bit worried about being betrayed by Scott McLean."

Scott appeared to be genuinely moved by what he had said. "That's really very touching. But does it mean I can't tell anybody?"

Brian smiled warmly. "Tell a soul and I'll have to kill you."

"That's kind of what I thought, but I just wanted to get it straight. Now, what's next with the time machine?"

"I'm glad you asked that. The next item on the agenda is to send a living, breathing human being on a time voyage." Nervously hesitating, he continued without losing eye contact with Scott. "But, I'll be needing a pilot."

Scott looked back casually. "Not a chance. I'm not your man."

"What do you mean, 'not my man?' You're perfect for the job. Look at yourself. The courageous firefighter performing brave rescues. The compassionate paramedic saving lives. You're a *stud* Scott ... the *original* stud. Besides, where else am I going to find someone I can trust to work with me on this? I need your help, man."

Scott stared quizzically at his friend, realizing for the first time what Brian was driving at. "You weren't kidding, were you? You'd really like to put me in that infernal contraption and send my butt into the space-time ... thing."

"Yep."

"Just like that? Yep? Then it's Alpha, Michael, Foxtrot to your old buddy, Scott? I don't believe it." He walked over to the window and put his unopened beer on the sill, ran his fingers through his hair, then turned around and leaned against the window frame.

"Sorry. I was hoping you'd be as psyched about time travel as me."

"Psyched doesn't even come close to describing my feelings about it. In fact, I'm downright flabbergasted by the whole concept of time travel. But, how about you going somewhere in time and letting me stay here to keep the home fires burning?"

"I'll think about it," Brian said, patronizing him. "Do me a favor, though. You think about it, too."

"Oh, I'll think about it. I won't consider doing it, but I'll certainly think about it."

"Fair enough," Brian said, nodding his head.

"Hey, what're you two plotting out here?" Jo Daniels said, coming through the door from the house wearing a frumpy gray sweatshirt, white sweat pants, and Birkenstocks. Her brown hair was still damp from the shower.

"Hi, hon," Brian said.

Scott looked around and said his greetings to Jo.

"Did you talk him into it?" Brian tried to shush her, but wasn't quick enough. "What? Oh, oops." She covered her mouth with both hands. "You haven't told him yet?"

Scott was already nodding his head. "Uh-huh. Uh-huh! The man says to me, 'I wouldn't trust anybody in the world but you to know about my time machine. I couldn't wait to tell my best friend about my time machine.'" He looked over at Jo and smiled, then gazed at his friend with an exasperated look spreading across his face.

"Of course I told Jo, but she doesn't count. She's only—"

"Only what?" Jo interrupted with a stern look, the nostrils of her pug nose flaring slightly. "She doesn't count?"

"You're goin' down, man," Scott said, backing away.

"Only what, Brian?" She put both hands on her hips and stared daggers at him with her dark brown eyes. "What am I *only*?"

Brian hung his head. "Only my wife, but I didn't mean it the way it sounded."

"Only your wife." Scott pointed a finger at him as he turned toward the door. "Good call, Brian." He headed for the door, then stopped and turned around to add a little more. "I'd better go now. It looks like you two might wanna be alone." He turned back around and exited the shop.

Jo was standing nose to nose with her husband, her hands still planted firmly on her hips, her jaw locked into a scowl. "Well?"

"You know what I meant, don't you? I could never keep anything from you. It's just natural to share everything with you."

She smiled and threw her arms around his neck and whispered in his ear. "A lot of women wouldn't believe you, but I know you too well, Daniels. Grovel for me anyway."

Brian couldn't help but smile. "What I meant was, that you're more than just my friend. You're like a part of me, my partner, so how could I not tell you first?"

"That's not bad," Jo said, kissing his ear and making him melt. "But you still owe me."

"What?"

"We haven't christened the time machine yet," she said sweetly.

Brian stepped back and stared at his wife.
"You aren't serious."
"Dead."
Brian grinned and headed for the ship. "What is it with you new age women, anyway?"
"We've been repressed for thousands of years, dear. Now it's our turn to rule." She pointed to the ship. "Into the cockpit and make it snappy."
Brian slipped into the ship, then poked his head part way up out of the hatch. Jo pushed it back down, stepped out of her sandals and climbed in after him.

* * *

"You two go get jammies on and we'll make some chocolate chip cookies," Patty said to Melissa and Casey as they walked into the house.

Patty and Scott had just returned from taking the kids to Wendy's for dinner and it was Casey's turn to choose. He always chose Wendy's.

"I have to admit, that Dave really knew how to throw together a tasty sandwich."

"No kidding." Scott hung his car keys on the hook. "And he made a pretty good baked potato, too. What a guy, that Dave was. A real stud muffin." She reached in a cupboard and got a package of chocolate chips, then stopped and said, "I'll go get the kids moving if you'll start getting cookie stuff ready."

"Check."

Later, the McLeans were sitting together on the carpeted living room floor. They'd all had their fill of fresh hot cookies and milk. Patty was reading a story book to Missy, Casey and Scott. Listening to her read to the kids was one of his very favorite things.

When she finished reading the book, which was about fire engines, Casey asked his father, "Did our grampa really wear that old hat into fires?"

"He sure did. Sometimes, he even drove the team of horses that pulled his fire company's steamer wagon."

"Cool," Casey said.

"Coo-woh," Missy repeated, wide-eyed and serious.

Scott had to stop and laugh at Missy, so Patty continued to tell the two children about their great, great grandfather, John Patrick McLean, Jr.

"He fought fires back when they didn't have anything but horse drawn fire wagons, and the horses lived right there in the firehouse alongside the firemen. The horses were like family to them, just like your daddy and his friends are at his station. And do you know what?" She stopped talking to the kids and turned to Scott. "You haven't ever told the kids about Grandpa Packy, have you?"

"No, well, I've told Casey a little bit, but not much. I was waiting until the time seemed right."

"Who's Grampa Packy, Daddy?"

Scott pulled Missy over to his side and began telling his children the story about how little Packy McLean decided to become a fireman.

When he finished, Patty told the kids about the leather-bound diary. "Your dad has a journal that Packy started writing when he was younger than you, Case." She poked him in the belly and started him giggling.

"Yeah," Scott said. "I'll have to find it so we can read about it in the exact way Grandpa Packy told it."

"Get it, Dad," Casey begged, jumping over into Scott's lap.

"Get it, Daddy," Missy chimed.

Scott thought for a moment. "I'm not sure where it is, but I'll look for it in the morning. It might be in the basement in one of the boxes."

"Can we look for it?" Casey added.

Scott looked at his 7-year-old son, the same age as Packy was when he made his career choice. "Okay. Both of you can look for it in the morning and then we'll all read it together. Now, I think it's time for bed."

He turned to Patty for backup and she nodded.

"Go brush your teeth and I'll be right up," she said to the children as they jumped and ran screaming up the stairs to the bathroom.

Scott and Patricia were on their way to the stairs when the phone rang. Scott offered to get it so his wife could go tuck in the kids.

"Hello."

"Scott. Brian. Do you have a second?"

"Sure," Scott said, starting to clean the mess in the kitchen.

"Have you given any more thought to my proposal?"

"Brian, I really can't consider doing that. I have too much to live for. Even if it's perfectly safe, I can't go off joy riding in your machine and leave my family here to fend for themselves. I need to stay here and fend with them. You should understand that."

"But you could go off for a day, a week or five years and we can bring you back at the same time you left. It wouldn't even take a minute in real time."

Scooping up the rest of the cookies from the countertop and putting them in the cookie jar, Scott said, "That's not the point. I just plain don't want to go off on some adventure into the unknown."

"All right." Brian sounded disappointed. "I'll give you more time to think it over."

"Sorry, man," Scott said, rinsing a sponge and wiping off the counter tops. "I won't change my mind."

"You're right. It is a lot for me to ask, isn't it?"

"You could say that." Scott wrung out the sponge and put it back on the sink.

"I just did."

"Oh, yeah, I forgot. Hey, I'd better go, Bri. I want to help tuck the kids in."

"Okay, I'll talk to you later." But before Scott could hang up the phone, Brian stopped him. "Hold it!" he shouted into the phone.

Scott put the phone back up to his ear. "What is it?"

"Before you hang up, let me give you something to think about."

"I'm listening."

"Just food for thought. I've been doing some thinking about it and I came up with an idea."

"Pray tell."

"How would you like to be present, in person, at the Great Chicago fire? Or be there to actually see the San Francisco earthquake and conflagration? You could do it, Scott. You could see the Coconut

FIRES OF TIME * 93

Grove fire or even help out at the Triangle Shirtwaist Company fire."

Scott felt the sensation of blood draining from his face and he began to get lightheaded. He didn't have a response. In fact, he was totally speechless.

Brian continued. "Think about it. No pressure. Maybe you could drive a steamer wagon or help Benjamin Franklin start America's first volunteer fire brigade in Philadelphia. What was it, the Union Fire Company? Think about this. Maybe you could even meet John Patrick McLean."

Scott finally interrupted Brian's sales pitch. "No fair. This is dirty pool."

Brian decided to back off. "I'm sorry. That was hitting below the belt, wasn't it? Just forget I said a thing. Pretend I didn't even call." He paused, then added, "G'night. Talk to you tomorrow."

Brian hung up and left Scott standing in the kitchen holding the telephone receiver and listening to the dial tone.

* * *

Lying in bed after getting Casey and Missy to sleep, Patty and Scott talked in the dark.

"Who called a little while ago?"

"Brian," Scott said, seeming preoccupied.

"Is anything wrong?"

"No, not really. I'm just thinking."

"About what? Or is it a secret?"

"Yes and no. I promised Brian I wouldn't say a word, but then I found out he'd already told Joellen."

"The time machine?" she asked innocently.

"What?"

"Are you talking about Brian's time machine project?"

Scott sat up in the bed. "You know about it too? What? Did Brian take out a newspaper ad or something? How many people has he told about *our little secret?*"

Patty sat up on the bed with her legs crossed and turned to face Scott.

"Jo told me about it this afternoon while you were with Brian. She said the four of us are the only people in the world who know about it." Patty took hold of his hand. "Besides, dear. A time machine? Do you honestly think, for one instant, that Brian Daniels or anyone else on this planet could build a time machine that actually works?"

Scott sat thinking, silently thinking.

"What did he want?"

"Who?"

"Brian, when he called."

"Oh, on the phone," Scott said, taking Patty's other hand in his. "You wouldn't believe what he asked me." Scott stopped and looked harder, trying to see his wife through the surreal vision of semi-darkness. "You haven't seen a demonstration, have you?"

"Demonstration? Are you trying to say it works?"

Scott laid back down beside his wife and held her in his arms.

"Let's wait until tomorrow when we can pay Brian a visit."

* * *

The next morning, after everybody was out of bed and finished with breakfast, the two McLean children went on a hunt for the journal. It took about forty-five minutes to find the old, leather-jacketed diary, but by the time they found it, Grandma McLean showed up to take the kids with her for the day. Missy gave the journal to Scott and made him promise to read it with them when they returned in the evening. After they'd gone, Scott and Patty were left sitting together at the table.

"I talked to Jo already," she announced. "She told us to come on over whenever we're ready, so when do you want to go?"

"I'm ready now," Scott said, folding the newspaper and laying it on the table. "Let's be gone." As they got up from their chairs to leave, Scott added, "Just a second, let me leave this here." He put the journal on top of the refrigerator and they continued out the door.

Brian and Jo were waiting in the shop when the McLeans stepped through the door.

"Hi you guys," Brian said.

Jo smiled. "You wanna go for a ride, Patty?"

"Right," Patty said, walking around and studying the time machine. She touched the side and ran her hand around on the gleaming green paint. "Have you two been planning something?"

"Not really," Brian said. "You already know about the project, so we talked and decided you really should see what it's all about. After all, you are one of the chosen few, ya know?"

Stepping up onto the platform, Patty said, "Is it for real?"

Scott went over and took her hand. "Why don't you decide for yourself?"

Brian clapped his hands together and rubbed them vigorously. "Okay. Let's do it, folks." He stepped up on the platform beside Patty and opened the hatch.

"I talked him into going for a spin and taking me along," Jo said, pointing toward Brian.

"You ready, Joellen?"

"You bet, Brian," she answered, moving over to the machine and climbing up on the platform with him.

"All right, you guys," Brian said. "I've already set the controls for the same trip Schrodinger took yesterday. We're getting set to go, so you can explain to Patty what's going to happen, Scott. Okay?"

"Ten-four," Scott said, taking Patricia by the hand and leading her off the platform and over to the side of the shop near the base computer. He began describing to his wife the basic operation of the vehicle when Brian interrupted.

"By the way, this trip will be my very first ride in the ship. I'll talk to you when we get there."

"Good luck," Scott said.

Jo was already inside the cockpit when Brian climbed in and closed the hatch from the inside. Scott finished explaining to Patty what was going to take place and she listened quietly with obvious amusement.

"I didn't take it seriously either, just watch. Oh, and when it starts to make a racket and begins to spin, close your eyes until after the flash."

"Flash?" Patty said, showing some surprise.

"Flash. You're not gonna believe this."

FIRES OF TIME * 97

The time machine went through all of its startup procedures and then made a tremendous crack and brilliant flash.

"It vanished," Patty declared in amazement. "Where are they?"

Not yet comfortable with the whole concept of time travel, Scott was still awed himself. "If what Brian told me is correct, they're somewhere, or sometime, traveling along the space-time continuum."

"Serious? Do you really think it's possible?"

"Keep watching. I didn't think it was possible, but I know what I saw." Scott pointed to the empty spot in the garage. "Look right over there and you'll see it too."

At that instant, a small fist of a cloud began to form, then enlarged to its doughnut shape. After the flash of light, the ship emerged from the aperture and came to rest on the floor, causing Patty to let out a squeal. It had no sooner stopped when Patty and Scott heard the hatch's locking mechanism being turned.

The hatch opened and Brian poked his head through. "Hey," he said.

"How was it?" Scott asked.

"Lemme look," Jo hollered from inside the ship. She stuck her head up behind Brian's and looked around the shop.

"We really did it!" she said excitedly, grabbing Brian's shoulder and shaking it. "We really did it, hon!"

Unconsciously, Scott stroked his mustache. "I have a question for you. What if you two got out of the ship and let it come back on its own? What kind of an influence would that have if you stayed one minute ahead in time forever? Would you be all screwed up or out of sync for the rest of your lives, or do you think it'd make any kind of difference?"

Brian gave him a puzzled look. "I never thought about it before, so I honestly can't tell you one way or another. Sorry."

Jo butted in. "Well, let's not try to find out. I don't want to chance it."

Glancing at his watch, Brian agreed, "Me neither. We have forty-five seconds."

Brian and Jo ducked backed down into the cockpit and the McLeans heard the latch slowly being turned.

After the ship returned to its original time, the four of them went into the house and sat at the kitchen table.

"Now I know why Schrodinger is always so mellow after each trip," Brian remarked.

"Me, too," Jo grinned. "I'm just about as relaxed as I ever get, like I took a Valium or something."

"Right on," Brian nodded.

Joellen looked puzzled. "Why does it cause this?"

"I wondered that too, so I did some research." He paused for a minute to glance at the others. "As you guys can well imagine, there isn't an awful lot of information available about the effects of time travel on the human body, so I had to do some of my own experimenting."

"Small animals?" Scott asked sarcastically.

Brian smirked. "Still nursing that grudge, eh?"

Scott laughed.

"In all honesty, I did use a small animal. Schrodinger." He glanced at Scott, who was smiling and shaking his head in mock disgust. "I hooked some monitoring equipment up to him when he went on three of his trips and found every trip the same. His blood pressure dropped, along with his pulse rate. And he was very relaxed. The nearest I can figure is that the drastic change of moving through time slows the metabolic rate and relaxes the body." He turned to Jo, then added. "Sorry I couldn't come up with some other breakthrough kind of explanation, but I'll keep working on it. That's what the experiments are all about."

His wife smiled and patted him on the arm.

Nobody spoke for a moment until Brian looked at Scott. "Do you want to try it?"

Scott stared at his hands momentarily, then looked up at Brian. "Let me tell you a couple of things. I've thought of little else since you called me last night. The things you said to me were really unfair, but effective. You hit me right where I live, just the way you planned it."

"And?"

"And I've thought about it a lot."

"What did he say last night?" Patty asked.

"He dangled a carrot in front of me, Patty" Scott said. "A big, juicy carrot. My good friend offered to send me on the trip, or trips, of a lifetime. My lifetime, anyway. He suggested that I could travel in time to some of the greatest events in the history of fires." He paused a few seconds. "You know? The Great One in Chicago? San Francisco in 1906?"

"Wow!" Patty said to Brian, her eyes widening. "That's harsh, Daniels. Do you go around offering drugs to recovering addicts, too?"

"You could go with him if you wanted," Brian offered.

"Thank you, no," she said emphatically. "Besides, I'm still a bit overwhelmed by the whole thing. It's a difficult concept to grasp right away."

"Yeah, I know." Looking at Scott, Brian asked, "Well, any decision yet?"

"I'm still thinking."

"How safe is it?" Patty asked.

"We came through all right and ol' Schrode always came back looking and feeling pretty darn good," Brian remarked, leaning back in his chair with both hands behind his head. "In all honesty, your guess is as good as mine. It seems very safe and serene as long as things go right, but if something went terribly wrong. Who's to say? I can't promise nothing will ever go wrong, but I can promise that I'll do everything within my power to keep that from happening."

"I never doubted that for a second, but this is all very mind boggling," Patty said, turning in her chair to face her husband. "What are you thinking now?"

He hesitated and peered into his wife's eyes, looking for some new sign. "I think I'd like to try it."

"That's my boy!" Brian said, dropping the front legs of his chair back to the floor and leaning out across the table on his forearms. "When do you want to go?"

"I don't know. What do you think?"

"Anytime you're ready."

"Okay," Scott said nervously. "Patty and I will need to have a good long talk about it first and I'll let you know what we decide."

"Cool," Brian said.

Scott looked intently at his friend. "But I won't do it if Patty has any qualms at all." Patty and

Brian turned their heads and when their eyes met, he said sincerely, "I'll respect whatever decision you make."

Patty smiled at him without speaking.

* * *

The back door flew open as Missy and Casey ran into the house at their usual speed — warp. Grandma McLean was returning them from the day's adventures.

"Hi, Mommy. Hi, Daddy," Missy called out as she ran upstairs toward the bathroom.

Casey went over to where his parents were sitting and related the tales of the day in one long, run-together sentence.

"Gramma took us to the sports park and I got to ride the slick track cars but Missy couldn't cause she didn't come up to the bear's hand he was holding out. It was real cool. Then we rented some videos and went back to Gramma's house and watched 'em."

"Sounds exciting," Patty smiled. "What videos did you see?"

"Two really neat ones." He turned to his grandmother and asked, "What were they called, Gramma?"

Rosalyn McLean smoothed the skirt of her colorful dress. "Oh, we watched *Back To The Future*. And that Paul Newman one with the fire ... *Towering Inferno*."

Patty looked at Scott to see his reaction. With a wry smile on his face, he looked at the floor and just shook his head.

"I don't believe it. Maybe it's an omen."

"That is pretty weird, Scott," Patty agreed.

Looking confused, Rosalyn said, "What are you two talking about?"

"Nothin' Mom," Scott said, smiling at Patty. "It was just something we were talking about earlier today."

Heading for the door, Rosalyn said, "I have to go now. I still have a few things to get done this evening."

"Let me guess, Mom," Scott said. "The kids didn't really get into the Paul Newman movie and you're going back home to watch it again."

"Oh, Scott." She was obviously embarrassed. "You know me too well. But that man is still a hunk. And Steve McQueen was a firefighter in the movie, too. Oh, don't get me started. You kids take care, now."

"Bye, Ma," Patty grinned with a wave.

"Bye, bye kids," Rosalyn said.

They all told her goodbye and she went out and pulled the door closed, with Scott still laughing at her.

"She's really something, my mom," he said to Patty. "She used to always say, 'that man can park his shoes under my bed any time he wants.'"

Patty smiled. "Did you know she buys his salad dressing because his picture is on the label and she can look at it while she eats?"

Scott nodded and started to speak, but was interrupted.

"Daddy," Melissa said, tugging on Scott's finger. "The story, remember? Get the Grampa Packy book."

After getting the children ready for bed and popping up some popcorn, the whole family gathered together in the family room to read Packy McLean's journal.

Opening the leather-bound journal and thumbing wistfully through some of the pages, Scott said to the kids, "I used to look through this a lot when I was a little boy. My favorite things were always the pictures that Packy drew."

Patty watched on, smiling at how excited Scott was to share his childhood treasure with his own kids. She adored that little boy side of him and wished he'd let it out to play more often.

Showing everybody one of the pages, Scott said, "See, he tried to draw pictures of the things he was writing about. There must be hundreds of these little drawings in here. When I was young, I thought it looked just like a dictionary the way the pictures sit out to the side of the each page beside the subject. But my grandma told me why Packy drew the pictures in the journal." Scott paused while the kids pointed excitedly to the pictures, then went on. "She said that when he started it he was only six years old, so he mostly drew pictures and left the rest of each page blank. Then, when he was about ten or eleven, he went back and wrote what he remembered about each day. Sometimes the pictures he'd drawn helped to remind him of what happened on that day. Grandma said 'that's why there are more of the pictures in the first part of the journal.' He drew more in the younger years and wrote more in the later ones."

"Read it to us, Dad," Casey said.

"Okay, but we can only read part of it tonight. Where do you want me to start?"

"Can I say?" Patty said promptly. "I'd like to hear the part we talked about last night. You know, when Packy was seven, and the big fires."

"Sounds good. Is that all right with you guys?"

"Yes," Missy and Casey said together.

Scott proceeded into the journal, reading about the boys fishing, the fires, and Packy's plans to be a fireman. Reaching the finish of the Great fire, Scott handed the journal to the kids so they could look at the pictures. John Patrick McLean wasn't the greatest artist, which sometimes made it difficult to figure out what the pictures were supposed to represent.

Missy looked closely at the page, counting the pictures in the margin. "... fibe ... sis," she reported. "Sis pishers."

Everyone looked at the page and counted.

"You're right, Missy," Patty said. "There are exactly six pictures on the page we just read."

"Look, this is a steamer wagon with hot cinders and stuff flying out behind it," Casey said, then pointed to another picture. "This might be the bathtub they put in the kitchen."

"Yeah, the bafftub," Missy said.

Casey held the journal for Scott to see, then pointed to a picture. "What's that one, Dad?"

Scott looked at the picture. It seemed to be a drawing of firefighters putting water on a fire while some other firefighters were busy rescuing someone from a burning building. Packy had tried to imitate the signature, "Currier," at the bottom of the picture.

"The only thing I could ever figure out was that he must have been trying to copy one of the lithographs from the side of a fire wagon. Each firehouse had a fancy picture of their own design painted on the side of their fire engine to identify it as their fire company, and many of them were painted by a former New York fireman named Currier. They were very competitive then, and even gave nicknames to their engines."

"What was Grampa Packy's named?"

"Not yet, Case. We'll find out more about that later on in the journal."

Scott closed the treasure and sent the kids off to brush their teeth. Watching his son walk up the stairs, he noticed for the first time that Casey looked a lot like the descriptions he'd heard of 7-year-old Packy McLean. A lean boy with a shaggy shock of light brown hair and green Irish eyes that sparkled whenever he smiled. Turning to Patty, he noticed she was watching the kids with a loving smile on her lips.

"You make beautiful children, Patricia," he said softly.

She turned to Scott, still smiling. "You're right. We do, don't we?"

* * *

The next morning, Patty and Scott hadn't yet discussed the time machine. Standing in the doorway between the living room and kitchen, Patty was the first to mention it.

"Are you thinking about Brian's ship?"

Sitting at the bar deep in thought, Scott turned to her and answered. "It's all I can think about. You'd have to admit, it's an interesting dilemma to be in, whether or not to take a trip through time. Not your run-of-the-mill kind of everyday decision, ya know?"

"This is far and above my realm of reasoning. If I get thinking too deeply about it, the whole thing overwhelms me. Like when I try to ponder ideas like space and infinity. Does that make sense to you, Scott?"

"Absolute sense. I'm there. I was thinking earlier about what it would be like if some high-falootin yahoo got in his limo and started giving directions to his chauffeur."

Using his best British accent, Scott went off on a verbal tangent similar to the one Brian did the day before:

"Good morning, sir, his driver might say. And where might we be planning on traveling to on this beautiful day?"

"Oh, didn't I tell you Jeeves? You'll be taking us promptly to 1906."

"Ahem, 1906 what, sir? You'll need to tell me the street name, in order to find this 1906 address."

"Oh my, you don't understand. We're not going to a street, we're going to 1906. The year. Come, come, get my things, we mustn't be late. After all, 1906 ..."

He stopped and looked at Patty, who was staring intently at him like he'd gone completely nuts, then finished the sentence.

"...isn't going anywhere, is it?"

After a few long seconds of silence, Patty spoke. "No, it isn't," she said quietly. Then stepping over to her husband and sitting on his lap, she put her arms around his neck and looked him directly in the eyes. "But *you* are," she said softly. Scott thought about it and said nothing. "You have to do it. Your

FIRES OF TIME * 107

best friend has offered you your dream. Think about it. I laid awake most of the night thinking about it."

"What if I don't want to go?"

Patty didn't acknowledge what he'd asked as being a valid question. "You want to go, hon. You have to go. I want you to."

Scott was puzzled. "Aren't you going to try to stop me or tell me how dangerous it is?"

"Number one, I don't have the slightest idea how dangerous, or safe it is and neither does Brian. But could it be more dangerous than firefighting?"

"Number two, how could I possibly stand in the way of your fulfilling a dream?"

"You are really something," Scott said lovingly.

"Thanks, babe. Just hurry back to me."

"Brian said it wouldn't even take a minute. I just hope it's safe."

"Scott, sometimes I think your friend Brian loves you more than I do. Do you realize how very fortunate you are to have a friend like that?"

"Yes I do, and next to you and the kids, I've never been closer to anyone else in my entire life."

"There you are then. He isn't going to do anything to jeopardize the life of his closest friend." She kissed Scott long and hard, then added, "There'll be a lot more of that waiting for you when you get back."

Scott hesitated briefly. "Do you want me to go right this minute?"

"No time like the present."

They both thought about what she'd said and laughed.

"Is Brian off work today?"

"Jo told me he's off for the next two weeks. Now, get out of here before I start having second thoughts."

Scott went into the family room and kissed the kids, giving them both big, strong hugs. He walked toward the back door and picked up his paramedic tool pouch. Picking up his small, black duffel, he put the pouch inside the nylon bag and zipped it closed. He noticed Patty watching him and shrugged his shoulders.

"You never know, ya know?"

She nodded and watched him start out the back door. He stopped and turned around.

"Do you want to come with me to watch the historic event?"

"If it's all the same to you, I think I'd like to stay here with the kids ... after all, you're only going to be gone a minute, right?"

"I wouldn't have expected anything else from such a great mom. I love you."

"Go."

* * *

Brian walked out through the door between the kitchen and the shop. Wearing Levis, high top Adidas and an off-white, short-sleeved trash shirt with three buttons at the neck, Scott was standing on the time machine's platform, looking in through the hatch.

"Ready to go, Scotty?"

"All set. Make it snappy before I lose my nerve."

"Have you decided where you want to go?"

"San Francisco. Wednesday, April 18, 1906, at 0510 hours."

"You got it, my man," Brian said, turning on the computer. "It'll take me a few minutes to program in the information. Why that particular time?"

"That was three minutes before the earthquake hit."

Brian stopped what he was doing and turned around, looking warily at Scott with a furrowed brow. "Do you really want to be there before it hits? Wouldn't you rather arrive shortly after the earthquake? Just to be safe?"

Scott stepped over to the computer console and explained his feelings to Brian. "If you're going to all the trouble of sending me to 1906 San Francisco, I'm not gonna miss the main event. Didn't you say you can put the ship down in a designated spot?"

"Within reason."

"Within reason?" Scott stepped back and gazed suspiciously at him.

"About a hundred yards or so. Would that be good enough?"

Scott thought it over. "Yeah, it would. I want to land in a spot that'll be safe from both the earthquake and the fire."

"You'll have to help me then. I don't have the foggiest idea what was safe and what wasn't. I believe you're the resident expert in that particular area."

"Telegraph Hill was safe for a while. Can you put me on Telegraph Hill?"

"Lemme look." Brian pulled up a screen on the computer that showed a map of the United States. As Scott watched, Brian made the map change to that of California, and then to San Francisco. Zooming in, the scientist soon had a full screen map of Telegraph Hill. He picked up a pencil and scratched some numbers on a notepad, then said, "There, that ought to do it."

"What are those numbers?"

"Coordinates for latitude and longitude. Gotta have those to put you in the right spot."

"Oh."

"All right, my friend," Brian said. "I believe we're set. For this first trip, I've programmed the ship to take you to San Francisco on the morning of Wednesday, April 18, 1906, at 0510 hours. When do you want to come back?"

"I'll have to get off of the hill by Friday morning before the fire overruns it. How about nine o'clock?"

"Okay then, it'll return automatically at 0900 hours on Friday, April 20, 1906. You still with me?"

"Sure. But I have a question. What if I want to come back earlier than that? Can I override the computer?"

"You can," Brian said, pointing out the keyboard located in the cockpit. "It's like using any other computer. You do know how to use a computer, don't you?"

Scott gave his friend an annoyed look. "You just show me what I need to do here, egghead. I'm not completely stupid."

"My, my, we're a bit testy this morning," Brian said as he showed Scott how to manually operate the ship's computer.

"I've put a password in so no one else can get in and steal your ship. It's a toughy Scott. I hope you can remember it."

FIRES OF TIME * 111

"What is it?"

"FIRESOFTIME," Brian said triumphantly. "Can you handle that?"

"Brilliant, Brian. Really brilliant."

"You can override at any time before nine on Friday. That time can not be changed to a later time by you. This thing comes back precisely at nine on Friday. If you choose to override the onboard computer to come back early, you have to put in the password, turn both keys and hit enter. If not, be there no later than nine, because I don't want to have to go back there looking for you, okay?"

"Check, no later than nine on Friday."

"Good. Climb on in, my friend, and let's send you on your way."

Scott climbed into the cockpit and fastened his seat belt, even though there seemed to be no real need for it. Brian had explained that the seat belt was mostly for looks. He stowed his duffel under his seat, and as Brian was closing the hatch, Scott stopped him.

"Can I take one of those half gallon jugs of water?"

Brian took a plastic milk jug filled with water from one of the storage shelves and handed it through the hatch to Scott.

"There you go. Anything else?"

"Yeah. When will I be back here?"

Brian looked at his watch. "About sixty seconds after you leave."

"Copy that. Is there anything else I'm supposed to do? Any instructions about time travel taboos or anything?"

Leaning into the hatch, Brian offered a few words of advice. "This thing about interrupting the space-time continuum? It may be just theory, or it could be a hard fact. I don't know. So, this first trip, you're going to observe. Try not to do anything or touch anything that could change history. Observe, Scott — just observe. As far as anything else goes, I don't know that either. Play it by ear and use that great common sense of yours."

"Ten-four," Scott said with a nervous smile.

"See you in a minute, my friend." Brian closed the hatch, then added, "Good luck."

Scott double checked the hatch on the inside and gave Brian a thumbs-up.

Sitting inside the ship, Scott heard the loud hissing of the high pressure air tanks and knew it was too late to turn back. The machine operated with extreme efficiency, going through all the required steps in under fifteen seconds.

One hundred and eighty-six thousand miles per second, he thought. *What in the hell am I doing here?*

Out loud he said, "This is absolutely insane."

Chapter Seven

Following the brilliant flash of light, the ship was thrown into darkness, the only light being the bluish glow from the computer monitor screen. Scott looked around the interior of the cockpit and thought, *This thing could use a dome light*. He felt a slight vibration as the outer shell quickly slowed down and came to a complete stop. Watching through the porthole in the hatch, the blackness turned to a cloudy gray, flashed brightly, then faded to black again. Feeling quite mellow, he thought, *They were right, this is very relaxing*.

Suddenly, he was acutely aware that the ship had stopped moving. As he strained to see something through the porthole, he realized the blackness he was seeing was filled with stars.

He undid his seatbelt and thought, *I wonder where I ended up?*

Then, reaching up, he turned the handle on the hatch and opened it a crack. *It smells like the ocean. Can it really be?*

He pushed the hatch the rest of the way open. The firefighter from 2002 stood up through the hatchway into the outside darkness.

"No way. No way," he told himself.

Climbing from the ship, Scott secured the hatch and stepped down from the small platform. He walked toward a clearing in the high bushes in which the ship had landed, saying to himself, "Nice shot, Bri."

The time machine was concealed by the bushes.

Working his way to a spot where he could see out to both the east and the south, he saw the faint beginnings of a sunrise, then scanned around below in the pre-dawn darkness and saw the city. Scott stood in absolute awe at the sight before him: San Francisco, 1906.

He leaned his head way back and yelled toward the sky, "You did it, Brian!"

Turning slowly in a circle, with his arms spread fully out to his sides, he yelled it louder, "You did it! I don't believe it, you really did it!" Still turning around in a circle and yelling, his jubilance was abruptly cut short as a tremendous jolt threw him to the ground.

* * *

Moments later, a voice called out from somewhere in the darkness. "Who are you yelling at?"

As he was getting back up, Scott squinted his eyes to see where it had come from and saw the figure of a man walking toward him. He appeared to be in his early thirties, maybe five-foot-ten or so, with a lean build. His dark wavy hair, parted in the middle and combed toward the back, was cut very trim and neat.

"Are you talking to me?"

The man surveyed Scott with his soft, brown eyes. "Were you doing all the yelling?"

Scott looked around, then back at the man. "Yeah."

"Well then, who were you yelling at?"

"No one in particular," Scott said, glancing at his watch and sitting back down on the ground.

The man continued walking toward Scott and stood right beside him. "Are you all right there?" He reached out his hand to Scott and said, "Here, let me give you a hand up."

"No, I'm fine, but you'd be wise to sit down and brace yourself for a minute." Looking at the Indiglow readout of his watch again, Scott continued. "Another big tremor is gonna hit in sixteen seconds."

The stranger stared intently at Scott's watch. "What makes you think that?"

"Trust me for a second and sit your butt down here on the grass."

"Do you fancy yourself as some kind of prophet or something? I believe I'll stand, thank you."

"Suit yourself," Scott said as the second shock hit, knocking the man to the ground.

The ground shook for what seemed like an eternity, but was really only sixty more seconds. The sound the earthquake created was a very loud, tremendous rumbling, just as deafening as Scott had imagined it would be. Continuing after the earthquake stopped, the sickening sound of buildings crashing to the ground in the distance added a terrifying quality to the already alarming event. The scraping and squealing was bone chilling, as brick and mortar crumbled and dredged along the twisting steel skeletal structures of many of the buildings.

I don't believe this is happening, Scott thought as he listened to the resounding whoomp of some building's upper floors and roof impacting the ground. *Am I really sitting in the middle of the San Francisco earthquake? In the year 1906?*

The sensation he experienced while riding out the earthquake was nearly indescribable, reminding Scott of one of the eyewitness stories he'd once read.

Credited to both a Stanford University professor named George Davidson and a man from Salt Lake City named Sam Wolf, was the quote: "The earthquake came from north to south, and the only description I am able to give of its effect is that it seemed like a terrier shaking a rat."

That pretty well sums it up, Scott thought.

He turned to speak to the stranger, but the man was no longer beside him. Searching in the darkness, Scott spotted him lying on the ground about ten feet away.

"Hey, are you all right over there?"

The other fellow got up and approached Scott again. "I'm okay, but how'd you do that? How did you know it was coming? Is there another on the way? If so, when is it going to happen?"

"It started out at two minutes. We're down to under a minute now."

The stranger hurried the rest of the way and planted himself on the ground next to Scott. He held out his right hand and introduced himself.

"Tyler Hunter. Dr. Tyler Hunter."

Scott shook his hand and started to reply, but stopped short. *I wonder if I'm supposed to use my own name.* Brian hadn't talked about what to do in this situation, so he decided to go the better safe than sorry route.

One of the historical names he had been thinking of popped into his head. With no more hesitation, he said, "Samuel Wolf. Dr. Samuel Wolf from Salt Lake City. Here comes another one."

The aftershock was severe, but short, lasting only about five seconds. McLean and Hunter heard the horrendous crashing of more buildings. The two men could hear the iron beams of some building screeching as they were twisted by the immense power of the convulsing earth. Rivets holding the steel structures together were ripped from their openings and fired like bullets through the collapsing edifice, echoing ricochets through the darkness for seconds afterward.

Scott stood and held out a hand to assist Dr. Hunter to his feet.

"Is that the end of it?"

"Yeah. Well, there will be a couple more, but they shouldn't be too bad."

"Tell me, Sam. How are you able to predict the arrival of an earthquake?"

"Oh that." Scott tried to think of a plausible explanation and came up with nothing, so he simply said, "I've studied quite a bit about earthquakes."

"I see." The doctor acted as if McLean had actually made some kind of sense. "I'm impressed."

"Don't be. It was nothing."

"You say you study earthquakes. Does that mean you are a doctor of geology?"

Scott worked enough years with doctors to know how some of their egos operated, so in order to establish a more equal relationship with Dr. Tyler Hunter, being a doctor himself could be beneficial. He also reasoned, that with his medical schooling and years of experience, a paramedic of 2002 would probably be able to hold his own with most doctors of 1906. Surely a gamble, but conceivably worth the effort.

"No sir, medicine," Scott said.

I could tell the man I'm a paramedic, but to a person of this part of the century, I might just as well say I'm from the moon. Or the future, huh, Scott? A smile formed on his lips at the thought.

Scott finished pulling Dr. Hunter to his feet. "Boy, I surely picked a fine time to visit San Francisco."

"Where are you from?"

"Portland. Portland, Oregon. I'm here for the medical conference. Is that why you're here?"

Scott was taken by surprise, so for lack of anything better, he said, "Yep." Then he thought to himself, *Wow, I'll have to be very careful here. I've only been in town ten minutes and I'm already painting myself into a corner with what started out as one small deception.*

Fortunately for Scott, he knew the history of the earthquake. He knew there would be no conference, therefore, no one would know he wasn't really Dr. Samuel Wolf of Salt Lake City. *Unless, of course, I run into the real Samuel Wolf who may or may not be a doctor. Let me see. Where did Wolf spend his time during the next few days? Oh, yeah. He was in the Market Street district and then worked*

FIRES OF TIME * 119

his way down to the ferry. Oh well, I guess all I can do is watch out for him.

"What are you hoping to learn from the conference?" Scott asked in hopes of finding out about the subject matter of the gathering, and just possibly, learning how to proceed with his own masquerade.

Dr. Tyler Hunter played into Scott's hands perfectly. "I'm an orthopaedic surgeon and I'm teaching one of the classes myself. I hope to glean as much trauma information as I can, being the conference will be covering a wide range of trauma related subjects."

Scott appeared to be genuinely interested, pondering what the doctor had just revealed. *By the time you're finished here in San Francisco Dr. Hunter, you won't need any medical conference on trauma. You'll have enough experience to be Portland's resident expert on the subject.*

Interrupting Scott's train of thought, Tyler said, "Do you have a specialty?"

"Burns," he said without thinking.

"Fascinating."

Way to go Scott, he thought, berating himself. *Pawn yourself off as a burn specialist right at the start of the greatest conflagration in American history.*

With that in mind, he realized the fires would soon be starting. "Uh, Tyler," Scott said quietly.

"Yes?"

"There's one other thing."

"Please tell me."

"There's the matter of the fire."

"The what?"

The attention of both men was suddenly drawn to the sprawling city below them. The darkness was interrupted by a tremendous eruption of flames brightening the entire sky above them. While Dr. Hunter and "Dr. Wolf" were chatting, scores of fires had started around the city. What attracted their attention most, looked to be some very tall buildings burning.

"Is Market Street on fire?" Tyler asked quietly.

"Sure looks like it."

The burning buildings looked like giant, hundred foot torches, lighting up the entire business district in the Mission and Market street areas. Dr. Hunter realized that what was transpiring was far more serious than a small tremor.

"What's going on here? You seem to know everything before it happens. What are we supposed to do now?"

Trying to decide just how far to go with his answer, Scott spoke calmly to his new acquaintance. "Tyler, listen closely to me. I can't tell you how or why I appear to know some of the things I appear to know. Does that make sense?"

The doctor gazed blankly at him. "Go on."

"You're going to have to trust me to lead both of us in the right direction. Can you do that?"

This is all very strange, Dr. Hunter thought. *The man seems to know all that is about to happen. And when. He appears to be a learned and reliable man, perhaps to be trusted.*

"I'll go along with you for the time being, Sam. Is that agreeable?"

"Fair enough. Now, we need to go down and offer our services in whatever way we can, because

I believe there are going to be a lot of people needing bone and burn docs. Will you be able to do whatever we may need to do?"

After a few seconds, Tyler responded. "I'm all right."

"Great, let's get ready to go."

"I'm as ready as I'll ever be."

"Hold on for a minute," Scott said. "I ... I ... need to pee."

He ran through the bushes to the time ship. Opening the hatch, he reached in and retrieved his small duffel bag and the half gallon jug of water Brian gave him. After securing the hatch, he unzipped the bag and inserted the water jug, then ran back over to the doctor.

Scott might have used some poor judgement when he made the quick decision to bring along his small nylon duffel bag. Even though it contained a host of useful tools, it was possible that some of the items in the bag could cause him problems if seen by anyone in 1906. It was also quite possible that those very items could be of great value to him while visiting 1906.

"Let's hit it, Doc," Scott declared, emerging from the bushes.

The two men started down the hill in the direction of Washington street, and as they walked, they talked.

"What were you doing on the hill so early in the morning?" Scott asked.

"I've visited San Francisco many times, and I've tried to watch a sunrise from Telegraph Hill on each visit."

"How did you get up here?"

"I walked from my hotel, the Occidental. It's only about a mile down the hill from here on Montgomery. Why were you on the hill, Sam?"

Scott thought briefly. "I'm just trying to see as much as possible while I'm in town."

"It sounds as if the two of us have a great deal in common. Where are you staying?"

"I just arrived. But I haven't had a chance to get a room. Do you need to try to get any of your belongings from your hotel?"

"I didn't carry much of value with me," Tyler said. "Other than a picture of my wife and children. I would like to find that, but it can be replaced, if necessary."

Scott stopped and asked, "Children, how many?"

"We, my wife Molly and I, have two children. Billy is seven and Sarah is three years old. Do you have children?"

"Yes we do. My wife's name is Patty and our son Casey is seven. Our baby girl, Melissa, is three years old."

"Interesting."

"Yes, it is."

"We aren't very far from the Harbor Emergency Hospital and they might need some help there," Tyler said.

Recalling what he could about what had and hadn't been destroyed, Scott remembered that Harbor Emergency had been heroically saved by firefighters from Engine Company Number One, who had stayed right by the hospital and protected it from the fire. Navy ships pumped salt water from the harbor and provided the firefighters with enough additional hose lines to save the hospital and the ferry building. The hospital also served as an infirmary for treating hundreds of the injured during the fire.

"An excellent choice. Now, all we have to do is find our way there."

"I know right where it is, Sam. If we can find our way to Market and East Streets by the ferry building, we'll be able to locate the hospital from there. Judging by the sound of the crumbling structures, there must be extensive damage. I would imagine there will be quite a number of people with injuries, so I'm sure they can use our assistance."

"That's putting it mildly."

"Excuse me?"

"Never mind, Doc, we have a long way to go, so let's get truckin' and see what we can do to help."

"Truckin'?"

"Never mind."

Suddenly, Scott remembered what Brian had said to him. "You're going to observe, Scott. I don't know which is the right theory to believe, so try not to do or change anything. Observe, Scott," he had said. "Just observe."

That may be tough, Brian, he thought. *That just may be tough.*

Scott McLean, aka, Dr. Samuel Wolf of Salt Lake City, was on his way to join in the chaos with Dr. Tyler Hunter of Portland, Oregon.

Chapter Eight

Tyler and Scott stepped out into the pandemonium in progress at the intersection of Montgomery and Greenwich streets. Huge chasms had opened in the ground, leaving gaping holes in streets that had been smooth asphalt only half an hour earlier. Walls of buildings were still falling into the street, causing entire upper floors and roofs to crash down with thunderous force. They literally exploded when they hit the ground, launching enormous cluster bombs of wood, plaster and lath.

Everywhere they looked, houses and buildings were beginning to burn. Some had already been devastated by the earthquake. Some were entirely intact. It made no difference to the fire because it had no sense of right or wrong. Nor did it use any reason. The Beast had no preferences, prejudices, or personal desires. It simply moved with the wind or in the direction of the fuel, consuming everything in its path.

Adding to the din of the collapsing structures, were the nightmarish screams of pain and anguish filling the air from all directions. People were running every which way, none of them paying any attention to Scott and Tyler. Horse drawn wagons filled with people and household belongings raced down the side streets. One wagon, the two horses galloping furiously, rounded a corner onto Montgomery street. Halfway through the turn, a huge pile of debris blocked the way, causing the horses to rear back and attempt to veer away from the roadblock.

"Look out, Tyler!" Scott yelled as the wagon turned violently and rolled over in the street, spilling the family and their possessions onto the ground.

Scott and Tyler ran to their aid, assessing their injuries and finding them to be nothing more than bumps and bruises.

"You folks were pretty fortunate," Tyler said as the two men helped to reload the wagon.

The wagon pulled away and they resumed their trek, captivated by the turmoil around them. They made their way for many blocks before making a turn in the direction of Market Street.

Coming to a large pile of smoking debris on one side of the street, Tyler called out to Scott, "Over here. I've found a clear path on this side of the street."

"On my way," Scott said, stepping gingerly over and around what appeared to have been a brick chimney. He made his way to Dr. Hunter's side and they picked their way along the thoroughfare.

Smoke was building up in the air and making it difficult to see, even though the sun had started its rise in the morning sky. The going was getting difficult as the two men found it more of an effort to get enough air into their lungs due to the heavy smoke.

Tyler stepped between a splintered wooden beam and the front of a large, three story house just as the roof collapsed onto the top floor, pancaking all of the floors together on the ground. The front wall ballooned out and pushed the doctor's lower right leg into the splintered end of the beam. He let out a yell as he fell to the ground with his leg pinned between the two objects.

"Where are you, Doc?" Scott called through the immense cloud of dust and smoke.

"Right here. I'm right in front of you about five feet, and my leg's caught."

Stooping down in the rubble beside Tyler's leg, Scott assessed the situation. "Is there much pain?"

"It isn't too bad."

"Where does it hurt when you move your toes and foot?"

The doctor moved his foot around. "No pain of any consequence. Do you think you can free my foot?"

"I'll do my best," Scott said, looking around in the haze for some kind of a lever.

Finding an eight foot length of wood, he proceeded to wedge it against the end of a four foot piece of wooden beam. Placing the end of the shorter beam against the side of the house next to Tyler's lower leg, he put his shoulder under the lever and lifted. He managed to move a small area of the wall, allowing Hunter's leg to drop to the ground.

"There you go."

The doctor sat on the ground with his pant leg pulled up, examining his right ankle. He looked up at Scott. "Thanks. You're quite resourceful."

Helping Tyler up, Scott said, "No problem, let's get moving."

Scott stopped when he heard a mournful moan coming from somewhere in the rubble of the collapsed house. Both men turned and started making their way toward the sound, then listening intently, they heard it again. It was a woman's voice.

They launched a search, grabbing chunks of plaster-and-lath and pieces of wood and tossing them to the side. Finally, after lifting up a section of the roof, Scott spotted a young woman lying in the rubble.

"Are you hurt, ma'am?" he said, heaving the roof section out of the way.

"It's my leg," she groaned. "My leg is stuck and it hurts something terrible. Will you please help me?"

Tyler knelt down in the dross pile of what had been a house to survey the situation. He felt down along the lady's lower leg and found it pinned below a large beam, then hooked his hand under the beam and gave it a heave. In doing so, he caused more grief to his own back than to the beam.

"She's really stuck in here, " he said to Scott. "We have to get this beam off her leg and I can't budge it."

"Any ideas?" Scott said as he knelt down on the other side of her leg. Turning to the woman, Scott asked her name.

"Jennifer," the 23-year-old earthquake victim told him. "Jennifer Brody."

"Jennifer? Do people call you Jenny?"

She nodded her head and managed a pained smile with her quivering lips. "What happened? Was it an earthquake? I was sleeping in the upstairs bedroom and I suddenly found myself falling through the air. You arrived here so fast and my leg hurts so much, can you help to get me out of here?"

Scott smiled. "We'll get you out of here, Jenny. Hang tough while we figure it out."

"Hang tough?"

Scott hesitated, then said to the 1906 woman, "I'm sorry, Jenny. I meant ... bear with us while we decide how to get you out of this."

Her hazel eyes were wide open, reflecting her feeling of helplessness in being at the complete mercy of two total strangers. "Do I have a choice?"

Scott smiled sympathetically. "I wish you did. By the way, I'm Sam and this is Tyler."

She managed a wan smile and nodded at Tyler. "Pleased to meet you. Thank you for stopping to help me."

The doctors tried to find a way to get Jenny's leg out from under the beam. The problem was most of the house sitting on that very beam. Scott thought of all the equipment he generally had at his disposal for heavy rescues. *We could have her out of here in five minutes if we had a couple of air bags.*

"There must be six tons of junk on this beam," Tyler whispered to Scott. "There's no way we can move it without finding a team of horses or a block and tackle."

"It doesn't look like that's going to happen, so let's figure out some other way."

"Whatever it is, it had better be quick," Tyler said tensely, pointing over Scott's shoulder.

Scott looked back to see what Tyler was so concerned about and saw it. Less than two blocks away, a wall of fire at least fifty feet high and a hundred feet wide was bearing down on them and consuming everything in its path. Houses, buildings, sheds and wagons were all being destroyed by the raging Beast as it raced toward the two rescuers and their unfortunate victim.

"Damn," Scott said quietly. "That's all we need."

He stood up and looked for some scrap to use as a lever. The force of the collapsing building had reduced everything but the greatest of the beams to splinters, making the search for a large, lever-sized piece of wood fruitless.

"What are you doing? We don't have enough time to try to move this beam. We wouldn't be able to do it anyway because of the weight."

"Something has to be done. We can't leave her here and we sure as hell can't stay here and nurse her back to health!" Scott yelled at the doctor.

"I can see that!" Tyler said back in kind. "Get down here and help me with this!"

Jenny's eyes darted frantically back and forth between them, hoping they would quickly figure something out.

"Okay, let's move it," Scott said. "Do you want to try to pull it out?"

"We have no choice."

Tyler leaned down close to her and yelled to be heard over the roaring noise of the fire, "We're going to try to pull your leg out from under the beam, Jenny. It will be painful."

"Do what you have to do, but please get me out of here."

She stared, terrified at the approaching conflagration. Her face showed the tension of both fear and pain while her glistening eyes reflected the firestorm that was bearing down on them.

"Ready?" Scott said, as they both gripped Jenny's leg. "Here we go. One ... two ... pull."

The two men pulled on the poor woman's leg as hard as they possibly could with no results — except for Jennifer Brody's blood curdling scream.

"I'm sorry, Jenny," Scott said.

Jenny didn't hear a thing because she'd already passed out from the excruciating pain in her leg.

Scott turned back to Dr. Hunter. "What do you want to do now?"

Tyler glanced dreadfully at the raging sea of flame. "Let's try to pull it out again while she's still unconscious."

They pulled on her leg again and it still didn't budge.

"I'm going have to take the leg off, Sam. There's no other way to get her out."

Scott surveyed the situation around them and thought, *He wants to do an amputation here in this mess, in 1906, with no anesthesia. If she makes it through the cutting, she could bleed to death, and even if she doesn't bleed out, there are no antibiotics in this time. She'll probably die from infection.*

He looked back at the fast approaching fire and quickly decided they had no other choice. "We'd better get crackin' then, it's getting mighty warm here."

Dr. Hunter reached his hand down to just above Jenny's ankle and probed her lower leg. He could feel that it was badly broken, which would reduce the time needed to perform the surgical procedure. He looked at Scott. "The bones are already severed, so this shouldn't be too difficult. Do you have a knife or something to cut with?"

Scott remembered the contents of his duffel. He reached in and got one of the items, handing a green, plastic handled scalpel to Tyler. "Try this, Ty."

Tyler examined the scalpel and started to say something, then stopped. He hesitated briefly, then said, "You don't happen to have a lantern in there also, do you? I can't see a thing down here."

The fire raged closer by the second, the heat becoming almost unbearable, causing sweat to literally pour from their faces. Scott pulled his mini mag-light out of his paramedic holster.

"We don't have time for questions, so don't ask any, okay?" he said firmly, while twisting the mag-light, creating a brilliant beam of light, and aiming it down at Jenny's ankle. "Go to it, doctor."

Tyler looked at the marvelous little lantern and started to say something, but Scott was quick to silence him. "Don't ask. Just cut."

The heat was beginning to sear the sides of the faces of the two rescuers and Scott could see the taut features on Tyler's face. Doctor Hunter was very frightened, but he was holding up well under the circumstances.

The men didn't realize that their patient had regained consciousness until Jenny spoke up. "I know you don't have any choice but to cut off my foot, Tyler. And as fast as that fire's coming at us, you'd better be quick about it."

FIRES OF TIME * 133

Tyler looked into her dark eyes. "Do you understand the seriousness of what we're about to do?"

Jennifer looked right back into his eyes. "I realize I'll die right on this very spot if you don't, so it doesn't matter to me if you gnaw it off, so long as you get me out of here alive."

Tyler quickly sliced off a large piece of her pale blue nightgown and handed it to Scott. "Give me some light."

Scott held the light on the leg as Dr. Hunter, with no further hesitation, made a deep incision, causing Jenny to scream once again. She grabbed a handful of Scott's perspiration-soaked hair and pulled his head nearly down to her side, but before he could react, she relaxed her grip. Her hand went limp and her scream tapered off to nothingness as she passed out from the pain for the second time.

"Go for it," Scott said. "She's out again."

The roar of the fire was deafening and the heat so intense that Scott could smell the hair burning on his arms. He began having second thoughts about being a time traveler. *This has got to be a dream. Who'd have ever thought I'd be stupid enough to put myself in a situation as bizarre as this?*

Tyler reached down and finished the job of amputating Jenny's ankle and foot. He reached over and took the piece of nightgown and lifted the leg from the rubble, pushing the bandage over the severed end.

"We could use a tourniquet," he yelled over the noise.

"In due time," Scott yelled as he picked her up and ran through the rubble that had been Jennifer Brody's house, tripping once and almost falling.

With Tyler running along beside them and grabbing a handful of the back of Scott's shirt, he managed to stay on his feet.

With the raging inferno licking at their heels and not even daring to slow up and look back at it, they ran down the debris strewn street to a safer spot in the next block.

Scott laid Jenny on the ground as Tyler knelt down to look at her injury. "We need to fashion a tourniquet for this. She's going to lose too much blood."

Scott reached in his bag and grasped a rubber tourniquet that had a Velcro fastening strip. To Tyler, he said with conviction, "I want you to do something for me."

"All right, Sam."

"Promise you won't ask any questions about me until this is all over. I'll explain everything to you then. Okay?"

Tyler looked a little puzzled. "Whatever you say."

Scott pulled the tourniquet out and attached it to Jenny's leg as Tyler leaned down close and checked it out, touching the velcro with his fingers. He then pulled the green, plastic handled scalpel out of his shirt pocket and examined it.

Looking back and seeing the scowl beginning to form on Scott's face, Tyler said, "Okay, no questions. I promise — but when this is over ..." His voice trailed off as he turned back to his patient, who was waking up again.

Still weak and a bit dizzy, Jenny looked in the direction of her house. "Is my home gone, Tyler?"

"I'm afraid so, Jenny. The fire destroyed what was left of it within minutes of our escape."

He removed the makeshift bandage from the injured leg and examined it closer in the daylight, seeing that it was a clean cut, severed almost totally when the beam landed on Jenny's leg. Scott removed a small athletic towel from his bag and handed it to Dr. Hunter.

Tyler took the towel, read the GOLD'S GYM monogram on it and smiled at Scott. "Thank you. You must have read my mind. Do you think we could find a small amount of water to clean this up?"

Reaching back into his duffel and getting the water jug, Scott said, "Show me where to pour it."

Tyler pointed out what he wanted as he held the leg up a little higher for Scott to pour some cool water over the wound.

"That feels nice," Jenny said. "Thank you."

Tyler wrapped the towel tightly around Jenny's injury and tied the ends together just below her knee. Motioning to Scott to soak the bandage with more water, he placed the velcro tourniquet back on her leg.

"This should heal nicely providing we get you to a hospital soon. It appears the beam did most of the job of severing your foot before we arrived, so we only finished the job. I'm sorry we weren't able to save it for you. I admire your strength. You're a very courageous person."

Jenny leaned back against a tree and flashed Tyler a smile of gratitude. Looking back and forth between the two men, the young woman said, "You two rescued me from certain death in my collapsed house. And then, the fire. You saved my life. Thank you. Thank you so much."

"I'm glad we were here for you."

"Sam called you Doctor, Tyler," Jenny said. "Are you a real medical doctor?"

"Yes I am and so is Sam, here," Hunter said.

"Well, how do you like that? Somebody up there must like me."

"Somebody must," Scott said warmly, wondering if Jennifer would have actually lived through the earthquake if he hadn't been there. He started to think about what had transpired, pondering his intervention in the events of the day.

Did I do anything wrong in helping Tyler to save this woman? Should she have died in that fire? Should I have let her die? I guess it doesn't matter now because what's done is done and history will have to live with it.

Jennifer chuckled. "Robert is not going to believe this. No sir, he won't believe it even after he sees it."

Both Tyler and Scott stared at her.

Scott looked confused. "Excuse me?"

"My husband, Robert Brody. He isn't going to believe this happened to me."

Tyler smiled. "You have a husband? Where is he?"

"Oh, he's at sea. His ship is due to come in any day now and I always wait at the dock when he arrives."

"You probably won't be able to do that this time," Tyler said. "He'll most likely have to find you."

"Why were you laughing just then?" Scott said.

The pretty and petite woman brushed her short, brown hair behind her ears and smiled again. "It's a joke Robert and I have shared since first we were married. Every time my husband prepares to go back to sea, I try to talk him into staying with me. He always promises to quit sailing, you see, but I know the sea is in his blood." She paused and gazed out toward the ocean. After taking a deep breath, she continued. "I tell him every time he leaves that I cannot wait until he loses a leg in a rigging accident, or to a shark, so he will be forced to walk on a peg leg. For after that takes place, on the night before he is to leave me again, I shall take his peg leg and toss it into the fireplace, obliging my sailor to stay at home with me forever."

The two doctors smiled at her.

"As much as my leg hurts, I still have to laugh," she said, managing a smile. "Can you imagine the look on his face when he finds out that his sweet wife now has a peg leg? No, of course you can't. You've never laid eyes on my man." Jenny hesitated, gazing out at the smoke filled San Francisco sky with tears welling up in her sparkling eyes. Beginning to cry, the tears streaming down her cheeks, she turned to Tyler. "How will I ever stop him from going back to sea now? Tell me Doctor, would a man ever stay with a woman who walks on a peg leg? Perhaps it isn't such a comical turn of events after all. Perhaps my Robert will turn right around and go directly back to sea."

"I don't know about your Robert," Tyler said. "If it were me, I'd stay home to care for you now and never leave your side. And if your seafaring husband has a lick of sense, he'll feel the same."

Scott had drifted off into thought again, trying to remember the historical details of the disaster. *We need to get to Market and East Streets. Let me see, downtown Market Street is toast, so we'll need to avoid that area. And the entire wharf will be in a state of total chaos, especially around the ferry building and the hospital. Whatever we do, it should be soon because this whole area of the city is going down. Or is it up?*

Intruding in Scott's thoughts, Tyler said, "Ready to move?"

"That's a good idea." Scott rose to his knees and moved over beside Jenny.

"How do you want to do it?"

"For now, we can take turns carrying Jenny," Scott said to Tyler as he picked her up and carried her toward the street. "The important thing is to stay ahead of the fire and—" he stopped mid-sentence and motioned to the street, hurriedly saying, "Stop that car, Ty! Quick, before they drive by!"

Tyler ran out and stood in the middle of the street, waving his arms at the driver and yelling at him to stop his automobile. The driver tried his best to drive around the doctor, but Tyler kept moving in the street to block his path. The vehicle came to a halt and the driver, a pompous looking man with a full gray beard pulled himself up behind the steering wheel and hollered over the windscreen at the doctor.

"What *are* you doing my good man? I'll thank you to please get out of our way so that we may continue our escape from this demon of extirpation!"

"I'm a doctor," Tyler explained, "and so is my associate. We need to get this lady to a hospital posthaste and we intend to take her in *your* automobile."

"I have no time for transporting her or—"

He was interrupted by the prim and priggish looking woman seated in the auto next to him. "We do *so* have time to help a fellow human being,

Andrew. Now get out there and help those men to put that poor girl in the rear seat. And be quick about it."

"Yes, dear. Of course you're right. I don't know what took hold of me to be so selfish." Commander Andrew Cornish, U.S. Navy, retired, hurried around and opened the rear door, helping Scott to place Jenny Brody onto the back seat of the automobile.

"I'm very sorry," he said to Tyler. "Please forgive my avaricious and impertinent behavior." Then turning and holding the door open for Tyler and Scott, he motioned them into the vehicle, saying simply, "Gentlemen."

Safely seated in the rear seat, Tyler reached out his right hand and introduced the three in his party to the commander and his wife. The commander responded with a handshake and his own introductions.

"Commander Andrew Cornish, and this lovely lady is my wife Emily, the one who keeps me on the straight and narrow, as you have doubtlessly surmised."

"Very pleased to meet you all," Emily Cornish said, smiling at the passengers. She looked at Jenny's leg, then put her hand over her mouth and recoiled slightly. "Oh my, you've been badly injured, dear. What may I do to help?"

Jenny smiled at Emily. "I'm very grateful for the transportation, ma'am, but I believe everything else is under control, due to the help of my own personal doctors." She paused. "They saved my life, you know."

"You don't say," Emily said with a look of surprise.

"I *do* say. They rescued me from the rubble of my collapsed home just ahead of the conflagration."

"Speaking of the conflagration, we had better continue our journey. What is our ultimate destination Doctor?" the commander asked of either Tyler or Scott.

Scott spoke up and answered the question with a question. "Do you know how to get to Harbor Emergency Hospital?"

"Yes I do, and barring any calamities, we should be able to get there by turning at the next crossroad," Andrew Cornish said with confidence, now exhilarated at being in a position to help somebody in need. He hadn't felt that way since retiring from the Navy six years before, and he'd almost forgotten how good it felt.

"I'll have us there in a trice," he said to Scott as he accelerated the automobile down the hill, dodging the crowds of people and the tremendous amounts of debris in the street.

* * *

The small group of people in the Oldsmobile Touring Car drove through the streets amid the frenzied confusion that was the city of San Francisco, April 18, 1906. McLean sat in the back seat and observed, just as Brian had told him to do. There was chaos in every direction as the vehicle picked its way around piles of building materials, wrecked vehicles and even human bodies strewn about in the streets.

Emily's high-pitched voice broke the deafening silence. "Do be careful, Andrew. These poor people aren't able to watch out for themselves." Andrew gave her a reassuring pat on the knee.

"There, there my dear. Your munificent concern is duly noted."

They had to turn from one street to another to avoid the fires, the crevasses, and the crowds of refugees fleeing the raging inferno.

"We shall have to search out a provisional course," Commander Cornish advised his charges. "I'm afraid this once great city's plight will slow our progress considerably."

Enthralled, Scott watched as history unfolded before his eyes. He saw people and events he'd only read about as they traveled through the city. People were riding in wagons filled with all the belongings they had managed to save before fleeing their homes. A young couple pushed two baby carriages around a cavernous split in the street. The carriages were piled high with their only remaining possessions, and their two small children were nestled cozily amid the heaps of clothing.

Automobiles driven by the wealthy moved alongside, many of them ignoring everything in their paths and even running into and over the pedestrians filling the roadways. Thousands of terrified people fled on foot to escape the fire as it devoured their homes and threatened to consume their very beings.

Man, woman and child alike carried trunks, bags and boxes on their backs filled with whatever was left of their lives. The throngs moved along every street, some pushing and shoving everyone out of their way while many stopped to help others in need of assistance.

The Cornish auto passed through entire blocks of homes that had been leveled by the force of the earthquake, and more neighborhoods that had already been consumed by fire. At one intersection, Scott saw a crew of firefighters trying to get water from a plug for their pumper, only to find there was no water. Virtually all of the city's wooden water mains were destroyed by the earthquake, rendering the fire department helpless to the ever-expanding firestorm. Two more fire department pumpers sat in another block where the fire had overtaken them. One was still burning and the remains of the other was smoldering.

In every direction, Scott could see burning buildings and the rubble of tremendous structures dropped by the earthquake. He saw skeletons of tall buildings, their steel inner structures twisted and sagging as a result of the heat. Buildings that had been touted as being earthquake proof or fire proof or both ... were neither.

Coming to one intersection, they were stopped at a roadblock by soldiers. "All able bodied men are required to help bury the bodies of the dead," a sergeant declared after walking to the front of the auto. He pointed to Scott and Tyler, then growled, "You two, get out of the car and follow me."

As they were exiting the rear seat, the commander intervened. "These men are doctors, Sergeant, and they have an injured patient to which they are attending."

"Out of the way, old man," the sergeant ordered the commander. "Or you will be shot."

"Now just a minute," the retired officer said determinedly, stepping from the vehicle. "These men are needed elsewhere to tend to the living."

With no hesitation, the sergeant rushed to the driver's side of the vehicle, pushed the commander back into the auto and leveled his pistol at the man's head.

"I would just as soon shoot you as argue!"

As Emily Cornish and Jennifer Brody watched in horror, he pulled the gun's hammer back and said loudly to all that could hear, "Let this be a lesson to all of you!"

An army captain walked briskly toward the automobile of Commander Cornish. "Stop, Sergeant! What is the trouble here?"

"This old man is interfering with the recruitment process, Sir," he said to the captain.

The captain looked closely at the driver and then back at the sergeant. "Do you know who this gentleman is?" Turning back to Andrew Cornish, he asked sincerely, "Are you all right, Sir?"

The commander sat straight in his seat. "I think just barely, Captain Steele. Just barely."

The captain turned to the sergeant and ordered him to put his pistol away. "And do not remove it again unless you are looking down the barrel of another weapon."

Addressing the commander again, the captain said, "What is the problem here, Commander Cornish?"

Andrew Cornish explained the situation to the captain, pointing out the severe injury of Jennifer Brody. At that, Captain Steele reached into his shirt pocket and withdrew two badges with red crosses on them.

"You will need to wear these doctor's badges on the front of your clothing, sirs," he said to Tyler and Scott as they climbed back into the vehicle. He turned to the couple in the car. "I'm sorry Commander, Mrs. Cornish, for this unfortunate turn of events. It seems as if the circumstances have caused some of us to misplace our sense of values."

Calling to another soldier to bring an ambulance flag which bore a large red cross, he fastened it to the commander's auto, then added, "This ambulance flag, along with the doctor's badges, should assure your safe passage to the hospital, Sir. And please allow me to apologize once again, Commander." The army captain saluted the retired navy man as they pulled away.

Driving from the intersection, they heard the captain reprimanding the soldier. "Sergeant, that officer you nearly killed is one of the most decorated naval war heroes in our country's history. You are hereby relieved of duty at this post. Report at once to your lieutenant for reassignment."

"Thank you, Commander," Scott said. "That was a brave thing you did for us back there."

"Perhaps. Or immeasurably foolhardy, I'm afraid. I was incognizant of the austere chastisement for resisting the dominion of the military this day."

"It does seem a bit harsh," Scott remarked.

Tyler leaned closer to the front seat. "The captain said you were a hero, Commander. Would I be forward in asking what it was you did?"

"It was many years ago. So long, in fact, that I languish to summon up the recollection."

Emily turned to face the back seat. "Andrew has never been willing to talk about what happened out there on the sea. The only thing I was ever able to learn of it was that he was responsible for saving the lives of nearly two hundred men in the face of a dreadful battle."

"Wow, I'm impressed!" Scott told the Commander.

FIRES OF TIME * 145

"Don't be, young physician," Andrew said. "I discharged my duties as any other man would ... faced with comparable circumstances."

"I hear that," McLean said. "I hear that."

This has got to be the most fascinating thing I've ever seen, Scott thought. *Or that I'll ever see.*

After all the years he'd spent in the fire service, Scott should have known better than to think something like that.

* * *

Several blocks ahead of the commander's automobile, a boarding house was burning. The four story hostelry was damaged by the first jolt of the earthquake, the front of the building having moved approximately two feet. The movement of the foundation forced the entire street facing facade to collapse out into the front yard, piling wooden beams, siding and brick on the small lawn. The yard was only fifteen feet deep and was on a slope of about forty degrees, which allowed the fallout from the structure to spill down over the sidewalk and part way into the street.

At the time of the collapse, the electrical power was still live and sending current to all parts of the boarding house. As the earthquake ravaged the house, the wiring was yanked through the walls and torn from the fixtures throughout the building. Several small fires were started inside those walls and ceilings. Lacking enough oxygen for combustion, the tiny hot spots could only smolder until one or more of them burned through the lath and plaster to the unlimited supply of fresh air. Even though all the power in the city was cut off shortly after the earthquake, the electricity within the walls of the boarding house had already done its damage.

Earlier that morning, after the earthquake had finished its destruction, all of the boarders managed to escape from the house unharmed. They were grateful that Providence had seen fit to spare them from injury and death. The women gathered the children together on a clear area of lawn across the street while some of the men made their way back into the house to check for stragglers. Finding none, they exited the house and waited with the women and children for help, or something, to arrive.

After waiting patiently for an hour or so, they realized it was pretty much every man, woman and child for themselves. By that time, all of the kids were hungry, so the adults decided to check out the house for safety.

A few of the men went back into the building, checking and testing the structure for strength and hidden dangers. On finding it surprisingly sound, they gave the okay for everyone to go back in to collect their belongings and foodstuffs. They were able to clear some of the rubble away from the front stairs to allow the residents to work their way up to their rooms. Many of the rooms sustained little damage, offering the boarders a false sense of security.

The large stove in the main kitchen was still operable, so Mrs. O'Grady, the owner of the boarding house, decided to go ahead and fix a nice breakfast for everyone. The sweet, plump little grandma set about her business as if nothing at all had happened. She stirred the banked coals, stoked up a good fire in the stove and began preparing the morning meal.

FIRES OF TIME * 147

* * *

Maria Rodriguez took her two children, Andrella 6, and Marco 5, by the hands and led them through the house and up the stairs to their third floor apartment. It wasn't really what could be classified an apartment, two small bedrooms and an even smaller sitting room. They shared a hallway washroom with the other third floor boarders.

Maria and the kids were still dressed in their nightclothes, having dashed from the house at just after 5:13 A.M. Since their rooms weren't damaged, Maria decided to get the children and herself dressed in the apartment, rather than gathering up clothing and returning to the outdoors.

Marco and Andrella spoke fluent Spanish, but 29-year-old Maria preferred to speak English with her children. They had moved to America from Chile over a year before and Maria wanted very much to help her children adapt to their new country. She worked hard as a housekeeper at the Grand Opera House during the day and occasional evenings cleaning one of the mansions on Nob's Hill. Every penny Maria earned went to support and care for her little Marco and Andrella, for they were all she had in the world.

"You kids find your play clothes and get yourself dressed," Maria said. "After I am changed, we will go to the kitchen, because Mrs. O'Grady is working to fix you a nice breakfast. Do you understand?"

"Yes, Mama," they said.

After dressing, Andrella went to the sitting room and looked at her storybook while she waited for her mother, but Marco had other plans. He just had to see what everything looked like after all of that shaking in the morning. He sneaked quietly past his sister, slipping into the hallway on his way to the stairs. Engrossed in her book, Andrella had no idea he had even gone.

* * *

The young bank teller, Sally Higgins, held onto Amanda Clark's arm to steady her as she crept up the stairs to the front door of the boarding house. The widow Amanda was a very close friend of Lorraine O'Grady and had been for many years. After both of their husbands died, Mrs. O'Grady asked Amanda to move into the house with her. She did just that, and stayed for the next ten years.

The two widows shared the household duties until Amanda's crippling stroke in July of 1905. Since that time, Amanda could get around with her partial paralysis, but sometimes needed a helping hand to navigate anything difficult.

Sally moved from her home in Oklahoma to the glamorous city of San Francisco nearly five years earlier when she was only seventeen years old. She started working at the Nevada National Bank right after turning eighteen, enjoying the job and the way she was treated by her employer. Sally missed her family, but being with Amanda Clark helped to fill that void because she often reminded Sally of her own grandmother back home in Oklahoma. Sally enjoyed helping Amanda whenever she could because she dearly loved her elderly friend.

Amanda and Sally found their way into the big kitchen just in time to help Mrs. O'Grady squeeze oranges for the orange juice. Lorraine O'Grady got the two of them started and returned to her cooking stove to finish preparing breakfast. Mr. Brown entered the kitchen and sat down, observing the routine activity of the women. Their actions could have made a person think it to be just another normal day.

E.W. Brown, the fiftyish and rotund newspaper columnist that lived on the second floor, described his thoughts and feelings of the scene. In his column on the morning following the earthquake, he wrote:

> "I was sitting in the large country kitchen watching my landlady as she hurried about the room executing her duties in preparing breakfast for the boarders in my house. Oh, the smells of bacon and sausage links sizzling in the big black skillets, and hotcakes on the griddle. I savored the taste of freshly squeezed orange juice from oranges picked right outside that very kitchen's window only last evening. Mrs. O'Grady plopped a tremendous dollop of butter on a dish in the center of the oaken table, to be used generously on stacks of hotcakes and the toasted slices of bread, still steaming hot from the oven.
>
> "Does this sound like a perfect morning on a perfect day when all's right with the world and life couldn't be more pleasant? Oh, if it only were. As I gazed across the large, oaken table and out through the ample foyer to the front door of the house, something was indeed not right. To begin, there was no front

door to be seen, for it had been broken into splinters. I looked up to see the grand oaken railing and found I was looking at a badly twisted, much shortened version of the original. The finely milled upright bars were poking out in all directions, broken and splayed with splinters where the ends were wrenched from their moorings. The lower third of the staircase sagged downward in the direction of the missing front door, for the entire foundation of the very large house had moved at least two feet. The four story brick and wooden facade was nothing but a tremendous mound of useless rubble, heaped high and covering the front yard. All of the damage I've described was accomplished in less than three minutes by the force of mother nature, the earthquake.

"How could the world seem so peaceful inside the room while such devastation existed outside the kitchen door? Mrs. Lorraine O'Grady, that's how. While our entire city was lying in ruins — crumbled and broken — our whole world, as we knew it, was still being destroyed by the demon fire, Mrs. O'Grady made our small boarding house world feel safe. She went about her normal daily routine, taking care of her boarders and letting man, woman, and child alike know that all was not lost. By her actions, Lorraine O'Grady showed us that even though our city is lost, our jobs may be lost, our homes and even many of our lives have been lost, life will still go on. Life will be hard for a while, but will improve after time and be happy once again. We still have each other to lean on in this time of grief and need, and when this time of calamity runs its course, life will again be good. The Mrs. O'Gradys of the world will see to that.

"The rest of the world thanks you, Mrs. O'Gradys, each and every one of you."

Chapter Nine

Naomi and Ray Ellis finished changing out of their nightclothes and started toward the stairs from their fourth floor room to go to the kitchen. The door to the Strueberg apartment was standing open as they walked past, so Naomi tapped on the door and called into the sitting room.

"Yoo, hoo, is anybody home?"

"In here, dear. We'll be out in a minute, sit down please," Sonya Strueberg called out in her strong German accent.

Naomi pulled Ray into the room by the hand and they sat on the small davenport just as a little boy came running into the room and jumped across both their laps. "Hi, let's go eat," said 2-year-old Michael Strueberg.

"Michael, you little rascal, how did you learn to talk so well?" Ray tickled the boy, causing him to giggle exuberantly.

Naomi tousled Michael's hair and added, "The amazing thing is that he doesn't even have an accent.

I really want one of these, sweetheart. When can we have one?"

Ray, a soft-spoken schoolteacher, smiled. "As soon as we can make one. We won't stop trying, my dear."

Karl Strueburg called out to them from the other room. "Is Mrs. O'Grady fixing breakfast?"

"I think so, Karl," Naomi replied. "We'll wait here and walk down with you when you're ready."

"Give us just a few more minutes," Sonya said.

* * *

Vincent Miller was in his room on the second floor gathering up his belongings. Everything he owned could be packed in his one small suitcase, so he packed it all. *I know I should be hurrying to get to my station,* the 25-year-old San Francisco fireman thought. *I probably should have already been there, but I really needed to be wearing something other than my nightshirt. I'd better grab a bite of breakfast before I go, because who knows when I'll have another chance to eat?* The strapping young man picked up his suitcase and left the room on his way to the kitchen.

"Let Vince dish up his food first so he can get to work," Mrs. O'Grady said to the other boarders at the table. "I'm sure he's needed on the job as soon as possible."

"Thank you ma'am," Vince said, filling his plate with food.

Already seated at the table when Vincent Miller sat down were E.W. Brown and Amanda Clark. Sally Higgins had gone up to her second floor room to dress and grab a few of her possessions while Mrs. O'Grady was busy fussing about the kitchen, making sure everyone was taken care of.

Sally put the last of her toiletry items in a small bag, then placed it in the suitcase on her bed. She turned to pick up her other pair of shoes and stopped short. The smell of smoke had been in the air all morning because of the many fires burning in the city, but the smoke she smelled was closer. More pungent. She hurried to the door of her room and opened it, finding the hallway filling with smoke. Leaving her suitcase behind, Sally ran through the second floor hallway yelling, "Fire! Fire! The house is on fire!"

Upon reaching the staircase, instead of making her escape while she had the chance, she went up to warn the others. When she got to the third floor landing, Sally yelled down the hall, "The house is on fire! Get out, the house is on fire!" She didn't even go into the hallway, but continued up the stairs to the fourth floor.

When Sally stepped into the fourth floor hall, the smoke had already begun to fill the top story of the boarding house. The level of the heavy smoke was down to six feet, so the bank teller leaned forward and continued through the hallway, still yelling, "Is anybody up here? The house is on fire and we have to get out!"

Ray poked his head out of the doorway of the Strueberg's apartment to see what all the commotion was about. Seeing the smoke, he panicked and ran back into the apartment, leaving the door wide open.

"The house is on fire!" he yelled. "The whole place is burning! We have to get out of here! Come on, Naomi!"

Naomi picked Michael up and followed Ray out the door into the hall, as Sally ran on down the hallway shouting, "Fire!"

Ray and Naomi stooped down and scurried for the stairway end of the corridor, then worked their way to the top of the stairs and started down, but the rising smoke was too thick and hot to allow passage. Running back up the stairs, they headed for the window at the end of the hallway.

Karl and Sonya emerged from their bedroom to see what was happening and found nobody there. Not even their 2-year-old son, Michael. What they did find was a sitting room full of thick smoke, so they thought Michael was hiding somewhere in the apartment. The two German immigrants commenced a search of the apartment for their son.

"Mama," Andrella Rodriguez said to her mother as she pushed open the bedroom door. "Someone was yelling in the hall and I don't know what she said."

"Okay, baby," Maria said. "I'll be out in just a minute."

"All right, Mama," the little girl calmly said. "There is some smoke in the sitting room, what should I do?"

Maria felt a chill wave of panic and dropped her hairbrush on the dresser. "What? Where is your brother?"

"I don't know, Mama, he must have gone someplace."

"Oh, my God!" Maria screamed. "Where is Marco?"

Andrella began to sob. "I don't *know*, Mama."

Maria saw she was upsetting her daughter, so she stooped down to hold her. She put her arms

FIRES OF TIME * 157

around the little girl and said calmly, "I'm sorry, baby. Let's you and I try to find Marco."

"Okay, Mama," Andrella said, sniffing and wiping her eyes.

The fire had broken through a wall in an empty room in the rear of the second floor and spread rapidly throughout that floor. When it reached the stairs, the open stairwell acted as a chimney to spread smoke and fire up to the third and fourth floors. By the time everyone on the upper floors was alerted to the danger, half of the boarding house was involved in flame. All of the boarders above the second floor were trapped by the encroaching fire.

In the kitchen, Vince Miller had barely finished his breakfast when he heard Sally yelling.

His strong voice boomed, "Let's move it! Everybody outside!"

He took Amanda Clark by the arm and led her from the kitchen, through the foyer and out the front door. After helping the widow to cross the street, he ran back to the house, passing Mrs. O'Grady and E.W. Brown on the front steps. The fireman went into the boarding house and started up the stairs, only to be driven back down by the smoke and heat. He ran back outside to see if there was another way to get to the upper floors.

When he looked up, he saw Ray and Naomi Ellis climbing out a window on the fourth floor to a perch on the piece of roof jutting out from just below the window. He could see that there was hardly anything supporting that section of roof due to the earlier collapse of the front portion of the boarding house.

"Stay where you are so we can try to rescue you!" he yelled. He noticed Ray was holding the Strueberg's child.

Still not knowing Michael was with the Ellis couple, the Strueberg's continued their search of the apartment for their lost boy.

* * *

There was little question that Emily Cornish was excited about everything taking place around her. "Oh, my! Look at that burning house!"

As they drew closer, her husband maneuvered the vehicle through many obstacles, including people, to jockey the automobile to a spot in front of the house.

"Hold it," Scott said. "It looks like someone may need a little help there."

"You're right," Tyler said, pointing up to the fourth floor of the building. "Look up there."

They heard someone from above. "Help us get down!" Ray yelled from his perch. "Will somebody please do something?"

He was holding Michael in one arm and holding onto the house with the other. Naomi clung tightly to Ray and Michael, her eyes darting around insanely in stark terror. Michael didn't seem to share that fear with her as he giggled and talked a blue streak.

The fireman, Vince, called back to them from the street. "Hold on for a minute and we'll find a way to get you down."

Ray yelled back to him. "We don't have many more minutes left. Hurry, please!"

FIRES OF TIME * 159

"Stop the vehicle Commander, maybe we can help," Scott told the driver.

Andrew Cornish brought the auto to a stop just past the burning boarding house, and as he shut off the motor, Scott and Tyler jumped to the ground.

When they reached the group of people gathered in the street in front of the house, Scott said, "How many people are in the house?"

Vince Miller turned to them. "I'm not exactly sure, but I believe there are six adults and three small children. The only ones we've seen though, are the three near the roof." He pointed to Naomi, Ray and Michael, then added, "We have to get them down from there before the whole place goes up in flames."

Scott moved onto the sidewalk to get a closer look at the situation up there. The section of roof under them was all that was left of the eave, formerly running the entire length of the house. They were on an eight foot remnant that had only one joist holding it in place when there should have been at least four under a section that size. If that one joist broke, they would fall nearly thirty feet into the pile of broken and splintered building rubble.

"I think we can get them down. I'll be right back," Scott said to Vince, remembering the rope, carabiners and figure eights in his bag.

He ran back to the commander's auto, grabbed the black nylon duffel from the rear seat and ran back toward the house. Fire was shooting out of every window on the second and third floors on the east side of the house, and it was showing in all of the fourth floor windows.

"Holy cow!" he yelled.

The boarding house was an old mansion divided up into fourteen separate apartments and rooms. The brick facade on the imposing, four-story building stretched around the entire circumference of the exterior up to just below the second floor windows. The rest was wooden siding painted a pale yellow. On the back of the house were two small decks, one each on the third and fourth floor levels. A porch wrapped completely around the house, except the sections in the front and on the right side, which had become debris in the yards on those sides of the house.

Scott scanned the exterior of the building. He thought, *It's good that you like a challenge, Scotty, cause this definitely fits that category.*

Searching for a way to get to the people on the fourth floor eave, he saw the ends of two large beams jutting out. Nearly three feet of an eighteen-inch wooden beam poked out right below the uppermost gable of the roof, and another one at the third floor level.

Judging from the jagged and tangled appearance of the outside wall, the facade had probably exploded as a result of the earthquake. Siding, stud work and even lath and plaster protruded from the front wall, providing handholds and footholds all over the surface.

Scott turned to Vince. "This looks almost too good to be true. Are you coming with me?"

"Lead the way," Vince replied, sensing Scott knew what he was doing.

Scott ran up the steps to begin his climb over and through the mountain of trash. He carefully picked his way around the dangerous looking projections, like shattered pieces of siding that stuck out of the rubble with sharp, splintery ends. Electrical wiring was strung tightly throughout the mess and razor sharp pieces of sheet metal protruded from many places. Nothing seemed to be very stable, with many of the handholds held in place only by electrical wiring. Most of his footing shifted with every step.

Reaching the highest point possible on the refuse pile, McLean grasped a piece of the wooden siding and tugged, testing it for stability. Finding it strong, he pulled himself up enough to get one foot in a hole in the wall. Climbing higher, he traversed the wall from left to right, using anything he could grasp to ascend the wall. While he climbed, the fire was growing, along with the panic and overall danger.

He yelled down to Vince, "You stage on that lower beam and I'll let you know what to do!"

Vince did as he was told.

* * *

Karl Strueberg pushed the mattress into place against the door of the bedroom. He had already closed the transom and wedged some towels in the crack under the door, but smoke poured into the room in spite of those efforts. Sonya was stripping sheets off the bed and tying them together to make a rope. She cried and talked non-stop while she worked with the sheets.

"Michael, oh Michael," she cried. "Where could my beautiful little boy be, Karl. Where could he be?"

"I don't know, but we're sure he wasn't in the apartment. I am hoping and praying Naomi took him outside to safety."

"What if she didn't?"

"I looked into the hallway and saw the smoke and fire," Karl said. "Just pray to God, my love, that someone took our son to safety. Now help me push this bed nearer the window."

Karl grabbed hold of the brass headboard and began swinging that end around in the room while Sonya pulled the foot of the bed toward the window. With the bed in place against the wall, Karl went over to his wife and held her in his arms, looking lovingly at her tear-streaked face. He could see the fear in her eyes and the stress in her drawn visage. Each feature was highlighted by the blackness of the soot the smoke in the room was depositing in every moist crevice and line.

"Be strong my love. It will be all right."

Karl and Sonya had endured more hardship in their lives than most people would be able to tolerate. Already nearing forty years old, they met on a ship while immigrating to America in 1899, fell in love, and were married in New York City right after the turn of the century in March of 1900. The immigrant couple, having read and heard much about the opportunities for immigrants in San Francisco, rode the train across the country to the west coast in May of 1902.

Karl tried to wipe some of the black soot from Sonya's face, but only succeeded in smearing it. He kissed her forehead and she held him closely for a moment.

Suddenly, she jerked back and said rapidly, "If Michael is safe from the fire we have to get out of here. He needs his mother and father."

Karl smiled at his wife's new resolve. "You are right, Leibeschon, do you have the sheets tied together?"

"Ja."

Karl took one end of the sheet rope and kneeled down beside the brass bedpost nearest the window. He laced the sheet between the post and the first bar and wrapped it back around the brass post. After tying it off, he ran the length of the makeshift rope through his hands, checking the fabric for tears and the knots for strength.

By the time he threw the rope of sheets out the fourth story window, black, choking smoke had filled the room and was pouring out around him through the window's opening. Sonya leaned as far out and down as she possibly could, trying to reach some fresh air. She looked all around outside the house for someone to help them, but the only people she could see were the refugees trudging along the street in the front.

She screamed, "Help us! Can't you people hear me?"

Sonya was ignored by all but a few who glanced her direction with expressionless eyes.

Karl tugged at her waist as he told her what to do. "Turn and go back out the window with your feet first, and I will assist you."

"I'm afraid of falling. Will you go with me?"

"I don't know if the sheets will hold us both, so you must go first. I'll start down after you reach the ground."

With Karl steadying her, Sonya climbed onto the windowsill and turned on her knees until her feet were pointed out of the window. She grabbed the inside of the sill with both hands and managed to slide out the window and down the side of the house, hanging from the room by her hands several stories above the ground.

"What do I do now?"

"Just hang on. I'll help you to get the rope."

He held the rope at her side, pried her left hand from the window sill and placed the rope in it. As he held the sheets over in front of her and patiently helped her to wrap her legs around the makeshift rope, black smoke billowed out through the window and engulfed him. The smoke caused Sonya's eyes to burn and tears to flow so heavily that she could no longer see. They were both choking and coughing enough that Karl worried his wife would fall from the sheet rope, but he still pried her right hand from the window sill and placed it around the rope.

"Start sliding down the rope," he said to her.

"I'm afraid."

"Please hurry," he said, staring lovingly into her eyes as soot blackened sweat dripped from his face.

The mattress blocking the door burned away and the room started burning, instantly creating unbearable, searing heat. Sonya slid down the rope to the first knot, her feet becoming tangled in the sheet momentarily. She felt her way around the knot with her feet and continued down the rope. She was still dangling in the air twenty-five feet above the ground when Karl leaned out the window as far as he could go without falling.

Sonya had worked her way over several knots in her descent when she looked down to see how much further she had to go. Her feet were inches from the end of the sheet rope, but she was still hanging fifteen feet above the ground.

"Karl!" she screamed. "The rope isn't long enough to reach the ground! What should I do?"

Karl didn't hear her over the noise of the roaring fire consuming the room. He had already climbed out onto the rope, hoping it would hold them both. He stopped momentarily at eye level to the window sill to take one last glance back into the blazing room. The whole room was involved in flame and the sheet rope around the bedpost was burning.

A voice called from below. "Slide the rest of the way and let go. I'll try to catch you." Tyler Hunter was standing on the ground below Sonya, waiting to break her fall when she let go.

As frightened as she was, Sonya slid down until she was at the very end of the sheet rope and let go. Tyler threw his arms around her waist just before she hit the ground, breaking her fall. He then lowered her safely the rest of the way.

Karl was at the third floor level on the rope, sliding down as fast as he dared and hoping his wife was out of the way. When the fire finally burned through the knotted sheets, the rope let go, dropping Karl from a height of about twenty feet. He fell through the air, still half blinded by the smoke. When he hit the ground, his legs buckled from the impact, spraining both ankles then tossing him forward onto his arms, breaking his right arm and collarbone. He had burns on his hands and arms and his hair was singed.

Sonya screamed again.

Tyler ran to Karl and examined him.

"Is he all right?" Sonya asked.

"He'll be okay, ma'am," the doctor answered knowingly.

Suddenly, she turned and cried out, "Michael! Where is my baby?"

* * *

Scott managed to climb all the way to the large beam at the apex of the roof and tied himself off to it with a fifteen-foot harness rope, leaving half of it dangling. While working his way there, he talked with the three victims and tried his best to assure them that he would get them down.

Fireman Vince Miller waited on the jutting beam at the the third floor level while Scott tied a carabiner to the upper beam with the remainder of his harness rope. He removed his fifty foot length of half inch rope and slipped it through a figure eight. Clipping the figure eight to the carabiner, he dropped one end down to Vince.

"Hold onto that end and I'll tell you when to pull on it!" Scott shouted.

Vince nodded, examining the strange blue rope the man dropped down to him. The brightly colored polypropylene rope was like nothing he had ever seen before. Scott then proceeded to lower himself to the level of the eave.

"Hi, are you all right?"

Naomi stared fearfully at the stranger hanging in mid-air in front of her. "Let's see if we can get you down from here, okay?"

No response.

"I'm going to tie this rope around your waist and that man down there will lower you to the ground."

"Vince," she said.

"Excuse me?" Scott said, glancing apprehensively at the smoke billowing from the window behind her.

"Vince. His name is Vince. He's a fireman."

"Really," Scott said thoughtfully to Naomi as he looked down. "That could turn out to be good."

"I trust him," she said.

"That's even better," he said, knowing that having her trust would help tremendously. "Now, what's your name?"

"Naomi."

"Naomi," Scott repeated, "I'm Sco ... Sam." He finished tying the rope around her waist and looked at Michael, asking his name.

"Michael Karl Strueberg," the boy answered.

Scott was taken aback by the articulate speech coming from such a tiny child. He smiled warmly at Michael. "Okay, Michael Karl Strueberg, how would you like to hang onto your mom and ride down on the rope?"

"She's my friend," Michael said as he let Ray and Scott lift him over into Naomi's arms.

"I'm not his mother," Naomi whispered to Scott.

"All right, Michael. I need you to hug Naomi around the neck real, real tight. Can you do that?"

Michael nodded as he put his little arms around her neck, squeezing so hard that she couldn't breathe. Scott noticed the choke hold and had the boy ease up a bit.

Ray adjusted the eyeglasses on the bridge of his slender nose, then said, "We'd better hurry here. There isn't much time."

The smoke was getting thicker and hotter and flames were beginning to shoot out of the window below them.

Scott shouted down at his 1906 colleague to take up the slack in the rope as he slid the other end up under Naomi's arms. He looked down to tell

Vince to wrap his legs around the beam and saw that the fireman had already done so. Vince's back was braced against the wall with his legs locked tightly around the beam as he held the rope securely in his hands.

Scott called out to him. "Are you ready, Vince?"

Vince looked up at him with a quizzical expression on his face, and thought, *How does he know my name?*

"I'm ready!"

Scott turned back to Naomi and explained what was going to happen. "I'll help you to get off and away from the eave. I know it's scary, but you'll be safe. Vince is going to lower you and Michael to the ground. Okay?"

"I ... I can do it," she said, squeezing Michael tighter.

"Hurry," Ray pleaded.

"All right Vince!" Scott yelled. "Pull on the rope a bit and we'll start them down!"

Vince pulled down on the rope, lifting Naomi and Michael slightly off the eave as Scott moved them out and away from the house. Scott quickly explained to Naomi to get the rope off as soon as they were safe on the ground.

Scott shouted, "They're all yours, Vince! Take 'em down!"

Hand over hand, Vince began lowering Naomi and Michael to the ground. The figure eight, with the rope sliding through it, worked to help slow the descent. Naomi and Michael were clinging tightly to each other. But the second they touched the ground, Naomi slipped out of the rope and let it drop. Still carrying Michael, she scrambled over the scrap pile

FIRES OF TIME * 169

and down to the street just as Sonya Strueberg rounded the corner of the house calling for her son.

"Mommy!" Michael cried, breaking from Naomi and running to his mother.

"Michael!" Sonya called out, running into the street. The petite, dark haired lady with the black-tear streaked face picked up her son and hugged him close. "Michael, oh, my Michael. Thank God you're safe."

Vince yelled. "The rope's coming back up!"

Black smoke encircled Scott and Ray up on the fourth floor. Fire was erupting from all the windows on every floor and even breaching the outer wall itself. Fingers of flame licked at the beam where the ropes were tied.

Scott pulled the rope back up and took the loop that had been around Naomi, then slipped it over Ray's head and under his arms. "Are you ready?"

Ray didn't have to be asked twice. With flames darting all around him he slid to the edge of the eave. "Aren't you coming?"

"Don't worry about me," Scott shouted over the din of the roaring blaze. "Just get out of here!"

"Take him away!" he yelled to Vince. "And when he hits the ground, get down yourself!"

Vince took up the slack and dangled Ray in the air, then lowered him down through the clouds of black smoke to the safety of the ground. Vince scrambled down from his perch with fire burning the hair on both his arms and his head.

Scott pulled the rope back up, removed the figure eight, and got busy untying his harness rope. The smoke was so bad that he couldn't see or breathe and he was coughing so much he could hardly manage to tie the half inch rope onto the beam. After finally getting it tied off, there was fire shooting out and around the beam, threatening to burn the rope away.

"That's not good," Scott said when he saw what the fire was doing.

He fumbled with a carabiner and the figure eight, attempting to get the beener hooked to his harness. Placing his feet against the edge of the eave, he pushed himself away from the encroaching flame, but when he pushed off, he heard a loud cracking. The one joist holding the eave snapped and the whole thing fell crashing to the scrap pile below, exploding in a spectacular display of sparks.

Scott was left hanging below the beam from his harness, swinging slowly back and forth in the smoke. He looked at the fire and carefully scrutinized his desperate situation.

He told himself soberly, "Well Scotty, you may have just gone and done it this time."

Tyler was helping Karl Strueberg limp into the street when Commander Cornish showed up to assist him. A crowd of people stood watching the front of the house go up in flames, the black smoke billowing out and up into the bright, blue sky.

To the commander, Tyler said, "Where is my friend, Sam?"

Andrew Cornish pointed to the top of the house. "The audacious physician failed to descend from his perilous precipice doctor. I'm afraid he was last seen suspended from a tether amid the lofty timbers."

Along with the rest of the gathered crowd, Tyler looked up at the house and could see nothing but smoke and flame. A collective gasp went up from the crowd when the eave fell and crashed to the ground in a hail of sparks. A few seconds later, something below the front gable near the top pitch of the roof fluttered out from the house and back into the roaring fire.

Standing near Tyler, Vince knew what it was. "That was the rope."

"What?" Tyler said.

"That was the strange blue rope we used to rescue them."

When the smoke and dust cleared enough for them to see the front of the house, there was no sign of Scott McLean.

* * *

After alerting everyone in the boarding house to the fire, Sally Higgins ran all the way down the fourth floor hallway to the back of the house to escape the flames, only to find more. She tried to get into a room near the back, but the door was locked and she couldn't break it. She climbed out the hallway window and stood on the small balcony, looking down three stories to the roof of the porch on the back of the house.

Smoke poured out of the window all around her, the heat of the fire intensifying. Thinking of jumping, Sally searched through the smoke to try to judge how far the jump would be, but when she leaned out, she heard someone yell from below.

Maria Rodriguez stood on the third floor balcony with Andrella, and pleaded, "Help us! Somebody help us!"

"Maria," Sally called. "Is that you?"

Maria looked up through the smoke and saw Sally's shape on the deck above her. "Yes. Who is there?"

"It's me. Sally. I'm above you."

"I can barely see you. What are we going to do?"

"I must get down to you. Where are the children?"

"Andrella is here with me. But we cannot find Marco."

Sally hesitated briefly, then added, "I'm sure Marco is safe with someone from the house. He's a very resourceful little boy."

Sally decided to make a move, so she inched her way over the wrought iron railing and climbed down to hang from the floor of the small porch with the intention of jumping to the balcony below. Hanging by her hands and looking down at the distance to the next floor, she realized she'd made a big mistake. She tried to pull herself back up, but her arms just weren't strong enough. There were no footholds and nothing to climb down on and her arms were beginning to weaken. She would soon have to drop and hope to land on the balcony or fall twenty-five feet to the porch roof below.

Looking up, Maria yelled to Sally to hold on. "Someone should be here soon to help us!"

Sally knew better. She knew the entire city must have been wiped out by the earthquake and there probably wouldn't be anyone around to come to her rescue. She could also see that she was going to have to drop. Possibly to her death. Hanging in the billowing smoke, she got weaker and more light headed by the second.

I'm never going to see my home and family again, she thought. *Grandmother will be heartbroken.* As the smoke made her groggier and her hands and arms grew weaker, she began to lose her grip on the balcony, along with her grip on reality.

She prayed. "Please, God. Spare the lives of Maria and Andrella and little Marco. And if it's not too much trouble, Lord, I could use a small miracle here myself."

She prepared to drop, her fingers slipping closer to the edge, when something brushed by her face. Sally stared at it, not understanding what it was.

"Grab the rope!" a voice called from above.

Sally thought she'd already died and the angels had been sent from heaven to hoist her up. She continued to stare at the bright, orange rope.

The voice was closer. "Grab onto the rope." A strong hand closed around her right wrist and began to pull her back up to the railing. "You need to give me a little help there ma'am, if you have the strength."

Sally was lifted up to the railing where she put her feet on the outer edge of the balcony floor. She looked into the dirty face of a very handsome man with a mustache who looked good enough to her to be an angel.

But why would an angel have such a dirty face? she thought.

"Are you an angel?"

"No ma'am, I'm not an angel," he grinned. "I've been called a lot of things, but angel hasn't generally been one of them."

"Who are you, then?"

"I'm sorry, my name is Sam. And you?"

"Sally," she answered. "Sally Higgins."

"Well, Ms. Higgins, I believe we had better get out of here."

"Whatever you say, Mr. Sam."

Scott stood on top of the railing flipping his harness rope to release the loop from the cornice piece above. It slipped off and fell down in a heap on the balcony floor. He jumped down and tied one end to the railing. He figured he could use his other rope on the third floor and manage to get to the roof of the porch from there ... if they hurried. The Beast had already foiled some of Scott's plans and it would probably be more than willing to go another round.

He tossed the end of the rope over the railing. "Have you regained enough strength to hold this rope and slide down to that next balcony?"

She looked at Scott through the ever thickening smoke, and grabbed the rope. "I'm sure I can make it. I don't want to think about the alternative, do I?"

"Not really," he said as she stepped off the balcony and slid down the rope.

Fire had built up to the point that Scott could see he was about to put himself in peril again. He leaned over to watch Sally and saw her climbing down from the railing and stepping onto the third floor balcony. He wasted no time in getting down to the next floor, where he met Maria and Andrella Rodriguez. The four of them were only fifteen feet from the roof and twenty-five feet from safety.

There was much less smoke on the third floor deck because the hallway didn't extend all the way to the window on that floor. An apartment covered the entire rear of the building. Maria and Andrella had piled mattresses in front of the door and plugged the cracks with anything they could find. The fire and smoke, however, were only delayed, not defeated.

Maria, Andrella, Sally, and Scott were the last living people in the house and nobody in the front had any idea if they were dead or alive, or where they were trapped. The first and second floors were both completely involved, with the fire spreading to the underside of the back porch roof. The third and fourth floors were completely involved except for the apartment by the deck.

All four had taken in a large amount of smoke on their journeys, causing them light-headedness, headaches and agitation. Maria was on the verge of a nervous breakdown, pacing back and forth on the tiny veranda with her dark eyes darting furtively in all directions. She looked like a person that was ready to lose it at any minute. She chattered to her daughter in Spanish and English, alternating them so quickly that it was all nothing but gibberish.

"I'll tie this rope to the railing and drop it over the edge," Scott said. "Then we can slide down to the roof below us."

Maria glanced at him with eyes like a caged tiger.

He smiled at her. "It's okay, Maria. We can do it."

She wasn't convinced. Ten feet below, at the second floor level, the brick facade ran along under the window forming an eight inch ledge running clear across the back of the house. The porch roof, still intact, was only a few feet below that.

Piece of cake, he thought. *If we hurry.*

He noticed the roaring of the fire, bombarding them from every direction, along with snapping and crackling sounds. It sounded like the whole house was beginning to crash right down upon them. Scott reached out and took hold of the rope hanging from the fourth floor balcony, giving it a tug. When it fell, he gathered it in, examining the burnt end by spinning it around in his fingers. He glanced up.

"We'd better get moving," he said to the group. "I think I've figured out what we need to do."

Sally was on her knees on the floor comforting Andrella. "Everything will be all right, dear. I'm sure Marco is safe and sound."

Maria fingered her rosary beads and prayed fervently in Spanish for the Lord to deliver Marco safely to her. Preferably in a safe spot on the ground.

Scott interrupted Maria's prayers. "Are you ready to get out of here?"

"Si. I mean yes."

He smiled at Maria's attempt to speak only English, even in her time of greatest fear. "Come over here by the railing so I can show all of you what we need to do."

The smoke around them had grown so thick that visibility was nearly zero. Scott tried to show them what he wanted, but he could no longer see the roof of the porch through the smoke. To Sally and Maria, he said, "Can you two get down the rope?"

They both answered that they could.

"I'll take your daughter down, if that's all right with you," he said to Maria. "You two go first and we'll follow."

"No, please. Take my baby down first and we will follow. Please!"

He looked at Sally with a question on his face.

"Yes, go!" she said.

"Come on, Andrella," Scott said. "I'll carry you down the rope. Doesn't that sound like fun?"

Andrella shyly nodded her head as Scott kneeled way down for her to climb on his back. He led her around behind his back, holding both her hands high in the air, then pulled her arms around his neck and placed her hands together. "Now hold on real tight, Andrella, and wrap your legs around my belly. Yeah, that's the way," he told her after she did as she'd been instructed.

Scott stood with Andrella, then went to the railing and stepped up and over it, standing back on the balcony floor on the outside of it. He kneeled down and grabbed the rope securely in both hands and pushed off with his knees, hanging in front of the balcony in the billowing smoke.

"Are you holding on tight?"

"Yes sir," she said directly into Scott's right ear.

Scott started to say something to the women just when the fire broke through the mattresses into the room and moved rapidly across the ceiling in search of oxygen. It blew out of the window and up into the fresh air causing Maria to scream. She scrambled up and over the railing to get away from the inferno.

"I think the rope will hold all of us!" Scott yelled over the noise. "Let us get part way down and then follow!"

Hand over hand, he started down toward the next floor, hoping there would be enough rope to get to the roof of the porch. Maria and Sally eagerly awaited their turn while watching Scott and Andrella disappear into the smoke.

"Hold on tight, Andrella," he said over and over to the girl.

Carefully, Scott took them quickly down the rope, his feet suddenly hanging in mid air. He'd reached the end of his rope and couldn't see anything through the smoke. Andrella coughed violently and Scott was afraid she might fall, so he reached out with his feet toward the wall and felt the brick facade, which meant he was within a few feet of the roof. Above, Maria and Sally had climbed on and started down the rope, causing enough movement that Scott knew he'd better get out of the way.

"Oh, well," he said. "Hang on Andrella!"

He let go of the rope and jumped away from the house. The porch roof was closer than anticipated and his feet hit the surface sooner than expected. His legs buckled, tossing him over backward. Trying to avoid landing on the small girl, Scott twisted his body and rolled on to his left side, his face scraping against the shingles. He let out a grunt and pushed himself up onto his knees, pried the girl's hands from his neck and helped her to stand up on the surface of the roof.

Rising and taking Andrella's hand, he moved them a few feet away from the side of the house to make room for the two ladies to land.

"You stay right there and don't move," he said to Andrella, moving back to find the rope.

He reached up to take hold of the rope just as Maria dropped into his arms, knocking him down. Both of them fell to the roof, and before they could get out of the way, Sally tumbled over on top of them.

"That worked out real well," Scott said sarcastically as he stared up at the burning boarding house.

The four-story wall began to bulge and Scott knew it was coming down soon. He jumped to his feet and picked up the little girl. "Come on, we have to get off of here. Be careful and follow in my footsteps!"

Scott tested the strength of the surface with every step as they moved carefully toward the edge. Large pieces of the siding and roofing fell through the smoke and hit the porch all around them. Scott took Andrella by one hand and swung her over the edge of the roof, dangling her in the air while he got to his knees. He lowered her to just about two feet above the ground and let go. She landed like a cat.

To the two women, he said, "Keep moving. Times-a-wastin'!"

Maria jumped, landing on the lawn and rolling just before a big piece of the wall hit the top of the porch, jolting it so hard that it sent Sally flying toward Scott. She crashed into him and they both tumbled off the roof toward the ground, landing in a heap on top of an overstuffed chaise lounge. The chaise broke under the pressure and they rolled out onto the grass unscathed.

"Run!"

They ran for the very edge of the large backyard and dropped, exhausted, in the shade of a tree. As they sat and watched, the big old boarding house collapsed and burned to the ground.

* * *

Following the collapse of the boarding house, Maria left her daughter in the care of Sally and frantically ran around the west side of the still burning, collapsed structure in search of her little Marco.

"Marco! Marco!" She screamed his name and prayed to God at the same time, not having any idea where to begin looking.

When she got to the street in front, the throngs of slow moving people made it impossible to see more than a few feet in any direction. There was no way to spot a small boy through the melee. She fought her way to the other side of the street, still calling out Marco's name past the deaf ears of the swarming mass of refugees.

"Where are you, my little Marco?"

Sobbing, she elbowed her way back and forth through the street several times and collapsed on the sidewalk near the grassy area across from the boarding house. The same grassy area where the residents of the house met after the earthquake, and where they were currently gathered.

"Maria," someone said. "Thank the heavens you're all right."

Maria looked up to see Naomi Ellis reaching out to her. Naomi kneeled down and put her arm around Maria's shoulders.

"We thought you were gone. Where are the children?"

Naomi looked around for Marco and Andrella.

Maria fell into Naomi's arms weeping. "My Marco. My beautiful little Marco. I can't find him. Have you seen him? Has anybody seen my Marco?"

Naomi didn't quite know what to say, being aware that nobody had seen the little boy. She comforted Maria and looked at Mrs. O'Grady for support as the landlady scurried over to them.

FIRES OF TIME * 181

Looking around, she didn't see Andrella. "I'm sorry. We haven't seen him, but we'll start searching."

"Was he with Andrella, dear?"

"No, no. Andrella is with Sally and the man who rescued us from the house."

Naomi appeared quite surprised. "A man? Is his name Sam?"

"I think so," Maria said.

Naomi watched Sam die in the fire. Or, at least she thought she'd seen him die. "How, Maria? How did he rescue you?"

"He came from above. The angels sent him from heaven to save us."

Hmm, Naomi thought. *That might explain why he didn't die.*

Mrs. O'Grady didn't quite understand all that was going on and asked, "And Sally is safe then?"

"Si."

"Oh, Thank God," she said as Naomi helped Maria to stand.

They walked over to the lawn and sat on the grass, and Mrs. O'Grady began organizing a search party for Marco.

"Mama! Mama!"

Every head in the group turned to see Andrella running from Sally and Scott to her mother's arms. They were all happy to see Sally and Andrella, but, at the same time, saddened that it wasn't Marco.

Vince Miller spotted Scott and hurried over to him, with Tyler right behind. "Doctor Wolf. Your friend, Dr. Hunter, told me who you are. I'm very happy to be able to meet you. Alive, that is. We all thought you were dead."

"So did I," Scott said. He glanced at Tyler and smiled. "Hey, Ty, how's it hangin'?"

Tyler shook his head and laughed. "You're an amazing man, Sam. I don't know how you did it, but I'm glad to see you made it out alive."

"Me too."

Vince dragged Scott over to where the other residents were gathered so they could properly thank him for his efforts. Always somewhat embarrassed by personal accolades, Scott humbly told them they were welcome and tried to get away as quickly as possible.

Vince then pulled him off to the side to ask him some questions. "How do you know so much about rescues, Doctor? You've surely done it before."

Wanting nothing more than to get moving, Scott said, "I've done some firefighting."

"Really?"

"Really."

"And then you became a doctor?"

Scott nodded and smiled. "Yes, Vince. I was a fireman long before I became a doctor. In fact, I haven't really been doctoring all that long."

"Why did you decide to become a doctor?"

"Oh, I just sort of stumbled into it. It seems like one minute I was a fireman, and then the next minute, I was a doctor."

"I see, but I'm sure it wasn't all that easy. Can I ask you another thing?"

Scott warily nodded.

"Where did you get that rope? I've never seen anything like it in my life."

And you probably won't again, Scott thought. *Unless your life turns out to be a very long one.*

FIRES OF TIME * 183

Tyler interrupted. "I've learned one thing about Sam, Vince. You're better off to just not ask any questions. Besides, we have to go. We have two patients to get to the hospital."

Scott cocked his head. "Two?"

"Two, Dr. Wolf," Tyler said. "The commander consented to allow us room for another patient. A gentleman by the name of Karl."

"Let's hit it then," Scott declared.

The two doctors walked away from the boarding house residents toward the Cornish automobile to a chorus of thanks from the grateful fire victims. Scott stopped and went back to Maria, who was sitting on the grass sobbing quietly, rocking back and forth with Andrella in her arms.

He kneeled down beside them and hugged them both. "I'm sorry, Maria."

Maria turned her blackened and tear streaked face to him and thanked him. "May God bless you," she said as he stood and walked back to Tyler.

"Hi, Doctors," Jennifer Brody said as they climbed into the vehicle. "It's good to see you."

The men got seated in the rear seat, cramped as it was getting. "Sam, this is Karl Strueberg," Tyler said, introducing the man seated between Jenny and himself.

Scott nodded to him. "Pleased to meet you. You look like somebody beat you up."

Karl managed a small smile through the pain. "I wish it had been only that, Doctor. Then, maybe I wouldn't hurt so much."

"I hear that."

"Shall we persevere upon our odyssey gentlemen?" Andrew Cornish said. "To the Harbor Emergency Hospital?"

"Oh, quite," Scott said pompously.

Tyler smiled and Emily Cornish turned around to Scott with an approving grin on her face.

The commander slowly maneuvered his auto back into the crowded roadway. He jerked to a stop when a police officer stepped in front of the car.

"Oh, my," Mrs. Cornish gasped. "We came close to driving into that policeman. He should be more careful, especially when he has a small child with him."

Scott spun his head around to get a look at the officer and saw a dark haired little boy pull his hand from the officer's and run away.

"Mama! Mama!" the boy yelled excitedly as he ran through the crowd of refugees.

Scott turned around in the seat and got to his knees so he could see out over the back of the vehicle, just in time to see the boy disappear in the swarm of people.

"Marco!" Maria yelled as she rose to her feet and dashed into the street to pick Marco up in her arms.

As the commander drove away, Scott saw Maria carrying Marco from the street with Andrella walking alongside, her arms around her mother's waist, hugging both her mother and her little brother Marco.

Scott turned around and sat back down in the rear seat with a contented smile and a trickle of tears running down his face.

Jenny looked at him. "What's the matter, Dr. Sam? Are you all right?"

Scott smiled even more. "I'm fine. You know, things could always be worse."

"I hear that," Tyler laughed.

Scott turned with a surprised look at hearing Tyler mimic his own style of talk.

"Oh, listen to that, won't you," Andrew Cornish said as he turned and chuckled at Scott. "I postulate your chum has plainly transcended your previous raillery."

Everyone in the automobile laughed, except for Karl, who didn't have the foggiest idea what any of them were talking about.

Chapter Ten

Scott McLean rode in the back of the commander's Oldsmobile Touring car, taking in the sights of 1906 San Francisco. He was actually living the history he had only read about for so many years. He saw recognizable buildings burning and knew when others were going to start to burn. Looking out over the bay, he saw the ships coming into the port, and knew the Navy ships were going to play a huge part in saving many areas of the city.

Bringing Scott back to the present, Tyler said, "Would you assist me with this? I'm going to change this dressing and could use your help, doctor."

"No problem," Scott said, turning in the seat to help Tyler lift Jenny's leg up to where they could work with it.

Tyler removed the tourniquet that was holding the bandage in place with a ripping sound familiar to only Scott. Every head in the car turned at the sound because nobody else in the group was accustomed to the sound of Velcro being pulled apart. Doctor

Hunter then carefully removed the bandage from the young lady's injured leg, exposing the severed end of her ankle.

He examined it closely and uttered an occasional, "Hmm." Looking over at Scott, he inquired, "How does it look to you?"

Scott looked at the injury and saw that it appeared to be amazingly clean and neat. The procedure the doctor had performed under such trying circumstances was carried out very nicely. It needed some surgery, of course, to finish trimming and sewing it up, but probably would have healed fairly well as it was.

"You did an outstanding job. You know, I'm genuinely impressed with your work."

"Thank you."

Tyler had barely finished changing the dressing on Jenny's leg, when the occupants of the vehicle were startled by the sound of a tremendous explosion. Then another.

"What was that?" Emily Cornish gasped. The white haired lady straightened her wide brimmed hat and retied the ample silk scarf that shaded her fair skin from the sun. She reached over and poked her husband's arm. "What is happening? Hasn't there been enough destruction?"

"I'm not sure," the commander said, "but I'm convinced that whatever it is, we shall not be aggrieved by its ferocity."

Andrew Cornish's plump and rosy cheeks were flushed a bright red and his two chins were pulled taut with tension underneath his beard. The commander had been through enough dangerous and life threatening situations that he knew not to panic the others in his charge.

He turned his head to face Tyler and Scott. "What are you gentlemen pondering in relationship to this situation?"

Dr. Hunter looked immediately to Scott for an answer, pretty well knowing Scott would be able to explain the new development.

"What?" Scott said.

Tyler looked knowingly into the face of his new friend. "You know what's happening, don't you?"

Scott stared back and wondered what must have been going on inside the early twentieth century doctor's head.

Every eye in the vehicle was on Scott. "Firebreaks," he admitted finally. "The army troops are blowing up buildings with dynamite to create firebreaks to stop the spread of the fire."

More explosions rocked the city. It was beginning to sound more and more like a battleground as dynamite was detonated in other parts of town. Scott was trying to concentrate on everything taking place and didn't want to miss a single thing. It seemed like his eyes weren't big enough to take in all that was happening. He was trying to observe, and didn't really want to be bothered by anything else at that juncture. The time traveler wanted to see it all, which was impossible, and he found himself wishing he'd used enough foresight to bring along a camera.

Man, pictures of this would look really nice in my office with the rest of my collection. His thoughts were quickly interrupted by Tyler.

"Can we get to Harbor Emergency, Sam? Is Harbor Emergency even going to be there if we do make it?"

Scott was beginning to tire of playing the secrecy game with Tyler Hunter. The doctor was a good man with good intentions and Scott sincerely liked him. He didn't deserve to have his head messed with, but Scott just couldn't tell him the truth. At least not yet. He had to keep up the masquerade for a little while longer.

"We'll be all right. Trust me," Scott said assuringly.

Tyler leaned across the seat and clasped his hand around Scott's left wrist. "In the city of San Francisco today, the very earth has betrayed us. The winds are blowing into the city from virtually all directions, fanning the flames of this vast holocaust. Mother Nature herself seems to have turned against us, and it seems there is little to trust. But I do trust you, Sam. If there is only one thing in this city I do trust, it's you. You've proven several times this day that I can trust you over all else."

Scott looked at his partner, feeling guilty for the untruths he'd told the man. *Thanks a lot, I really needed that,* he thought. *If you only knew. I've betrayed you more than anyone today, but I'll make it right before I go.*

Scott looked at the driver of the auto. Commander Andrew Cornish was an interesting individual, with his pompous airs and highfalutin way of talking. He was obviously a man of good taste, judging by the clothes he wore. Tan colored pants with a matching vest over a ruffled shirt with bloused sleeves. Scott noticed a gold watch chain snaking from a pocket in the vest to a belt loop on the man's pants. He wasn't wearing a jacket, although Scott was sure one existed that matched the pants and

FIRES OF TIME * 191

vest. The commander's gray beard and hair lent a sophisticated look to the large and portly gentleman.

The watch chain caught Scott's attention. "Can you tell me what time it is, Commander?"

"Eleven thirty-five, my good man," he said, reading the face of the intricately engraved gold watch. "We have undeniably occupied a monumental segment of our morning with this rescue activity. I must explicate, however, that it has all been exceedingly exhilarating and inordinately rewarding."

Scott turned away from the others as much as possible in the cramped seat to reset his Timex, unaware that Tyler was watching.

Tyler had already noticed the Indiglow instrument in the darkness of morning when they were still on Telegraph Hill. He'd noticed many things about Scott during their day together in addition to the tools in his black duffel. Sitting back in the seat, Dr. Tyler Hunter contemplated the many oddities surrounding Dr. Sam Wolf.

I don't understand, he thought, as he gazed at the colossal clouds of smoke rising into the sky in every direction. *This man showed up in the city at the beginning of this terrible calamity with precisely the right knowledge and skills needed. And all of those remarkable tools in his small black bag seem to have been designed for just such an occasion as this. It's all very confusing. Perhaps Maria Rodriguez was on the right track. Maybe the angels did send him from heaven to help us in our time of need, for some of the tools he uses and the things he's done don't seem to be of this world. The fire swallowed him up and he emerged unscathed. No, there is some plausible explanation, I'm sure. But, as a physician, I learned long ago to never scoff at miracles. I would only hope that he finds it in his heart to explain it all to me.*

Another series of explosions brought him back from the depths of his thoughts.

"Oh my, but that is so unnerving." Emily shuddered as she put her arms around her husband's large arm and squeezed.

"There, there, dear," the commander said, patting his wife's knee. "It will be all right. I'm quite sure."

The Cornish auto made a left turn from Sansome onto Broadway in the direction of the wharf. The handful of people on board the official ambulance could have seen across the bay if it had been a clear day, but with smoke enveloping the whole city, they could see no more than a block in front of the car.

Andrew turned to the passengers in the rear. "Please allow me to apologize for the circuitous route which I have navigated in pursuit of our ultimate destination. I'm afraid the disrepair of the roadways made an undeviating course quite unattainable."

Scott and Tyler couldn't help but smile.

"That's quite all right, Commander," Scott said. "We're grateful for the safe transportation to the hospital. You've been quite gracious, and we appreciate all you've done."

The crowd of refugees in the streets grew larger as they drew closer to the Union Ferry Building. They were still riding in the auto, but progress had slowed to a snail's pace. Scott's first view of the scene at the wharf was nothing short of awesome. Thousands of people pushed their way toward the ferries that offered them escape from the stricken city, and they looked the same as the refugees Scott had been seeing all morning long.

San Francisco of 1906 was a true melting pot for the people of the world, with humankind of many races thrown together in the frantic rush to outrun the disastrous fire. Chinese, Japanese, Germans and Latins were shoulder to shoulder with French, Italians, Spaniards and Dutch. The nationalities represented in the commotion had all been run out of their individual ethnic communities by the earthquake and fire to join the multi-national mad dash toward the one common goal. To get the hell outta Dodge.

The scene outside Harbor Emergency Hospital was bedlam. Fire department vehicles were set up in every available spot. Firemen worked fervently to protect the hospital from the encroaching fire while a constant, unending stream of injured poured into the infirmary. Steamer wagons were positioned at the hospital for the duration of the fire to protect the building, with U.S. Navy ships pumping salt water to the steamers.

* * *

When they finally wound their way to the vicinity of Harbor Emergency, the lines were not lines at all. They had become the rhythmic and pulsating, integrated hoi polloi. It appeared it would be a very long wait to get within shouting distance of the hospital, longer still to get in.

"It looks pretty bleak," Scott observed.

"Perhaps," Tyler said. "I know one of the doctors that works here, on normal days, that is. If I can work my way up to the door to find Dr. Schmidt, perhaps I can talk my way in."

"Wait a moment, Doctor," the commander said. "It appears the Navy is helping with the operation. I wonder ..." He abruptly exited the automobile and added, "I shall return."

Hurrying away into the crowd, his voice could be heard above the din calling out to someone. "Ensign Judson! Ensign Judson!" He disappeared into the mass of people.

Karl Strueberg had been silent during the entire trip, sitting quietly and listening to the conversation of the others in the vehicle. Scott studied his face and noticed the occasional grimace Karl made because of the pain. The injuries the man suffered were causing him an untold amount of grief, yet he silently endured the pain. He was grateful for what had been done for him and didn't want to cause anyone to have to bother with him. He could see they had plenty to do in just taking care of the young lady and getting them all to the hospital.

Scott leaned over to touch Karl's shoulder. "Are you all right?"

"I'm all right, thank you, sir."

"You look like you're in a lot of pain."

"Yes, I am having much pain, but so far I have been able to endure it."

"Where do you hurt?"

Karl pointed out his right collarbone and upper arm. "The place you touched, Doctor. Right there, and here on my arm."

"Anywhere else?"

"My hands are very painful from the burns. And my arms."

Scott reached over, carefully taking Karl's hands and turning the left one over as he examined both hands and arms. Karl had first and second degree burns covering most of his left hand, and about fifty percent of his left arm, with additional first degree burns on part of his right hand. Scott felt bad that he hadn't noticed the amount of burned surface earlier. Finding a towel on the floor of the car, he shook it off and gently laid it around Karl's burns. Reaching into his duffel, he took out the bottle of water and poured enough of it over the towel to completely soak it.

The relief from pain showed in Karl's face as his body relaxed back into the seat. "Thank you, that feels very good. Thank you."

Tyler was watching with a quizzical look, wondering why Scott was putting cold water on the burns. "Is this a new procedure I haven't heard about?"

Scott was so accustomed to the method of using cold water to treat burns, that he hadn't thought about the treatment being different back then.

"Yes it is," Scott answered. "The water accomplishes several things, the first being pain relief. It also stops the burning process, because after a burn occurs, enough heat is still present for quite some time to keep burning deeper. And if you put salves or butter on the burn, you can turn a first degree burn to second or second degree to third. Salves and butter actually trap the heat and allow the burn to worsen, and they can even introduce bacteria that start infection."

Tyler looked thoughtfully at Scott. "You know, that makes a lot of sense."

Scott explained further. "Salves, and especially butter, contain germs that can introduce serious infections in burned areas where the protective layers of skin have been damaged or destroyed."

"Fascinating. Are there other new procedures that haven't yet reached us here on the west coast?"

"Possibly. I'll try to let you know if we come across anything in the next day or so."

Because Doctor Hunter had shown himself to be a competent surgeon, Scott was a little surprised that he already had to explain a new treatment to him. And something so basic.

"Thank you. I'll appreciate any new knowledge I can gain from your expertise."

"Do me a favor, Ty."

"Yes?"

"You do the same for me."

Tyler smiled at his friend and agreed to share any of his knowledge, thinking, *What could I possibly tell this miracle man about anything? I don't know that he's a heavenly being, but if he is I want to learn every new procedure or treatment he can teach me. Wouldn't an angel know everything, even things that haven't yet happened?*

"Doctors!" Commander Cornish announced as he approached the automobile. "We may now proceed forthwith to the infirmary."

He introduced a middle-aged naval officer who was accompanying him. "This, gentleman, is Lieutenant Welden, an old and dear friend of mine. He shall be escorting all but my sweet wife and myself into the hospital."

The lieutenant motioned to one of his men to bring a stretcher, and then moved around to the right side of the car to assist with removing Jennifer Brody from the rear seat. Several sailors arrived, and under Scott's direction, placed her on a canvas stretcher.

Scott thanked Emily Cornish for helping them and stepped to the front of the vehicle where the commander was standing.

"Thank you, Sir," Scott said, shaking the commander's hand. "If you don't mind my saying, I've learned this morning why you are so well respected. I'm honored to have shared this experience with such a compassionate couple as you and your lovely wife. Thank you again and I wish you well."

Commander Cornish flashed him a smile. "You are most welcome, Doctor Wolf. I'm most pleased to have made your acquaintance."

Scott hurried away to escort Jenny through the crowd while, with the help of two Navy medical people, Tyler assisted Karl from the other side of the Oldsmobile. Tyler walked past the commander as they headed toward the hospital and thanked him for his help.

The booming commander's voice called out. "Doctor Hunter!"

Tyler stopped and turned around to look at the retired Navy man.

"Thank you for the comeuppance this morning. You helped in bringing me and my pompous attitude back to earth where I belong. Thank you so."

Tyler smiled at him and waved as he disappeared into the mob of sick and injured surrounding the hospital.

* * *

"Doctor Hunter? Is that you?" A small, dark haired man in a white smock called to Tyler as he worked his way around the beds and medical personnel inside the hospital.

Tyler waved and called back to him. "Henry. Yes, it *is* me."

The man reached Tyler and his small entourage and took Tyler's hand in a firm handshake. That he was very pleased to see Doctor Hunter showed in the warm look on his face.

"I don't know what act of providence has brought you here Doctor, but I am delighted to see you." With a sweeping hand, he continued. "As you can see we have been deluged with patients from the disaster and are in dire need of assistance. Orthopaedic, burns, internal surgeons. In fact, we need help of every kind."

"I'm here to do whatever I can to help," Tyler said. Motioning to Scott, Tyler introduced him to the doctor. "Dr. Henry Schmidt, Dr. Sam Wolf, burn specialist."

Doctor Schmidt's eyes lit up when he heard burn specialist. He reached out and took Scott's hand. "Doctor Wolf, I am very happy to meet you. I know the good Lord sent you, I just know it."

Tyler looked at Scott and smiled, saying to Dr. Schmidt, "I believe he did."

Scott shook the doctor's hand and told him he was glad to make his acquaintance. Pointing to Jenny and Karl, he said, "We've brought a couple of our own patients with us. Is there anywhere we can put them for treatment?"

"Follow me," Henry Schmidt said, moving among the patients in search of empty bed space.

The Navy medics followed Dr. Schmidt, carrying Jenny Brody on the canvas stretcher and assisting Karl Strueberg in limping through the hospital.

The scene inside Harbor Emergency Hospital was a bit more organized than the bedlam on the outside. It was a more structured chaos, being orchestrated by the nurses and doctors. As they moved between the beds, Scott saw scores of suffering people. Nurses were scurrying around, carrying pans of water, bandages, sheets, and medicine. They assisted doctors who were performing surgeries right in the beds, sheets hung around them to provide some semblance of antisepsis and privacy.

Dr. Schmidt stopped the medics and pointed out a bed for Jenny among the other orthopaedic injuries. Dr. Hunter helped to move her onto the bed and immediately went to work removing her bandages and calling for a nurse to bring him some morphine for his patient. As he followed the now smaller entourage further into the hospital, Scott glanced back and saw Tyler moving around to other orthopaedic patients, assessing injuries. *Tyler's doing triage and doesn't even know what it is,* he thought.

They entered a small hallway and emerged in another ward. Dr. Schmidt motioned for the medics to place Karl in a bed and then stepped over to Scott's side.

"We have many burns in this area. Although I've not heard of many doctors who specialize in burns, I am ever so grateful to have you here. There are several nurses here to assist you, and I will give you more doctors as they become available." The doctor waved his arm in another sweeping motion, then added, "I leave you to your work. Thank you."

He said something to Karl in German, making him smile, then left the burn ward with the Navy medics. Scott looked out over the large room containing more than twenty beds and took a deep breath. Letting it out in a sigh, he thought about the situation. *Well McLean, look what you've gone and gotten yourself into now.*

Suddenly, a nurse touched him on the shoulder. "I will be your assistant, Doctor Wolf. My name is Margaret Vail."

Scott turned and smiled at her, then looked back out over the beds and thought, *Oh well, I guess I'm better than nothing for these people.*

He turned back to Margaret. "What should I call you?"

She smiled at him. "You may call me Nurse Vail, or Maggie. Either one is fine."

He grinned. "Okay, Nurse Vail, I'll call you Maggie."

"Very good, Doctor," she said, managing a slight smile.

Scott leaned over and whispered to her. "You can call me Sam. I expect we will keep this very informal for the next while. Maggie, if you could find me a smock and show me where to wash up, we'll get started."

"This way," she said, taking him by the arm and leading him to a small cubicle.

Scott found a basin of water, and some smocks hanging on a wall. After cleaning up and donning a dingy white one, Dr. Sam Wolf stepped out of the cubicle and went to work.

During the ensuing twenty-four hours, Scott worked with over a hundred burn patients. Some had relatively minor burns while others were much more serious. He counted twelve that died and didn't give much hope to quite a number more than that.

Scott learned a lot about early twentieth century medicine and taught some new things to the nurses and doctors at the hospital that day. He learned they had an abundance of morphine, ether, and chloroform, but no IV fluids like Ringers Lactate or Normal Saline to put into their patients. The treatment most needed by many burn patients was fluid replacement.

At one point, Scott began treating Karl Strueberg's burns and summoned Tyler to assess his other injuries. After reducing the dislocated shoulder, Tyler set the broken humerus in his right arm. Scott showed Tyler and the nurses how to debride the burns and wrap them in the cleanest dry bandages they could find.

"Sam," Tyler said from the doorway. Scott turned and acknowledged him. "Jenny wants to see you before she leaves. I've finished with her surgery and they are taking her to Mare Island."

"Where?"

"The Navy has hospitals on both Mare and Goat Islands. That's where they are taking our patients after we stabilize them."

"Oh," Scott smiled slyly. "I wondered where they were all disappearing to before I could give them my bill."

They walked over to Jennifer Brody's bedside where medics had just slipped her onto a canvas stretcher and she took hold of both their hands.

"Thank you, Doctors, for all you did for me." Her eyes welled up. "There is no way I could ever thank you enough or repay you."

The medics picked up her stretcher and started moving through the hospital toward a side exit, with Scott and Tyler walking alongside.

"You don't have to repay anything, Jennifer," Tyler said. "We were coming this direction anyway."

She smiled.

"Good luck, Jenny," Scott said. She waved as they carried her out the door. To Tyler, Scott added, "Nice girl."

"Very," Tyler answered, watching until she was out of sight.

Scott winked at Tyler as he headed back to his work in the burn ward.

* * *

On Thursday afternoon, Tyler retrieved Scott from the burn ward and took him out the back door onto an enclosed patio where other medical personnel were milling around. They sat at a small table and a nun showed up with a tray of food for them. There was fried chicken, bread, iced tea, and chocolate cake. The two men hadn't eaten in a long time and were nearly starving, so they ate voraciously, finishing everything on the tray in minutes.

Sitting back in his chair with a glass of iced tea in his hand, Scott smiled at Tyler. "You eat like a pig."

Tyler wiped his mouth with a napkin from the tray and chuckled at Scott. "A very satisfied pig, thank you. From one pig to another, I might add."

They both laughed.

Looking around, they noticed that virtually everyone who came outside did the same thing. They sat down, had food delivered to them, and then

FIRES OF TIME * 203

wolfed it down in a matter of minutes. The nun walked over and took the tray from the table, smiling warmly at them.

"Thank you, Sister," they said at the same time.

"You're welcome," she smiled.

Scott had his feet up on one of the other chairs at the table with his filthy, dirty, formerly white shoes resting on the seat. The Adidas cross-trainers were white with black and blue trim and soles. Tyler was staring at the strange shoes made of strange materials, wondering about the strange man who was wearing them.

"I've been hearing good things about you," Tyler said. "Everybody is talking about some of the treatments you're using. You've impressed many people, including me. Where did you learn all of these new and innovative medical procedures?"

"There's a burn unit in Salt Lake City where they know all of the newest treatments and also develop new ones. The unit is both innovative and impressive."

Scott had heard of the Intermountain Burn Center at the university, but had no clue as to when it had been started. For that matter, he had no idea if the university itself had even been founded in 1906. He counted on Tyler to not know either.

"I haven't heard about it. It must be gratifying to be so far ahead of the rest of us. I've heard you taught some new treatments to doctors in other fields, too. Are you going to tell me about yourself soon?"

"In due time," is all Scott said.

Suddenly, a ruckus started near one of the other tables. There were doctors and nurses running to aid someone at the table. A doctor was standing by the table choking, his lips turning blue. Another doctor pounded him on the back as a nurse ran past Scott carrying some kind of forceps. She handed them to the doctor and he proceeded to look and probe in the other doctor's mouth.

"I can't see a thing," he said. "It must be too far down."

Another doctor yelled to him. "Get him inside and we'll open up that trachea. It's the only way."

Scott was watching with so much interest that he almost let them do it. "I don't think he needs a crycothyrotomy."

"What?" Tyler asked.

Scott could see the man was about to pass out, so he jumped and ran to the back of the stricken doctor and wrapped his arms around his abdomen. Making a fist with one hand and placing his other hand over it, he performed the Heimlich maneuver. He gave three abdominal thrusts, inward and upward, and forced a large chunk of chicken to fly out of the man's mouth and land on a table several feet away.

Scott continued to steady the doctor until he was breathing normally and the cyanosis began to disappear from around his mouth and nose. He released him and turned him around.

"Are you all right now?"

The doctor was still shaken, but seemed to have recovered without too much trouble. "Y ... yes, I am. Thank you, Doctor. Thank you very much. What did you do to me and how did you do it?"

Everybody on the patio gathered around amidst a hum of chatter, waiting anxiously to hear the man speak.

Oh, shit, Scott thought. *I've just introduced the Heimlich maneuver before Henry Heimlich ever thought of it. Come to think of it, he hasn't even been born yet.* The whole group of doctors and nurses stood in silent anticipation, staring at Scott while they waited for enlightenment.

Oh well, sorry about that, Dr. Heimlich, but I don't have much choice. Scott proceeded to explain the principle behind the Heimlich maneuver to the medical professionals. When he finished, they gave him a small round of applause, and the stricken doctor thanked him again. As they dispersed back to where ever they had been, Scott heard them talking to each other about that amazing doctor.

He listened and thought, *You're blowing it, Scotty. You may have helped a few people, but you're really screwing up.*

He walked back over to his table where Tyler was sitting and shaking his head.

"You are an amazing man. I can't wait to find out who you really are. You are going to tell me, aren't you?"

McLean just nodded, then turned and went back inside the hospital to tend to his patients. They worked the rest of the night without a break until Scott worked his way to a point where there was no one waiting for him. He decided to take a break and started out the back door. The morning sun hit his face.

"Oh my God!" he said out loud as he checked his watch. "Whew, six-fifteen, probably plenty of time."

He hurried back inside and went to the burn ward to hang up his smock. As he turned to leave, he spotted Margaret Vail. He went over and gave her a big hug.

"Thank you for all you did. You are, by far, the best nurse I've ever worked with." Then he hurried out the door to find Tyler.

Maggie stood dumbfounded, not knowing why he had hugged her or where he was going. She heard a man's voice call to her from the other side of the room and went over to the doctor who was standing by a bed reading a chart. When she got there, he stopped reading and looked up from the chart.

"Nurse Vail," he said. "I am Doctor York and I supervise a hospital in Oakland. I would like very much for you to come to my hospital to help supervise my nursing staff. You will be well paid and have a private room in the nursing quarters."

"But why, Doctor? Why would you make such a generous offer to me? You first set eyes on me only last evening."

"I heard what the good Dr. Wolf told you. If a doctor of his stature thinks so very highly of you, I have every confidence that you are just the nurse I've been looking for."

Maggie was nearly unable to speak, but managed to thank the doctor. He gave her the directions to his hospital and asked her to be there the following Monday morning. She agreed.

Scott wanted to say goodbye to Tyler and thank him for his friendship, but he searched the entire hospital and was unable to find him. He'd looked in every possible place. Twice. It was pushing six-thirty and he had to leave.

He wandered over by fire engine number one and took a couple of laps around it, taking in all the details his eyes could absorb. He admired the gleaming brass and chrome of the boiler and smokestack and the beautiful lithograph on the side, designating it as Engine One. He chatted with the engineer for a few minutes, then turned to leave. A hand touched his shoulder from behind.

"Where are you going, Sam?"

"I've been looking for you to tell you I have to leave now. There's really no time for any explanations and I don't have any choice in the matter. I figured you'd want to stay here longer."

He put out his hand to shake Tyler's, but the doctor didn't respond with his own hand. Instead, he took hold of Scott's forearm and pulled him away from the steamer. "I'll go with you."

"Ty, you don't have to come with me. I can find my way back, so you can continue your work."

Tyler stopped and stared Scott squarely in the eye, a determined look in his own eyes. "Do you think you can run off without any explanations?" He hesitated briefly. "You've filled me with more questions than I could have ever imagined and assured me for two days that you would explain it all to me when this is over. Am I wrong about that? Am I mistaken in that assumption?"

Scott was trapped. The doctor was absolutely right about the promise, and after all they'd been through together, he did deserve to have some of his questions answered. Scott solemnly nodded his head, then said in a low voice, "You're right. You're one hundred percent right and I apologize for thinking differently."

He thought to himself, *Besides, I could probably tell the 1906 doctor just about anything and he'd never be able to share it with anyone else. If Tyler told a farfetched time travel story like that to anyone at all, he could end up in the insane asylum.*

Scott pondered it all for a moment. "Don't you want to stay here at the hospital? I mean, couldn't they still use your assistance here?"

"They can do without me for a few hours. And I need a break from here."

"Okay, Doc," Scott said. "We have to get going."

"To where?"

"Back to Telegraph Hill. Let's go. Time's a wastin'. We have to get there before nine and I don't know if it will take one hour or three. Better to get there early than late."

He turned and headed off in the direction of the ferry building with Tyler right on his heels.

* * *

The fires had spread ten-fold in the forty hours they'd spent at the wharf. Most of the area they traveled to get to the hospital was already destroyed by the fire, with much of it still burning. Telegraph Hill hadn't been touched by any fire, yet. But it would be before the day was over. The two men were fighting against the flow of the fleeing refugees, still numbering in the thousands and still moving toward the ferry building.

They elbowed their way past the ferry building to the corner of the next block. Looking up that street, a few blocks of which had obviously been consumed by fire sometime earlier, the two men turned off of East Street.

"Okay, let's do it," Scott said, and the two of them started running.

They jogged through the burned out blocks full of tons of earthquake debris, much of it still smoldering. Some streets were impassable, forcing them to double back and take alternate routes. They even picked their way right through the middle of some of the devastated blocks, climbing over walls and foundations and down through basements filled with piles of smoldering rubble. Just a few blocks short of their destination, they caught up with the firestorm. Less than a block ahead, a wide wall of fire blocked their path.

Scott stopped running and leaned forward with his hands on his knees to catch his breath. Tyler caught up and rested also.

"Now what? How are we going to get through the fire?"

"Good question, Tyler. I wish I had a good answer for you."

I really wish I had an answer, he thought. *Wow, here I am, the resident expert on this fire and I don't remember learning about the exact spread of the fire at this point. We could end up being unable to get to Telegraph Hill. Way to go, McLean.*

They stood and watched the fire roar through a wood frame section of San Francisco like a freight train, consuming literally everything in its path. Nothing escaped the devastating conflagration and nothing the firefighters did seemed to slow it down. Scott had fought a lot of fires in his career, but he'd never even imagined anything remotely close to what he was seeing in 1906 San Francisco, California.

"Unbelievable," Scott said grimly. He turned slowly, scanning out over the city. "Man, the destruction. This is unreal."

He checked his watch again, it was six fifty-five. "Well, we need to find a way around. Any ideas?"

Tyler surveyed the area, looking for any possible avenue through the inferno, but it looked hopeless. "I think we'll have to go back down and around. Maybe we could go down by the bay and work our way up the back side of the hill."

Scott thought it over and agreed. "Good idea. Shall we get started?"

The doctors took off again, running down toward the docks. They ran until they reached East Street and turned to go north along the wharf. As they hurried toward their goal, the fire came closer. Finally, looking ahead less than a block, they saw there was no passage through. The fire extended close enough to the bay to cut them off. The fire department had steamer wagons battling the blaze at that point, blocking their way completely.

Without hesitation, Scott ran alongside a steamer. Then, amid shouts from the firemen to stay back, he ran into the water of the bay and began to swim out and around. Dr. Hunter followed right behind and the two men found themselves in the San Francisco Bay, attempting to out-swim a conflagration. They swam a few hundred feet out and could then see that the distance out and around the fire was no more than two city blocks. Scott stopped swimming and began to tread water, waiting for Tyler to catch up.

Scott yelled to him, "Do you think you can make it?"

Tyler swam up and stopped to tread water beside Scott, "Is there another way to get there?"

"I think we already missed the ferry. Wanna wait for the next one?"

Laughing, out of breath and working to stay afloat, Tyler answered, "You can wait if you want, but I don't think there will be another one along. The water's too rough."

Scott laughed and agreed. The winds blowing in from the bay were tremendous. In fact, the huge fires in the city created a chimney effect, causing wind to blow in from all directions, fueling the fires as they grew and spread ... creating stronger winds to feed more oxygen to the fires ... causing them to grow and spread ... and so on. The wind wreaked havoc on the bay, creating waves for Tyler and Scott to contend with.

The men swam side-by-side, bobbing in the waves as they worked their way toward the shore. It took them about twenty-five minutes to make the swim and they washed up on the shore in the yard of some kind of manufacturing plant, lying out on the ground and panting to regain their breath.

"You're quite a swimmer, Tyler."

"I was on the swim team at Dartmouth."

"Really? Dartmouth? You went to medical school at Dartmouth?"

"No, I did my undergraduate studies there. I went to medical school at Harvard."

"Serious?" Scott sat up and leaned on one arm. "Harvard Medical?" He turned around and sat with his legs folded, facing Tyler. The doctor was lying back on both elbows on the slight incline of the embankment. "Why did you go clear back there?"

"There aren't many good medical colleges here on the west coast, so a young man has to be willing to travel to attend the best schools. That's why I traveled to the east."

"I'm impressed. Not only that you're a Harvard graduate, but because I watched you work for two days. You're a very good surgeon, Doctor Hunter."

"Thank you. That means a lot to me, coming from you." He paused and looked at himself and at Scott. "Look at us. I think I've discovered a new side of myself today. Daring and impetuous. Think of what we just did."

"Pretty fun, huh? I think you always had it in you. You just needed someone unbalanced, like me, to drag it out of you."

Tyler stared at Scott momentarily with a smile forming on his lips. "You may be right. But I must admit it has been very exciting."

They rested and discussed the swim for a few more minutes before Scott stood up and held out a hand to Tyler. "Shall we go and have some more fun?" He pulled Tyler up from the ground.

Tyler stood. "I'll follow you."

They began walking through the storage yard of the business and found their way to the street, then began their run toward Telegraph Hill. After running one block and turning at the corner, they were enveloped by dark, acrid smoke. The heat was intensifying and the roar became louder. The pair of medics had managed to run right into the path of the fire. A sudden gust of wind came along and removed most of the smoke for a few seconds, enabling Scott to see how close they were to the fire. Too close, less than a block.

He grabbed Tyler's arm and pulled him off the street and up through the middle of the block, around the still standing houses and onto the next street. There was less smoke and they could see that if they continued on, moving parallel to the fire, they would soon be at their destination. Exhausted as they were, they ran on.

They ran through several blocks of nearly deserted streets, putting the conflagration behind them and the hill directly in front of them. After running half the way up Telegraph Hill, they dropped onto a grassy area to rest. They laid there on the ground catching their breath and coughing from the smoke they'd been in. After relaxing for a few minutes, Scott checked his watch: 7:20. *We made good time,* he thought. *Maybe now we can kick back for a little bit.*

"How hungry are you, Ty?"

"Very hungry. Why? Do you have some *food* in that magical bag, also?"

"As a matter of fact, I do. And I apologize for not remembering it sooner. I just plain forgot I had it."

"I forgive you. Bring it out, I'm famished."

"Me too."

Scott opened his soggy duffel and removed two military MREs and read what was written on them. "What would you like? Barbecue beef or chicken-ala-king?"

"I don't know. What's the difference?"

"Unfortunately, it's pretty hard to tell," Scott said.

"I'll take the Chicken-ala ... what was it?"

"King. Chicken-ala-king."

Scott handed the chicken meal to his friend and watched his reaction, which was just as he'd expected. Tyler turned the MRE around in his hands, reading the directions, the ingredients, and one other thing. Printed on the outside of the sealed plastic pouch was: USE BY JUNE, 2004. He read it over and over, then slowly raised his eyes up to meet Scott's gaze.

"What does this mean, Sam? Use by June, 2004?"

Scott tried to remain nonchalant, tearing open his own pouch before answering. "It means to eat it before 2004. These things keep for a real long time."

"Ninety-eight years? And what is this, anyway?"

"They're called meals ready to eat, MREs," Scott answered. "U.S. Army rations."

"From what century?"

Scott hesitated, then asked, "Do you need some help opening it?"

"You aren't going to tell me, are you?"

Taking the pouch from Tyler, Scott showed him how to open the pouch and dumped all of the goodies out in his lap.

"Start eating and we'll talk about it," he said, removing the plastic container of water from the duffel. "And we have a little bit of drinking water left here."

The two men sat on the grass and ate their MREs, drinking water from the plastic milk carton. With good reason, Tyler Hunter was bursting with curiosity about the strange man that had become his friend in such a short period of time. He watched as Scott worked his way through the various courses of the MRE, using his Old Timer pocket knife to slice open each plastic sealed package. Scott was still half soaked and dirty, with some rips in his clothes, scrapes on the left side of his face and minor burns on his hands. Hair was burned off both his arms and he looked very, very tired, but he zipped right through the MRE packages like a pro.

"Sam, is there anything you aren't able to do?"

Scott looked seriously at his new friend, wondering what this was leading to. His face was gaunt from the pressures of the last two days, but his eyes showed a tenderness and understanding for the doctor's quandary. Knowing that Tyler Hunter had to be going crazy with questions about what he'd seen, Scott was at a complete loss about how to proceed.

"Yes, sir. There are many things I can't do. In fact, I'm a man just like yourself. I'm not magic or super-human or anything like that."

"Maria Rodriguez called you an angel, sent down from heaven to rescue her and Andrella."

"You don't believe that, do you Tyler?"

"After watching you, what should I believe? You know more about medicine and emergency treatments than anyone I've ever met. I learned more about trauma treatment in one day from you than I could have learned in ten of those conferences. You climb up on buildings and rescue people, using tools I've never seen before. You know when earthquakes are going to happen and seem to know what the results are going to be. And that bag. You have that bag made of—" He reached over and pinched a fold of the nylon bag in his fingers and rubbed it around in between them. "I don't know what it's made of. That bag is filled with some of the most marvelous things. Things I've never seen or heard or even dreamed of before." He paused for a moment to collect his thoughts. "You put your arms around that choking doctor and performed a life saving treatment that I've never before seen. What would you call a maneuver like that?"

"Uh, you could call it any kind of maneuver you'd like. I don't believe it has a name ... yet," Scott grinned.

"Who are you, Sam? Where are you from? Really?"

"I'll tell you all about it when we get back up on the hill."

"Why? What's on the hill that's going to make any difference?"

Scott took a swallow of water. "One very important thing, and you pretty much have to see it to believe it."

There was a long, silent pause as the men sat and thought about the events that led up to this moment. Both of them were thinking about their wives and children.

"May I ask you one more thing?"

"Shoot."

"I'm worried about my family. I don't know if the earthquake extended all the way up to Portland and I've been sick with worry about my wife and children. You seemed to know all about the earthquake before it happened, so what else do you know? I mean, did it damage Portland? Do you have any way of knowing?"

Scott stared at Tyler with a very deep look on his face while he pondered what the man had just asked him. Of course he knew what happened and it wouldn't hurt to tell him.

Tyler could tell by the knowing look in Scott's eyes that he knew the answer. "You know, don't you?"

Scott knew that a man shouldn't have to worry needlessly about his family. After the selfless way

FIRES OF TIME * 217

Tyler had worked to help others during the crisis, his mind needed to be set at ease.

Breaking into a smile, he said, "You deserve to know. You're a good man and you have a right to know about the safety of your family."

Tyler said nothing, waiting to hear more.

"The earthquake extended north, but not anywhere near Portland. It was primarily in the San Francisco area."

Tyler looked confused, his forehead furrowed. He started to ask another question and stopped short, then went back to eating his meal. "May I borrow your knife? This stuff covering this food is tough. What is it made from? What is it called?"

Scott was still smiling. "Oh, what the hell. It's made from petroleum and it's called plastic."

Ty gave him a puzzled look. "Oil? It's made from oil?"

"Yep."

"How?"

"I don't know how they do it, I just know they do."

They had finished eating, so Scott gathered up the remnants of the MREs and put it all in his duffel. "Ready to climb the hill?"

"Yes, I am," Tyler said as he rose to his feet.

He gave Scott a hand up and they commenced their hike to the top of Telegraph Hill. When the arrived at the grassy spot where they'd started their friendship an eternity earlier, Scott checked his watch: 8:07. Almost time to go home.

"What now?"

Scott contemplated the question for a moment. "No time like the present. Come on, I want to show you something."

He motioned for Tyler to follow him in through the bushes to where the time machine was waiting. When they stepped into the clearing, Scott pointed to the ship and said, "This is why I waited to get you up here on the hill. You needed to see this."

* * *

Tyler's awe was genuine. He stood and stared at the shiny green time machine, with all its wires, tubing, tanks, and other gizmos.

"Any questions, Ty?"

He slowly turned toward Scott. "It never occurred to me. I mean, I wouldn't have guessed. You're from outer space? You're a Martian?"

A grin spread across Scott's face as he clapped Tyler on the back and declared, "No, my friend, let me show you."

He led Tyler over to the ship and began his explanation. "First of all you won't be able to tell anyone about this. I know you won't, because if you do, everyone you tell will think you're absolutely nuts and you'll end up in the insane asylum. Secondly, my name isn't Sam, it's Scott. Scott McLean. Sorry about that," Scott said meekly. "Are you still with me?"

The confused doctor nodded his head.

"This contraption you're looking at is a time machine. I came here from the year 2002 to observe the earthquake and fire, but I got a bit carried away with trying to help."

"You're from the future?" Tyler asked very quietly. "Honestly from the future? From America's future?"

FIRES OF TIME * 219

"Yes," Scott said, checking his watch. "And I now have forty minutes before this thing leaves for 2002."

"Your name is Scott? Are you really a burn doctor?"

"I'm really a firefighter paramedic," Scott admitted.

"Paramedic? Is that some kind of future doctor?"

"No, it's a whole new addition to the field of medicine — at least from your standpoint. A paramedic is someone who is schooled in emergency medicine and trained to perform emergency advanced life support procedures in the field before moving patients from the scene."

Tyler's soft brown eyes looked thoughtfully at Scott. "I see. And medicine is so far advanced in 2002, that a paramedic can do many times more, right where the accident happens, than a doctor like myself can do in a fully equipped hospital in the year 1906. Is that correct?"

"In many respects, yes. Paramedics are trained to perform many advanced life support procedures in the field that were previously done only by doctors in the hospital. Because of the advancements in medicine and technology, much more can be done to treat emergency patients right where they lie. And many of those procedures weren't developed until later in this century, especially the ones requiring specialized equipment."

"Like that powerful lantern of yours?"

Scott stopped and stared at Tyler, thinking of just how far we had come in the last century. He reached in his bag and took out his mini mag light, handing it to his friend and demonstrating how to twist it to turn it on.

"This light is very useful, but it's a far cry from being considered specialized equipment. Anyone can buy one of these for about ten dollars at any variety store."

"Variety store?"

Scott dropped his head down and shook it in semi disbelief. It seemed like nearly everything he mentioned from the future either didn't exist in 1906, or it had changed so dramatically as to make it foreign to Tyler Hunter.

"I'm sorry," Scott said. "I'll explain variety stores later. Let me stick to what we were discussing."

"Specialized equipment, right?"

"Right. The flashlight isn't specialized." Scott paused to think, not knowing quite where to start. Or stop. "One of our most basic pieces of equipment is a portable heart monitor. It weighs around fifteen pounds and can be taken anywhere we go. It monitors heart rhythms, showing the rhythms both on a screen and tracing it onto paper. We can also transmit what we see on the screen from the scene in the field to the emergency center of nearly any hospital, enabling the personnel there to see what we're seeing. This machine will also do many other procedures that haven't yet been developed in 1906. For example, de-fibrillation, cardioversion and external cardiac pacing."

Doctor Hunter was mesmerized. He had heard of a new heart monitoring machine that could draw on paper, but had never seen one. The rest was nothing short of fascinating.

"What is accomplished by all of those procedures? And what did you mean when you said you could see the heart rhythm on a screen?"

Scott stopped short and wondered how to explain a monitor screen to him. "I'll get back to the screen later because it's kind of difficult to explain. Now, what is ultimately accomplished by these procedures, is to be able to go to the patient with serious heart problems, problems threatening imminent death, and keeping them alive until we can get them to a hospital for further life saving treatment."

"Such as?"

"Surgery."

"They perform surgery on the heart?"

"Yessir, they do," Scott said. "You wouldn't believe what they can do."

"I don't believe what you've already told me, so go on."

"Bypass surgery, for one thing. The arteries of the heart are actually bypassed by taking veins from the legs, or arteries from the arms, and sewing them to the cardiac arteries, forming new blood vessels to carry the blood around the blocked ones. They also do heart transplants. They can even remove a person's heart and temporarily replace it with an artificial heart until a suitable donor can be found." Scott paused to carefully select his next words. "They've performed transplants of both heart and lungs at the same time."

Tyler looked confused. "But where do they find replacements for such vital organs?"

Scott smiled, realizing that it may have horrified Dr. Hunter to think of mad doctors wrenching the hearts and lungs out of screaming patients. "Before they die, people offer to donate their organs. They carry donor cards. Wait, I'll show you."

Scott took his water-logged wallet from his back pocket, removed his donor card, and handed it to Tyler. As the doctor stared at it, Scott continued.

"You see, I carry this card with me so it may be readily found, in case I die suddenly in an accident. Doctors can keep my body functioning with the aid of machines, even after brain death, until final permission is given by my family. If viable, my organs would then be removed and shipped to any part of the world and transplanted into a waiting patient. It is a very sophisticated system."

"You would actually give your heart and lungs to someone else? A total stranger in France or somewhere?"

"I'd be dead. I wouldn't have any more use for them. But they could be used to give life to someone else. It would be rather selfish of me to take useful tissue and organs to my grave if they could be used to save a life or give someone back their sight."

Tyler shook his head. "They transplant eyes?"

"Doctors also transplant kidneys, livers, pretty much anything. And, oh, yeah, something that may interest you especially since you're an orthopaedic man. They can replace many of the joints in your body with plastics or special alloy steel. You can get a new hip or knee if you need it."

"I'd love to hear it all," Tyler said.

"And I'd love to tell you, but ninety-six years of advancements would take a long time to detail. Much longer than I've got right now," Scott said as he again peeked at his watch.

"May I see inside the ... time machine, before you leave?"

Scott looked at his watch. "I only have twenty-nine minutes left, so we need to hurry." He climbed up on the platform, opened the hatch and looked inside the cockpit. "Climb up here and take a look."

Tyler climbed up on the platform and looked inside. "Aren't we going to get in?"

Scott shrugged his shoulders. "Yeah, sure, but we'd better hurry." He went in through the hatch first then helped Tyler to climb into the cockpit, checking his watch again after they sat down facing one another.

Scott gave Tyler a tour of the ship's interior, explaining briefly how the time travel was accomplished. When he got to the computer, he realized that it had a screen similar to that of an EKG monitor.

"You asked me to tell you how we could see a heart rhythm on a screen," Scott said, pointing to the computer monitor's screen and turning it on. "This is what I meant by a screen."

Tyler nodded. "Does everybody in the future go time traveling?"

"No, they don't. This machine was built by my best friend in his garage, and as far as I know, I'm the first time traveler." He glanced at his watch again. "Seventeen minutes. You have to get out of here pretty quick or you'll end up in 2002."

"All right, Sam, I mean Scott. I just want to tell you how much I appreciate the knowledge I've gained from—"

A loud hissing noise interrupted Tyler. Suddenly, the ship started to vibrate slightly. Scott checked his watch and saw 8:44.

"What's the deal?"

He frantically looked down under the seat at the onboard computer. The digital readout showed 09:00 hours. The hissing had reached a crescendo and Scott heard the electric motor kick in.

"What's happening?"

"Well, it looks like the commander's watch was slower than the clock on the ship's computer. I'm afraid you'll be coming back home with me."

"Can't I jump out?"

"It's probably not a good idea," Scott answered, reaching up and closing the hatch. "Sit tight and fasten your seatbelt."

It was even too late for that.

Dr. Tyler Hunter from Portland, Oregon, was on his way to the future with Scott McLean, leaving Dr. Sam Wolf of Salt Lake City behind.

Chapter Eleven

Scott unlocked the latch on the cockpit hatch. "Are you all right?"

The doctor was sitting on the seat across from Scott, trying to see out through the porthole in the hatch. He checked himself visually, looking at his hands and arms, then the rest of his body. After palpating himself over most of his body, he responded, "I am. I'm just fine. In fact, I feel very relaxed, Sa—Scott."

Scott stood and pushed the hatch into the fully open position and poked his head out, then stood straight up. Brian was standing over by the computer console watching.

"Scott," Brian said, greeting him and staring at him as if he were seeing a ghost.

"What?"

Still staring at his friend's appearance with a look of general disbelief, Brian finally spoke. "You look like hell. What have you been doing for the last minute?"

Scott looked puzzled at Brian's statement about the last minute and attempted to put everything in perspective. Brian had literally been waiting only a minute of real time for the ship's return, yet Scott had been gone for more than two days. The time spent in 1906 had been very real time to Scott. He had spent two days and was virtually two complete days older than he was when he left that very spot one minute earlier. Brian had only aged one minute in that same amount of time. Patty's statement about time travel being mind boggling, like trying to comprehend the concept of infinity, couldn't have been more accurate.

Maybe we should have arranged the trip to use up the same amount of time for Brian here in 2002, he thought. *If we do another trip, it should be done in real 2002 time. If I'm going to age two days, Brian should age the same two days.*

Scott motioned with his hand for Tyler to sit still and be quiet for the moment. The weary time traveler needed a few minutes to figure out how to tell Brian about the new development.

"I've been busy. You know, observing."

"Right," Brian said with a suspicious look. "You do look like somebody beat you up. In fact, you look like something ol' Schrodinger would bury in the sandbox. Let's get you out of there so I can hear all about it." Brian took a step toward the ship with the intent of helping Scott out.

"Uh, Bri?" Scott held up his hand to halt him. "Before I get out, there's something I should tell you. *You* may want to beat me up after you learn what's happened."

FIRES OF TIME * 227

Brian stopped in his tracks and waited to hear whatever earthshaking news his friend had to share with him. "Shoot."

"Well, it's this way ... I mean, there's—"

"What's the problem?" Brian interrupted, perplexed by the way his normally cool friend was acting. "Is it something serious?"

Scott pursed his lips and nodded his head. "Serious? I believe you'll probably see it that way."

"Come on, Scotty. What's going on?"

"Okay, here's the deal." Scott hemmed and hawed around a little longer, then decided to let it all out. "Oh, hell. I've returned with a passenger. His name is Tyler Hunter and he's a doctor from Portland in the year 1906. We didn't mean for this to happen, it just did. I hope you can do something about it."

Brian stood expressionless in the middle of the shop, then broke into a grin and shook his head. "I thought for a minute there really was a problem. All joking aside. You look bad enough to need some medical attention."

For the longest time, Scott stared blankly at his friend. "I feel just as bad as I look. And I'm not in much of a joking mood." He reached down, tugging on Tyler's arm, and the doctor slowly stood up through the hatch. "Brian Daniels, this is Dr. Tyler Hunter. Ty? Brian Daniels."

Of course, Brian was in a state of shock. Not talking or moving, he stood staring at Tyler as if he were from another planet. He didn't even appear to be breathing. Only staring.

"It's a pleasure to meet you, Brian," Tyler said genially. "I certainly apologize for causing you concern." He turned to Scott and inquired about Brian's condition.

Scott climbed out of the ship and stood on the platform. "I would imagine he'll be just fine. After he recovers from this nervous breakdown, that is." He reached a hand out to the doctor and added, "Let me give you a hand out of there."

Tyler climbed out of the ship, stepped down to the garage floor, and began looking around the shop as Scott stepped down to face Brian. He tried to read in his best friend's face what was going on in his head, but couldn't find a clue. Brian was mesmerized, watching Tyler while the visitor moved slowly around the room investigating everything.

Scott stared at his old friend. "Are you all right? You don't look very good."

Brian cleared his throat and removed his glasses. After cleaning them on his shop rag, he put them back on and raised his right hand, wagging his finger.

"Do you know what I would have said if I'd been asked to name all the things that could have gone wrong on this trip?"

"I think I have an—"

"Quiet!" Brian quickly shouted. "That was a rhetorical question. I would have probably said something like losing the ship with you in it. Or maybe having an accident that caused you serious injury ... or even you dying somewhere out there on the continuum."

Scott interrupted. "Brian—"

Brian held up his hand to silence Scott again and continued to speak. "But do you want to know what would have never entered my mind? I would never have imagined that you would possibly bring back a time hitchhiker." He shook his head and kept talking. "No way, Scott. I would never have thought of that one."

"It was an accident. Honest."

"I believe you," he said, glancing at Tyler. "But what do we do now?"

Scott went over to the small bar fridge and reached in, grabbing a beer and tossing it to Brian. He took two more out and turned to offer one to Tyler, bumping into him as Tyler peeked over his shoulder to look at the refrigerator.

Tyler accepted the beer from Scott, just as Scott was telling Brian, "I don't know. I'm really counting on you to come up with something, ya know?"

Brian turned and walked around the shop, glancing at Tyler as he opened and closed the refrigerator door. Running his hand through his long, dark hair and pacing, Brian stopped near the computer console and turned to face Scott. "The fact is, your doctor friend is here from 1906 and standing in my garage. We can't change that. Even if we send him back, he'll still have this memory, I think."

While he was talking, Brian stepped over to the fridge and showed Tyler the power cord. "It runs on electricity." Turning back to Scott, he conceded, "So, we'll just have to go on from here and make the best of it."

Then for some reason, a strange smile spread across Brian's face, startling Scott.

"That's your mad scientist look. What are you thinking?"

"Like I said. We'll just have to make the best of a very weird situation," he said, turning to Tyler and taking his hand in a friendly handshake. His mad scientist look changed to friendly and warm.

"Welcome to my home, Doctor. This is so exciting, don't you think?"

Tyler managed a nervous smile. "It is, but it's also frightening for me. Overwhelming would better serve to describe my feelings."

"I understand," Brian said. "Wait until you see outside of this shop. It should astound you."

"Is that a good idea? Shouldn't we be getting Tyler ready to go back?"

"In due time," he said, brushing off Scott's attempt to act responsibly. "Right now, this is very exciting."

"May I ask you a question, Brian? Are you a scientist?"

"Yes Tyler, I am."

"Does that mean you're a doctor?"

"I have a doctorate degree, if that's what you mean. But I don't answer to doctor."

"Excuse me?"

"What I mean is that I don't use the title of doctor. I didn't earn my degree in physics to become Doctor Daniels. My degree came as a result of my doing what I love to do, studying physics. In actuality, I hold a second doctorate degree in mathematics, but that doesn't make me a doctor in the accepted sense. I happen to feel that the title of doctor should be reserved exclusively for medical doctors, because to most of the people in this country, myself included, doctor means medical person, not some egghead physics scientist."

Brian began to pace the floor again.

"I didn't know you felt that way, Bri," Scott remarked.

Brian stopped pacing. "You don't call me doctor, do you?"

"Well, of course not. But I happen to know you'd rather be called 'captain.'"

Brian tried to stare Scott down, but couldn't hold back a laugh at his own expense. After regaining his composure, he said, "You've told me about going out on medical calls and finding doctors at the scene who start barking orders at you, only to find out they aren't really medical doctors. I remember you telling me about the time a doctor at the university was telling you how to run your heart attack call."

Scott nodded and smiled. "I remember it, too."

"And when she started giving you bizarre orders, you asked her what kind of doctor she was? What was she, a doctor of history?"

"Yeah, and I made the comment that she should let us work on the patient today, and tomorrow, when it's history, she could study it." Scott paused, closed his eyes and slowly shook his head. "After she complained about me, I got to have a chat with a deputy chief the next shift."

"Well, when I have someone tell me they're a doctor, in an emergency situation, I want them to be a doctor. Of medicine."

Scott laughed at Brian's remark and glanced at Tyler, who was looking back at him, sporting a knowing smile.

"I don't think that's the same thing, Scott," Tyler said. "You were an excellent doctor in 1906."

"Thanks," Scott said graciously.

Brian glanced furtively back and forth between the two of them. "Doctor? In 1906?"

"It's a long story. I had a difficult time observing and not getting involved just a touch. You know me."

"Yes, I do," Brian agreed. "What else did you do?"

"Oh, nothing much," Scott said meekly, taking another drink of his beer and looking down at the floor.

Brian turned to Tyler. "Did he do more?"

"A little."

"A little? How much is a little?"

Tyler looked to Scott for guidance and Scott shrugged his shoulders in submission, so he told it all. "Not much, really. Let me see." He looked thoughtfully at the ceiling, gathering his thoughts, then went on to explain. "Together, we amputated a young lady's leg to rescue her from certain death by fire. Next, we were nearly shot by the military, and then Scott scaled the outside walls of a burning building to rescue several people, nearly being killed himself. We made our way to the emergency hospital where we spent nearly forty hours treating the injuries of hundreds of earthquake victims."

Staring at Tyler, Brian was past the point of dumbfounded. He took a step forward, removed the beer from Tyler's hand and popped the top to open it. Handing it back and then pointing to it in Tyler's hand, he quietly said, "It's a beer."

To Brian, Tyler said, "Should I continue?" Brian still appeared shocked. The doctor looked at the can in his hand and continued. "Scott taught those of us at the hospital many new ways for treating trauma, especially burn injuries." He paused and looked at the can again, examining the top where Brian had opened it. "Hmm. This is truly interesting." He looked back up and added excitedly, "Oh, another thing. He saved the life of a very prominent physician who was choking, by using only his hands and arms."

Brian looked at Scott with a quizzical stare.

Scott shrugged his shoulders, nodded and mouthed the word Heimlich, then said, "You can pick your chin up off the floor. It wasn't that big a deal, Brian. Really."

"Is that it?"

Tyler nodded to Brian.

Turning back to Scott, who had a guilty smile on his face, Brian said, "You mean you didn't singlehandedly go out and stop the conflagration? Or rebuild the entire city before returning home?"

Trying to act indignant, Scott said, "Now you're just being silly. You know I'm all thumbs when it comes to construction work." Pausing, he added, "I did manage to put the fire out though."

The laughter that followed broke the final bit of tension.

Over their laughter, Brian said, "Okay, let's decide what to do about this time traveling stowaway."

* * *

Scott stepped through the back door of his home and found Patty working at the computer in the family room. He watched her for several minutes, thinking about all that had transpired since he last saw her. Two long, tiring and exciting days had passed for him, but she had last seen him about an hour earlier. He needed desperately to take a shower, shave, and get into some clean clothes. Some decent food seemed like a good idea, too.

He put his bag on the floor and crept quietly down the four steps into the family room, trying to sneak up behind her. His smell preceded him. Patty twirled around on her chair to see what kind of horrible creature had entered the room and saw Scott hunched down a few feet behind her.

"Whew," she said. "You're ripe. What've you been doing in your adventures with Brian?"

"Oh, not much," he said casually. "Just got back from two days in San Francisco."

Patty took a good look at him and recoiled at the sight. She stood and walked a complete circle around him, inspecting his whole body. She couldn't believe her eyes. "Honey, you not only stink, you look terrible."

She touched the scrapes on his face and took his hand in hers, looking closely at the burns. Rubbing her hands up his arms, she could tell that a lot of hair had been burned off. His face and arms looked like they were sunburned on top of all the other injuries.

"Are you hurting? Can I help?"

"I just want to clean up and maybe I'll feel human again."

"Are you hungry, babe?" He nodded. "Why don't you go get cleaned up while I fix us something to eat. I want to hear about every minute you spent there. It had to be exciting, just look at you. But I can't begin to describe how awful you look."

"Thanks a lot. Brian said I looked like something his cat would bury in the sandbox."

She shook her head. "No, he's wrong about that. You look much worse than anything that cat would bury."

"Thanks again."

Scott trudged up the stairs toward the shower. A long, hot and steaming, wonderful shower. Patty exited her work, shut down the computer and went to the kitchen to make them some lunch.

* * *

Meantime, Brian took Tyler into his home and showed him to a bathroom so he could take a shower. Brian had to teach him how to operate the bathroom fixtures in order to make the shower put out water.

Tyler was fascinated by nearly everything he saw in the house. After he showered, Tyler spent the rest of the afternoon exploring with his host. Brian had more fun than he could have ever imagined, having a living, breathing human being from the past to show around. Some of the simplest things were the most interesting to the time traveler. Things that were commonplace to people of the twenty-first century, like the blender and telephone, and beer and carbonated soft drinks in pop-top cans. The microwave was especially fascinating to him.

Tyler sat mesmerized on the sofa, listening to The Eagles play *Hotel California* from a CD on Brian's stereo system. Brian cranked up the sound until the two of them could feel the bass as well as hear it. Tyler read the words from the CD jacket as the song played.

"What does it mean?"

"What's that?"

"The song. I read the words while the song played, but it doesn't make any sense to me. Is it because I don't live in this day and age that I don't understand it?"

Brian smiled, "Hotel California is a rock-n-roll classic that everybody loves. Nobody really knows what it means. Most of us have our own personal interpretation of the meaning, but quite frankly it's really just the music we like."

Tyler seemed puzzled. "I guess I don't grasp the customs of the people of 2002."

"Hey!" Brian said, interrupting. "Let me play you something you might relate to a little better." He searched through his cd's and found one with some classical composers on it. Skipping through it, he played a Rossini classic for Tyler, *The William Tell Overture.*

After listening to the entire overture, Tyler was nearly breathless. "I am very impressed with your music machine. It makes the same sound as a symphony in a concert hall."

"That's why I bought it," Brian said. "Come on, let's go outside for a while."

He led his visitor out to the back yard. While in the yard, a Life Flight helicopter flew over the house, frightening Tyler. He ran for cover on the patio.

"It's all right!" Brian shouted. He waved for Tyler to come out and watch it. "Hurry, come see it before it's gone."

Tyler went to the edge of the patio and looked tentatively at the helicopter. "What is that thing?"

"It's called a helicopter." He could see that Tyler was visibly upset. "Are you okay?"

"What is it doing? What does it do? What is it for?"

"That thing scared the bejeebers out of you, didn't it?"

"I don't know what it was. But yes, it certainly frightened me. What is it?"

"It's a flying machine. That particular one is called Life Flight. It's a flying ambulance."

"Ambulance?"

"Yep. Helicopters can land just about anywhere, right in this yard if they needed to. That makes them more versatile for rescue work than a regular airplane."

"Airplane? What is an airplane?"

"I'm sorry," Brian said quietly, motioning for him to take a seat on the patio.

Brian sat down and explained it all, from airplanes to the space shuttle, air ambulances and ground ambulances.

The information overload began to show, so Brian talked Tyler into going back into the house.

Just then Jo arrived home from work. Brian greeted his wife with a kiss and introduced their guest. Joellen couldn't have been a nicer host. She sat Dr. Hunter at the kitchen table, poured them some coffee and set out to learn all she could about her houseguest.

She sat and listened with fascination as Tyler told of his adventures with Scott in San Francisco, explaining how he was unable to comprehend the amount of devastation and suffering. The stories that didn't surprise her though, were the ones about Scott's rescues and compassionate acts toward the people of 1906. Jo and Brian had long admired Scott's many abilities, and his willingness to use them to help other people. It was obvious to Jo that Tyler Hunter also admired him, but she got the feeling he may have thought everybody in 2002 was the same as Scott.

"Scott is a special case," Jo told Tyler. "The world could use a few more just like him."

Tyler seemed puzzled by the statement. "Do you mean Scott is the only person like that?"

"Oh, no," she smiled. "There may be a lot of people like Scott. There just aren't enough of them."

Tyler looked sincerely across the table at Jo. "He is a very good man. He seems able to do most anything he attempts, such as medical treatments, and rescuing people from fires. Yet he is compassionate and very humble. Humility is one of the greatest virtues and Scott is a genuinely humble man. He does many heroic things, yet he expects no recognition for what he does."

"I understand," Jo said. "He seems to feel like what he does is what anybody else would do in the same situation, when most people in the same situation would simply panic. Or they just plain wouldn't know what to do or how to do it. But, to Scott McLean, those things just come naturally."

During their conversation, Brian told Tyler that Joellen had a college degree in Media Communications. And that she and Patty had attended the university together and that both were in the communications department, but in different areas of study. Tyler was impressed, but when he learned that Jo actually worked at the place where the television pictures originated, he was enraptured. He listened intently to Jo tell about how the programs are put together. She explained how the cameras operate and how the signals are transmitted through the air, or cable, to be viewed on televisions in the home.

Brian walked into the kitchen with a video camera, taping their conversation. Then they all went into the other room to watch it on the TV. Brian plugged the camera into the VCR and played it back for Tyler.

"I don't quite know how to describe it," Tyler humbly said. "Everything is so different, so marvelous. Even your small, insignificant things are so remarkable. You live in an incredible time. You people are truly blessed to live in an era of such convenience."

The kitchen door opened and Patty yelled, "Hello! Anybody home?" She and Scott walked in through the kitchen and into the living room.

"Doctor Hunter," Patty said as she moved across the room to shake Tyler's hand. "I'm Patty McLean, Scott's wife. Scott told me all about San Francisco, and you. He has great respect for you and I couldn't wait any longer to meet you."

Tyler stood to greet her and shook her hand. "I'm honored to meet you as well, Patty." The doctor stared at her for a moment then continued. "Scott has told me many good things about you."

Scott sat down on the fireplace hearth and looked over at Doctor Hunter as he chatted with his wife. After a few minutes, he said, "Tyler, you look a lot better than you did earlier. Where'd you get those new duds?"

Tyler looked at his clothing. "While I napped, Brian went someplace and bought them for me. How do you like them?"

"They're great," Patty smiled, pointing out each item of clothing to Scott.

"Will you look at this? Dockers pants, nice looking Nikes and Brian's Hard Rock Café Las Vegas T-shirt?"

Scott surveyed Tyler's new clothing and grinned. "You look quite studly. Do you think it would be all right to wear that outfit back to 1906?"

"Probably not, the shoes maybe. And I think it would be all right to wear these nice looking pants," he said.

"And the shirt?"

Brian looked up. "Not on your life. He's only borrowing my Hard Rock Café Las Vegas T-shirt."

Scott laughed. "Aw, come on. Where's your sense of adventure?"

"It isn't that, Scotty. I wouldn't care about him going back with the logo on it. But I do care about having to go to Vegas again to get another shirt. By the time I got out of the casino, that shirt cost me seven hundred dollars."

Scott laughed and Jo gave Brian a disgusted look, remembering his uncharacteristic, irresponsible behavior when they went to the Hard Rock Casino.

"I remember the incident. You were pretty mad at yourself over that."

"He wasn't the only one," Jo added.

Brian hung his head slightly. "I don't know what came over me that night, but I did promise myself that I'd never go into a casino again."

Tyler was watching and listening to them talk, looking back and forth between Brian, Scott, and Joellen. "If I may interrupt." They stopped and turned to look at Tyler. "When do you plan to send me back?"

Scott contemplated the question. "Have you thought about it, Bri?"

Brian looked puzzled. He hadn't even given it a minute's thought and it bothered him because, as the scientist, he should have already addressed the situation.

"I don't know. We probably should have already done it, but I guess we got caught up in the fun of having you here. I apologize for that."

Tyler went over to Brian, put his hand on his shoulder. "You don't have anything to be sorry about. I've enjoyed this as much as you. Probably a lot more than you." He stepped away from Brian and, stammering a bit, continued. "I ... I have a favor to ask of you if you don't think it would be too much trouble, or maybe something you shouldn't do."

"You can always ask a favor," Brian answered. "What is it we can do for you?"

Taking a seat on the sofa, Tyler said, "Would it be possible for me to visit a hospital?" Standing back up, he started into the kitchen, stopped and turned around, then added, "If it would be too difficult, I understand." He turned and pulled a kitchen chair from under the table and sat down, noticing Brian and Scott exchanging glances.

Brian was the first to speak. "As far as I'm concerned, that is a reasonable request, but it wouldn't be up to me. Scott's the one who would have to set up something like that." He looked at Scott, raising his eyebrows and cocking his head.

Scott was sitting on the loveseat with Patty, holding her hand. She gave his hand a squeeze to let him know that she would support him in whatever decision he made, but he didn't hesitate at all. "Tyler," he said. "I'd be honored to take you on a tour of a first rate hospital. I'll call first thing in the morning to see if we can make some special arrangements."

Tyler smiled and thanked him, then turned to Brian. "Do you think I could go back home after visiting the hospital? I miss my family." He got a bit choked up, swallowed and sniffed, then went on. "Do you have to send me back to San Francisco, or is it possible to send me right to Portland?"

Brian smiled and nodded. "Portland shouldn't be a problem, Doctor. I'd be more than happy to send you back to your home."

"Thank you," Tyler said with a smile. Then a look of sincerity spread over his face as he added, "You know, it is comforting to see that the world will still have good people like all of you in the future."

"Thanks," Brian said.

"I have another question," Tyler said of anybody who wanted to answer. "On this shirt. What does it mean? What is Las Vegas? And one other thing, what does it mean by Hard Rock? Haven't rocks always been hard, or has there been some kind of major geological change in the last ninety-six years?"

Smiling broadly, Scott answered. "Those are good questions. How 'bout we tell you all about it over dinner?" He turned and looked around the room. "Anybody up for fast food?"

Tyler looked puzzled, but Patty took him by the arm and assured him he would like it.

"I'll have to take the kids," Patty said.

"No problem. We can all go in the Caravan," Scott replied.

They all went out the kitchen door, Patty on her way to get the kids, the others headed for the McLean's silver-blue Dodge Caravan for transport to some fast food joint.

FIRES OF TIME * 243

* * *

It was nearly ten o'clock the next morning when Scott and Tyler backed out of the driveway in the Caravan to go to the hospital. Scott had lined up permission for them to observe the performance of a total hip replacement surgery at eleven. He didn't tell Tyler about it, planning to take him to the observation theater as part of the tour. He'd told the hospital administrator that Tyler was a close friend, a physician from Portland who was visiting with him. The administrator, William Singer, was a friend Scott had known since starting with the fire department, so there was no problem in setting up the tour.

"I told the hospital administrator you're a doctor from Portland, Tyler. All he knows is you wanted to see the hospital I work out of most of the time. You need to remember to not let on about *when* you were a doctor from Portland. Okay?"

Tyler nodded. "How fast are we moving? It seems to be awfully fast."

They'd just driven onto the freeway, so Scott told him, "About sixty-five."

"Sixty-five what?"

"Sixty-five miles-per-hour."

"Shouldn't I be hanging onto something?"

Scott looked over at him. "You have your seat belt on and there's a passenger side air bag, so you should be safe."

"I'll have to trust you on that. But it does seem that we're traveling quite fast."

"Well, I suppose we are. But that's the way it is nowadays. The whole world travels fast all of the time, in fact, too fast. Everyone's in a hurry to get somewhere to do something, often with little regard for the safety or feelings of anyone else. You do learn to live with it, though."

The doctor looked out the window at the cars speeding past in the fast lane. "It would make me nervous to live at a pace like this all of the time."

"You know, that may be one of the great problems of living in our time. Far too many people are nervous most of the time." He pointed out the right side of the windshield, then said, "Over there, the dark brick building. Do you see it? That's the hospital."

Scott merged over and eased onto the off ramp, exiting the freeway. Pulling to a stop at the light, he waited for it to turn green.

"Why are we not moving?"

Pointing to the stoplight, Scott explained the way the lights operate. "You see the number of cars everywhere? If we didn't have the traffic lights, we'd all be running into each other at every intersection."

A few minutes later, they pulled into the parking garage, parked the van, and walked to the entrance to the hospital. Tyler stepped toward the door to open it and was startled by the automatic doors sliding open. He stopped in his tracks and waited for Scott to go ahead of him.

"How did the doors open?"

"They're automatic," Scott said, stopping between the two sets of doors. He pointed to the tiny red electric eye above the center of the doors and told Tyler how they operated. Then, he put his foot out to where it would trigger the inner set of doors and they magically opened. "This type of door is used in many businesses and large buildings," he explained.

"They are very convenient when you have your arms full of packages or groceries or something."

"Fascinating," Tyler whispered, his head moving in a steady motion, watching around the frame of the doors. "Such a strange and wonderful time you live in."

Bill Singer greeted them warmly when they walked into his office, shaking both their hands firmly. Scott made the introductions and they sat and chatted for about ten minutes. He handed them name badges. Tyler's read, Dr. T. Hunter, and Scott's simply read, S. McLean. Singer offered to accompany them until they reached the surgical suite and the tour began.

The first part, through the administration offices, was brief and uninformative. Uninteresting would better describe it. They toured some of the floors, working their way to the ICU and CCU wards. Bill Singer maintained a quiet narration as they walked through.

In the Cardiac Care Unit, Scott pointed to an EKG monitor and whispered to Tyler, "That's what an EKG screen looks like."

Tyler nodded his head in recognition.

Doctor Hunter was like a child at Disneyland, his eyes unable to take in all he wished to see. Fascinated as he was, though, he was able to maintain the dignity of a 2002 physician, never letting on just how excited he really became. They reached the observation area of the surgery suite just in time to see the surgeons open up the patient's hip. Tyler sat on the edge of his seat, his face nearly against the window so he could see every detail. Scott kept an eye on him the whole time so he could watch his reactions during each part of the operation.

Tyler's face went through a range of reactions, expressions and emotions.

Other than a well dressed elderly gentleman sitting in a far corner, the two were alone in the observation theatre. Scott noticed the gentleman looking over at them, even staring at times. Tyler, however, was oblivious to everything but the events taking place before him in the operating room.

Scott explained some things to him as they went along. "They're using a combination of synthetic materials on this one. They've grafted bone around some of the steel and it will knit together to form a strong bond. Except, in many ways, it will be stronger than the original parts."

Tyler was nearly breathless at the thought. At times, he held his breath for so long he nearly passed out. There was so much going on around the patient that he couldn't keep up with it most of the time. Surgeons and nurses worked together in a perfectly orchestrated performance of the marvels of modern medicine.

The great climax came when they finished closing the large incision and installed the equipment to drain excess fluids. Scott had to touch Tyler and remind him to breathe at one point, eliciting a nervous smile. After watching the anesthesiologist remove the endotracheal tube and stimulate the patient to begin breathing on his own, Tyler let out a tremendous sigh of relief and slumped back in his seat, wiping perspiration from his brow.

"How did you like that?" Scott asked quietly.

Tyler merely smiled and shook his head in disbelief at the question. Scott tugged on his sleeve and led him from the room so they could finish their tour. Tyler didn't say a word during the walk to the

FIRES OF TIME * 247

emergency room. When they arrived, Scott introduced him to some of his friends, nurses and doctors who worked in emergency.

"This is where I spend a lot of my time," Scott said. "Let me show you around."

Scott showed him some of the rooms and most of the equipment. Then, while they were standing in one of the cardiac care rooms, a paramedic rescue called in on their way to the hospital with a cardiac arrest patient. Scott and Tyler stood off to the side and watched the drama unfold in the room. Many doctors, nurses and respiratory therapists hurried into the room carrying equipment, pushing carts and setting up monitors, oxygen lines and IV sets. They were all ready and waiting for the paramedics to wheel the cardiac patient through the door.

One nurse came through the other door with her hands full of syringes and suture packs, stopped next to Scott, and read Tyler's name badge. "Hi, Scott," she said. "Just slumming on your day off?"

Scott smiled and nodded to her. "Sometimes it's good to watch others work, Kami."

She nodded and glanced at Tyler again.

Scott introduced them. "Doctor Tyler Hunter, Kami. Kami, this is my friend, Tyler. He's an orthopedic surgeon from Portland." She held out her hand, full of supplies, as Scott finished the introduction. To Tyler, he said, "Kami is one of my favorite nurses and oldest friends. We've worked together for nearly twelve years."

"Pleased to meet you," Tyler said as he held out his hand.

"Likewise, Doctor," she smiled. "Would you mind holding this stuff for me? I think we're gonna get real busy here in just a sec. Thanks."

He took the syringes and sutures from her as she turned to help prepare for the patient. When she moved past Scott, she quickly whispered in his ear. "He's cute, McLean. Is he ...?" Scott nodded his head and she winced, then added, "What a shame."

Scott smiled and glanced at Tyler, who was caught up in watching the preparations for the controlled chaos that was about to take place.

"This is what I do," Scott said to Tyler as the patient was wheeled into the room by the paramedics and moved from the stretcher to the hospital gurney.

CPR had been administered before the medics had converted the heart rhythm to one that would sustain life. The patient had IVs running, monitors attached and had been intubated. They had a ventilator attached that was breathing for the patient through the ET tube at a rate of about sixteen breaths per minute.

Tyler was once again awestruck. "Was all of that done to the patient somewhere outside the hospital?"

"Just a second, Scott said. He went over and talked briefly with one of the paramedics to learn the details. He returned to explain them to Tyler.

"This is a 58-year-old male who was found pulseless and non-breathing in the back yard of his home. Cardiopulmonary Resuscitation was performed until they were able to bring back a viable heart rhythm. Now he'll be admitted to the CCU we visited earlier, and if he needs it, surgery may be performed to repair his heart. It all depends on how well he responds to the initial treatment by the paramedics, nurses and ER doctors."

Tyler stood wide-eyed with gaping jaw, watching the swiftness with which the ER staff worked on the patient. In a relatively short period of time, the patient was wheeled out of emergency on his way upstairs to the cardiac care unit.

He was out of breath again as he turned to Scott. "I'm impressed with what you do. Overwhelmed would better describe my feelings. Now I understand why you were so calm and efficient in San Francisco. The fastest pace at Harbor Emergency didn't compare to the slowest pace I've seen here today."

Scott smiled. "Let's get out of here. I'm hungry and it's almost five o'clock."

They left the hospital and walked to the parking terrace where Tyler stood by a fifth level concrete wall gazing at the hospital.

"I felt extremely inadequate in there today, Scott. This made me realize how far we have to go from 1906. Can you imagine? I've actually heard respected physicians declare that medicine has gone just about as far as it will ever go. If nothing else, I'll be able to laugh at them from a more knowledgeable viewpoint."

Reaching the Caravan, Scott smiled at his new friend. The two men got in and started the drive back to the McLean home.

$$* \quad * \quad *$$

The next morning, Hunter stood in the shop near the kitchen door watching Brian replace the high pressure air bottle under the machine. After he finished the job, Brian rolled out from under the time machine. Sitting up on the creeper, he folded his arms around his knees and stared at Tyler, wondering what could be going on inside the man's mind.

Looking back at Brian, Tyler contemplated the same thing about the scientist.

"It's all set to fly," Brian announced. "It won't be long and you'll be back home in Portland." He paused and looked quizzically at the doctor, hoping to elicit the information he needed. "First, we have to figure out where you want me to put you in the city and when you want me to put you there."

Tyler was hesitant in his response because he was wavering on what to do. He wasn't sure if he should go back to San Francisco to help out at Harbor Emergency Hospital, or follow his heart and go back home to his family.

"I have a question for you," he said. "What do you think I should do? I know I could do some more good if I were to go back to San Francisco to help in the hospital, but I would like very much to get back to my family."

Brian got up from the creeper and walked over to the computer console. "I'm afraid that's a decision I'm not qualified to answer. It does seem to me, though, that you've already served above and beyond the call of duty at the hospital. According to Scott, you put in a lot of hard time there and helped to alleviate a great deal of pain and suffering. If you miss your family, I'd suggest you go home."

Tyler smiled briefly. "With all due respect, you haven't told me anything I didn't already know."

The kitchen door opened and Jo, Patty and Scott stepped down into the garage. Jo went to Tyler and took his hands in hers. "I want to tell you how much I enjoyed having you here with us. This has been a very exciting two days and I'm sad to see you leave, even though I know it's what you need to do."

Scott looked over Brian's shoulder at the computer screen, which was still relatively empty. "Where's the travel itinerary, Bri? Aren't there supposed to be some, you know, numbers and stuff?"

Brian slowly turned his head around to face Scott nose to nose. "I'm waiting for some input from the traveler. He's in a bit of a quandary as to where he'd like me to send him, Portland or San Francisco."

Scott turned around to Tyler just as Patty started talking to him.

"Go home Tyler," she said. "Your family needs you."

"She's right, you know," Jo said. "You've done enough to help the people in San Francisco."

Tyler looked back at Scott, who was nodding in agreement. "I agree. You did much more than your share to help, and you deserve to go back home now. Get over here and help Brian figure out your destination."

Tyler nodded and walked over to the computer console, huddling with Brian. Scott, Patty, and Joellen watched as Brian figured the latitude and longitude, along with the time coordinates, for Tyler's trip back home.

"Okay, I think we're ready," Brian declared. "Do you have everything you need, Tyler?"

"I ... I didn't bring anything with me."

Brian nodded as he went over and opened the hatch on the time machine.

"Your chariot awaits, sir."

Tyler stepped over to where Scott was standing and held out his hand, but Scott hugged him instead. "Thank you, for all you taught me. And for your friendship and hospitality. I'm grateful for having met you."

Scott smiled and stared momentarily at his friend from the past. "Thank *you*, Doctor. Thank you for all you did for *me*. And I wish you well, my friend."

Patty and Jo both hugged Tyler and said their farewells, as did Brian. Tyler climbed up into the ship, and just before he shut the hatch, they could see his glistening eyes as he waved a final goodbye. He closed the hatch and pushed the handle into the locked position.

"Here we go." Brian typed GO on the computer and pressed ENTER.

Doctor Tyler Hunter left 2002, never to see it again.

The ship set down in a field outside of Portland on the morning of April 21, 1906. Tyler opened the hatch and climbed out, then walked about twenty feet away to sit on a large rock. He watched the ship for five minutes until it came to life and disappeared from his sight.

He sat on the rock for quite some time thinking about all that had happened since he first boarded the train to attend the conference in San Francisco seven days earlier. Reaching into the pocket of his Dockers pants, he removed some objects. He held in his hands a packaged syringe, with needle, several packages of sutures, and quite by accident, Scott's mini mag flashlight. Imprinted in his mind were images of many other marvelous tools of the future.

Back in 2002, parts of history had changed dramatically, especially those connected in any way to Dr. Tyler Hunter. Scott and Brian's memories of the new history were slow in coming, leaving them quite unaware of the later accomplishments of their friend, Ty.

Chapter Twelve

One week after the Caufield fire, Josh Evans and Tony Escobedo sat at the kitchen table in station five discussing it. Tony was having a hard time forgetting the incident. He raised himself up on his elbows and leaned toward Captain Evans.

"I don't know, Josh. There was just something about the circumstances of that fire I haven't been able to come to grips with. Something's still bothering me and I can't seem to nail it down."

"We did lose a child on that fire, Tony," Josh said, taking a sip of his soda then setting the can on the table. "Losing anyone under those circumstances is tough, but when it's just a kid ... even after all my years on the job, I still have a hard time with any kind of call involving kids. Especially when they're badly hurt or killed. So you have a right to be bothered by the incident."

"Thanks."

"Has it been keeping you up nights, or causing any kind of physical stuff?"

"No, nothing like that, Cap. It's just been kind of eating at me, you know. But taking real small bites."

"I can relate. You think you're gonna be able to handle it? Can I help out somehow?"

"I'll be okay with it, but I guess it wouldn't hurt to talk about it though. That can make you feel better."

Josh sat back in his chair, folding his arms across his chest and nodding his head. "Been there, Tony. Many times. You can't discuss it with anybody outside the department, like family, because they just can't relate. No one can understand unless they've been there themselves. I recall going on a three week vacation the morning after a really bad one and I was a basket case by the time I got back."

"What'd you do then?"

"Matt Johnson was my captain at the time. I was still an engineer. It was a multiple child abuse thing, real ugly. Anyway, a lot of the crew had problems with that one. Matt called for a CISD team, but had them wait until I got back on shift to hold the debriefing, just in case I needed it. I really appreciated what they did. I still feel like I owe Matt one for doing it for me. Of course, the rest of the crew agreed to wait also, which was good of them."

"That's cool," Tony said. "I don't believe I need a CISD debriefing, but if anybody else would like it, well, it couldn't hurt."

"I'll keep my ears open. And you do the same. Okay?"

"Ten-four, Cap."

Tony stood to leave the kitchen. Josh got up and went out the other door on his way to the vehicle bay.

The doorbell rang and Tony turned to go answer it, but when he walked through the hall toward the front door, he saw Captain Evans letting a family of four into the station. He turned around and went back to the kitchen.

Looking at Josh's name badge, the woman said, "Captain, I'm Susan Caufield. Do you remember me? I'm afraid I was quite hysterical the last time you saw me."

"Yes, I do remember you. And under the circumstances you had every right to be upset," the captain said.

"Thank you. This is my husband, Dan, and our children, Natalie and Jason," she said, introducing her family to the captain.

"Happy to meet you." He winked and smiled at the kids as he shook Dan's hand.

Dan started to say something, hesitated and started again. "We came to thank you and all of your crew for what you did for our family."

Josh stopped him before he could say more. "Before you go any further, let me get the company together so you can talk to all of us at once." He turned to walk down the hallway toward the kitchen, then spun back around. "Come on back to the kitchen with me while I find everyone."

The Caufield family followed Josh back to the kitchen and sat at the table with Tony while they waited. The same table the firefighters sat around when Matt Johnson told them about station three's crew finding the body of Nate Morgan.

Evans walked into the kitchen with the rest of the firefighters following. The captain introduced the crew to the family and told Susan to go ahead with what she had to say.

"I think Jason and Natalie have something to tell you," she said while motioning for the kids to talk.

Natalie went over to Dennis Graham and handed him a big card made from a piece of poster board. "Thank you for saving me from the fire and thank you for keeping it from burning up my house, 'specially my daybed."

Dennis smiled and thanked the little girl as he opened the card to read it to the others. The kids had drawn a fire engine and ambulance sitting in front of a burning house that looked a lot like their own home. Inside, there was a drawing of firefighters carrying two kids from the burning structure. Printed across from the drawing on the inside were the words: Thank you firefighters. We love you.

All four members of the Caufield family had signed the card with colored markers. Graham handed the card to Traci Kingston to pass around the room. The burly engineer was noticeably touched.

The captain interrupted. With his hand on Traci's shoulder, he said, "This is Traci Kingston." Pointing to McLean, he continued with the introduction to the Caufield children. "And that guy over there is Scott McLean. They're the paramedics that found you kids and brought you out of the fire."

"Thank you for rescuing me and saving my life," Jason said to Scott and Traci.

"You're welcome, Jason," Traci told him. "We're glad we were there to help you and real happy to see you're doing okay."

Jason's gray eyes sparkled. "Oh yeah, and Mom made you some pies."

Tony leaned out over the two apple pies on the table and smelled the aroma with a long, deep sniff. "Dudes! They smell totally fantastic!"

"Down boy," Graham barked at Tony.

"That's very kind of you Mrs. Caufield," Josh said. "We appreciate it when people go out of their way to thank us. It makes us feel like we're doing a *little* good, anyway."

Dan Caufield removed his oval-shaped eyeglasses to stare into Josh's eyes. "A *little* good? What you people did for us was nothing short of a miracle. You saved our children's lives." He paused and looked around the kitchen at each one of the firefighters with tears forming in his eyes. "These two kids are everything to Susan and myself and we can never thank you enough for what you did. You'll always be heroes in our eyes. Thank you."

The kitchen fell silent for a minute or two before Susan added, "The pies are just a small gesture to say thanks. If we had it our way, we'd give you all raises or something, but they could never pay you enough for what you do."

"We'd sure be willing to let 'em try," Tony remarked. They all laughed, breaking up the heaviness of the mood, then Tony said to Susan, "Did you ever think of running for mayor?"

They all laughed again and the family chatted with the crew for a while before McLean gave them a tour of the station and equipment. Following the tour, Scott walked to the front door of the station with the Caufields. Susan told him about the problems their neighbors, the Morgans, had been having since the death of Nate.

"Kathy doesn't sleep at night and she had to be put on tranquilizers and sleeping pills since it happened," she explained. "Her son Tim blames himself for the death of his little brother. He made himself so sick over it that he had to be hospitalized and now they have him in therapy with a psychiatrist. The poor boy is only thirteen and he's carrying a burden like that. I feel so sorry for him."

The revelation about Nate's family was unusually upsetting to Scott, making him think about how devastating it would be if it was his own family. Even so, he'd seen so many people die in so many ways. Why had this one affected him so strongly? He never even saw Nate, let alone the rest of his family.

Susan was apologizing for dumping on Scott when he interrupted her. "I'm sorry Mrs. Caufield. But can I ask you something? Do the Morgans have any other children? I mean besides the brother, Tim."

"No, Tim is all Kathy has left."

"You said, all Kathy has left. Isn't there a father?"

"It's all very sad, I'm afraid. She lost her husband less than two years ago. The whole family was ice skating on the lake when Nate fell through the ice. He was seven at the time. His dad, Erik, jumped through the hole to save him, skates and all." She hesitated briefly, her eyes glistening with tears. "They were under the ice for the longest time and then Erik managed to hand Nate up through the ice to his mom." Susan's voice broke and she stopped talking.

Dan finished it for her.

"The paramedics said they were able to save Nate's life because it was a cold water drowning. Even though he was under the ice for over twenty minutes, he recovered with no side effects. But Erik disappeared back under the ice and it took weeks to find his body. Those kids lost the best father, and Kathy lost a great husband."

After a short silence, Scott spoke. "I remember hearing one of the medics talk about that one. It was a tough call."

Susan was crying. "Why do things like this keep happening to such nice people? Kathy just doesn't deserve it."

"Nobody deserves to lose a member of their family ma'am," Scott said sadly. "And to have it happen twice, I don't know. I don't know how they go on, I really don't. I've seen it over and over and I just don't know where people get the inner strength to recover from such tragic losses."

"That's the problem," Dan said. "It looks like Kathy and Tim Morgan have run out of inner strength."

"That's very sad," Scott said. He looked out into the parking lot at the Caufield kids getting in the car. "How is Jason handling all of this?"

Susan sighed. "Jason has cried a lot and still has nightmares about the fire. Sometimes he wakes up crying, sometimes yelling. He woke the other night yelling at Nate to stop, drop and roll. It just broke my heart. And I keep thinking that if I hadn't gone across the street to Esther's house to borrow some cinnamon for the pies I was making ... if I had just stayed home."

Scott could see the pain in Susan's face. The sorrow and sense of loss showed in her tear-filled eyes. She looked tired, like she hadn't been getting much sleep lately. They stood in silence for a minute or two until Scott spoke.

"If anything comes up that you think I might be able to help with please call me." He wrote his home phone number on a post-it note and handed it to Susan. "Or if I can help in any way with Tim and his mother."

Dan took a card from his wallet and wrote his home phone number on the back. "And if you hear of anything that might help the Morgans, would you please call us?"

Scott nodded his tacit agreement.

"We'd better go now," Dan said quietly, taking his wife's arm. He looked back at Scott. "Thank you again for saving our children. We're truly grateful."

"I know you are. And you're most welcome."

Scott watched the Caufield family get in their car and drive out of the front parking lot of station five. He was thinking about the surviving members of the Morgan family and wondering why some people have to endure such horrible tragedies in their lives.

"Wow, that was a heavy scene," he said softly as he turned and walked back to the kitchen, sitting down at the table. "Sometimes this job really sucks."

"Excuse me?" Keith Ryan said, stepping through the other door and taking a seat across the table from McLean.

Scott looked over at the young rookie. "Hey, Keith. I was just jabbering to myself."

"Are you okay? You looked like you were in the Bahamas or something."

"I was just thinking about those kids. You know, sometimes it can really get to you around here if you let it."

"You know, I thought I was all prepared by the training to handle my first fatal fire." Keith paused and breathed deeply, then continued. "But I wasn't ready for what happened. We had a good knockdown on the fire and two good saves. Then we found out later that we missed a boy. But not only did we not save him, we missed him altogether. I guess that's what made it worse. I know Chief Johnson assured us he was dead before we got there, but it was kind of upsetting for me."

"That's at least three of you," the captain said, rubbing his chin and looking very thoughtfully at Scott. "I'll call for a CISD team to set up a stress debriefing. Should be able to get them here by next shift. Think that'll be soon enough?"

Scott nodded. "Good idea."

"What's a CISD team?"

Evans answered. "I'm sorry, Ryan. You probably haven't had the chance to hear about that yet. It's an acronym for Critical Incident Stress Debriefing team. The teams are put together from a pool of psychiatrists, doctors, nurses, firefighters, paramedics, and police officers from around the state. They can assemble a stress debriefing at a moment's notice. We use them once in a while."

"What do they do?"

"It's all very informal. Like any other group therapy, we talk it out and put it behind us."

"It really helps, huh?"

"It seems to," Scott said. "Most of us thought it was a crock when the department bought into the idea of the CISD team. We thought it was a stupid, very 'today' thing to do. And being the macho shitheads we can all be at times, nobody wanted to admit they couldn't handle everything thrown at

Keith hesitated briefly. "Can I tell you something?"

"Shoot."

"That was my first fatal fire. In fact, that was the first fire I've worked with injuries of any kind. I've had a hard time dealing with it, but I figured it was because I'm new. I haven't told anyone what I've been feeling."

Scott sat up in his chair and leaned on the table. "Don't hold it in, Ryan. Don't ever hold it in. You need to talk it out with someone. Everybody on the crew has been there and they're all more than willing to talk about it. They may even be struggling with it themselves, so you could be helping them."

"I, uh, I thought maybe I just wasn't able to handle the job the way all of you other guys do. Everyone in our engine company seems so invincible that I didn't think anything affected any of you. That's why I was leery about telling anyone how I felt."

Josh Evans walked into the kitchen, rinsed a glass in the sink and leaned over to put it in the dishwasher.

"Hey, Cap," Scott said. "Are you having any problems with the Caufield fire?"

Sitting down at the table and pondering for a moment, Josh admitted, "I'm really not. But Tony shared some of his feelings with me. Are you two having trouble with it?"

"Yeah, we've been talking some about it," Scott said.

Fire captains have a tendency to fret about the rookies in their charge. Josh looked worriedly at Keith. "Are you okay?"

them. I know I was skeptical before I attended one of the debriefings. In fact, I fought tooth and nail to keep from going to that first one because I didn't have a problem with the incident, but they made me go anyway. After it was over, I could see it helped a few people. It's no panacea by any means, but it does sometimes help."

Scott paused and sat up straight in his chair, then continued. "We've all since learned that no matter how tough we are, or think we are, some of the tragic things we see happening to other people can get to us. We bury the feelings away and let them fester without ever realizing it and they sit somewhere back in our psyche eating away at us."

"Right," Captain Evans said. "Tony told me this one wasn't taking very big bites."

Scott smiled. "That's Tony's way of describing to what degree something bothers him. You know Tony and his way with words. He'll always tell you what size bite something's taking. It's a pure Escobedo-ism. Weird, but unambiguous."

The revelation that the veteran firefighters, his personal demigods, were vulnerable to the same feelings was quite an eye opener for Keith. "Are you going to arrange for the CISD team to come?"

"I'll go make some phone calls right now," Evans said as he got up from the table. "Matt will need to be there. And '3s' crew."

"Thanks, Cap," Scott said.

Alert tones sounded: *"Station Five, respond code three, man down, 7365 South Mineral Road. Patient is unconscious, but breathing. Time out: 1934."*

Rising from the table Scott waved his arm and said to the rookie, "Come on, Ryan. Let's go see what we can do for this butt-breather."

Butt-breather? the rookie wondered as he followed McLean from the kitchen and out into the bay. *Is that possible?*

* * *

Brian was sitting on his patio working on some project with his laptop computer placed on the glass top of the patio coffee table. Scott walked through the gate in the cedar fence and entered the backyard.

"Hey Bri."

"Scott. What's happening?"

Scott walked on over to the patio and pulled a lawn chair closer to Brian. Sitting down, he said, "Do you believe in fate?"

Brian stared at him with a wary look.

"Really, Brian. I'm being serious."

"Why are you asking something like that? What happened that I don't know about?"

"I just wanta know what your feelings are on the subject."

"That all depends. Fate in what context?"

Scott thought about it for a moment. "Like dying. As in do you think fate dictates when we're supposed to die? Is there a designated time set up for each one of us to bite the big one?" He paused briefly, locking his blue eyes with Brian. "Like in the words of that great philosopher, David Crosby, 'To every thing — is there a season?'"

Brian gave him a cynical look. "Do you mean the same great philosopher that later gave us the sage advice, 'If you can't be with the one you love, love the one you're with?'"

"No, that was his friend, the Sage Stephen Stills."

"Oh yeah, that's right," Brian grinned. "So what are you driving at?"

"Forget what I'm driving at for a minute, okay? I just want to know what you think about the part fate plays in our lives, and deaths."

"Jeez. I really never gave it a whole lotta thought. I guess I just figure that when you die ... you're dead."

"Thanks a lot. You're a big help."

"What do you want me to say? I don't really have any strong feelings one way or another about fate. Sometimes it seems like fate is playing a part in our lives, but look at what happened with the people back in 1906. If fate played a part in the death of that woman, Jenny, then you changed fate. So if you can sometimes change fate, then it isn't as all encompassing as some people would have us believe. I suppose I figure we cruise through our lives making things happen for us, but then, some of the time shit happens. Maybe that's what fate is, Scotty. When shit happens. That's fate. The rest of the time, we make our own destiny."

"So, you think that maybe fate plays a part, but only part of the time. Is that what you're saying?"

"I guess."

"That's pretty wishy-washy."

"You're right. But who knows? I don't have the answers. I'm just speculating like everybody else. As we've recently learned, we do have the ability to change history, but who's to say if we can change anything that was originally dictated by fate. Maybe we're only able to change those things that happened by chance. Take San Francisco for example. Maybe fate dictated the deaths and injuries of a whole bunch of those people, but not everyone. So some of them, like Jennifer Brody, were just caught in the middle of a big, fateful calamity. Which would put them in the 'watch out, shitsa happenin' and you're in the way' category. There's just a lot of possibilities, Scotty. I don't know."

"I don't know either. It's quite a puzzle, isn't it? Some people go around their whole lives tempting fate at every turn and they never get caught. Yet others never take a chance and constantly have accidents."

"Right, some people tempt fate all their lives, don't they? Like you maybe? You know, I've always marveled at the way you tempt fate. You've spent your whole life doing dangerous things, like when you went sky-diving that time. And when you went hang-gliding over the ocean on our Mexico trip. How about what you do at work all the time? Fighting fires is just about as crazy as you can get, wouldn't you say?"

"What do you mean?"

"Tempting fate, living on the edge, taking chances."

"Well, I guess I've probably believed in fate all along and not even realized it, you know? I've always had this feeling that when it's my time to die, I'll die. So if it's my fate to die at age seventy-five from colon cancer, then I'm not really taking much of a chance by fighting fires at age thirty-four, now, am I?"

"That's an interesting way to look at it. But you could also end up maiming or crippling yourself and still manage to die from colon cancer at age seventy-five."

"Ah," Scott said, holding one finger in the air and then bringing it down to point directly at Brian. "If it were my fate to live my life as a quadriplegic, maybe. But if that was the case, I'd end up crippling myself in some other way, like slipping on a bar of soap in the shower."

"Okay, I know you well enough to realize when you're leading up to something. Come on, lay it on me."

Scott gazed off in the distance momentarily and tried to form his thoughts into something that would convey the intensity of his feelings. "Do you remember the fire, a week or so ago, that killed the little boy?"

"Yes, I do."

"We also pulled two other kids out of that house and they came to my station last night with their parents. They brought us a homemade thank you card and some pies. Delicious, I might add."

"The card or the pies?"

Scott ignored Brian's attempt at humor and continued.

"Well, they told me about the family of the boy who died, what's left of it."

"What do you mean, what's *left* of it?"

Scott just blurted out the rest. "You wouldn't believe it, Bri. This family's been slam-dunked by fate, if that's what caused it. Two years ago they were just a nice little family of four. Nice parents doing their best to raise two nice boys. Now they are a mother and a 13-year-old boy, doing their best to just keep from going over the edge. It's really bothering me and I don't quite understand why. I don't get involved with victims from work, never have. But something about this has gotten stuck in my craw and I can't get it out. I even gave those people my home phone number and told them to call me if anything comes up that I might be able to help with. Do you believe it?"

"This isn't like you, I know. I've never heard you talk like this about any call you ever worked before. You just went through the San Francisco earthquake, man. What could be more upsetting than that?"

"I wouldn't think anything could be worse, except that I didn't work with any critical children. And I certainly didn't have to live with the families afterward." Scott paused. "Maybe it has something to do with those things."

"Are you just trying to get it off your chest, or is there something you think I can do to help?"

"You can help."

"How?"

"I want to go back and try to change it. I want you to send me back to that day."

Brian was shocked, unable to make a sound. He stood and walked off the patio, then around in the yard holding his head in both hands. Staring at Scott, he stood very straight and tipped his head back, running his hands through his long hair. Brian was truly agonizing over the prospect of using his machine for personal reasons because he promised himself he would never do that. After a few minutes, he went back to the patio and sat down. He gazed at his friend and started to say something, then stopped. Scott spoke instead.

"I'm serious. I feel a need to try and help."

Brian finally managed to say, "You can't go back and try to change all the wrongs that have happened in the world. We just have to accept certain things and I think death is one of them. I made myself a promise a long time ago that if I ever got that thing to work I would only use it for experimental purposes. I thought if I used it for one personal thing, then it would be easy to justify using it for more ... and more ... maybe even personal gain. I promised myself."

"I don't want to make a habit of it, but I need to try this one time."

"I don't know, Scott. I—"

"Brian!" Scott growled, his eyes furrowed. "I'm not asking you to send me back twenty-five years so I can buy up a bunch of IBM stock. I want to go back eight days to try to help a nice family. Jeez! You could even justify it as being experimental. Call it an experiment to see if we can change destiny."

"Let me think," Brian said. They sat in silence for several minutes with Brian staring out at the blue sky and Scott staring at Brian. Finally he spoke. "One time. We have to limit this kind of rescue mission to one time. Is that agreeable?"

"Thanks. It's agreeable."

"I'm dead serious about this. One time, and if you screw something up, you can't keep going back there to try to get it right." Brian shifted in his chair, then leaned forward toward Scott, saying softly, "This kind of thing could snowball into something we can't handle. So remember, no matter what comes up in the future, this is it. The one and only personal rescue mission. Okay?"

"All right, one time," Scott meekly answered. "Agreed."

* * *

About an hour after the conversation on the patio, Brian was lying on the garage floor under the time machine monkeying with the battery. He charged both batteries and re-filled the compressed air tank before every voyage of the ship. After tightening the last cable, he rolled the creeper out from under the ship into the open. The physicist inventor removed his John Lennon glasses and wiped them off with a clean part of his T-shirt, then wiped the sweat off his face with the same shirt. After putting his glasses back on, he rolled back under the ship to finish his pre-flight check.

"Got it ready?" Scott asked, entering the garage.

"Almost there," Brian answered, grunting while he tugged on the high pressure air bottle to make sure it was secure. "I wouldn't want this thing to start dropping parts in the middle of a trip. Know what I mean?"

"I hear that. Good call, Bri."

Brian scooted out into the open again. "Like brand new. Should be good for another trip or two, providing you don't take a lot more people out for joy rides."

Scott gave him a small smile. "Ty was just one man and I didn't have any choice in the matter, short of beating him up and throwing him out. And I couldn't do that 'cause I really liked the guy."

"Do you have everything you need?"

FIRES OF TIME * 271

Scott checked his pockets and duffel bag. "I think so. All I really need is my cell phone." He held up his phone for Brian to see.

"Phone numbers?"

Scott held out his left arm to reveal two phone numbers written on the back of his hand. Each number had a name scrawled beside it. One was Caufield and the other, Morgan.

"I've got the numbers of both families in case something goes wrong. I don't think it will, but the Caufields could have an answering machine or something and not pick up right away. Know what I mean?"

"Good thinking. Ya done well," Brian said, climbing into the cockpit to check out the inside.

Scott reached into his pocket and took out a slip of paper, then climbed up on the time machine platform and looked down into the cockpit. "I drove past the Caufield house this morning on my way home from work and saw an empty house two doors up from theirs. It had a for sale sign in the yard, so I figured nobody would care if I nosed around a bit. The back yard is completely surrounded by big bushes that would hide the ship if you put it down there. What do you think? Could you pinpoint a location that closely?"

Brian poked his head out of the hatch, his nose inches from Scott's. Shaking his head, he said, "Didn't I put you down in the right place in San Francisco? Ninety-six years ago?"

"Yes you did," Scott said quietly. "But that was ninety-six years ago. Do you still have what it takes?"

"Get in the ship before I end up sending you to Baghdad, in January of ninety-one," he said sarcastically, exiting the ship.

Scott handed him the slip of paper with the address on it and started to get in the ship. He stood on the floor of the cockpit and leaned on the frame of the hatch to talk with Brian, watching him cross over to the main computer console. Holding the slip of paper, Brian read out loud, "8743 South Hempstead Drive. Is that the right address?"

"That's it."

"What about the time?"

"I want to give myself enough time, so if you put me there at 1620 hours, I should be all right."

"Okay, give me a few minutes to figure my coordinates and I'll have you on your way. Oh, yeah. How long do you want to stay?"

Scott hesitated. "I figured about half an hour, so I guess until about 1650 would be cool."

"Sixteen-fifty hours it is. Now plant your butt in the cockpit and I'll send you on your way."

"See you in a minute. And thanks," Scott said, pulling the hatch shut over his head.

"No problem," Brian said to himself, knowing the hatch was already shut. "No problem at all, and I wish you luck on your mission of mercy, my friend."

Brian finished entering the time and place coordinates, tapped the enter key and covered his eyes.

* * *

Scott reached up and unlocked the hatch, then pushed it all the way open as he stood. He poked his head through the opening into the bright afternoon sun and scanned the yard. It was another fine shot by Brian to put the ship down precisely where it needed to be. Scott recognized the back yard, the bushes and the empty house. Still holding the cell phone in his hand, and with the pertinent phone numbers written on the back of his other one, he climbed out of the cockpit and sat down on the ship's platform.

"Oops," he said to himself as he got up and climbed back into the cockpit to check the time on the computer's clock. He reset his Timex to read 1622 and climbed back out to sit on the ship's platform. Composing his thoughts, he went over the script in his head.

He thought, *I hope she buys this. She sure wouldn't believe the truth at this point in time.* He flipped open the phone and began punching in the Caufield's number.

Susan Caufield stood at the kitchen sink slicing apples for the pies she was making. She was thinking about what an absolutely perfect day it had been. She was all prepared for the next day's parent teacher conference, and the only thing left to do was to shake hands and smile pretty.

Susan laid the strips of pie crust dough in a criss-cross pattern on the tops of the two pies. She reached into the cupboard for the finishing touch, cinnamon. "Oh, shoot, no cinnamon," she said aloud as she looked further. Finding none, she picked up the phone and called her friend, Esther Adamson, to ask to borrow some cinnamon. Esther told her to come right over and get some, so she turned the oven on to preheat and went upstairs to check on her 6-year-old daughter, Natalie. The little girl was sleeping soundly on her white daybed.

She should be all right for a few minutes, Susan thought. She started down the stairs to run over to Esther's house when the telephone rang. She wanted to ignore the ringing, rather than take time to go back to the kitchen to answer it.

"Ooh," Susan said, stopping just inside the front door and turning around. "I'd better get it." Hurrying into the kitchen, she answered the phone on the fourth ring.

"Hello."

"Mrs. Caufield?"

"Yes, this is Mrs. Caufield."

The man on the phone said, "My name is Joe Pack. I'm known to the kids at school as Officer Friendly. Is Jason there yet?"

Susan worried at having a policeman from the school call for her son. "No, Officer. He's over at his friend's house. May I help you with something?"

"As a matter of fact, yes," he said. "The boys are on their way over there from Nate's house right now. Let me explain, Mrs. Caufield. We're having a problem with some of the kids making dangerous devices from cans of aerosol hairspray and butane lighters. I have reason to believe that Jason and Nate are two of the boys involved in this, and quite frankly, I'm worried for them."

"I don't understand, Officer. What would you like me to do, talk to them about it?"

"Yes ma'am, that's exactly what I'd like you to do. Now, will you please wait for them to get in your house and then take the items away from them? I'm certain they'll be carrying a butane lighter and a can of hair spray."

FIRES OF TIME * 275

"How could you possibly know that? The boys have been playing over at Nate's house since they got home from school."

"I'm going to have to ask you to trust me, Mrs. Caufield. Please wait for them and check for those items. It's very important to keep them from injuring themselves."

Susan thought the guy was kind of weird, but he *was* talking about the safety of her son. So, weird or not, it probably wouldn't hurt to wait a few minutes. "Okay Officer, I'll do it. And what was your name again?"

"Joe Pack, ma'am. Officer Joe Pack. And thank you Mrs. Caufield for your cooperation. Bye now."

"You're quite welcome," the school principal said in a low voice. "Goodbye."

Hmm, she thought as she hung up the receiver of the phone. *I'd better check on that guy tomorrow with Jason's principal.*

Suddenly, the kitchen door opened and Jason and Nate stepped through it.

"This is gonna be so cool," Nate said as the boys walked into the kitchen. "Tim showed me how to—"

Nate walked right into Susan, who was still standing by the phone. Both boys were silent as they stared up at Jason's mom. They had guilty looks on their faces.

Jason tried to be cool as he meekly said, "Hi, Mom."

Susan smiled at the two obviously guilty boys standing before her. She let them stand and simmer for a moment before confronting them. Holding out her right hand, she said, "All right boys, let's have it."

"Have what, Mom?"

Still smiling, Susan told him. "I wouldn't get in any deeper, son. Let me have the lighter. And the hair spray."

The two boys turned their heads and stared wide-eyed at each other. They were definitely looks that said, *"How did she know?"* Jason sheepishly handed the lighter to his mother. She took it and held her hand out for Nate to do the same with the hair spray can.

Nate took the can from behind his back and slowly handed it to her. "Is it 'cause you're a principal that you knew we had this stuff? Can you read minds or something?"

Jason nodded vigorously. "Yep, she can."

Susan was actually a bit surprised that they really had the items the officer said they would have, but she was grateful he'd called. Her smile faded as she inspected the things in her hands. She looked back at the boys. "Do you want to tell me what you were going to do with these things?"

Jason hung his head, saying very quietly, "Make a fireball."

"Excuse me?"

He looked up at his mother, then back at the floor and said it again.

"A fireball? In my house? You were going to make a fireball inside my house?"

"In my room," Jason admitted slowly. He looked his mother in the eye, then added, "I'm sorry, Mom. I'm real sorry."

"I'm sorry, too," Nate said swallowing. "It was a dumb idea."

Interrupting, the phone rang and Jason grabbed it.

"Jason, honey, this is Esther across the street. Is your mother there?"

"Yeah, she's right here," he said. He started to hand her the telephone but Esther stopped him.

"You don't have to get her, Jason. Just ask her if she's coming over to get this cinnamon, would you?"

"Mom, are you going to go across the street and get the cinnamon?"

"Oh my, I forgot all about that," Susan said. "Tell her I'll be right over."

"She'll be right over ... okay ... bye." He hung up the phone and turned back to his mother.

"We're not through talking about this," she said while holding the hairspray can and lighter up in front of her. "I'd better run over there, but I expect you to be right here when I get back. Do you understand?"

Jason nodded. Susan turned to leave the kitchen, then stopped. "Natalie is napping and could wake up any minute. I wanted to be here, so will you please listen for her and see that she knows somebody's home with her?"

"Yeah ... Mom? I can run over and get the cinnamon for you."

Before she could protest, he was out the front door and down the steps with Nate right on his heels, yelling, "Wait up, Jase!"

Susan watched the two boys go and said to herself, "They really are good kids."

Scott stood on the ship's platform and watched the neighborhood for any sign of smoke. He couldn't see or smell anything, so at 1648 hours, he climbed into the time machine. Standing up through the hatch opening, he took one last look around, then smiled and thought, *It may have worked. I hope it worked.* He pulled the hatch down and locked the latch. The computer's digital clock changed to read 1650 and the machine started its warmup.

In Brian's garage, a small, gray cloud appeared and enlarged. With the familiar brilliant flash, the cloud disgorged the time machine through its doughnut hole aperture. By the time it wound down to a halt, Brian stepped onto the platform.

* * *

Eight days earlier, Scott followed the pathway that was marked by yellow lines on the asphalt of the training facility. The color of the paint reminded McLean of the yellow crayon the police use to mark the outlines around dead bodies and he thought, *I hope they have enough left to paint a line around my body in a few minutes.*

Watching McLean closely, Graham yelled out, "Pace yourself, Scott! Three minutes and fifteen seconds!" Scott continued to walk an even pace along the pathway.

Suddenly, they were interrupted by the dispatch alert tones.

Dispatch: "Rescue Five, Engine Five, Ambulance Three, respond code three, auto-pedestrian, 8765 South Hempstead Drive. R.P. states two victims, one is still down. Time out: 1652."

As Engine Five turned onto Hempstead Drive from 8700, the crew could see a white pickup truck sitting in the middle of the block, angled over against the curb. Just to the rear of the truck, lying in the center of the street, was the motionless body of a child. A boy stood a few feet away from the body holding onto his upper left arm with his right hand.

Dennis Graham pulled the engine onto the scene, positioning it near the curb opposite the pickup truck. The squad pulled right up near the child in the street.

Captain Evans: "Engine Five, Rescue Five at scene. We have two patients. Roll a second ambulance to our location, code three."

Dispatch: "Copy. Engine Five, Rescue Five at scene at 1658, break." Dispatch keyed another set of alert tones. *"Ambulance Seven, respond code three, assist Station Five on auto-pedestrian, 8765 South Hempstead Drive. Time out: 1659."*

McLean and Kingston hustled over to the child in the street and began to assess him. He was pulseless and non-breathing. Escobedo and Ryan arrived at their sides with some of the equipment. Evans and Graham went to the boy standing off to the side and assessed his injuries.

"Let's move it, guys!" Traci yelled. "We gotta get him out of here!"

The siren of Ambulance Three was heard approaching the scene, then shutting down before pulling up beside the medics.

EMT: "Ambulance Three at scene."

Dispatch: "Copy Ambulance Three at scene at 1703."

One of the EMTs on the ambulance yelled over to Scott. "What do you need, McLean?"

"Full spinal!" he shouted back.

Susan Caufield and Kathy Morgan stood on the sidewalk, holding onto one another, horrified at what they were seeing in the street. Captain Evans noticed, but didn't have time to check on them. He and Dennis were applying a vacuum splint to the left arm of the other boy.

Josh heard someone yelling on the other side of the street and looked that direction to see what was happening. He saw the white pickup truck with the driver's side door standing wide open. The left headlight was broken from hitting the upper left arm of the one boy. The hood had a dent on the front where it hit the other boy's head. The lettering on the door said, Jones Construction Company. A young man no older than twenty was sitting on the edge of the seat with his head buried in his hands. An elderly lady stood a few feet away yelling at him.

It was Esther Adamson, Sunday school teacher and chairperson of the city's Citizen's Movie Decency Committee. The sweet, elderly grandma, easily offended by any kind of profanity, stood yelling at the boy.

"You son-of-a-bitch ... you son-of-a-bitch ... you've killed that child! I've warned you over and over ... *you son-of-a-bitch!*

She kept it up until a police officer finally took her by the shoulders and walked her away from the pickup where she began to sob uncontrollably.

Within minutes, the firefighters had the child on a backboard with full spinal immobilization. He was intubated and the medics were performing CPR on him as the rest of the crew lifted him onto the stretcher and moved quickly to the ambulance. As an EMT closed the back door of the ambulance, Traci, Scott, Tony, and Keith were already getting bilateral, large bore IVs started, hooking him up to the EKG monitor, and attaching the ventilator to his endotracheal tube.

With lights and siren on, the ambulance pulled away from the scene, enroute to the hospital. When the ambulance turned the first corner, a car passed in the other direction, then drove to the scene and pulled up into the driveway of the Caufield home.

Dan Caufield got out of his car and ran to the end of the driveway, watching in horror as his wife picked up the T-shirt the paramedics had cut from the unconscious boy's body. She stepped back to the curb and looked sadly at Kathy Morgan as they both started crying. The T-shirt, hanging limply at Susan's side, fell and draped over the curb when Kathy embraced her in sorrow.

Dan reached down to pick it up, but the small hand of a 9-year-old boy beat him to it. All three parents watched as Jason held up the faded orange Mickey Mouse T-shirt with one hand, then dropped it to his side as he also began to cry.

Nate Morgan was on his way to the hospital where he was pronounced dead shortly after reaching the trauma center.

* * *

A worried looking Brian Daniels was standing on the platform of the ship when Scott unlatched and pushed open the hatch. Scott stood in the opening and stared him in the eye.

"What's up?"
"You don't know?"
"I just got here. Know what?"
"Did you manage to talk with the boy's mother?"

"Yes," Scott said. "She sounded like she was going to cooperate. But I don't know if she did."

"Climb on out of there and we'll talk for a while until it comes to you."

Scott climbed out of the ship and stepped down on the platform. Brian was already walking across the shop. They both sat on the platform and Brian said, "Did you see what happened?"

"No, I didn't. I watched until the last minute or so and didn't see or smell any smoke in the neighborhood, but I don't know if I was able to change anything."

"I don't know either, Scott."

Scott stood and paced around in the shop for a few minutes, stopping back in front of where Brian was still sitting. He was very deep in thought, trying to remember something, anything different about the incident, but coming up with nothing.

"Shouldn't we be able to remember if it turned out different?"

"I would think so, but we don't have enough experience with this to know exactly how it works," Brian said. "Maybe it'll come to us later or something. I don't know."

"This is strange. You'd think that if it had turned out differently, we'd remember the new way it turned out."

"Like I said, maybe something will come to us later. Then again, maybe not."

* * *

After putting the kids to bed later that evening, Patty and Scott sat together in the family room. Patty at the computer and Scott on the sofa reading the newspaper. Patty finished what she was doing, turned off the computer and walked over to sit beside her husband.

"What did you and Brian do today?"

Scott thought about it. "I went for a ride in the time machine to try to change something that happened about a week ago, but I don't know if I did any good."

Patty sat up and turned to face him. "I don't understand. What are you doing? Trying to intentionally change the past?"

"I was having a hard time dealing with what happened on a call last week. One of the families involved in it came to the station last night and thanked all of us, but that only made it worse." Scott took both of Patty's hands in his and stared into her big eyes. "It wasn't easy, but I convinced Brian to let me go back and try to change the event, except I don't know if I did. It's kind of weird. You'd think I'd remember if anything was different, wouldn't you?" He slumped back into the sofa, still holding onto her hands.

Patty studied Scott's face and saw the frustration in his eyes, but didn't know how to help. "What call was it, hon? Did I know about it?"

"Sure you did. It was the one involving the kids in the fire. Two boys set the house on fire and the one boy died."

Patty stared at him with a confused look on her face, trying to remember something about it. "I don't remember you telling me anything about that."

"Of course you do," he said, puzzled, sitting up straight on the sofa. "We talked about it the next morning. You saw me on the news and told me how bad you felt about it."

Slowly she moved her head from side to side, indicating that she was at a complete loss about it.

"The two boys. Over on Hempstead. Nate and Jason. We found Jason and brought him out. Nate's body was found later. Remember?"

Patty was even more confused because she remembered a different incident on Hempstead. "I remember the two boys getting hit by the pickup truck over on Hempstead last week. One died and the other had a broken arm. You worked the call and felt bad about it. Was there another one that I don't know about?"

If Scott had been in a cartoon, a light bulb would have lit up brightly above his head. "Now I remember," he said suddenly. "It just came to me ... oh, Patty!"

"What? What's the matter?"

"I remember what happened. I only changed the *way* the boy died. Now I have both memories, Patricia."

Slumping back into the sofa, Scott stared blankly at the ceiling and attempted to gather his thoughts. He was struck with the realization that he was responsible for making Nate go through another fatal accident. Knowing full well that a person could only die once didn't change the two memories in his head. Scott vividly remembered the 9-year-old boy being killed by fire, then in an auto-ped accident.

Slowly turning his head to his beautiful wife, he expressed his grim feelings. "Do you know what I've done, Patty? Do you realize what I've caused that boy to go through? And his mother? I've killed him a second time!"

"You didn't kill him."

He shook his head vigorously, then buried it in his hands. "I know I didn't go right out and kill him. But I caused him to suffer a second time. I caused his mother to have to watch him die in the street." He sat back up and gazed at Patty through watery eyes. "Why did I do it? Why did I meddle in the past? Who was I to think I could change fate? God? Did I think I was God or something?"

Scott stood and paced the room, ending up standing and staring out the small window in the front door. "This is the stupidest thing I've ever done." He went over and knelt in front of her, taking her hands in his. "What can I do?"

She lovingly expressed her feelings. "You're going to put it behind you and learn from it. That's all you can do. What you did was done with the best intentions, it just turned out wrong." She leaned forward, putting her face just inches from Scott's. "It looks like some things, like death, have to be accepted. You tried. You learned. Let it be."

Scott sat back on his heels and stared at her. "You really know how to dig down deep and pull out words of wisdom. Thanks, babe."

He laid his head in her lap and they quietly discussed the strange way the memories had come and gone. Scott gaining one and Patty losing the other. The time lapse between Scott's returning and the memory appearing.

After the talk, Patty suggested, "Why don't you call Brian and talk it over with him. It may be beneficial for both of you."

Scott smiled at her, then got up and went to call Brian.

Brian retained both memories, too. He also ended up with the same feelings of guilt and regret at what they'd done.

Before hanging up, Scott inquired, "Do you think the old memory will fade after a while and leave only the new one?"

"We can only hope. But we lived through both events today, so we may be stuck with both memories."

"You're probably right."

"You know, it may be for the best after all," Brian said. "This is a lesson we don't want to forget."

"I hear that."

Chapter Thirteen

Joellen knocked on the door and walked into Patty's kitchen. She opened a cupboard and got a coffee cup, then poured herself a cup with cream and sat on a stool at the bar.

"Did you and Scott talk about the trip he took to Hempstead Drive?"

Patty stopped sifting through some receipts from the laundromats and looked sadly at Jo. "Yes, he had to explain it all to me, because I don't remember anything about the fire. He said that he and Brian are carrying both memories around with them. It's so sad. Scott's having a real hard time dealing with it because he feels like he shouldn't have meddled with fate, or destiny, or whatever you want to call it."

"I don't have any memory of the fire either, but I still feel bad for them, and the families of those boys." She sat back and sipped her coffee, then put the cup on the bar and turned to face her friend. "What do you really think about all this? I don't think Brian ever considered any of it when he was working on the time machine. I mean he worked half his life to design and build it. He put his heart and soul into the thing and never once did he consider something like this happening."

"What did he think was going to happen? What kind of plans did he have for the machine?"

"Oh, he had truly noble plans to explore the capabilities of time travel and carefully document every detail he observed in his research. But he never accounted for the human factor."

Patty smiled. "You mean the McLean factor, don't you?"

Jo laughed. "Scott is one of a kind. There's no way he could observe an emergency situation and not get involved. He has to help, that's the way he is. In fact, I think he'd really get into taking short trips all over the place to try to fix everything bad that's ever happened to anyone."

Patty grinned. "Yeah, they could start up a rescue service that goes back in time to change the outcome of tragic events for their clients."

"Right, they could call it Rescues-*R*-Us."

"Uh-huh," Patty laughed. "I'm sure a service like that would prove to be quite lucrative. They could take a video camera along on their rescue trips and record rescues to help sell their service on those late night TV infomercials."

"Really, I can picture it all now. With video action in the background, they could say, 'What you're seeing is live video of an actual rescue. We can do the same for you. You say Grandpa was run over by a garbage truck and the family's embarrassed about it? We can change that. Sure, there have been times we weren't able to bring 'em back, but we've always managed to change the circumstances. And we can do the same for you. If it turns out it was just dear old grandpa's time to go, we could probably arrange for him to get hit by a Lexus. Or maybe a Mercedes. Your family shame will fly out the window as friends and neighbors file past his casket and see that fine Mercedes symbol imprinted on his forehead. He'll go out with a flair and the family will maintain their dignity.'"

Jo and Patty both laughed. "That's gross, Jo," Patty managed to say. "But funny."

"Why is it that disgusting things like that are funny?" Joellen grimaced and said, "Maybe we're just sickos."

"Could be."

Suddenly, Jo's expression changed. "Seriously Patty, both Brian and Scott are having some trouble dealing with what happened to the families."

"You have to admit though, they helped the older brother of that boy who died. Scott said he should no longer feel the guilt about causing the death of his little brother. And the other boy, Jason? Scott also told me he'd been having nightmares, so he might have an easier time now."

Jo reflected on that. "You're right, but now the guilt's been transferred to the boy who was driving the truck."

Patty reached over and took hold of Jo's hand. "Didn't you hear about that boy?" Jo shook her head. "He was driving on a revoked driver's license, and as it turns out, he's been arrested three times in the last year for drunk driving. And he'd been drinking the day of the accident."

"Whoa," Jo whispered.

"That's not all. Scott's captain said the kid got belligerent with the police and they had to handcuff and restrain him to get him in the police car. He was yelling about moron parents letting their stupid brats run around in the streets."

"Nice kid," Jo said.

"Exemplary. Another thing they said was that the police estimated he was going nearly sixty in a twenty-five mile-an-hour zone."

Jo continued shaking her head in disapproval. "Makes it kind of hard to feel sorry for him, doesn't it? I mean, I feel sorry for any young person who's destroyed the rest of his life, but it's difficult to drum up any pity for him."

"I understand what you mean There's also another way to look at it. It removed a dangerous driver from the streets. Who knows how many people he might have killed if he was still out there driving."

Jo perked up. "You're right, so Scott may have accomplished something after all. Sad as it is, the only person killed was the boy who was apparently destined to die anyway."

"Right. Scott altered things a bit, but the outcome seems to have been already decided. Not to change the subject, but I will. I was wondering, has Brian thought about discontinuing the trips or stopping the experiment?"

"No, he'll just be a lot more careful in the future to plan things out better, ya know?" Patty nodded. "He did say he'll never again allow the ship to be used for personal reasons. In fact, he said that under no circumstance would he allow any more personal rescue missions. He told me, even if it were one of his own relatives, it would be over his dead body."

"Well, I think they've proven they can't change fate, so what would be the use in trying?"

Joellen nodded. "You know they're planning another big trip. They're out on our patio working on it as we speak."

Patty jerked up straight on her stool. "To where? I mean, when?" She dropped her head down and shook it in frustration. "Oh, you know what I mean."

"Uh-huh. And I have an idea that they're planning on sending Scott to Chicago in the year 1871."

Patty looked up at her. "The Great Fire? Oh, I don't know. I'll worry more, especially after the way he came back last time, from San Francisco I mean. He was so beat up."

Jo put her hands on Patty's shoulders and looked her in the eye. "I know what you mean, but I'm sure he'll be much more careful this time. Hopefully they've learned something from the events of the past week."

"I sure hope so, but what about this trip to Chicago, Jo? Did they tell you anything about it?"

"All I know is what I overheard when I was out on the patio and listened to them talk about it for a few minutes. They were deciding what to do about the time lapse here in 2002 while Scott is back in 1871."

"I don't understand."

"It sounded like they've decided to trade minute for minute. If Scott is in Chicago for thirty hours, he'll actually be gone from 2002 for the same thirty hours."

"Why'd they decide to do it that way?"

Jo cleared her throat. "Well, Brian wants to experiment with different variations to see if there's one best way to do it, and I think Scott wants the rest of us to age at the same speed as him."

Patty smiled. "That sounds fair enough." She rose and put the coffee cups in the dishwasher. Walking around and sitting at the kitchen table she added, "I have another question for you. How many of these trips do you think Brian wants Scott to take?"

"Patricia, if you're real worried and don't want him to do any more trips, just tell him. They might be disappointed for a while, but I know they'll both respect your wishes."

"Yes, I am worried. But I worry every day he goes to work, so I'm used to that part of it. But having him gone for a long time, in 1871? I'll have a harder time with that than I did when he went to San Francisco for a minute."

"He was there for more than two days," Jo said, stepping from her stool to the table and taking a seat to Patty's left.

"I know that, but it was only a minute for me and that didn't give me a whole lotta time to worry. You know?"

Jo gave her friend an understanding nod and said nothing.

After a few minutes of silence, Patty said, "I don't want to discourage Scott from going to Chicago. Do you realize that his Grandpa Packy was there?"

"Uh-huh."

"What I'm getting at is, that if I had the opportunity to pick any gift in the world for Scott. Anything at all, with money being no object—"

"It would be the trip to 1871 Chicago," Jo finished.

Patty gazed serenely at Joellen. "Yes. I can't think of any other thing on this earth that would even compare with a trip to the Great One. No, I wouldn't do anything but encourage him to go on this dream trip. I may feel differently about additional trips after he gets back, but there's no other place that would mean nearly as much to him."

Jo stood and took a few steps toward the back door, then stopped and turned back around. "You could go with him, you know. It could be like a second honeymoon or something."

Patty laughed. "That's not my idea of the ideal honeymoon spot. I've heard it got rather hot, and I'd prefer to stay in a honeymoon suite that isn't on fire. Scott can have it all to himself, thank you."

"I think I'd go if Brian were going."

"Not me, thanks. I would never travel in that thing. To be completely honest, a team of wild steamer wagon horses couldn't drag me into it for any reason."

"Chicken."

"That's me."

"Hey," Jo said, grabbing hold of Patty's arm and pulling her toward the back door. "Let's go over and see how the Chicago plans are coming."

* * *

Brian and Scott were so engrossed in what they were doing, they didn't even notice when their wives entered the back yard. Jo and Patty walked right onto the patio before Scott turned to look at them.

"Hey," Scott said.

"Hey," Joellen said, sliding a chair over and taking a seat beside Brian at the table. "How're the plans coming along?"

Patty pulled out a chair and sat on his other side.

Brian looked up at Patty, then glanced at Jo. "They're coming along great, so far at least. We're planning this trip much more carefully than San Francisco." He turned to look at Patty, then continued, "We weren't going to send him away without talking to you first, honest."

Patty smiled and slowly nodded. Scott looked up at Patty and grinned, then went right back to the map of old Chicago.

Without looking back up, Scott said casually, "What do you think, hon? I'll be gone longer than before, so maybe it will seem like I've really been on a trip this time." He sat up straight and reached onto the table, taking hold of Patty's hand. "We weren't planning on doing it for a couple of days and I'll have to get someone to cover one shift for me, so we have plenty of time to discuss it."

Smiling warmly, Patricia stared right into her husband's eyes and responded to his statement. "From where I sit, there isn't any need for discussion. Of course I'll worry about you, but not any more than when you're on shift. I may have a change of heart after you get back from the Great One, but I want you to have this just as much as you do. There isn't anything I want more than for you to take advantage of this unbelievable opportunity. Except getting you back safely."

Brian and Jo smiled approvingly at each other, and Jo was about to say something but Patty cut her off.

"I hope you appreciate the fact that you get to travel back in time," she said, squeezing his hand. "Back in time to your roots. That's where it all started. Have you thought about that? Grandpa Packy. The Great Fire. All the things handed down to you through the stories and the journal. You've heard and read about them your entire life and now you have the opportunity to actually see some of it." Patty shifted a little in her chair, but kept eye contact as she finished. "Go, Scott. Go see it all and live it all, then come back home to me in one piece."

"I think I'm gonna cry," Brian said, sniffing and wiping his eyes.

Scott lifted the map up and tossed it at Brian, covering his head and face. Patty and Jo started punching him on both arms.

"Okay, okay," Brian pleaded, slinking down in his chair to get away from the hail of punches. "I'm sorry. I was only kidding, honest." They stopped slugging him and he sat back up in his chair. "That was a beautiful speech, Patricia," he said sincerely.

"Thanks."

Scott locked eyes with his wife again. "I feel a lot better about it, knowing I have your support. Thanks for always being there for me. I hope I can find a way to repay you."

"Not a chance, McLean," Joellen said. Scott turned and looked at her as she completed her statement. "I happen to know that she's always dreamed of traveling to the moon."

Patty turned and looked disgustedly at Jo.

"It could probably be done," Brian said quietly as he picked up a calculator from the table and did some figuring. "Yep, we could jump you into the continuum and have you there in about—"

"Enough!" Patty yelled, holding both hands out in front of her. "I've never wanted to go to the moon, and as a matter of fact, I don't even want to go for a spin around the block in that machine. This girl is keeping her feet firmly planted on this very earth!" She stomped both her feet and pointed one finger at her wristwatch. "And right here in this very time!"

"Ahem."

All four of them jerked their heads around at the sound of someone clearing his throat. An elderly gentleman was standing in the middle of the gateway holding the gate wide open. He had mostly gray hair and was wearing an expensive suit, but aside from that, he had a gentle face and soft, brown eyes.

"I'm sorry to startle you, but I didn't want to interrupt your conversation."

They all stared at the stranger, because each and every one of them felt like they'd met him before. He was probably about five-ten, with a medium build, but something about his overall appearance, especially his face, was quite familiar. More so to Scott, who felt certain he'd seen the man somewhere.

The visitor couldn't help but notice the stares, so he quickly assessed his appearance. He looked for something out of place on his suit and reached discretely down to check his fly. Having done that, he spoke.

"I've come to speak with the McLeans and the Danielses. It looks like I found the right place."

FIRES OF TIME * 297

Brian broke the quartet's silence, standing and greeting him. "Yes sir, you did. I'm Brian Daniels and this is my wife, Joellen," he said as he put his hand on her shoulder. He motioned to Patty and Scott. "They are Patty and Scott McLean. And you are?"

With a huge grin, he walked over to the table and held out his hand to shake theirs.

"My name is Hunter. Scott Hunter. You folks have no idea what a thrill this is to meet all of you. My grandfather first told me about you people when I was ... well, before I was old enough to attend school."

When he paused, the silence was complete. Every person seated at the patio table was frozen in place, too stunned to move or speak.

He continued. "Grandpa must have told the stories to me a thousand times, but there's one question I need to ask before I continue." He looked intently at each one of them. "You have already met my grandfather, Dr. Tyler Hunter?"

All four heads nodded in unison, slowly and silently.

"May I also ask when you last saw him?"

Silence.

He smiled. "I'm terribly sorry to shock you all this way. I'm afraid I underestimated the impact this might have on all of you, considering I've had my entire life to prepare for this moment. Oh, and I suppose I thought you would all know about his history by now. I guess not, judging from your reactions. May I sit down, please?"

Joellen was the first to recover somewhat from the shock and motioned for him to sit on the loveseat swing. They all followed him with their eyes and turned in their seats as he walked across the patio and sat in the swing, placing his briefcase on the patio. Scott Hunter couldn't wipe the smile off his face, his excitement thoroughly unrestrained.

Suddenly, Joellen spoke. "Tyler ... your grandfather. I don't—"

Interrupting, Hunter laughed and shrugged his shoulders. "I'll bet you don't."

Jo continued. "He was just here last week."

Looking at Scott, Hunter said, "Did you really meet my grandfather in San Francisco?"

Scott nodded his head.

Hunter looked over at Brian. "And you built the time machine?"

Brian nodded his head. Scott Hunter was elated. He stood and stepped over to the table, reaching out to shake all their hands.

"I apologize for acting so giddy. But this is the single greatest thrill of my life!"

Joellen stood and went to Hunter, taking hold of his shoulders and turning him to face her. She put her arms around him and hugged him tightly.

"Welcome to our home, Scott Hunter," she said genially.

She then turned and asked them all, "Anybody want a soda? We've got a wide selection, cola and diet cola."

They each told her what they liked and she went into the house, returning a few minutes later with the drinks.

It took a little while for the shock to wear off, but when it did, they talked enthusiastically with Scott, the grandson of Tyler Hunter.

"Your name," Scott McLean said.

"Yes," he said. "I am your namesake, Scott. And I'll tell you up front, I've always been proud to be named after such a man as yourself."

Surprised, Scott said, "What in the world did he tell you about me?"

Sitting at the table in one of the vacated chairs, Scott Hunter said, "I suppose you don't realize what kind of impact you had on my grandfather. You see, when you showed up in 1906 with a few of your 2002 tools and all of your 2002 knowledge and skills, you loomed much larger than life to Tyler Hunter. He told me that at one point in time he honestly believed you to be an emissary from God. An angel from heaven."

"I remember that," Scott said, smiling at the memory. "He thought I was either an angel or a Martian."

Hunter went on. "You remained larger than life to him when he visited here. The way you treated him, the fascinating things you showed him, watching the paramedics bring a patient into the ER, and all the other wonderful things you shared with him."

"You know about all that?" Brian asked.

Hunter looked knowingly at Brian. "I know every little detail of the whole thing. From the adventures in San Francisco, to the exact time and place where he arrived back in Portland. Let me tell you about that, the place he landed. One parcel at a time, he bought up the property around it. There was a huge rock — the place he sat to watch the time machine disappear — sitting on the property. He ended up with a few hundred acres of ground around that spot and that's where he built the family ranch and business. I grew up on that ranch, and it was the most wonderful place in the world for a small boy to spend his early years. The ranch has a rather unique name. It's called the—"

"Lemme guess," Patty said. "Hard Rock Ranch."

Hunter smiled. "Very good. You remembered the Hard Rock Café Las Vegas shirt. We still have that shirt and the pants. The Nikes are there in the case also, but they're as worn out as a pair of shoes could possibly be. You see, he didn't wear the clothes again, but those Nikes were possibly the single most comfortable shoes in the world at that time. He wore them for years and extracted every bit of possible use out of them."

Joellen, Scott, and Patty were all smiling, but Brian wasn't.

"Damn. I forgot all about getting that shirt back from him before he left." Brian stewed for a minute, then throwing up his hands, he added, "Oh, well, it was only a lousy seven hundred dollar T-shirt."

Jo broke in. "You said the clothes are in a case. Where is it located?"

He smiled and explained. "It's a display case that sits in the lobby of the family business office building. The clothing is folded and arranged so the lettering on the shirt doesn't show."

"Is there an explanation about the clothing and what happened in the display case, too?"

"Don't worry, Brian," Hunter said. "Your secret is still safe, and will remain that way. The plaque in the case simply states: 'Dr. Tyler Hunter arrived home from the earthquake in San Francisco with nothing but these clothes on his back. From nothing, he built this great corporation.' I'm the last person who will ever hear the time travel stories, and it's now a reality. I would never betray you, you see, because we owe everything to you."

"How's that?"

"If it hadn't been for you and Scott, my grandfather couldn't have built the largest medical supply corporation in the world."

"The Hunter Medical Supply Corporation!" Scott shouted out. "It just jumped into my head when you mentioned medical supplies."

Patty stirred. "What about it?"

"Nearly all of our medical supplies are from Hunter. In fact, Hunter supplies are what we use on all the rescues and ambulances."

"Why is that?"

"I don't know, Jo."

"Let me explain," Hunter said. "There is no rule, but we have always asked the fire departments around the country to be discreet about it. Most have been, which is nice. You see, any fire department that sends its requisition orders to our company is given priority. All fire department orders go to the front of the shipping as soon as they arrive. After filling the orders, they're shipped priority at no charge to the department."

"You say you ship the orders for free," Jo said. "Is that a big expense?"

"Oh, no, the shipping isn't too bad," he replied, looking around at the four people he felt he'd known all his life and noticing they were all a bit puzzled. "Maybe I wasn't clear enough. It isn't only the shipping that's free, you see. Hunter Medical supplies fire departments with all they need at fifty percent of our own cost to manufacture the products."

"Are you serious?" Scott asked.

"Oh, very serious."

"How can you afford to do that? Your company is taking a fifty percent loss on every item they send?" Hunter nodded. "It would cost a fortune to supply them all, especially if you're paying for the privilege of doing it."

"Scott, Hunter Medical Supply Corporation is the largest in the world. There isn't any other company even near the size of ours. In fact, we could supply every fire department in the world, free of all charges, and still make plenty of profit. Unfortunately, many of our other customers would likely take offense at such blatant favoritism."

"Instead what we've done is offer scholarships, all the way through graduate school, to all children of firefighters, so long as their grades qualify them to attend. They must maintain a certain grade point level in order to continue on, but if they do their part, Hunter Medical will keep them in school." He paused and smiled, studying their faces.

"We've put *some* students all the way through medical school and other doctorate programs. This program has always been the most gratifying aspect of my career, you see, I keep a close eye on the students in the scholarship program. They don't know it, but I personally watch to make sure they're treated fairly and given all the assistance, guidance, or counseling they need to keep them in school. I suppose you could say it's my pet project because I take a personal interest in the futures of each and every one of the kids. Probably more so than my father did. Or even my grandfather for that matter."

He picked up his soda and leaned back in his chair, taking a drink and setting the can back on the table. Leaning forward and speaking in a softer voice, like he was telling a secret, he continued. "I try to attend all of our students' graduations without anyone knowing. When I arrive at the ceremonies, I slip in and sit in the rear and then leave immediately when it ends. Sometimes I'm as proud of them as if I were one of the parents." Hunter stared at McLean and smiled slightly while searching his face for any sign of recognition. Seeing none, he said, "You obviously don't recall yet, do you Scott?"

McLean stared back for a moment until his eyes opened wide in sudden recognition. "I went through school and got my Fire Science degree on a Hunter scholarship!"

Everyone else at the table suddenly remembered, too.

"That's right. And you were, by far, my favorite student of all," Hunter said. "I sat in the back of the auditorium and watched your graduation ceremony. It remains as one of my all-time favorite memories."

"That's quite a rush, Scott," Brian said. "We were sitting near the back during your graduation."

Hunter laughed. "All of this was set up by my grandfather, and quite frankly, I wouldn't want it any other way. You see, he was always grateful to Scott for his success and this is one of his ways of sharing his success with others of the same ilk. In spite of all he accomplished in his lifetime, he remained the same humble and generous person throughout his entire existence."

Scott asked, "How did all this come about?"

"He had a few small medical souvenirs with him when he returned to Portland," Hunter said. "He had some sutures, one syringe, and one other item, let me get it." While Scott Hunter rummaged around in his leather briefcase, he kept talking. "My grandfather had what some people would call a photographic memory. He remembered nearly everything he saw when he was here. Being the type of surgeon he was, he couldn't bring himself to ignore all of those wonderful advancements that could be of so much benefit to the sick and injured, so he developed them earlier than they had originally been invented. Ah, here it is."

Hunter stood up and handed the item to McLean.

"A mag light," Scott said, looking a bit puzzled.

"Correction, *your* mag light. He had it in his pocket when he arrived back home. He swore it was an accident and I believe him. In fact, he always felt bad about accidentally taking it, so I promised I'd bring it to you. You know, he could have invented the flashlight, but he told me he didn't want to be greedy. Grampa could have invented many other non-medical items also, but he steadfastly stayed with only medical equipment. Like I said, he was a very honest and humble man."

"Was? Did he die?"

"Yes, Patty," Hunter said with a fond smile. "He died in 1960 at the age of eighty-eight."

Jo gasped as she and the others were taken aback by the revelation.

"Wow," Patty said as she slumped down in her chair and dropped both arms down to the sides of it. Shaking her head, she went on. "He was just here last week and now we hear he's been dead for forty-two years. Time travel gets more mind-boggling all the time."

FIRES OF TIME * 305

Going through his briefcase again, Scott Hunter came up with an envelope. "This is for all of you, from my grandpa. I promised him that I'd deliver it." He handed it to Brian, who opened the yellowing old envelope and removed a letter from Dr. Tyler Hunter, dated June 16, 1958.

Brian read it aloud:

Dear Scott, Brian, Patty, and Joellen,

I have asked my grandson, Scott, to contact you on this day in the year 2002, considering you wouldn't know about me at any point in time before that. I was never able to adequately thank you for all you did for me. In gratitude, I have strived to repay your kindness by sharing my good fortune with others. In that vein, my grandson has been instructed to deliver to you a token of my appreciation for the contribution you kind people made to my successful career.

As I was unable to share in your friendships throughout my life, I can do little else than try to reach out from the past with this small gesture. I am acutely aware that it isn't much, but I sorely need to feel as if I was able to have you share in my success, as my success stemmed directly from the time I spent with the four of you. You have my sincere apology, should any of you find this bequest either insulting or inappropriate.

Please feel free to do with it as you desire. Whether you choose to keep it, use it to further your research, or give it to charity, it matters not.

> *Scott, I am returning something I accidentally borrowed from you and I do apologize for taking it. I didn't realize it was in my pocket when I left.*
>
> *Thank you all again for befriending me and may God bless and watch over you and your lovely families.*
>
> *Your friend, Tyler Hunter*

After Brian finished reading the letter, Hunter handed an envelope to Scott and Patty, then turned and gave an identical envelope to Brian and Joellen.

"I was asked to deliver these envelopes to you and answer any questions you might have about them."

They opened the envelopes and found a single stock certificate in each one. Each stock certificate bore the Hunter Medical Supply Corporation name and was in the amount of five hundred shares.

"I'm afraid grampa wasn't in a position at that time to leave you more, but we are now in the position to give you as much more as you request."

"Don't be silly," Scott said. "You don't owe us anything. We honestly liked Tyler, and anything we did, we did because of that. Besides, this would be a good little college fund starter for the kids. No, Scott, this is more than ample. Thank you very much."

Looking closely at the stock certificate, Brian added, "He's right, you don't owe us a thing. How much is each share worth, anyway?"

Scott Hunter smiled broadly. "For one thing, you don't need to save for college, because your children's education will be fully funded, being firefighter's children. And you, Brian and Joellen, if you have children, are the single exception to the firefighter rule. Your kids will also have their education paid for."

Jo lost the ability to catch her breath for a moment. Even though they hadn't been able to have children, they fully intended to adopt before too long.

Scott Hunter went on with his explanation. "The stock value is rather difficult to explain, because if you look closely at the certificates, you'll see they're dated 1956. There have been many, many increases and splits in our stock since that time. I checked with my chief accountant before coming here and he informed me that each share of that particular Hunter Medical stock is now worth approximately three thousand dollars on the current market. Now, like I said before, if that isn't adequate, all you need do is let me know how much more you need and I'll see that you receive it."

After recovering from the shock of learning the huge worth of the stock, McLean looked at Brian, who was slowly shaking his head. Scott knew exactly what it meant. He gave Brian one distinct nod, indicating he understood and agreed.

He then looked at Scott Hunter, pausing for only a moment. "Let me explain something to you. We don't want to sound ungrateful, because we realize your grandfather truly felt he owed us something for inadvertently helping him in his success. We know he was a good man with a good heart and he wanted to share his good fortune with us. I for one am impressed with him for the integrity he showed with his knowledge of the future. Actually, most men would have used every bit of their new found knowledge to make as much money as possible. Tyler, although he became rich, didn't exploit the opportunity. He was generous with his success, and from meeting his grandson, I can see he taught his family to live by the same values he chose for himself."

"Thank you," Hunter said. "I—"

McLean held up his hand. "Wait a minute, I'm not quite finished explaining. When Brian finished building his time machine, he told me he had only one hard and fast rule. That rule is a good one and I happen to support him in it. He said that he would never, under any circumstances, allow his machine to be used for personal reasons, especially if it involved making personal profits from its use. Out of respect for my closest friend, Brian, I'll have to decline the stock certificate."

"I feel the same way," Brian said. "I can't accept this either. Not because it isn't legal, but because it goes against my principles. But I too am grateful for the generous offer."

Scott Hunter was not offended. The grandson of Dr. Tyler Hunter wasn't even the least bit surprised. What else could he have expected from the legends of a childhood spent with his grandfather? Brian and Scott had been larger than life to Tyler, and they came through, true to anticipated form, to his legacy, Scott. They turned down three million dollars without batting an eye. Hunter couldn't have been more thrilled. He stood up from his briefcase, then sat back down on the swing and leaned forward toward his four new, yet old, friends.

"I'm not disappointed that you can't accept it, and I want you to know how my grandpa would have felt about it." He stammered a little bit as he went on. "My grandfather counseled me about this very thing. I feel like he knew you'd turn it down, just by the way he always spoke of you. Although he had no idea the stock would be so valuable today, he wouldn't have been a bit surprised by your reaction and, quite frankly, neither am I. To tell you the absolute truth, I might have been surprised if you had accepted it."

While Hunter paused to catch his breath, Patty grinned warmly at Jo.

"Grandpa had a way of seeing through people, usually when he first met them. He could sense things about them, like their character, their honesty, their general spirit. He could be kind of spooky that way."

"I hear that."

"I'll bet you do, Scott," Hunter smiled. "He knew there was something very, very different about you the moment he met you, but he also had a strong feeling that you were a good man. No, a very special man. I watched him in action during most of my life and I can verify his innate abilities."

"Me too," McLean said, "and it took me a very short time to figure that out about him. He saw through me almost immediately and it was difficult for me to keep my secrets as long as I did."

Scott Hunter leaned back on the swing and stretched his arms, then settled back down on the seat. "All right then, what would you like me to do with the money from the stock certificates? That decision is still up to the four of you and I'd really like you to help with it. You can designate it to go for any purpose you choose, because it is still legally yours."

"Do you have any suggestions?" Patty asked.

"Well, you can set up trusts, give it directly to charities, or give it to someone else who needs it. It doesn't matter to me what you do with it, but I have a feeling you'll come up with the right decision."

"Do you mean we could give it to some family that's suffered a loss, or to help out with expenses for ... for just about anything?" Joellen said.

Hunter smiled and answered, "It's your money. My company will be happy to administer the funds if you like or you can handle it yourself. You make the decisions and I'll abide by anything you tell me to do."

"How about helping the family of that boy who was killed by the car?"

"Right, Patty," Jo added. "Or getting legal help for the young man that hit him, along with counseling to straighten out his life. He could probably use a lot of assistance in getting his life started after he pays all of his dues."

Brian spoke up. "Don't you guys have a fund to help burn victims during their recovery periods, Scott? Doesn't it pay to catch up all of their personal bills and then make all of the payments while they're laid up?"

"Yes, we pay their living expenses and all their monthly payments until they get back on their feet and back to work. So far, we haven't let any of them lose anything, like their homes, cars, stereos, furniture, and stuff like that. It allows them to recover from devastating burn injuries with less worry and more dignity."

Scott Hunter smiled and nodded his head in an approving and admiring way, becoming more and more proud to be associated with his four new friends.

Brian turned to Scott McLean. "Do they have burn funds like that in other cities? Or is it something unique to our fire department?"

McLean leaned forward, picked up his soft drink and responded. "There are various kinds of burn funds all over the country, but I don't know if many of them go in and do the kind of thing we do. You see, the way it started was when a friend of one of our firefighters was badly burned and out of work for an extended length of time." He paused to take a drink of his soda. Placing it back on the table, he added, "The firefighter saw his friend lose his car and his home to repossession, then suggested we do something to help with those particular problems the burn victims face. One thing led to another and our burn fund was the result."

"I've never heard of such an interesting kind of charitable fund," Hunter admitted. "It's so thoughtful, and provides such a compassionate and vital service. Are others included in the fund, or is it used exclusively for firefighters?"

"Oh no," McLean said quickly. "Firefighters aren't included in the burn fund. We have our own safety nets set up in other ways. Our burn fund is used exclusively for assisting the burn victims in our city who suffer debilitating burn injuries."

"That makes it even more compassionate," Hunter said.

"We could have Scott start one up in his home town of Portland," Brian said.

"That'd be pretty cool," McLean said.

"Those are all very fine ideas," Hunter said. "You don't have to make any decisions right now, by any means. Spend some time and work it out to the satisfaction of all. We can get back together and set it up another day."

To Scott Hunter, Patty said, "You're staying for dinner, aren't you? We can have a barbecue, and you have to meet the kids."

With tears in his eyes, Scott Hunter hesitated, then said, "I wouldn't miss it for the world."

Chapter Fourteen

After eating dinner, they were all sitting in the McLean's family room talking. Casey had already shown the leather-bound journal to Scott Hunter, and Missy was sitting on Grampa Hunter's lap. She was showing him her Dr. Seuss book, *Fox in Sox*.

"Daddy reads it to me and he's so funny. He mitses up."

"Mixes up, that's a nice way of saying it, babe," McLean said.

"You should hear him," Patty laughed. "Sometimes it sounds like a fifty car freeway pile-up."

McLean spoke up in defense. "But I'm getting better. Someday I'll be able to read it perfectly. Missy might be fifteen by then, but I'll have it perfected. And I'll make her listen to every bit of it."

Hunter was still smiling broadly. "My grandfather was right, you have very precious children. He described them to me many times, but mere description didn't come close to reality. You're very fortunate."

"Thanks," Patty said. "But I have a question for you. Weren't you tempted to show up early while Tyler was here, just to get a glimpse of him? I know *I* would have been."

Scott Hunter looked earnestly at Patty and answered. "He made me promise I wouldn't do that. He felt that if I were to meet him, it could change the outcome of his life. He was a very happy man and didn't want to change a minute of it. I promised I wouldn't try to meet him. Could you imagine how strange it would be to meet your own grandson, who's nearly twice your own age?" He paused to shake his head. "But I *was* at the hospital when he went there with Scott. I couldn't resist seeing him as a young man, so I wangled my way into the seats of the operating theater."

"You were there!" Scott gasped. "You sly devil, that was you sitting over in the corner staring at us, wasn't it?"

"Guilty as charged. Other than my parents, I never loved anyone more than him. Can you blame me for taking the opportunity to see that man again?"

"Not in the least," McLean said. "Actually, I'm glad you had the opportunity to experience something like that. Though it could never happen, I've always wished I could have a chance to meet my great, great grandfather. I'm proud of you, Scott."

"It was a very poignant moment for me."

"I'll bet it was. You know, Tyler didn't even notice you, but I was wondering why that man kept staring at us. Now I know."

"He seemed so excited while he watched the surgery. Seeing it must have been so thrilling for him, I can't even imagine."

McLean thought it over and smiled. "I was sitting and talking with him and I still couldn't imagine what was really going through his head. The feelings he was having were nearly impossible for him to put into words."

Brian stopped playing with Missy to break in on the conversation. "Did you know he slept at our house that night? Jo and I stayed up quite late talking with him about many things. He *did* have a difficult time expressing his feelings, but he tried anyway. He told me he was so overwhelmed by the whole 2002 experience that his head was actually swimming. So when Scott took him to the hospital and then to the surgical theater, well, I guess the best way to describe it would be to say that he just about lost it completely. His actual words were, 'Once or twice, I thought I was coming down with the vapors.'"

They all laughed.

Sitting on the floor listening, Casey said, "What are the vapors?"

His father explained, "What it basically meant is that parts of your body, possibly your stomach, would go a bit haywire and give off gases, or vapors. Then, that was supposed to make you sick or crazy. It's an old outdated thing that doesn't really happen."

"Wow! That sounds really cool!" Casey grabbed his stomach and writhed around on the floor, shouting to his mother, "Mom, my stomach is really hungry and it's vaporizing. Quick, it's an emergency! I've got the vapors and I need Häagen-Dazs. Hurry, before I go bonkers!"

Everyone laughed as Patty told her son, "You're already bonkers and I doubt very much if Häagen-Dazs will cure that."

Laughing, Scott Hunter stood and walked over to the bottom of the stairs. He sat on the second step beside Joellen.

"Can I ask you something?"

Jo turned to face him. "Sure."

"What Brian said. My grandfather actually slept in your home?"

Nodding her head, Jo smiled and answered. "Uh-huh, he slept in our guest bedroom."

"This is becoming very strange. I didn't expect to run into anything strange, since I thought I already knew everything that happened. Seeing Grandpa and Scott in the hospital, then finally meeting all of the people I feel I've known my entire life. Now, thinking about him actually sleeping in your guest bedroom only days ago." He paused to reflect, then asked, "Would it be possible to see the room ... I mean, to maybe have a look around it?"

"Of course, Scott," Jo said. "I've got an even better idea. Why don't you stay in our guest room tonight? We'd be excited to have you."

"I—I already have a hotel room, Jo," Hunter said.

"You aren't required to sleep in it just because you rented it," Patty said warmly. "You really should stay over in their guest room."

"We can stay up and talk," Brian said, glancing over at Casey. "And eat Häagen-Dazs." Casey's head spun around to give Brian a scowl, then a pitiful, pleading look. Brian laughed and stared right at Casey. He spoke to everyone while he continued to stare at Casey. "Why don't we all go over and have some of that wonderful ice cream?"

Casey's pleading look changed to quizzical, as his eyes widened and seemed to ask, "Me too?"

"You too, Case," Brian smiled.

"Me too?" Missy asked.

"Of course. It wouldn't be a party if you weren't there."

The little girl ran giggling to her mom.

* * *

A little later, they were all sitting in Jo and Brian's kitchen eating Häagen-Dazs ice cream and talking. The kids took theirs in the other room to play video games. Scott Hunter related many of the stories his grandfather had shared with him as a youngster. Brian, Jo and the McLeans, told Hunter about some of the things Tyler had seen and done while he was visiting 2002.

"You know I have anticipated this day for so many years with great zeal, often wondering if it could possibly live up to my great expectations." Hunter paused briefly and cleared his throat. "But I must tell you, my greatest expectations didn't hold a candle to what I've found here. This is the single most exciting thing that's ever happened to me."

McLean spoke. "I'm glad we were up to par. This is no small event for us, either. It's the best thing to yet result from our time travel adventures and I'm happy it involved both of our families."

"Time travel. That's where it all began. Will I have a chance to see the ship?"

"Ship! You called it a ship!" Brian said brightly. "How did you know to call it that?"

"Grandpa always referred to it as a ship. He said you liked to call it that because it sounded more professional. He also said you liked to be called *captain*," Hunter added, grinning broadly.

Brian sat up straight looking surprised. "Seems he didn't miss a thing. Tyler had quite a sense of humor, didn't he?"

Scott Hunter leaned toward the center of the table. "My grandfather was one of the wittiest people I ever met. He was quick with a comeback and always had something funny to say. And yes, he had a great sense of humor."

Brian nodded with a thoughtful expression on his face and after a short pause, looked at McLean. "Would you want to go tomorrow?"

"I don't know. I have to get someone to cover my shift the day after tomorrow. I'll call around and see what I can do."

Brian nodded again, then turned to Hunter. "We're sending Scott on another time travel trip. If possible, you may not only have the opportunity to see the ship, you may get to see it leave our time for the past."

Hunter perked up. "Honestly? To where in the past?"

"Chicago, 1871. The Great Chicago Fire," Brian answered.

"I'll certainly stay for that," Hunter said. "This is a bonus I never even dreamed of."

"Come on, kids," Patty called to them as she stood up. "Let's go home now. Tell Brian and Joellen thanks for the ice cream."

"Thank you for the Häagen-Dazs," Casey said, moving toward the back door.

"Thank you for the Hojjen Dots," Missy repeated, walking behind Casey and imitating his every movement.

"You're both welcome," Brian and Jo said in chorus.

Scott stood to leave, but stopped to say, "I'll call you in the morning and tell you what I find out about that shift."

"Cool," Brian said happily. "See you later."

"Bye," Patty said as she waved and exited the house.

"G'night," Joellen added.

The McLeans left and the visitor stayed, sitting up late to talk with Jo and Brian. Brian remembered the short video he had taken of Tyler and Joellen. Scott watched it over and over, mesmerized by the video of the grandfather he lost so many years before. Following the screening, Brian gave the tape to the very grateful grandson.

Scott Hunter spent the night in the very same room his grandfather, Tyler Hunter, had stayed in less than two weeks before.

* * *

The next morning, Scott McLean got up early and began calling to find someone to cover his next shift. At the first station he called, he found a medic who owed him a shift. After making the necessary arrangements for the trade, he went over to Brian's garage to see if he was out working on the time machine. Brian had already been working in the shop for a couple of hours, performing his pre-flight check.

"We good to go?" Scott said after stepping through the door.

Brian looked up from the bolt he was tightening on the platform. "Morning. It looks like the ship's pretty much in order. When do you wanna go?"

"Oh, not until later this afternoon. I need to stay with Missy for a while this morning while Patty does some work at the laundromat over on Crystal Boulevard."

"Why isn't Missy going to the laundromat with Patty?" Brian inquired, standing and wiping his hands on a shop rag. "I thought she always went there with her."

"Patty's not going to the cleaners Mrs. Jelesnik manages. You know, the big one down on Jordan Avenue."

"Wow. Is Mrs. Jelesnik still alive?"

"Yeah." Scott smiled broadly. "She's way old, but she still knows how to run a store in the laundromat and cleaning business. That's one reason Missy likes going to the big store. She just loves Mrs. Jelesnik, and of course her playroom we built in the back boiler room. She has most of the comforts of home in there, with the carpeted floor, TV and VCR. Patty even got her one of those child-size recliners, so she thinks she's real grown up. The dead giveaway that she's only a kid is the large collection of Winnie the Pooh videos she watches from her recliner."

"Right," Brian smiled warmly. "It's not hard to envision her sitting there." He paused and patted the time machine lovingly on the side. "You never told me what you decided on where to put this baby down in 1871. Let's get the old Chicago map and make some decisions about time and location."

Scott stepped up on the platform and dropped his black nylon duffel into the cockpit through the hatch. Stepping back down, he answered, "I have a couple of pretty good spots in mind, but nothing set in concrete. Let's throw a study on the map and figure it out."

They went out to the patio table and spread out the map of old Chicago to begin their work.

"Okay, Scotty, amaze me with your vast knowledge of yon days of yesteryear Chicago."

Scott gave him a sour look and leaned out over the map. Pointing to an area in South Chicago, he said, "Somewhere in this vicinity." He pointed out a specific street and continued. "This is DeKoven street, where the fire started. The O'Learys lived just about there, at 137 DeKoven." He touched the map, showing Brian the location.

"Seriously, did Mrs. O'Leary's cow really kick over the lantern and start the fire?"

Scott sat down in a chair. "The fire really started in the O'Leary's cowshed. A peg-legged neighbor named Daniel Sullivan was sitting on a lawn across the street. When he saw the fire, he began yelling, 'fire, fire.'"

"That makes sense," Brian said.

Scott gave Brian a disgusted smile, then rattled on. "Old man Sullivan did his best to run over to try to put it out. When he got inside the shed, the heat was so intense he only had time to let some of the animals loose. He almost bought the farm when a calf ran into him and knocked him down, but he hung on to the calf and led it out of the shed. Another neighbor, Dennis Rogan, woke up and ran over to the

O'Leary's and tried first to save their new wagon. Since the wagon was already toast, he decided to go ahead and wake up the O'Leary family."

"What about the cow?"

"Keep your shirt on, I'm getting to that. Later, a board of inquiry met to determine the cause of the fire. Only one fact was solid; the fire started in the O'Leary's barn. Even though the consensus of the board was that the cow did indeed kick over the lantern, nobody ever really proved it and in 1998 the City of Chicago absolved the cow of all charges. In fact, some people thought ol' Peg Leg Sullivan really started it. Oh, and one other interesting thing. One of the only structures in the neighborhood that wasn't destroyed was the O'Leary's cottage."

"Really?"

Nodding his head, Scott said knowingly, "Most of the neighbors were really pissed about that."

"So, in your long-winded, roundabout way of saying it, nobody really knows if the cow kicked over the lantern."

"That's right, but you asked me to wow you with my vast knowledge. Didn't you?"

"Yeah, sorry. You did dazzle me with brilliance instead of baffling me with bullshit. Didn't you?"

"Does it matter?"

"Not really. I just hope you're as knowledgeable as you think, so you can stay alive while you're there."

"Not to worry," Scott said assuringly.

A voice interrupted from the back door of the house. It was Scott Hunter, who'd been standing in the doorway listening to their conversation.

FIRES OF TIME * 323

"You two are a joy to listen to. It must have been absolutely perplexing to my grandfather."

"At times I think it was," Brian confessed. "But he seemed to enjoy listening to our mindless drivel."

Taking a step toward them, Hunter said, "May I join you two in your planning?"

"Sure, have a seat." McLean patted the seat of the chair next to him. "We'd love to have you in on the planning stages."

Hunter stepped over to the table and sat in one of the chairs.

"I have an idea, Bri," Scott said suddenly. "I'm not quite as familiar with the area as I'd like to be, so could you put me in a spot somewhere down west on DeKoven? And then give me the information I need to come right back, if necessary?"

Brian stared at Scott for a few moments with the wheels turning in his head. He finally brightened up and suggested, "How about this? I'll send you to a spot near DeKoven and leave you there for five minutes so you can get out and see if the spot is all right. If so, I'll send you right back there. If it isn't a good place, see if you can scope out a better one so we can make the proper adjustments. Just try to be back in the ship within five minutes."

"Excellent idea. But how about seven minutes. You never know, ya know?"

"All right, seven minutes it is. Let's go get it all figured out on the computer so it'll be ready to go whenever you are."

They got up and started into the garage.

Hunter followed them through the door and said, "This is terribly exciting. I sort of wish I were going."

Brian and Scott both stopped in their tracks and Hunter came to a screeching halt.

Scott turned to Brian. "Are you thinking the same thing I am?"

Brian nodded and smiled. "It's got to be." Motioning to Hunter, he said, "It's only for seven minutes."

"Right."

Scott Hunter looked somewhat bewildered, glancing back and forth from Scott to Brian and back again.

Brian glanced toward Hunter. "How would you like to go along for a seven minute vacation in 1871 Chicago, Scott? The ship'll be coming right back—"

"And you don't even have to get out of the cockpit, if you don't want to," Scott said, interrupting.

There was a lengthy pause, for Scott Hunter was momentarily struck dumb. He was light headed and shocky, unable to believe his ears. Those heroic figures from his childhood had offered him a chance to ride in the time machine that carried his grandfather from 1906 San Francisco to 2002, then back to 1906 Portland, Oregon.

He choked up, and in a futile attempt, tried to swallow the lump in his throat. "A—Are you serious?"

"As a heart attack," Brian said. "I'll bet you'd really enjoy it."

"A tremendous understatement," Hunter managed to say.

"All right!" McLean said, clapping Hunter on the shoulder. "You can even sit in the same seat Tyler used for his trips."

Hunter was too stunned to speak, standing in silence and staring at the time machine with a magnificent smile on his face.

McLean winked at Brian and headed for the door.

"I'll be back later, Bri," he said. "See you then, Scott." As he stepped out of the garage, Scott Hunter was still frozen to the same spot, unable to fully comprehend what had just transpired.

* * *

McLean spent the rest of the morning with Missy. They mowed the lawns together and went out for lunch. When Patty got home from work, she and Scott made love and showered together afterward. They dressed, went down to the kitchen, and sat at the table drinking colas.

"You be extremely careful, babe," Patty told him. "We want you back in one piece."

Holding her hand in his, he replied, "I'll be okay. You'll have me back at about six o'clock tomorrow."

"I'll be lonely."

"Me too."

"Time should go pretty fast here, though. Casey will be in school and I'll take Missy with me to the big store. Mrs. Jelesnik and I are going over the month's books and it'll probably take all morning. So we should be all done with everything by the time you get back. Will you miss me?"

"I just told you that about two seconds ago."

"I know," she said lovingly. "I just wanted to hear it again."

Scott smiled and kissed her on the cheek. Whispering in her ear, he said, "I missed you when I didn't see you all day today. I'll be thinking about you the whole time I'm gone, and missing you every minute, in fact, I'll be a basket case until I see you again." He sat up straight on the chair and looked her squarely in the eye. "How was that?"

She scrunched up her nose and closed one eye. "Aw, you poured it on a little thick, but I still loved it."

The kids ran into the kitchen right between Scott and Patty and they gave both kids a group hug, squeezing real tight.

"A Missy and Casey sabwish," Missy said before she started giggling.

"That's right, sweetheart," Patty told her. "Give Daddy a hug and kiss, he has to go now." The kids hugged and kissed their dad.

Trying to squeeze the life out of him, Missy said, "I luzyou, Daddy."

"I love you too, babe." He paused and said, "You too, Case."

"I know that, Dad," Casey said.

Scott stood, said goodbye to them all and went out the back door on his way to Chicago, via Brian's garage shop. Brian and Scott Hunter were in the shop waiting for him to arrive.

"'Bout time, Scotty," Brian said as he stepped through the door. "It's almost five-thirty."

"Let's do it." Scott looked at Hunter. "You ready?"

"Whenever you are," Hunter answered nervously.

Scott McLean was wearing an old pair of brown Dockers pants, a faded blue, long-sleeved muslin shirt, and his ancient pair of brown, lace-up work boots. Scott Hunter wore the same expensive outfit he had on the day before, minus the coat and tie.

"Is that what you'd call period dress?" Brian asked.

McLean held his arms straight out from his sides and pirouetted in a circle. "Yes, how do you like it?"

"It's perfectly dreadful," Brian said. "Is that really how they dressed back then?"

"Yeah." Scott grabbed his belt and pulled the pants up slightly. "The pants they wore looked a lot like these."

He looked at Hunter, studying his clothes. "I think we may have to come up with something different for Scott here."

Hunter looked down at his clothes. "These probably are a bit much for that time."

"You could say that," McLean said.

"He just did," Brian replied.

"Oh yeah, I forgot."

Hunter shook his head and laughed. "You guys are really a pair to draw to."

Brian took some clothing down from the row of coat hooks to show Hunter. "How about these clothes, Scott? Do you think they'll fit?"

Hunter took the white, bloused sleeve shirt and black wool pants and held them up to himself. "If it's the dreadful look we're after, these certainly fill the bill. But they do look to be about the right size."

"Those look like something they'd be wearing in 1871," McLean said, taking a closer, second look at the clothing. His face suddenly lit up with recognition. "Where'd you get that stuff, Bri?"

Brian held up a halting hand to McLean. "You look like you're built about like your grandfather was, Scott."

"I've got almost the same build as he had, except I've put on a few extra pounds around the middle." He patted his not-so-big belly. "Why do you ask about my grandpa's physique, Brian?"

Brian smiled and winked in McLean's direction. "Because those are the clothes Tyler was wearing when he came to visit us. Do you think you can get them on?"

Once again, Hunter was struck with a nostalgic thought: the opportunity to wear the very clothes his grandfather wore only days before.

"Oh, I'll get into them, even if it means emergency liposuction surgery. This is such a thrill!"

"I think we even have his shoes somewhere here," Brian added, rummaging around in the pile of shoes by the door. "Here they are."

Brian carried the black leather shoes over to Hunter and laid them down beside his feet. "Looks like they may fit."

He gazed at Brian. "Thank you. Thank you very much."

"That's really cool," McLean said. "You're gonna look spiffy."

Hunter looked at McLean. "I think so. I honestly think I will." He picked up the shoes, tucked the clothes under his arm, then started in through the kitchen door. "I can't wait to get changed into these clothes," he added as the door closed behind him.

He stepped into the kitchen, leaving Scott and Brian to stand in the garage staring at the closing door, with slight, approving smiles. They wandered over to the computer and started figuring the coordinates for the landing zone.

Brian pointed to the picture on the computer screen. "Show me on the computer where you want to go. This is a magnified map of the southwest area of Chicago in 1871. You see all your favorite historical streets there. Jackson, DeKoven, all the way to Canal Street. Pick a spot and we'll make the travel arrangements."

Scott touched a place on the monitor screen. He pointed out a spot near Taylor and Ann Streets in the middle of a block, without the slightest idea of what he might find there. "How about right there?"

Brian zoomed in on the map and brought the blocks around the area to their largest possible size. Touching a key on the keyboard, dozens of lat and long coordinates appeared on the screen. He highlighted the appropriate numbers, and when he cleared the screen, they were automatically re-entered on the next one.

"What time do you want to arrive?"

"The fire started between eight-thirty and nine at night on Sunday, October 8, 1871, so six o'clock would be great."

Scott paid close attention to what Brian was doing. He thought, *It wouldn't hurt to learn how to fly this thing, just in case. If anything ever happens to force me into operating it, a lack of knowledge could be big trouble.*

"All done, my friend. All we need is Scott Hunter and we'll send you two on your way."

Just then, Hunter exited the kitchen and stepped down into the shop. "Did I hear someone say my name?"

"Right on," Brian said. "We're all set to—" Brian saw Hunter dressed in Tyler's clothes and did a double take.

McLean looked at the grandson and couldn't believe his eyes. Scott was older, granted, but he bore a striking resemblance to Tyler Hunter.

"Wow!" Scott said, nudging Brian with his elbow. "Will you look at that?"

"Already am." He motioned to Hunter. "Wasn't this same guy standing on that very spot a couple of weeks back?"

McLean stood motionless except for the dilatory back and forth movement of his head. "You'll get no argument from me, Bri. That's pretty amazing stuff."

Hunter looked himself over, seeing his body clad in an outfit consisting of some pretty rugged looking clothes. The clothing wasn't old or worn out, after all it was the garb of a respected orthopaedic surgeon. It was simply ninety-six years out of fashion, along with having been on Tyler Hunter's body while he lived through an earthquake and traveled through the worst fire in America's history.

The white shirt had a few small tears in it, the pants the same, and the whole ensemble couldn't have been dirtier. Or smellier. The black leather shoes, fashionable in their day, were scuffed up and terribly dirty, and they also appeared to be unbelievably uncomfortable.

Finishing his self survey, Hunter glanced back at McLean. "Do I look real spiffy?"

"That outfit is *you*." Detecting an unexpected feeling of respect, McLean was unable to tell if it was for Scott or Tyler Hunter. "But it's also *Tyler*."

"I consider that a compliment."

Brian shook his head. "You know the old adage, 'the clothes make the man.' In this case it looks like the clothes make one man. Those clothes turned you into your grandpa."

"Thank you so much," Hunter said, swinging his leg over the seat of Brian's mountain bike. He sat straddling the bike and holding onto the grips. "I'm feeling a pride I've not felt since I was a child when I spent time with my grandfather. My father was busy building a career when I was very young, but Grandpa had the time to give me. So you see, he and I were quite close." Hunter paused again to collect his thoughts, pushing off of the grips and standing over the bike with his arms folded across his chest. He cocked his head and squinted his eyes. "Did I tell you about our secret, my grandpa's and mine?"

Both Brian and Scott shook their heads and sat on the time machine's platform.

"Grandpa never did share the time machine secret with anyone but me. Not another living soul. He didn't think my father could handle it because he was so much more serious about life than grandpa or me. Not that Dad was less honest or compassionate; he was a good man. Grandpa chose to share it with me because we were so much alike. We were like kindred spirits, I suppose. Grandpa knew I would believe him and help him to carry out his many goals. And out of love and respect for him, I have enthusiastically done just that. My father often wondered why Grandpa did some of the things he did, such as the scholarships and the supplies to the fire departments. But he never wavered in his duty to carry out those wishes. His love, respect and loyalty were unshakable."

Scott and Brian sat very still and attentive, hanging on Hunter's every word.

"What I'm getting at is that no matter what it looks like, just wearing this clothing gives me that same childhood feeling of pride. He never treated me like I was just a child, except when he knew it was what I wanted or needed at the time. He always listened to my grade school problems and treated them, and me, with respect. We'd talk them out and he'd help me to solve them. I was treated like an intelligent human being by Tyler Hunter."

He stopped talking and gazed wistfully at the ship.

"I hope you take the clothes with you, Scott," Brian said warmly. "I'm sure you'd get much more from them than we would."

"Do you mean that?"

"Of course, Scott," McLean said. "Besides, they're rightfully yours since you're his heir."

"Thank you," Hunter said softly. He stepped off the bike, leaned it back against the wall, and started toward the ship. "Are we ready to leave?"

Scott and Brian stood back up and Brian moved over to the computer. McLean turned to face the ship, stepped up onto the platform and extended his hand to Scott Hunter.

"Let me give you a hand up."

Hunter grabbed his hand and stepped on the platform, then leaned over the top and looked through the hatch at the cockpit.

"You having any second thoughts?" McLean said.

"Nope. If anything, I'm more excited than ever. I'm ready."

"Me too. Let's do it."

McLean helped Hunter in through the hatch so the visitor could settle into his seat in the cockpit. McLean climbed in and stood up through the opening, facing Brian.

Without turning around, Brian said, "Any more questions, Scotty?"

"I'm cool. We'll be there for seven minutes while we scope out the area for the best spot. If we're not back inside the ship within the seven minutes, we miss the bus. Right?"

"Exactly. So anytime you're ready."

McLean sat down in his seat, pulled the hatch closed above him, and secured the latch. Seated directly across from him, Hunter stared him squarely in the eyes.

"Here we go," McLean said. "I think you're really gonna like this."

Hunter's mouth formed a smile as he heard the hissing of the pneumatics.

Within seconds, the system worked through the stages and created its brilliant flash of light as it leapt into the space-time continuum.

They were on their way to Chicago, circa 1871.

Chapter Fifteen

It was very warm and breezy at nearly five-thirty on Sunday afternoon, October 8, 1871. In his late 20's, Walter Appleton was reading a book out on the front porch when the baby began to cry. He glanced at his 22-year-old wife. With pale skin and reddish hair, Helen was still napping on an overstuffed glider. Setting his book down and rising from the chair, he went into the house and got 7-month-old Zachariah from his crib, then returned to the porch. As soon as he picked him up, the baby stopped crying, so Walter sat in the high-backed, wooden rocking chair and rocked his first born son in the warm afternoon breeze.

Walter was careful to not wake Helen, for she needed every snatch of sleep she could get. Zack had been keeping her up to all hours for several nights with a bad cold and she was worn to a frazzle. A Chicago City fireman, Walter had been kept up to all hours also, working overtime on the many fires around the city, so he hadn't been home to help Helen with the baby.

The parched conditions around Chicago, due to a very dry summer with less than five total inches of rain from July to October, had caused the first week of the month to be the driest ever, with unusually warm temperatures and daily winds. Most of the structures in the city of over 300,000 people were wood frame, from warehouses and woodworking mills, to stables filled with hay, grain and fuel for stoves and fireplaces. Large coal yards, paint and varnish factories, along with the custom of roofing with tar on tall buildings that fire hoses couldn't reach, all combined to make Chicago ripe for a devastating conflagration.

Walter had been notified to report to work on Saturday evening, his firehouse company working through the night fighting the tremendous Lull and Holmes fire. He arrived home at five in the morning and collapsed into bed from exhaustion.

Around two in the afternoon, he awoke with sore muscles, a nagging cough caused by smoke inhalation and a few small, minor burns. After bathing and eating a hearty brunch, he sat on the front porch and read part of the Tribune. Along about five o'clock, Helen laid on the glider and slipped into a much needed nap. Clad only in a white strap T-shirt and baggy red and white underwear, Walter read from a book and listened for little Zack to fuss.

It took about thirty minutes for Zack and Walter to drift off to sleep in the rocking chair. Helen was awakening, still groggy and somewhat bleary-eyed, when she saw something in the air in the middle of the front yard. Blinking her eyes, she tried to focus on the object, thinking it to be a small gray bird flitting around.

"Walter," she said. "Walter, wake up."

He opened his eyes and saw the same object begin to grow into a large gray cloud that nearly filled the small yard. As they watched in wonder, the cloud formed a small opening in one side, not unlike a doughnut hole. With a blinding flash of light, the hole grew in size to over five feet in diameter and right in the middle of their West Taylor Street lawn deposited a large, green cylindrical object.

Helen sat up on the glider and moved to the farthest corner she could push herself into, pulling her long flowered dress up under her legs as she huddled on her knees. Her brown eyes seemed to be popping right out of their sockets. Holding Zachariah, Walter pushed his back as far into the wooden chair as he could manage, then propelled the chair backward with his feet, wedging it into the corner of the porch railing. He held his son tighter and turned slightly in his seat to protect the child from any harm.

The Appleton couple heard some movement inside the object, then a scraping sound came from the top of the big green intruder. As they watched in fear, a portion of the top began to open up. A hand pushed it all the way back until it rested gently against the top of the green thing. Following the arm was the top of a head and a shoulder. Then came the complete upper torso of a handsome man in a blue shirt. The young parents sat in silence, for the appearance of the apparition was too much for them to fathom.

The man in the green machine scanned around the property until his eyes fell on Helen Appleton.

He scanned further, seeing Walter and little Zack, then looked back at Helen.

"Hi," McLean said, smiling timidly. "I'm sorry to startle you like this." He looked straight down into the cockpit at Scott Hunter and waved him up with a whisper. "You have to see this, Scott. We've landed in somebody's yard and they're sitting on the porch."

Hunter remained seated, staring at Scott as if he were on fire. "Are we really sitting in somebody's yard, or are you joking with me?"

McLean shook his head vigorously and motioned Hunter to stand up, then finally took hold of his shirt and tugged on it. Hunter slowly stood up into the hatch opening alongside McLean and gawked at the sight of the Appleton family on their porch.

McLean climbed out of the ship and jumped down from the platform to the grass. Stepping up onto the porch, he extended his hand to Walter in greeting.

"My name's Scott and we don't mean any harm. In fact, we've landed here by accident and will be gone in just a few minutes."

Walter meekly shook his hand, not uttering a sound. McLean turned and stepped over to Helen, taking her hand in greeting.

"Excuse me," he said. "I need to look around for a minute. This is my friend, Scott." He leaped off the porch and ran out across the yard, looking in every direction for a place to put the ship on his return.

There weren't many houses around to speak of, because it was mostly dry farmland. He spotted a house and barn about an eighth of a mile to the east, and another to the south, just about the same distance away. He hurried around the west side of the house to look for something in that direction and saw wide open spaces with some structures way off in the distance. Scanning to the north, he spotted a farmhouse nearly a mile in the distance to the northwest. There was a barn sitting nearby with tall dry weeds all around it. Scott squinted his eyes to focus in on it and thought it looked vacant. He studied the barn and the surrounding area to get the best bearings he could, and figured it to be just under a mile to the northwest. There were a few trees around the property with a hedgerow of bushes down both sides and across the back.

Whoa, could it really be? he thought, still studying the area around the farm. *If I can get the bearings just right, maybe Brian could put me down right in the middle of that yard. I'll have to ask these folks what they know about that place.*

Checking his watch, he saw he'd already used up two minutes and fifteen seconds. With over four minutes left before the ship would leave, he walked on around the house to see if he could find any better spots to land.

Hunter, still standing in the hatch opening, stared at the Appletons, feeling every bit as surprised as they. "That's a beautiful baby. Is it a boy?" Still sitting in stunned silence, Walter nodded. Scott was back to square one, not knowing what to say to the couple. "This undoubtedly seems strange to you, but please allow me to reassure you, we mean no harm. And we'll only be here for a few more minutes." Still fumbling for words, he added, "May I ask your names?"

Walter sat in silence, staring at the stranger, but Helen spoke up. "I am Helen Appleton and this is my husband, Walter." She paused and stammered a little. "And this is our son, Zachariah."

Hunter glanced at the baby and smiled, then said awkwardly, "You're very fortunate to have such a beautiful child." Looking closer, he noticed something didn't seem quite right with the baby. The child's color seemed to be pale and there appeared to be a slight bluish tinge around his lips. "Has your son been ill?"

Walter nodded. "He's been ill for several days, but it's the first sickness he's had since the day he was born. When he sleeps, his lungs seem to fill with liquid and he begins to choke." The young father paused and glanced worriedly at his tiny son. "We've been keeping a very close vigil on him."

"I'm sorry," Hunter said sympathetically. "I certainly hope he gets better soon."

Zachariah began to choke, so Walter stood and began patting his back. Helen jumped up and hurried over to take little Zack's arm and lift it as high above his head as possible, accomplishing nothing. The baby's larynx was completely blocked and he was starting to turn blue. Walter continued to pound on his back, but the phlegm from Zack's lungs held firm, allowing absolutely no air exchange.

"Lay him face down on your forearm and pat his back," Hunter suggested.

Walter complied by laying Zack on his forearm. With the baby's head down, he applied several back blows, to no avail, just as McLean rounded the corner of the house and stopped beside the porch.

"The baby's choking, Scott!" Hunter shouted. "His little lungs are congested and he's coughed some phlegm or something into his throat!"

McLean vaulted onto the porch. "Grab my black duffel out of the cockpit, Scott!" Hunter ducked down in the ship to find the bag as McLean reached out to the baby. "Keep holding him there," he said to Walter, placing his hands around the chest of the baby and squeezing in on the ribs. After three chest thrusts, the infant-type Heimlich Maneuver, the baby was still completely blocked, his lips and earlobes turning a grayish blue.

"I've got the bag, Scott," Hunter said, climbing out of the time machine.

"There should be a 50cc irrigation syringe and a piece of surgical tubing I took home for Casey to make a squirt gun. Get it out and attach the tubing to the syringe."

Hunter quickly removed the items from the duffel and deftly tore the Hunter Medical Supply packaging from the syringe. He attached the tubing to it and stepped over to McLean, handing him the makeshift suction unit.

As McLean turned to suction the baby, he heard a slight noise from the ship. A faint hissing sound. Glancing at his watch, he declared nervously, "It's time, Scott. Hurry, jump in and lock the hatch."

"What about you? I can't just—"

"Get in and go!" McLean yelled. "Have Brian send you back in ten minutes to get me. Go!"

Hunter stepped up on the platform, and with a grace and agility he didn't know he still possessed, hurdled into the cockpit and pulled the hatch closed only seconds before the photon race began.

"Cover your eyes," McLean told the Appletons, which they obediently did.

With a brilliant flash, the time machine vanished, leaving Scott McLean up the 1871 creek without a paddle.

He quickly turned back to Walter and took Zack from his arms, then placed the baby on the floor in front of him. He inserted the surgical tubing down into the trachea of the now unconscious infant and grabbed Helen's hand, placing it around the tubing.

"Hold this tube right where it is and do exactly what I tell you to do." Taking the irrigation syringe in his left hand, he used his right hand to slowly pull out on the plunger and extract a small bit of fluid. "Now, move the tubing further down his throat, slowly and gently."

With her hands trembling, Helen began pushing the tubing slowly down the small child's trachea as Scott pulled gently on the plunger. Feeling some resistance, he reached over and calmly took hold of Helen's hand to stop her. He pulled her hand up and they backed the tubing out slightly.

"Hold it right there."

He pulled on the plunger of the syringe again. Since the resistance still felt about the same after moving it up the trachea, Scott surmised it to be the blockage and not a part of the baby's anatomy. As he very gently continued the suction, the resistance gave way. He pulled a 10cc mass of phlegm up into the tubing, clearing the airway of the blockage.

"Okay, pull out the tube."

As Helen removed the tubing, Scott picked Zack up in his arms and began mouth-to-mouth resuscitation, checking for a pulse at the same time. He felt a pulse, a very rapid pulse.

Oh, man, we needed that, he thought as he continued breathing for the baby. After about a

FIRES OF TIME * 343

minute of rescue breathing, Zachariah began to breathe on his own, so Scott held him upright and turned him around face to face to better observe him. Zack was pinking up already and Scott breathed a little easier himself.

Zack started to cry, then quickly escalated it to a tremendous wail. McLean handed him to his mother who took him in her arms and held him close. Walter had moved from his chair and gotten to his knees on the floor by Helen and Scott.

He stared at his son. Then stared at McLean. "I don't understand."

"I'm sure you don't, uh, what was your name?"

"Walter, Walter Appleton and my wife, Helen." Touching his son on the arm, he said, "And this is Zachariah, our son."

Helen sat holding Zack as she rocked back and forth on the floor. "Thank you for helping my son. But what exactly did you do to make him breathe again?"

"Oh, we just sucked some of that nasty junk out of his throat."

"What is that piece of equipment you used? And how does it work?" Walter stopped momentarily, looking confused, then went on with his questioning. "Who are you and why are you here? And what is that green contraption?"

McLean smiled at Walter and held up his hand. "I apologize for intruding on you folks like this. We certainly didn't mean to land in your yard, or to startle you in any way. It's very difficult to explain to you, and I'm afraid we don't have much time, but the green contraption is a vehicle. A mode of travel from one point to another."

"A mode of travel from *what* point to another? Where did you come from? Is everyone there named Scott?"

"Only the men. I really wish I could tell you everything else, Walter, but I can't." Standing up with the syringe and tubing, Scott looked for the kitchen. "Do you have a container of water I could use, ma'am?"

She pointed through the living room to the kitchen. "You'll find a pitcher and wash basin in there on the sideboard. Please help yourself."

Scott went to the kitchen, found a drinking glass and filled it with water from the pitcher. Going back to the porch, he jumped down to the lawn and set the glass of water on the floor of the porch.

Turning to Helen, he explained, "This is the way to clean this suction unit."

He put the end of the tubing into the water and sucked enough water up to fill the syringe. Turning and aiming it away from the house, he depressed the plunger forcefully and squirted the entire amount into the yard, repeating the process once. He inspected it to make sure of the cleanliness, then stepped back on the porch and handed it to Helen.

"Hold onto this," he continued calmly. "You can keep him suctioned better with it and maybe avoid another crisis like this one. Do I need to explain its use to you, or did you learn enough the first time?"

Helen turned the simple, makeshift suction unit over in her hand and studied the little machine in wonderment. Looking back at McLean, she smiled warmly.

"Thank you for saving my baby. I'm very grateful to you, whoever you are. And thank you for

FIRES OF TIME * 345

this ... suction machine." She turned to Walter. "Do you think you'll be able to use it, dear?"

He nodded. "Yes, and I'll be here at home to help you instead of working like last night."

"We can only hope. As long as there are no more fires taking you away."

Scott whipped his head around and stared at Walter. "Are you a firefighter?"

"Fire ... fighter? I'm a Chicago City fireman. We've had an unusually high number of fires during the last week, so I've worked nearly every day and night. And if we have another tonight ..." Walter gazed at his wife. "...I will have no choice but to respond."

Helen reached out and took his hand in hers. "I'll understand if that happens. If so, Zachariah and I will be fine, so long as you keep the fire away from our home."

Walter smiled. "It would need to be a very large fire to extend all the way out here from the city and I doubt there will ever be another fire as large as the one last night."

Scott listened to their conversation, knowing exactly how Walter would spend the next day and a half, starting in just over two hours.

Glancing at his watch, he said, "Please stay on the porch, because my friend will be here any second. He should land in the same spot, so we need to be out of the way."

Walter helped Helen up as she held the baby. The small family sat on the glider while Scott sat down in the big wooden rocking chair.

Checking his watch again, he cautioned them. "Don't be alarmed when the vehicle arrives, and be sure to shield your eyes from the light."

Suddenly, the small gray fist of cloud appeared in the exact same place as before, first enlarging, then disgorging the time machine to rest gently on the grass of the front yard. The hatch opened and Scott Hunter stood up through the frame. The first thing he did was look at the baby to see if he was all right.

"Well, it appears the baby is doing okay, am I right?"

"Little Zack is fine," Helen said softly. "Thank you so much."

McLean stood and walked to the ship, putting one foot on the platform. "When do we return, Scott?"

"Right away, I'm afraid. Brian was a bit anxious about the situation."

McLean laughed. "Okay, we'd better get back." He turned to the Appletons and pointed to the northwest. "Is there a family living in the house about a mile in that direction?"

"The McLeans?" Shaking his head, Walter continued, "No, they moved nearly a year ago when John finished building the house over on Jackson. The people who bought the farmhouse haven't yet arrived from England to take possession. I'm afraid it's still vacant."

"The McLeans?" Scott repeated reverently. "John Patrick McLean?"

"Yes. Do you know him?"

"Yes, Walter. I mean no ... I mean ... kind of."

He was overwhelmed by the curious news until he remembered something in Packy's journal. Packy wrote about the fire when he was seven, but he started the journal when he was six years old.

He thought, *the name and address in the front of the journal. It wasn't Jackson Street. It was*

Harrison Street, so they must have moved shortly after he got the journal. I've never heard anyone mention anything about a move to Jackson. Scott shrugged his shoulders and thought, *I guess they had to move there sometime, so why not the year before? It's not so strange, Scotty. Yes it is, Scotty. Maybe not the move, but the coincidence of picking that very house to land the ship. That's pretty weird.*

"Scott, are you all right?" Hunter's voice jolted McLean out of his world of thoughts.

"Huh? Oh, yeah, I'm fine."

"You need to get in here. We leave in less than a minute."

McLean stepped the rest of the way onto the platform and climbed down into the cockpit. Standing up in the hatch, he faced the Appletons.

"I know you're still confused and I'm sorry for that."

"It doesn't matter who you are or where you came from," Helen said. "I know why you were here and I'm grateful to you. Thank you for the life of my son."

McLean waved and started closing the hatch, then stopped and stood back up. "One more thing. Get a couple more hours of sleep, Walter. You're going to need it."

Walter's eyes grew in size. "Why?"

"Tonight ... the conflagration ... this house will be safe. Jeez! Trust me. Just trust me."

"C—Conflagration?"

Scott nodded slowly. "Oh, Walter, what fire company are you in?"

"The Little Giant. Why do you ask?"

McLean's eyes widened. "Really? The Little Giant?"

"Yes. The Little Giant, why?"

"Wow, I'm impressed!" Scott said.

He pulled the hatch shut for the last time just when the hissing pneumatics started. Following the rest of the start-up process, the hunter green time machine vanished in a brilliant photon flash.

Helen and Walter sat and stared at the empty spot where the ship had been sitting. "I wonder why he wanted to know about my fire company?" Walter asked rhetorically.

Helen looked at her husband and smiled a knowing smile. "Probably so he can watch over you tonight."

"What?"

"Watch over you, my dear."

"What do you mean?"

"You should have figured it out for yourself. They appeared in our yard at just the right time to save the life of our beautiful son. They gave us a marvelous tool to keep it from happening again."

Walter moved on the glider to face his wife.

She continued. "They were familiar with that sweet McLean family, and he warned you of a conflagration that would require you to be well rested. Isn't a conflagration a very large fire?"

Walter nodded and Helen gazed into his eyes.

"Walter. Dear. Think about it. He even assured us that our home will be safe from the fire, so doesn't it seem sensible that those Scotts will be with you tonight to watch over and protect you?"

"But who is he to assure us of anything? It all sounds unbelievable to me."

"As unbelievable as that green carriage they were riding in?"

The young couple sat back on the glider, holding onto each other and their son Zachariah, contemplating the unknown meaning of their visitors.

* * *

Brian was sitting on the workbench beside the computer terminal when Scott pushed open the hatch to exit the ship. After both Scotts had climbed down into the garage, Brian grinned broadly and said, "It's good to see that some things never change, huh Scotty?"

"Whadda ya mean?" McLean said innocently.

Brian laughed out loud and continued. "You were only there for seven minutes. Seven minutes! And you managed to squeeze in the time to change the course of history."

"Not necessarily."

"Would that child have lived if you hadn't been there?"

"Jeez, I don't know," he answered, stepping over to the workbench computer. "He may have."

Brian looked at Scott Hunter. "What do you think? Would that baby have lived through the night?"

Hunter's eyes darted to McLean, then back at Brian. "I don't think he would have lived another five minutes. Scott's probably being a little too modest." He glanced back at McLean, who was busy writing down some information on Brian's notepad.

McLean stopped writing to look around at Brian and Hunter. "Okay, he would have died. Probably in less than five minutes, but I just happened to be there. There was a reason for that, you know. I didn't put us there at just the right time and neither did you, Brian. It was timed too perfectly to be called a mere coincidence, so we can't very well take credit for anything that happened. Call it fate or destiny or kismet, it doesn't matter. I think I was simply the tool performing the work for those forces, whatever those forces represent."

"And fate, destiny, and kismet knew they could count on you to get the job done," Brian said.

Hunter got himself a beer from the small fridge. "Do you mind?"

Brian shook his head.

McLean grunted. "Is that bad? Do you think I'd be better off to turn away and let life run its course?"

"Oh, no. It's not bad, it's just you. Vintage Scott McLean."

McLean had a sudden recollection as his eyes lit up with new excitement. "You aren't gonna believe this!" he said, handing Brian a slip of paper. "I've written down the directions here for the next landing zone, and wait until I tell you about it. I scoped out a good looking place to put the ship in Chicago and was trying to get some information about it from the Appleton couple. Walter Appleton informed me that the farmhouse had been empty for about a year while waiting for the new owners to arrive from England. The old owners, who built a new house over on Jackson Street were ... are you ready for this?"

Brian nodded, then took a deep breath and motioned for him to finish his story.

"The old owners were Mr. and Mrs. John Patrick McLean!"

Brian's jaw dropped.

"I didn't even know about any farmhouse, but I remembered there being an address in the front of Packy's journal. His name and address are inside the front cover, only the address was on West Harrison Street. They must have moved shortly after he started the journal. Can you believe it?"

Brian was still thinking about the irony of Scott blindly picking a landing zone in a completely unknown area of Chicago and ending up with a visit to grandma's house. He was having a tough time believing it. A tough time believing how any one person could possibly have as much perpetual dumb luck as Scott McLean.

"Oh yeah!" Scott said excitedly, interrupting Brian's thoughts. "There's one other thing." Brian leaned forward on the workbench with his hands gripped tightly to the edge. "The father of the baby, Walter Appleton? He's a Chicago City firefighter and he's part of the Little Giant steamer crew. Is that a trip, or what?"

Brian smiled a weak smile and slowly shook his head.

"The Little Giant, Brian! It was the first steamer engine on the scene of the fire. The crew didn't even wait for an alarm to sound, because the stoker, a man named Joseph Lagger, saw the flames from the lookout tower of their firehouse. One unit, the America hose cart, arrived there just ahead of them, but hose carts could only throw as much water as there was hydrant pressure. They carried a lot of hose, but had no pumps like the steamers."

"Hold it!" Brian said. "I realize you know a lot about the fires of the past. But you remember the names of the individual firemen on one of the steamers?"

McLean jumped up, sat on the workbench and gave Brian a disgusted look. He glanced over at Scott Hunter, who was sitting on the old kitchen chair nursing his beer. Quickly raising his eyebrows and throwing Hunter an 'I'm gonna mess with his head look,' he turned back to Brian.

"Not all of their names."

"How many men were on the Little Giant crew that night?"

Scott shrugged his shoulders. "I'm not sure."

"Really? You really don't know?"

"Nope. But I do know they were two men short when they left the station, because a pipeman named Frank Howard had been off sick for about a month. Another man, Michael Dolan, was home eating supper, but he ran after the steamer and caught up a few minutes later. So they probably started out with eight men and ended up with nine by the time they reached the fire. Maybe more, if Walter and others managed to show up."

Brian was shaking his head again. "I thought you said you didn't know how many."

"I have an idea, but I'm not altogether positive." He glanced back at Hunter, who smiled in return.

A bit exasperated, Brian hopped down from the workbench and faced McLean. He lifted his hands up in front of himself. "Let me get this straight. Frank was eating dinner and Dolan had been off sick for a month? If a guy was sick, they just did without him for a month?" Scott shrugged as Brian continued. "And Lagger was in charge?"

"No, no Bri," McLean said, smiling at the egghead's confusion. "William Musham was the foreman and Joseph Lagger was the stoker who spotted the flames from the tower. Dolan was home eating supper and Frank Howard was off sick."

"Oh, so Dolan wasn't sick after all, huh?"

"Not that night," Scott quickly answered.

Hunter was enthralled as he listened to them banter back and forth.

Timidly, Brian asked, "Not that night?"

"Nope, not that night," McLean smiled. "He got sick and went home at about noon the next day."

Brian gazed suspiciously at his best friend. "Serious?"

"Yep." Hunter was laughing out loud at them as Scott talked on, "Anything else you wanna know? Like who's on first?"

Brian stared silently at McLean for a several seconds. "No, thank you. And I don't care what's on second." After a short pause, he added, "Or third."

"I don't know about third," Scott said.

Hunter sat drinking his beer, looking back and forth between the two of them with an amused grin on his face.

Brian turned and stepped back over to the computer module. "Okay, enough of that. Shall we get going on this other stuff? You know, the trip back to Chicago?" Under his breath he whispered, "Not that a know-it-all like you needs any more information about the Great One."

Scott understood what he said and responded. "I heard that."

"No you didn't."

"Did so."

Brian glanced at Scott Hunter. "I should know better than to try to have an intelligent conversation with him. You just can't communicate with a creature like that."

Acting insulted, McLean said, "I do can communicate more goodly with talking kinds of conversations."

Brian finally joined Scott Hunter in laughter, then holding his pencil like a Groucho Marx cigar, he said, "Now, that's the most *intelligent* thing you've said all day." He turned back to the computer, looking at the notes McLean had written. "You're sure this will be close enough to the farmhouse for you?"

McLean hopped down and looked over Brian's shoulder. "I think so. It looked like it was close to a mile away. Not quite a mile, but pretty close. More north northwest than anything else."

Brian worked his magic on the keyboard, then cocked his head. "I believe you're set on the location. What about the times?"

Scott leaned over and placed his left elbow on the workbench, then rested his chin in his cupped left hand. "Hmm, let me think about it a bit." He turned his left cheek into his hand and looked up at Brian while he thought it out.

Brian could see the wheels turning in McLean's head while he sifted through all of his knowledge about the Chicago fire.

Finally, his eyes lit up and he stood back beside Brian where he could see the computer monitor. "I thought it over last night, but I want to be absolutely sure. The fire was still burning when it started to rain at about eleven o'clock on Monday night, but I don't need to stay that long. There are a few things I don't want to miss, though. I should be finished by about three-thirty on Monday afternoon."

Hunter stepped up behind them to see the computer monitor, and McLean asked, "Do you want to go back again, Scott?"

"No, thanks," Hunter said as he slowly lifted his hands up, palms open, in front of his body, and took a couple of steps backward. Then, stopping and lowering his hands, Hunter carefully put his thoughts into words. "Don't get me wrong. I'm tickled pink about having been allowed to accompany you on that short trip in time. It was such a thrill, but I'm afraid I don't share your affinity for large fires, Scott. Or my grandfather's, for that matter. But I do appreciate the offer."

"All right, Scotty," Brian said. "You can be done by about three-thirty, so is that when you want to come back?"

He put his hands up on the keyboard and started to type in the times, but McLean reached over and stopped him.

"If all goes well, I'll be clear over on the other side of Chicago at three-thirty with about three or four miles to cover in that mess of rubble and people. I could even end up having to swim across the Chicago river, so why don't you give me until about six. Does that sound okay?"

"Six o'clock it is. That'll be twenty-four hours, then. Are you sure that's enough time?"

"I should be fine with that."

"Just give me a few minutes to check out the ship and we'll be ready to go," Brian said as he went to the ship and crawled under the platform to change the air tank and battery. He called to McLean from beneath the machine. "Swim the Chicago River? Are you nuts? You don't have to answer that,

Scotty," Brian said quickly. "It was a rhetorical question."

McLean turned to Hunter. "Are you staying until I get back tomorrow?"

"No, I'll be leaving tonight. Just as soon as my pilot, Sonny, calls back from the airport."

"Your pilot?"

Hunter smiled. "Yes, as owner and president of the Hunter Medical Supply Corporation I have access to a corporate jet."

"I guess I just hadn't thought about it. Are we going to be seeing more of you?"

Hunter smiled again. "I'm hoping I can be a part of your lives from now on. It's been my wish since the minute my grandfather asked me to come here." He dropped his head bashfully and shuffled his feet, then raised his head back up and said, "If you wouldn't mind, that is. After all, I'm only a visitor here."

McLean smiled at the grandson of his friend, Tyler Hunter. "I can't think of a nicer person to have as a friend. I hope this will be a friendship to last our whole lives. My kids really love you, but I guess you already sensed that."

Hunter stared at McLean. "I was married for nearly thirty-five years before my sweet wife died. We were never able to have children, so I could sorely use a couple of surrogate grandchildren to dote on and spoil a bit. Do you think Missy and Casey are up to the job?"

McLean nodded.

After discussing the need to get together to set up the trust funds, Scott Hunter and Scott McLean said their goodbyes. Brian finished his pre-flight check of the ship and McLean climbed into the cockpit, standing in the hatchway before sitting down inside.

"We're all set, Scotty. Are you good to go?"

Before settling down inside the cockpit, he gave his two friends a thumbs-up, followed by a salute. Grinning sheepishly, he explained. "What can I say, I saw it in a movie." He sat down on the seat in the cockpit and closed the hatch.

Moments later, Brian and Hunter watched the time machine vanish.

Chapter Sixteen

Scott turned the latching mechanism, pushed open the hatch and stood up in the opening. As he surveyed his new surroundings through the dim light, the smells of a musty old barn filled his nostrils. Piercing shafts of sunlight, filtering through narrow slits in the barn's roof and walls, knifed down through the clouds of dust created by the arrival of the ship. The air in the barn was stiflingly hot and the absolute quiet, nearly deafening.

Opening the hatch, he stood and surveyed his new environs, noticing one of the barn doors was slightly ajar. *Looks like I can squeeze through there,* he thought. He threw the strap of his black duffel over his shoulder and climbed out of the ship. As he slipped between the two doors, he checked out the ship's landing zone.

"Way to go, Brian. You've done it again," he said to himself.

Brian had placed the time machine right in the middle of the abandoned barn formerly owned by the McLean family.

Scott stepped out into the bright sunlight of Chicago, Illinois, 1871. Surveying the barnyard, he saw two smaller outbuildings and a tall hedgerow of bushes. The shrubbery ran across the back of the lot and along both sides to a spot even with the back of a two story, wood-frame house. Beginning at each end of the hedgerow, a weather beaten picket fence ran down both sides of the house toward the front yard. The house was sided with white wooden panels, sorely in need of paint. A large porch ran across the length of the house on the back, with three wide wooden stairs leading up to it. The windows were all intact and the two doors on the back appeared to be in good shape and sturdy.

Probably locked, he thought.

He climbed the three steps to the porch and approached the first door. When he took hold of the doorknob, to his surprise and delight, it turned easily. The door swung open and revealed a large, airy kitchen. He stepped inside and stood in the middle of the floor.

To himself, he mumbled, "So, this is the same house Packy lived in when he started his journal."

He walked through the house, trying to find some remnant of the McLean family, quickly realizing that the entire house had been thoroughly spit-shined. There wasn't a trace of the former owners to be seen.

Standing back in the kitchen, he stared out the window lost in thought. *This place really doesn't do a thing for me, but why should it? I never heard of it until a little while ago, so it hasn't been a part of my life. So much for getting an extra little thrill out of this. I'd better get moving so I can see all the other stuff.*

"Oh, well," he said aloud. "What did I expect, anyway?"

With no more hesitation, he walked out the back door and around to the front of the house. Crossing the dried out, weedy front lawn, he exited the property through a three foot high gate in the weather-beaten picket fence and stepped out onto the side of Harrison Street.

Standing in the late afternoon sun he looked up and down the street and saw a one-horse buggy disappearing in the distance to the west. He turned to the east and saw virtually no activity, save for the dust being kicked up by the steadily increasing breeze blowing out of the southwest.

"Well Scotty," he said to himself, "San Francisco was pretty cool, but this could turn out to be the greatest adventure of your life."

* * *

It was just after eight in the morning when Patty loaded her bookkeeping paperwork in the Caravan. Melissa ran out and climbed into the side door, then on up into her car seat.

"Les' go to work, Mommy," she said determinedly as Patty leaned in through the door and hooked up the harness on the car seat.

"Okay, honey. Are you going to help me today?"

"Yes, Mommy. I'm going to help you work."

"Good. You're such a good helper," Patty said as she backed the car out of the driveway.

It took only a few blocks for Missy to think it over. "Mommy?"

"What is it, sweetheart," Patty said, looking in the rearview mirror at Missy.

"Can I watch my movies, cause I like to help you work, but I like to watch movies, too."

Patty couldn't help smiling at her cute little daughter. "Sure, honey. Sometimes it helps mommy get her work done when you watch your videos."

"Thank you, Mommy. I luzyou, Mommy."

"I love you too, baby," Patty smiled as she pulled the van in beside the cleaners and parked. "Here we are, honey."

Patty turned off the ignition, then reached back and undid Missy's car seat harness. When they walked into the building, Mrs. Jelesnik was already there, having opened the business at seven o'clock.

"Hi, Mrs. Deewezik!" Missy yelled as she ran to the elderly store manager.

"Missy. How's my favorite little girl in the whole world?" She picked Missy up and received a wonderful 3-year-old hug. "Are you going to play here with me today?"

"Uh-huh. I'm gonna watch Pooh Bear, cause it helps Mommy and I'm a good helper."

"Oh good, dear," she said as she put the child down. "I'm glad you're here."

"Good morning, Mrs. Jelesnik," Patty said, setting her armload of paper down on the counter. "I brought some new receipt books and the paychecks."

"Hi, Patty," she answered, watching Missy run off to her playroom. "That's great. We were almost completely out of receipts. Are you staying for a while?"

Patty went back and checked on Missy, who was plugging a video into the VCR. When she returned she replied, "I wanted to go over last months paperwork, so I'll be here for a couple of hours, I guess."

"I'm so glad." She smiled her grandmotherly smile. "I just love to watch that little girl play. She is the sweetest little thing I ever saw."

Patty smiled at her and glanced in at Missy. Looking back at Mrs. Jelesnik, she said proudly, "I think so, too."

A customer walked through the door and the manager went to help her, so Patty started taking items from a filing cabinet. Meanwhile, Missy was sitting on her little chair in front of her TV, fully engrossed in watching Tigger bounce around on his tail and sing his song about the wonderful thing about Tiggers.

Patty sat down at the desk against the wall behind the main counter and opened another file drawer, taking out the receipts for the previous month. She turned on the computer and went to work.

Just before nine o'clock, Mrs. Jelesnik called to Patty and asked if she could help with something in the front of the store. On her way to the front, Patty peeked in on Missy who was sitting in her little recliner holding her Pooh Bear and watching her Beauty and the Beast video. Patty smiled and walked up to where Mrs. Jelesnik was fussing with a necktie display rack.

"How can I help?"

"Oh good, you're here," the elderly woman said. "I've put together this new tuxedo display in the window and I need your opinion on it. Would you mind looking at it and giving me some ideas?"

"No problem. I'll go outside and see how it looks from the sidewalk," she said and started for the door.

"Thank you. Oh, while you do that I'll run back and find the missing piece for this tie rack. It might be on the shelf in the boiler room."

Patty nodded as she exited through the front door and stood on the sidewalk facing the big display window, while Mrs. Jelesnik walked back to the boiler room to find her missing piece of equipment. She noticed Missy watching *Bawooty an Beas'*, so she stopped and stood behind the small child-size recliner to look at the video. She raised her tiger-striped glasses to her face with the rhinestone chain hanging in a loop around her neck. As she watched, Belle refused to accept the Beast's invitation for dinner after he tossed her into a castle room.

Patty was standing on the sidewalk in front of the cleaners admiring Mrs. Jelesnik's new tuxedo display when a customer pulled his vehicle to the curb. He gave a short toot on his horn as he parked, and she waved to him. As he got out of his four-wheel-drive, Patty noticed something lying on the sidewalk. She squatted down to pick up the piece of litter and heard the customer drop his keys on the roadway. The sound caused her to glance under his parked Bronco just in time to see his hand reach down to pick up the keys.

* * *

Scott walked for about twenty minutes, ranging nearly a quarter mile, before arriving at the intersection of Harrison and Halsted. Upon turning south, he noticed a street intersecting Halsted on an angle from the southwest. He knew the street had to be Blue Island Avenue, since it was less than a block south of Harrison.

He began to question why he felt so much more wonderment about seeing familiar landmarks in Chicago than he had the ones in San Francisco. After all, they were his two favorite fires of all time.

Must have something to do with how busy I was in San Francisco, he thought. *I didn't really take much time to stop and smell the roses when I was there.*

He stopped in his tracks and gazed out Blue Island Avenue. *Take your time, Scotty. You've got twenty-four hours to watch some of the coolest stuff in our country's history. Just mind your own business and don't miss a thing.* Traveling south on Halsted, he shook his head and berated himself.

"That'll be the day," he said aloud.

He traveled about six or eight more blocks until he saw the street sign: De Koven Street. He stepped up in front of the sign and stopped to look closely at it. Reaching out to touch it, Scott ran his fingers over the surface and marveled at the thought of actually being on that very street.

He stepped into the intersection and stared east down De Koven Street, well aware of the great significance and feeling the sweet anticipation. As he continued east on De Koven, his eyes never stopped moving as they tried to absorb every detail, and imprint in his mind the image of every house, every barn, every single thing he was seeing on that famous street.

"Unbelievable," he said out loud, shaking his head.

The breeze didn't increase much during his walk and the air was still very warm. People were walking in the streets, driving wagons and buggies, standing on the raised wooden sidewalks chatting with neighbors, and sitting on their porches. It was a balmy Sunday afternoon in the western district of Chicago.

As he approached Jefferson Street, his heart began to pound faster. He crossed Jefferson and started into the next block, his heart racing as he got closer to his first destination. He felt as if his breath was being taken away, and lightheaded, like he might pass out. With his nervousness and excitement at its peak, he stopped and sat on the edge of the wooden sidewalk and stared intently across the street.

Catherine O'Leary's house, he thought. *It looks just like in all the pictures. The fence, the gate, the sidewalk, the cottage. I feel like I've been here a hundred times before.*

Patrick McLaughlin, who worked for one of the railroads, lived in the house in the front. He rented from the landlord, who lived in the abutting cottage directly behind him. Although there were no numbers on the front, Scott knew the address was the same for both the house and cottage.

"137 De Koven street," he said under his breath. "Bless you, Brian, for being such a genius."

The landlord, Patrick O'Leary, was a laborer who paid five hundred dollars for the property only seven years earlier. His wife Catherine ran a milk route in the neighborhood and kept five cows and a calf in the cow barn. The barn sat at the back end of the lot, right next to the alley running through the middle of the block. Taking one last look at the front of the property, he got up and walked down around the corner and up to the alley entrance. Two boys ran past him rolling a metal hoop with a stick. Scott moved out of the way as they went by.

Man, now this is more like returning to my childhood home ... except I've never been here before, he thought. *I guess I just spent a lot of time here in my imagination.*

Partway through the block, he approached the barn where Catherine kept her cows. He walked all the way around it, his eyes scanning and his mind documenting every detail of the small structure. Moving around to the open door on the side of the barn, Scott stood motionless, peering in through the doorway.

"There you are," he said to the cows inside. "Which one of you is going to kick over the lantern?" He leaned closer to the door and whispered to the cows. "Remember, just keep your mouths shut and they'll never be able to prove a thing." One of the cows looked him in the eye and mooed.

Laughing to himself, he stepped back from the barn so he could take in the whole scene and scoped out the entire O'Leary lot. When he had the overall view in his eyesight, he scanned around in wonder and thought, *Whoa. How am I gonna be able to handle this? It's so unreal, so overwhelming. So impossible. I know I can't possibly be seeing this. But I am. I'm standing here talking to Mrs. O'Leary's cows. In Mrs. O'Leary's cow shed. In Mrs. O'Leary's yard. On October eighth, eighteen-seventy-one.*

He shook his head in disbelief and smiled. Not just a smile, but a broad grin. As he stood there in the true fantasyland of his past, he was reminded of his childhood; flashes of himself, sitting beside his dad on the flowery living room sofa in Wisconsin. The velour sofa was green and gold ... and yellow, and red, and orange, and brown — pretty much every earth color one could imagine.

Man, that really was one ugly piece of furniture, he fondly recalled.

In his mind, he could hear his dad reading to him from Packy's journal. They were talking about the stories and trying to figure out what each of the little pictures really meant. When his memories became too vivid, his eyes clouded up with tears, but the smile remained. Not only could he hear his dad's voice, but he could feel his dad's hand on his shoulder and smell his Old Spice after shave. The memory of that smell transported him back to his childhood. The memories so real ... so vivid.

* * *

It was late summer, 1981. Thirteen-year-old Scott and his friend, Neal, were riding their bikes home from the swimming pool. They planned to stop at the hot dog place to get coney dogs. They always stopped at the little hot dog stand that looked like a circus train-car on their way home from swimming. It was very near the outskirts of the city, just down the street from the huge Feed Company silos. Four of the giant storage cylinders poked roughly a hundred feet into the sky, the tallest structures in that part of town.

"Come on, I'll race you to the hot dog place," Neal said as he sped up and jumped the set of railroad tracks on his bike.

"No fair, you got a head start."
"Wimp."
"Cheater."

Both boys were riding 5-speed, Schwinn Stingrays. They tore down alongside the tracks, racing for the next street. When they reached it, Neal skidded his rear tire and slid sideways to the sidewalk, making a perfect turn and taking off on the sidewalk toward the hot dog stand. Not far behind, Scott made the same maneuver, skidding onto, then across the sidewalk into the street. He over-corrected and nearly toppled over on the blacktop of the street, catching himself just in time. The young lanky Scott McLean raced after Neal, but Neal had too big a lead by then, skidding to a stop in front of the hot dog place while Scott was still half a block away.

Scott skidded to a spectacular sideways stop and jumped off his bike, leaning it against the wall of the circus car. Neal kicked down his kickstand, then let his bike fall to the other side and crash to the ground.

"Spaz," Scott said as both boys started laughing.

"I resemble that remark." Neal showed his big front teeth and looked at Scott, both boys still laughing. Scott pulled the door open and they started into the building, stopping when they heard the noise. Scott turned to look down the street.

"Fire engines!" They both ran back out to the edge of the sidewalk, watching for the engines.

"There it is!" Neal cried out, jumping and pointing toward the approaching fire apparatus.

An engine raced past with its lights flashing and siren blaring. The boys waved and the captain pulled the chain to blast the air horn for them. A ladder truck followed closely behind, trailed by a battalion chief.

"Let's go," Scott said briskly.

The boys jumped on their bikes and pedaled after the fire department vehicles as fast as they could possibly go. They could see the giant header of smoke about two blocks ahead.

Neal was breathless. "It looks like the silos are on fire, Scott."

"Far out!"

As they rode their bikes furiously toward the fire, more fire engines and trucks passed by. One of them was Engine 5.

"Hey, that's my dad's station. Hustle!" Scott shifted gears and pedaled faster, leaving Neal in his dust.

"Wait up, Scott. Hey, wait up!"

Scott just kept on going. When he got to the scene, he stopped his bike and looked for his dad. Neal pulled to a stop next to him.

"You see your dad?"

"Not yet. Keep your eyes peeled."

"Okay."

Scott spotted Engine 5 taking a plug and driving on to the fire, laying out two, two-and-a-half-inch supply lines. He jumped back on his bike and raced off to where he could get a better look, with Neal following. They stopped out on the sidewalk and stood over their bikes.

"Can't we get closer?"

"Nope."

"How come?"

"My dad told me it's okay to watch at a fire, as long as we don't get too close or in anybody's way. He said the firefighters have enough on their hands without having to take time to run a bunch of kids off. Besides, I think we have a great seat right here."

Neal looked over at the blazing silo. "Oh, wow! Wouldja look at that? It's hot clear over here, so those firemen must be scorching!"

"It's a big one, isn't it?"

Neal just nodded heartily, listening to the firefighters yelling to each other.

Captain Harry McLean stood out in front of his engine, sizing up the fire. He had on an airpack, with his facepiece hanging from the strap around his neck. He talked into his handheld radio, then yelled orders to his engine crew.

"They want us to set up a monitor to help protect the exposures of those other silos, and then drag a hand line to that window opening. There's too much fire to send any crews in, so let's hit it from the outside."

The ten-story-high silo was a quarter full of corn, dry and dusty — prime for an explosion. A product of incomplete combustion, heavy, black smoke was billowing out from around the roof and filling the sky. Smoke poured out of every opening in the building. The firefighters all knew that if the fire got enough air, it would either blow out the roof, or blow out the sides. Every firefighter dreaded fighting silo fires for just that reason. They were unpredictable, volatile, and extremely dangerous. The dust filling the empty three fourths of the silo could be highly explosive, making it a bomb that could go off at any time.

When Captain McLean and his company got near the small, square opening, he put on his facepiece. They worked their way to the window and poked the nozzle right into it, opening up with a full fog stream, hoping to cool the super-heated atmosphere. Shutting off the nozzle, Harry stuck his head as far into the opening as he could, and looked up into the huge silo. Through the thick smoke, he could barely see tiny fingers of flame jumping out into mid-air. Watching the fingers dance in the eerie, smoke-filled atmosphere was fascinating, almost hypnotic — and deadly.

Harry knew exactly what he was seeing and pulled his head back, ripping his facepiece from his face and yelling at his crew. "Get back! Go! It's gonna flash, run!"

The firefighters dropped the line and scattered, running for their lives. Harry took a couple of steps and stopped. He turned to make sure all of his men were clear, then spun around to run. The silo exploded like a bomb.

All of Harry's engine company made it to safety, except one. Captain Harry McLean was hit by the force of the explosion, slammed to the ground, and mostly covered by the debris. Only his gloved hand poked out from the pile of broken concrete and twisted rebar. He died instantly, along with seven more firefighters from other engine companies.

Scott watched the explosion knock his father across the ground and bury him with concrete. He didn't move from his position for at least two minutes, standing over his bicycle like one of the Queen's Sentries. His mouth half open to yell or scream, not a sound came out. His eyes literally squirted tears, drenching his face in salty moisture. Finally, a sound came out: a long, mournful, pained scream. A sound only a young son could make on seeing his father destroyed by the Beast that had stalked his family for eighty years.

"Daaaad!"

He stepped from his bike and ran for his father. One firefighter spotted him, recognized him, and saw where he was headed. He intercepted young Scott and grabbed for him, but Scott side-stepped and nearly got past. The man grabbed the back of the boy's shirt, holding him in place while his feet churned in the dirt. Scott spun around and leaned over, wiggling out of his shirt. He pulled his arms free and ran bare-chested toward his father.

When he reached the pile of concrete, he grabbed his dad's hand and pulled off the glove. Grabbing the hand, he tried to stand and pull his father free, using every bit of strength he had. As other firefighters arrived, they threw chunks of concrete as fast as they could, digging Harry's upper torso out in less than ten minutes.

Scott never let go of his father's hand, holding onto it tightly even after his dad was freed and loaded into the ambulance. He rode to the hospital with his father and held his hand until his mother arrived in the small, dimly lit room an hour later. She finally convinced him to let go, then took him home. But he never did let go of his dad, his friend, his hero.

Harry McLean's spirit never died in the heart of his son. Nonetheless, that was the day he began to have doubts about becoming a firefighter.

* * *

Like a dog shaking off the water from a bath, Scott shook his head vigorously to jolt himself back to reality, such as it was. As he watched the cows move slowly in the barn, he wiped the tears from his face. Then, without warning, a disturbing thought jumped into his head, bringing with it a curious realization.

I could stop this thing. I have the power to stop the Great Fire from even starting. All I'd have to do is be here at the right time and I could keep all the death and destruction from taking place.

This is pretty heavy stuff, McLean, he pondered as he moved even closer to the door and looked inside, trying to see the lantern. He couldn't see inside the dark barn well enough to tell if there was a lantern in it, and if there was one, it wasn't lit at that time. He didn't dare to go inside and look for it.

He stepped back into the alley. *I can't do anything to alter the fire,* he thought. *It's far too big a thing to change, and even if I could, Brian would probably kill me. No question about it, he'd absolutely kill me. No, the Great One was undoubtedly an action of fate, so even if I stopped it here in this barn, it would just spring up somewhere else, speaking from hard, personal experience. I would bet the conflagration was definitely important enough to fall into Brian's "shit happens" category.*

Scott turned and started back up the alley, then stopped to take one last look at the O'Leary's barn. *I'd sure like to stay and watch the start of everything, but I've got places to go and people to meet. Damn. If I stayed around to watch, I could be the only person in the world to know if the cow was really the culprit.* He turned back around and walked briskly to the end of the alley, slowing only to turn north on Jefferson Street.

As he neared the corner of Jefferson and Washington, a tall, skinny man was standing on his porch looking north in the direction of the Lull and Holmes fire of the night before. Scott could smell the smoke from the smoldering ashes, not yet dead.

"Looks like it's just about burned itself out," the man in the pinstriped suit pants and dingy white shirt said.

Scott stopped in front of the house and answered. "It looks that way. That was quite a burner."

"You a fireman?"

"Why do you ask?"

"Oh, it just sounded like the kind of jargon the firemen use. I have a friend who's a fireman is why I know."

Scott smiled. "I've been a fireman, but not here in Chicago. I guess the jargon kind of sticks with you."

"I knew it!" the man shouted triumphantly.

Scott discretely checked his watch, it showed 7:22. "Do you happen to have the proper time?"

He pulled a watch from his pocket and opened the face. "Of course I do. The time is now twenty past seven, my good man."

Close enough, Scott thought. "Thank you so much," he said as he turned and started up Jefferson. He waved at the man and shouted, "Thanks again and have a pleasant evening."

The man waved, then turned back to watch for smoke from the Saturday night fire.

That guy could use a hobby, Scott thought.

As he walked north, McLean removed his watch and put it in his pants pocket instead of back on his wrist. The closer he got to Van Buren Street, the stronger the smell of smoke became. When he reached the street, he stood at the corner looking at the remains of the four city blocks of rubble. *Whoa, that was one hell of a fire. The stories didn't do it justice at all,* he thought.

He spent nearly an hour walking around the four-block area, stopping and investigating areas of the burn. There were still several hot spots smoldering, but a hose cart was on hand to keep them from flaring up in the breeze. Over on the Jackson Street side of the fire, he managed to find the home of the commission merchant whose house burned with his elderly wife still in it. He stood and stared at the burned pile of those people's lives.

It was nearly eight-thirty when Scott stood in the doorway of the Jefferson Street firehouse admiring the steamer "Chicago." He pulled his watch out and checked it, exclaiming out loud, "Holy cow!" He stuffed the watch back into the pocket and said to himself, "I'm gonna be late."

Scott started running to the west toward the McLean house. He loped along Jackson Street at an even pace while he watched for familiar signs or landmarks. It was difficult to see in the growing darkness, even with the occasional streetlamp. Coming to an intersection, he spotted a street sign on the far northwest corner. He hurried over to it and read: Des Plaines Street.

"Okay, Scotty, you've only got a few blocks to go," he told himself. "Plenty of time."

He jogged on, stopping to search for signs at each little intersection. When he reached the next lighted street, he saw another sign on the southwest corner. *Not very uniform,* he thought as he trotted diagonally across the intersection.

Halsted Street, the sign informed him as he continued on, passing small street after small street with neither lights nor signs. It seemed he'd run about half a mile more when he reached the next lighted street, so he came to a screeching halt in front of a sign that read: Ann Street.

Whoa, how'd I get this far already? I thought there was another big one before Ann, but I guess I was wrong. He stopped at the intersection of Ann and Jefferson to check his bearings. And his watch.

Eight fifty-five, better get moving, he thought, walking briskly toward the west, fully aware that the McLean house was only two or three short blocks further. He walked on the south side of the street because he knew the house to be on the north, and he didn't really want to burst right in on the McLean family.

After traveling a couple of blocks further, he spotted a house that looked like it could be the one, so he moved very slowly toward the southeast corner and squinted his eyes to see in the darkness. The house on the northeast corner had a big porch with a glider sitting beneath one of the windows. There appeared to be two small boys sitting on the glider, and they were pushing it as hard as they could possibly push without launching the whole thing off the porch.

Is that them? Near the dark corner, he stared in wonder at the two boys, while sidling slowly toward the corner, taking very small steps. He was startled by a voice directly over his left shoulder.

"Look at that, would ya. It looks like another one."

Scott whipped his head around and saw a man standing beside him, but not soon enough to avoid stepping on the man's foot.

Looking down, then back up, Scott said, "Oops, sorry about that."

The stranger pulled his foot back unhurt. "It's all right, I walk on 'em myself. 'Cept I try to use the bottom part. Shoes seem to last longer that way."

"Good point," Scott grinned to the stranger with wide shoulders and a long nose. "Were you saying something to me before I stepped on you?"

"Yep. I said it looks like they've got another big one goin' again tonight."

Scott spun around to look off in the distance and saw an orange glow in huge clouds of billowing smoke. "It's started," he mumbled in quiet wonder.

"Huh?"

"Oh," Scott stammered. "It's nothing."

Suddenly, they heard a boy yelling, but in the darkness they couldn't see what was happening. It sounded like someone running into the street in front of the two men.

Hearing the clanging bells and horses hooves of the approaching steamer wagon, Scott said, "What's that?"

"Sounds like the clatter-wheels-a-hell," the stranger replied.

From out of nowhere, the steamer wagon careened around the corner with bells clanging and three horses stomping and snorting. The smokestack belched bright red ashes, cinders and clinkers, leaving brilliant orange streamers in the darkness.

Scott was mesmerized by the sight he'd read about in Packy's journal. "Wow, it's even more spectacular than I imagined."

FIRES OF TIME * 379

As Scott watched the approaching fire apparatus make the turn onto Jackson, the stranger suddenly reached in front of him, grazing his chin as he did so. "The boy!" the man cried out.

Scott jerked his head around and saw the right shoulder of the nearest horse almost touching Packy. With Scott standing in the way, the stranger's reach wasn't long enough to be of any use. Instinctively, Scott reached out his right hand and took a handful of the boys shirt, yanking him out of the street to safety. He held tightly onto the shirt while he watched the side of the steamer race past only a few feet from his own nose.

He looked through the darkness at his great, great grandfather's face and saw him staring intently at the hand that held onto his shirt. When the danger had passed, Scott slowly released the shirt and allowed the child to settle back down onto his feet.

He looked up at Scott and smiled with his whole face. Especially his eyes. Although he couldn't tell the color through the darkness, Scott knew those eyes were Irish and very green.

"Gee thanks, Mister," the boy said as he turned to run back across the street.

Scott watched the sight and sound of Packy McLean running out into the street and then back again to the yard. In the dim light shining from the windows of the house, he watched Packy sit on one of the front steps to force his misshapen shoe onto his foot. His brother George yelled at him the whole time and Scott laughed out loud. Packy jumped up and grabbed onto George's hand, trying to drag him in the direction of the fire. But George, being twice as big, dragged Packy up the steps and into the house.

What? Scott thought. *That isn't how the story goes. Packy's supposed to drag George to—*

The screen door suddenly flew open and Packy and George appeared in the doorway, each holding onto one of their dad's hands, dragging him out of the house. Scott laughed once again.

"You guys be careful," Maggie hollered from the doorway as the three McLean's ran from the yard and down Jackson Street.

Scott turned to the stranger. "Nice to meet you. I've got to go."

The stranger stood and stared at Scott as he walked away into the darkness of the night. In all the excitement and wonder of the moment, Scott didn't realize the significance of the act he'd performed only minutes earlier.

* * *

The laundromat was originally a separate business, attached to the cleaners by a common cinder block wall. Two openings had been made in the wall many years earlier. One was a small doorway in the rear, and the other, a ten foot breezeway in the extreme front. Large eight foot high windows ran the full length of the laundromat across the front and down the far side. Inside the very back of the building, a shop area held a large workbench sitting right against the rear wall.

The only person in the laundromat at the time was the maintenance man, Mel. In his sixties and with gnarled hands and a missing left index finger, Mel had been working in the shop since six that morning making a bracket to re-hang a change machine. He was a retired machinist who performed all the repairs on the equipment in both buildings. He was a wiz at what he did and he always wore dark green, long-sleeved coveralls, even in summer.

He muttered to himself as he carried the parts back to the grinder. "How the hell does somebody tear that machine halfway off the wall? It'll be a cold day in hell before they yank *these* brackets down. This is three-eighths-inch steel, for hell's sake."

There was no power when he turned on the grinder, so he knelt down to plug the cord into the outlet on the very back wall. He crawled under the workbench on his hands and knees, just plugging it into the outlet when the boiler in the back room of the cleaners exploded, knocking him against the back wall. He ended up under the workbench in a sitting position with his back pushed against the cool cinder block.

When the blast occurred, it followed the path of least resistance through the breezeway and small doorway, knocking out the front and side windowed walls. The common wall followed, allowing the explosive force to extend out through the rest of the laundromat. With no resistance from the outer two walls, the energy spread more out than up, but the impact did force the entire roof up a few feet. The rear wall endured the impact and remained standing to form a lean-to of sorts when the roof fell to the ground on the other three sides.

Mel received no injuries from the initial blast, but found himself hopelessly buried by the roof in a small tomb beneath the workbench.

"What the hell?" he said to himself out loud as he tried to see in the darkness.

Tiny pinholes of light filtered through the thick heap of wooden lath, plaster, chicken wire, and tarry roofing material. Putting his foot up against it, he tried to force it up, to no avail. "This is a hell of a mess!"

Patty was in a squatting position, picking up the litter from the ground, when the tremendous explosion rocked the entire neighborhood. The cleaners side of the building was blown up and out in every direction. She was hurled across the sidewalk like a rag doll, landing on her right side and scraping her leg and arm. Small pieces of glass were imbedded all over in her skin from the shattering display window.

As she lay on the sidewalk, pieces of wood, glass and concrete rained down on her, inflicting additional, albeit minor, trauma. Before the dust settled, she pushed herself up onto her hands and knees and sat back on her legs in a daze. She held up her arms and gazed stuporously at the multiple small cuts on both of them.

The haze began to lift, and when her head finally cleared, she whirled around and screamed.

"Missy!"

Vaulting to her feet, Patty started to run back inside the cleaners, but there was no door. The front of the building was bulged out to four or five feet in places from the force of the explosion. She dashed around the side of the building yelling Missy's name, but received no reply. She reached the back of the cleaners and found it mostly destroyed.

What wasn't collapsed in the pile of rubble, was scattered over a half acre area, except for one corner. That junction stood seven feet above the ruins, each wall a few feet wide at the bottom and angling jaggedly up to the corner to form a grotesque triangle. Building fragments, steel, concrete, and cinder block, sloped down from the corner to the cracked and cratered cement floor.

"Missy!" Patty screamed again as she scrambled over and through the huge mess of shattered building fragments that was, only moments before, her family's business and her little girl's playroom.

She stopped and looked around, turning slowly in a circle as her eyes darted in every direction, searching for a sign of Melissa. Listening for any sound of movement, all she heard were the sirens and airhorns of approaching emergency vehicles.

From the corner of her eye, she saw something move near a pile of shattered cinder block and clothing. She stumbled through the debris to the spot, dropped to her knees and dug in. Furiously throwing chunks of concrete and cinder block, she shoveled into the heap. A cloud of dust went up as she yanked dresses and hangers out and threw them over her shoulders. She called her daughter's name and clawed through the jagged rubble, her hands cut and bleeding through the layer of white powder. All to no avail. Exhausted and breathless, she stopped digging, leaning over on all fours, gasping to catch her breath.

"Missy!" she yelled, jumping up and running blindly from the devastated cleaners to the debris strewn parking lot, stumbling over wreckage with every step.

Out on the asphalt of the lot, Patty tripped over a piece of roof truss and fell. She painfully pushed herself up to a standing position and flailed her head around in desperation.

She saw her Caravan lying on its top a good forty feet from where it had been parked. The passenger side, the one she parked nearest the building, was nothing more than a gaping hole. Torn and twisted metal jutted out in gnarled and irregular sawtooth patterns, making the totaled van resemble a bizarre, Picassoesque sculpture. The sliding doorframe was torn away on one end and sticking up from the inverted undercarriage. Still attached on one side, the door moved slowly in the slight breeze.

"Melissa!" she cried helplessly.

She felt her knees weaken and start to tremble uncontrollably as her shoulders slumped and head drooped down impotently.

"Where are you, Missy?"

Her cries diminished, more feeble, nearly inaudible. Patty sank solemnly to her knees on a heap of crushed concrete, too shocked to cry.

The sirens were getting closer and someone was running across the parking lot to her aid.

* * *

The Great Chicago Fire started in Mrs. O'Leary's barn right on schedule, then spread through the neighborhood and beyond. The fierce southwest winds whipped it up and drove it to the northeast on a direct path toward the very heart of the beautiful Garden City.

From the beginning of the fire, everything went terribly wrong. Following the fire the night before, the fire department was woefully undermanned due to illnesses and injuries. Most of the firemen were exhausted, suffering from smoke inhalation and inflamed eyes. Some of the department's fire engines were down for overhaul and many more were simply beaten up by the fire and in need of repairs. The condition of the hose was dreadful because of age, wear and deterioration. It was also in short supply, which meant that if an engine lost any hose for any reason, there wasn't much to replace it.

A holdup in sending the appropriate engines to the correct places was caused by delayed and erroneous alarms. On and near De Koven Street, the Little Giant steamer, the America hosecart and the Chicago steamer waged a valiant battle until the America lost the water to its hose, and the Chicago suffered a mechanical breakdown. Although the breakdown of the Chicago was only temporary, it was enough time to allow the one-alarm fire to grow into a three-alarm.

Once the fire moved into the block north of the O'Leary's, the wind had grown stronger and whipped up the flames, spreading it further to the northeast. As the fire grew in size and intensity, it created its own powerful updrafts, adding to the already fierce winds. By ten o'clock, about an hour into the fire, the wind carried burning brands and debris through the air, far over the heads of the firemen.

The structures around the O'Leary's home were mostly made of wood, such as: frame houses, barns, sheds, and even wooden sidewalks. People emptied their houses of possessions and piled everything in the middle of the streets. The fire then used the stacks of flammable possessions as fuel to further its cause, with the piles of household goods enabling it to spread more easily. As it grew hotter and larger, the intense heat caused houses, yet untouched by the blaze, to billow with smoke and then burst into flames.

Literally thousands of people were in the streets, running from the fire. They carried whatever they could grab before leaving their homes. There were half-naked people carrying everything from iron kettles to pianos. An elderly couple was seen, dazed and confused, walking stark naked through the streets carrying a large wicker basket between them. The basket was filled with their own clean laundry.

As the masses trudged through the streets and alleys, burning embers and ashes rained down on their heads. The wind grew so strong that it picked up burning mattresses and large sections of roofs from houses and literally hurled them a mile or more, setting new fires further to the north. Sometime between ten and eleven o'clock, sparks were raining down on the people in the south area across the river, right in the business district. There was nothing the fire department could do to stem the fury of the Beast in its savage and relentless objective—consuming everything in its path until there was nothing more.

After wandering around town and watching the fire's progress from a safe distance, Scott worked his way back over to Jefferson and De Koven at about ten o'clock. He knew the Little Giant crew would be working in the Turner block on the east side of Jefferson, right where he'd been earlier, between De Koven and the alley. The Little Giant was working with two other steamer companies, the Chicago and the Illinois. In fact, those three companies ended up working together as a group for most of the fire.

As Scott approached on the west side of Jefferson, he saw the Illinois setting up, and the Chicago starting to throw water on the group of buildings. The Little Giant crew was at the other end of the row of two-story buildings pulling pipe, as they called the hose. There were five buildings, all owned by the same man, with businesses on the bottom floors and living quarters on the top. The three fire companies were the last line of defense in keeping the fire from crossing Jefferson and continuing west. They had their work cut out for them, because the immense heat from the fire on the De Koven block had already ignited the entire row of buildings.

Firemen were working in a frenzied effort to seize control of the fire, but the fire had other plans. It had burned into the attic of one of the buildings, then driven the fireman back down the stairs with the heat and smoke. McLean watched with great interest as they all spilled out the door into the street.

Commenting quietly to himself, he said, "Watch out, boys, she's in fine form tonight." He glanced up and down the street, then added, "And just getting started."

As he watched, there came the sound of a tremendous whoomp, followed by oohs and aahs from onlookers on the other side of Jefferson Street. Scott looked up and saw the fire reaching high in the air above the building the firemen had just exited. A section of the roof had collapsed, providing the hungry fire with all the oxygen it needed to roar up toward the sky.

Two firemen were scaling the outside of the building without ladders, one with a rope tied around his waist. In the same fashion as the modern day rock climbers, the one with the rope found fingerholds in the siding and window frames, and even on the signs on the building advertising the ales and wines inside Shultses Saloon. He made it to the top and tied the rope off to the brick chimney, then swung it over for his partner to grab. The other fireman gripped the rope and walked his way up to the edge of the roof.

"Excellent," Scott said, nodding his approval.

Once they were situated on the top, a bucket brigade began passing buckets of water to two people at the bottom of the rope. They fashioned a makeshift hook from a piece of metal and tied it onto the rope, then hooked two leather buckets full of water on, so the firemen could hoist them up over the edge and throw the water on the fire. The only real progress being made was that of the roaring fire, which threatened to run them off the roof at any minute.

"Scott!"

Standing near the Little Giant watching the heroic exercise in futility, McLean heard his name called by somebody next to the steamer. He turned toward the voice and saw the stoker waving him over. The stoker was responsible for keeping the fire burning in the boiler by feeding the fuel into it.

"Over here, Scott."

He walked over to see who it was and, lo and behold, it was Walter Appleton, wearing his high-peaked fire helmet and long turnout coat. His face was cherry red, streaked with black soot, and glistening with sweat. The perspiration ran a steady stream from his chin.

"Walter? Is that you?"

"Yes, it is," Walter said as Scott stepped right up beside him.

Scott broke into a grin. "Tell me, is Zack doing all right?"

Walter smiled and nodded vigorously while he tossed a large lump of coal into the boiler.

"Yes, he is. Helen and I, we used the suction machine on him twice more after you ... rode off." He stopped and shot McLean a funny look. "Is rode off a good way to describe what you did when you left our house?"

Scott nodded slowly. "Rode off is as good a way to put it as any."

"Zack was fine when I had to leave them, and Helen is real good with the suction machine. I'm not worried about my son with her. She's really a good mother. She'll stay up all night watching over him, I'm sure."

Scott nodded his approval and looked back over at the bucket brigade. *I know I can't do anything to affect the outcome of this thing and I know they ended up stopping the westerly spread here at these buildings, but maybe I could help them do it a bit faster and at a lower cost to the firemen's health. They could probably learn a couple of things for future use, too.*

He looked at the Little Giant's hose stream and saw it being played up over the edge of the roof. The stream was so dissipated by the time it reached the area of the fire that it turned to steam without ever reaching the flames.

Hmm, that's not doing a bit of good. They need to get a line up on top of that roof and put some serious water on that fire. They may lose the building anyway, but it's worth a try. He turned back to Walter and made a suggestion, prompting Walter to call the foreman over to discuss it.

The foreman sized up Scott from head to toe, then spat, "Who are you and what makes you think you know so much? Besides, why should I listen to you?"

Glancing back and forth from the other two men's faces, Walter had a thought pop into his head. He remembered what his wife said earlier: *"They appeared in our home at just the right time to save the life of our beautiful son. They gave us a marvelous tool to keep it from happening again. He warned you of a conflagration that would require you to be well rested. Doesn't it seem sensible that he'll be with you tonight to watch over and protect you?"* Walter stared at McLean's face and nodded in agreement with his wife.

He interrupted the foreman in mid-sentence. "We should listen to anything he has to tell us, Bill. Please trust me. He's quite knowledgeable and we don't have the time to argue about it."

The foreman glared sternly at Walter, glanced over at Scott, then back at Walter. "If you say so Appleton," he grunted. "Do you think we could put him in charge of your pipemen for a while?"

Walter nodded. "Yes, sir. That would be a good idea."

Bill gave Walter one firm nod, then turned to look Scott squarely in the eye. "Fair enough. My assistance is needed elsewhere, so I'll leave this building to you and pray to God Almighty that Appleton knows something I don't know."

Abruptly, he turned and hurried over to the pipemen with the hose, then pointed back at McLean. "That man is temporarily in charge. Do as he orders you." He then marched off to help somewhere else.

Walter turned to Scott. "You're in charge. What do you want us to do?"

Scott looked at the pipemen, who were moving their hoseline and checked out the situation on the roof. "Okay, shut down that hose line until I tell you to charge it again."

Walter complied by shutting down the water supply to the hose line. McLean hustled over to the pipemen and told them to stand by as he took the nozzle to begin draining the water from the hose.

"Find me a ladder if you can," he told one pipeman and the man scurried off in search of one.

Scott and the other pipeman dragged the hose over to the bottom of the rope where the bucket brigade was hooking the buckets. He took the end of the rope that hung below the hook and tied it to the hose just below the nozzle.

"It's all right," the pipemen told the volunteers. "This man is now in charge of this operation." He slowly moved them back with a gentle sweeping motion of his arm.

Scott looked around for any sign of a ladder, and seeing none, said to the pipeman, "If he arrives with a ladder, set it up right here."

"Yes, sir."

With that, Scott grabbed the rope and used it to walk up the side of the building. Reaching the top, the two firemen there pulled him over the lip and onto the edge of the roof. McLean immediately turned and started pulling the rope up to the top, bringing the nozzle and hose with it. The other men assisted in hauling it up and dragged a few feet of the pipe onto the roof. Scott untied the rope and tossed the end over the edge, looked at the chimney, then unzipped his duffel bag. He removed a fifteen-foot length of orange nylon webbing and wrapped it around the chimney.

One fireman touched Scott on the shoulder, causing him to stop and look around. The man worriedly said, "Excuse me, sir, but we cannot handle pipe of this size on a rooftop. It would sweep us right off and down to the ground, especially using the pressure from a steamer as powerful as the Little Giant."

"Stick with me, my friend," McLean said assuringly. "Just do what I tell you and we can all get down from this inferno a lot sooner."

The heat and smoke were extremely intense on the roof, with fire shooting up fifteen feet above their heads. He finished tying off the strap to the chimney, then turned around and hoisted the hoseline up near the long end of it.

"Hang onto this and keep it right there for a minute."

They held the hose up while McLean tied a loop around it just large enough to hold tight once the hose became pressurized.

Hearing a bump, Scott glanced over and saw the top three feet of a ladder poking up past the edge of the roof. He looked down and waved to the pipemen, motioning for them to move the ladder over directly behind the protection of the chimney.

Turning to the two firemen, he said, "Come on, let's get out of here."

One fireman started down the ladder as Scott and the other man moved behind the chimney.

By then, the fire was so intensely hot that Scott's shirttail started to burn. The fireman beat it out. "What now?"

"Grab hold of the hose, but stay to this side. It'll swing toward the back of the building when Appleton charges it. After that, hopefully, we can move down on the ladder and operate the pipe from there. Kind of like remote control."

"What kind of control?"

"Never mind," Scott said, motioning to Walter to give them water.

When the line was charged, it whipped around with the lower length arcing out toward the back of the building. The nozzle, firmly attached to the chimney, held fast. Its stream of water shot high in the air out over the street. Scott took another piece of strap, red nylon webbing, and tied one end tightly to the charged hose line, with the other end dangling down over the edge.

"You start down the ladder," he instructed one fireman as he pointed down.

He then noticed the very long end of the hemp rope they had tied to the chimney lying in a heap behind it. He tied that end to the lowest rung of the ladder that he could see above the edge of the roof and cinched it down, securing the ladder in place.

He handed the end of the red strap to the fireman and showed him how to pull it up and down and side to side, using only the strap and his hand to direct the flow to any spot he wanted. "You could even maneuver it from lower down on the ladder to get away from the heat if you had a stick hooked to it."

The fireman laughed out loud at the fun he was starting to have with his new toy.

"It's sort of like a hose elevator, or monitor. It should be somewhat user friendly."

Silently, the fireman gave him a funny look.

Scott took hold of the escape rope that was still dangling beside the ladder, then slipped out over the edge and gave the man a final word of advice. "When you shut down here, pull on the short ends of that strap and it'll come off so you can use it again."

The fireman turned to thank him for the help, but Scott was already scurrying to the ground with singed hair, eyebrows, and clothing. After stepping to the ground, he worked his way back to Walter and stood beside him to watch the action.

"I'm impressed with your idea, Scott," Walter declared. "And you did it all so quickly and efficiently."

They watched the work of the fireman on the ladder as he learned the tricks of operating the hoseline, becoming quite adept in only a few short minutes.

While the crowd of firemen and bystanders watched, the rooftop began to darken as the raging Beast was lowered to its knees and finished off by the pipeman on the ladder. Walter just happened to glance around and see the foreman standing two buildings over, smiling at him and signaling his approval.

He tapped McLean on the shoulder and pointed to Bill, the foreman. "Look over there. I'm not the only one you impressed."

Scott glanced over and saw the foreman wave. Scott waved back and nodded, thinking, *Well, Scotty. Who'da ever thunk it? You're fighting fire with the Little Giant crew on the Great One. I can't wait to tell Patty about this.*

Scott stayed with Walter until they finished with the Turner block, helping the foreman to direct the companies in firefighting operations. The Little Giant, Chicago and Illinois steamer companies were credited with halting the western advance of the fire and thereby saving the entire west district of Chicago.

Scott was counted among the heroic figures involved in the bitter battle, except no one knew his last name. Instead of writing about some guy named Scott, historians included him in their references to the hearty volunteers who fought valiantly alongside the brave firemen. After mopping up from the Turner block, the crews prepared to move on to another area of the city.

* * *

The three fire companies worked their posts at De Koven and Jefferson, then pushed the southwestern boundary on up to Taylor Street, one block north. After the fire died down in that area, the Little Giant was ordered east on Taylor to try to save the Chicago Dock Company from destruction.

As they prepared to respond, Walter got up in the driver's seat and called to McLean. "Are you coming with us? If so, climb on up here."

He patted the narrow one man seat beside him for Scott to use. Scott stared at Walter, the narrow seat, and the whole steamer, then nervously climbed up to sit beside him in the driver's seat. "You're the driver?"

Walter gave him a curious glance. "What did you think the stoker did when he wasn't stoking?" McLean shrugged his shoulders. Walter laughed, then said, "I'm one of the regular drivers, but the stoker is over helping on the Illinois. I'm doing both jobs tonight."

Scott smiled at his little joke and thought, *I'll be darned, you're a smart-ass, Appleton. You different firemen are all alike.*

"We're going south to Twelfth Street, over east to Canal, and then back up to Taylor," Walter explained. "Then we can go east on Taylor to the dock company. I don't know what we'd run into if we went more direct, so we'll take the safest route."

Scott nodded. "How hard is it to drive this thing? Are the horses difficult to control?"

"These horses are the best trained and mannered you'll ever find. I don't have to do more than nudge them one way or another to make them respond."

He looked around to see if the company was ready to roll and was told to wait two more minutes.

"Haven't you ever engineered a steamer wagon before?" Scott shook his head. "As knowledgeable as you are about fires, I would have thought you would have spent some time on a steamer."

Scott was still shaking his head. "Never had the opportunity. Not that I haven't wanted to. I've driven other types of fire apparatus, but never a steamer."

"Oh, right. Hose wagons. Do you want to give it a try?"

Scott's heart started racing and his hands shook. "I'd love to. Would it be all right?"

"It would be just fine. I don't think anyone in this company will mind a bit."

Walter handed the reins to Scott and directed him in how to handle them, telling him they had to hurry. Their response would be the equivalent of code-three, but they had no lights-and-siren. They responded — *bell*.

When he touched the reins to the backs of the three powerful horses, McLean found out what Walter meant about them knowing their jobs. They took off running at full speed and never slowed down until they reached the fire. They knew only two speeds: stop and top. Nothing in-between.

FIRES OF TIME * 397

They raced through the dark streets with the bell clanging, the horses loudly snorting, and the smokestack belching out thick, black smoke. Red hot cinders and clinkers flying from the stack left brilliant orange streamers trailing in the blackness of the night, exploding like bright orange snowballs when they hit the street.

Scott's hair blew in the wind and his eyes watered so much that the tears turned into small, icy streams, winding their way back across his cheeks and into his ears. He pumped buckets of adrenaline, causing his heart to race like the magnificent horses that were pulling the steamer he was piloting. He felt like he did as a kid when his dad took him on the monster roller-coaster on their trip to Cincinnati. His thoughts were running around in circles in his mind, allowing none to stay for more than a few seconds at a time.

I'm not supposed to feel like this anymore. I'm a grown-up now. I thought I'd done it all ... but driving a steamer wagon? The Little Giant steamer wagon? In the middle of the Great Chicago Fire of 1871? He shook his head vigorously, trying to jar the clutter loose so he could think straight.

Knock it off, Scotty. Just enjoy it and stop trying to analyze everything.

Nearly thrown from his seat, he guided the horse team around the corner onto Taylor Street and headed east to the dock company.

Almost over now, but oh, what a ride it's been, he thought as the Little Giant rolled to a stop beside the Chicago Dock Company under a veritable snowstorm of bright, red hot ashes.

While they caught their breath, Walter sat in the seat next to Scott, smiling his approval. "You did a great job. Are you sure you've never driven a steamer before?"

Scott smiled. "Trust me. I've never even been on a steamer before, but I've always wanted to drive one. Thank you."

Suddenly, Appleton jumped from the steamer and ran around to help unhitch the horses and throw blankets over them for protection from the rain of red hot sparks. To Scott, he yelled, "If you're staying with us let's get to work!"

McLean stayed with the Little Giant until sometime between three and four in the morning. He said his goodbyes to Walter and the rest of the company and headed out toward the west side.

Scott walked around burned out areas of the southern district to get to the untouched western section of the city. Once he knew he was safe, he headed north, skirting the areas damaged by the fire. After all, he was the only person in town who knew just what the fire was doing. Finding a park on the west side, an exhausted Scott collapsed on the grass and fell instantly asleep, not to wake until after eight.

* * *

The customer out in front of the cleaners, an off duty firefighter and friend of the McLeans, had shut off the engine of his red and tan Ford Bronco. When he exited the truck, he dropped his keys to the ground between his sandals, so when he reached down to pick them up, he too was bent over as the blast occurred. The Bronco saved him from serious injury as he received only minor cuts on his feet, ankles and one hand from bits of glass flying under the vehicle.

The passenger side of the Bronco was riddled by the barrage of building shrapnel. It looked like Bonnie and Clyde's car after the feds finished shooting it full of bullet holes. The windows were blown out on both sides and a tuxedo clad mannequin was hanging half in and half out of the front, right side window. The lifelike accident victim appeared to be a real person, as seen through the surreal aura of the blast site.

The firefighter was dazed as he stood up and leaned his back against the side of his truck to inspect his hands and feet. When he finally realized what had happened, he spun and ran around the back of the Bronco, stepping over and around the wreckage on his way to the sidewalk.

The good-looking, sharp-featured firefighter surveyed the razed structure and scanned the area, spotting Patty sinking to her knees on the heap of crushed masonry. Turning to run to her, he noticed the demolished passenger side of his vehicle as he ran by.

Great. My Bronco's toast, he thought without breaking his stride.

He reached Patty and knelt down by her, assessing her injuries as he spoke. "Patty. Patty," he said firmly, trying to get her to look him in the eyes. "Where are you hurt? Can you tell me? Patty?" She didn't answer. "Patty. It's Jeff. Can you talk to me?"

Patty slowly raised her head and gazed at him with dead eyes. She moved her head back and forth ever so slowly as she said quietly, "Missy. My baby."

Jeff jerked back and the color drained from his face. "Missy? Was Missy in there?"

Patty's head ceased its side to side movement and she began to nod slowly and deliberately. The emotion in her eyes changed to a pathetic, pleading stare. Quietly and listlessly, she pleaded, "Find her for me Jeff. Please find my baby girl."

He heard an engine company arriving and looked out to the street. The firefighters from his own station, "7s" were picking their way to the front of the disaster. "People are here to help, Patty. I'm going to leave you here while I look for Missy."

She touched his arm and begged him once more. "Find her, Jeffrey. Melissa needs me. Please bring me my baby."

Jeff left her and began working his way through the ruins in search of Missy. He made his way over the mounds of demolished masonry and wood that was intertwined with hundreds of metal hangers and clothing. Draperies, comforters, throw rugs, and all kinds of clothing items were scattered everywhere he looked. Jeff didn't know where to begin, so he simply began. Starting with the higher heaps, he launched a search for Missy McLean.

* * *

Scott raised his head from the black nylon duffel he'd used as a pillow. For a brief moment while his mind ascended through the dark reticular pathways of his brain he had no idea where he was. As his eyes began to focus, he saw people moving all around him, so he raised himself to his elbows and scanned the area. Hundreds, no, thousands of displaced refugees had filled in Scott's safe haven as he slept there on the grass.

"You woked up, huh, mister?"

Scott turned his head and found a small girl with light eyes and long brown hair standing beside him.

"Huh?"

"You woked up. I've been waiting for you to quit sleeping." She stood about four feet tall and was wearing a brownish dress that hung down below her knees.

"My name's Savannah. What's yours?"

"Scott," he said, still wondering what was going on.

Savannah held a sandwich in her right hand. A huge sandwich made from freshly baked bread that was sliced an inch thick. A quarter inch slab of ham was hanging out on all sides of the bread. Scott's salivary glands created a rapid release of tangy fluid onto the back of his tongue, making him swallow involuntarily. He continued to stare at the sandwich. He hadn't eaten since the previous afternoon, and that was before fighting fires for half the night and hiking all over Chicago. Scott was hungry. Real hungry.

Savannah held the sandwich out to him. "My mama told me to give you this. She said you'd prob'ly be hungry. Take it, mister Scott, it's awful good. I know cause I had a bite."

He took the sandwich from her hand and thanked her, then Savannah turned and ran away into the crowd. Scott held the sandwich up to take his first big bite and stopped. There was a small bite missing from one corner. He grinned.

Kids are the same, no matter where or when you go, he thought. He stood up and slung his bag over his shoulder, took his first big bite and started walking through the crowded park, taking in the sights.

Amazing, he marveled. *I've read so much about it and seen all the pictures of the crowds of refugees, but this is unbelievable.* There was a veritable sea of people stretching out over the lawns of the park. They were milling about, cooking and talking, even joking with one another about their new neighborhood. Scott heard one man joking with another about the tree he had decided on for his new home.

"Yep, I see a lot of possibility in this ol' tree. I won't need a dog cause it already has *bark*, and there's plenty of room to *branch* out. All in all, it seems like a darn good place to put down *roots*. In fact, I may not ever want to *leaf*."

Scott was astounded by the spirit of those people who had just lost everything they owned. While the entire sky to the east and north continued to billow with smoke and ash from the fire, the resilient escapees were already making plans to rebuild their homes and lives.

He took his watch out of his pocket and checked the time. It was nearly nine-thirty. He put it away and strolled through the rest of the park, devouring the fabulous ham sandwich along the way.

A kindly old man touched him on the arm as he was passing. "You look like you could use a drink there, son," he said, dipping a ladle of water from a large can and holding it out to Scott.

Scott took the ladle and drank it down, realizing he was thirsty. He drank down two more and handed the ladle back to the man.

"Thank you," Scott said. "I appreciate that a lot."

FIRES OF TIME * 403

"You're most welcome, son. We have to help each other out through this thing now, don't we?"

"We sure do." Scott smiled and waved to the man as he left the park, caught up in excited anticipation.

He walked from the park in the direction of the still burning sections of the city, captivated by the history taking place before his delighted eyes. He decided to just wander for a while and take in the sights.

It would have been a beautiful, sunny fall morning had it not been for the voluminous clouds of smoke filling the sky and blocking out the sun. The wind was still blowing, although not quite as hard as the night before. It was being created by the fire itself, with little help from the usual forces of nature.

He walked for nearly an hour. Finding a small retaining wall in the front of a yard, he sat and rested, checking out the sights and sounds of the city. He looked at the street, hard-packed dirt, narrow by western standards. A horse ran by, chased by a man and a boy. A girl hurried past carrying a box full of baby kittens. Scott could hear the roar of the fire several blocks away. The smell of smoke grew much stronger, the air getting hazier by the minute. Sounds were muffled by the thick atmosphere, exhibiting a pre-tornado or post-nuclear feeling. He drifted easily into thought in the quiet surroundings, but was startled from his contemplation when someone spoke.

"Excuse me, sir."

Scott turned and saw a man standing on the edge of the street, holding onto the halter of a horse that was hitched to a wagon. He was a big man, about as tall as Scott, but more stocky and muscular.

"You talking to me?" Scott asked.

"Yes, sir. I'm sorry to bother you, sir, but my family ... well, they're not really my kin ... I mean, I work for them and ... I need help, sir. Can you help me?"

He was a black man with short cropped hair, dressed in a baggy gray shirt and dirty gray pants. The pants were also baggy, with the pant legs barely covering the tops of his scuffed, brown lace-up work boots. He had a desperate, panicked look on his lean face. His brown eyes were bloodshot from lack of sleep and the irritating smoke that filled the air. Scott stepped into the street and approached the man.

"What do you need? I'll help if I can." Scott was kind of psyched about being asked to assist. The man stared nervously at Scott, almost like he was afraid of him, but still determined to get someone to help him.

"M—My name's L—Leonard. Leonard Martin. I work for ... I'm the handyman for the Bagley family. That's their house right over there."

Leonard pointed to a huge brownstone mansion down the block and across the street. It sat back about a hundred and fifty feet from the street on an enormous lot. It was surrounded by large, old oak trees. A gravel driveway ran from the street and circled in front of a big porch and entryway. The porch roof was supported by grand, white pillars, twenty feet in height.

It didn't take a genius to see that the poor guy was frantic. Scott had read accounts of some of the black people involved in the Great Fire. Many of them performed great heroics in saving the lives and property of their own families, and the people they worked for. He was also acutely aware that the civil rights movement in America didn't begin for another ninety years, which probably would account for Leonard's nervousness in asking a white stranger for help. He stepped over and placed his hand on the man's shoulder, gently nudging him in the direction of the mansion.

"I'm Scott, and I'd love to help you out. Lead on, my man."

Leonard smiled meekly and seemed to relax a bit. He started walking toward the house, leading the horse and wagon. "Thank you, Mr. Scott, sir. I'm grateful for your help."

Scott smiled at him. "My name is Scott, Leonard. Just Scott. You don't need to call me sir, or mister. Just Scott. Now, tell me what's happening here that's got you so all-fired upset."

"It's my family, Mr. Scott, sir! They've all gone plum crazy!"

* * *

Station seven's approach to the scene was blocked by the vast amount of cinder block, glass, clothing, and even washing machines littering the street. From one corner of the block to the other, the roadway was blanketed with wreckage from the blast. Tailboarders vaulted from the jumpseats and ran ahead of engine seven, tossing fragments aside to clear a path for both the engine and the ambulance. As they neared the site of the explosion, station five's crew started the same process from the other end of the block.

Captain Seven: "Station seven at scene."
Dispatch: "Ten-four station seven at 0905."
Captain Seven: "We have what appears to be an explosion in a business. Or businesses, I'm not

sure. It looks like it was of cinder block construction. There is no fire."

Dispatch: "Do you know the business name?"

Captain Seven: "There's nothing left to be able to tell—"

The captain stopped short and paused. *"Captain Five, Captain Seven,"* he said as he keyed the mike.

Captain Evans: "Captain Five, go ahead."

Captain Seven: "Is McLean on shift today, Josh?"

Captain Evans: "He's off duty today. What do you need?"

Captain Seven: "We'll need your medics over here with Patty."

Captain Evans: "McLean?"

Captain Seven: "Ten-four."

Captain Evans: "Rescue Five ... Escobido, Buttram..."

Paramedic Buttram: "Already on it, Cap." Tony put the squad into four-wheel-drive and started crawling up and over the debris strewn street. He drove it right up beside Patty and the two paramedics got out and hurried over to her side.

The sight greeting the eyes of the firefighters was incredible. What had been the Jelesnik cleaners and laundromat resembled old pictures of war-ravaged London during World War II. Aside from the grotesquely misshapen front wall and one rear corner, the cleaners side of the building was leveled. The old structure's wooden front door frame and window casings were broken and splintered, poking out in every direction. Shards of glass still clinging to some of the fractured wood moved gently in the breeze, clinking together to produce tinkling noises like back porch wind chimes.

Engine seven's firefighters were assigned primary search and rescue and spread out over the area of devastation searching for casualties. Ambulance seven's two EMTs grabbed some equipment and headed over to Patty. They assisted the paramedics in assessing her injuries, finding multiple cuts and abrasions, but nothing serious ... physically.

"We'll find her, Patty," Buttram said assuringly, kneeling down beside her and putting his arm around her shoulder. He talked to her softly, trying to offer some comfort. "They're searching right now and I'm sure we'll find her."

As she turned and stared at him with her blank eyes, they welled up with tears and she broke down, leaning limply into his chest. "Missy's gone, Tom," she said as she began to weep effusively, her body wracked with convulsive sobbing. "My ... little angel is ... dead."

Tom looked away because he felt his own tears start to flow.

The medics helped her up, walking her to the ambulance. She sat on the rear bumper and refused to leave without her baby.

Jeff, the off duty firefighter, was on his knees digging in the pile of rubble near the partial corner walls. He looked over on top of a three foot square of cinder block wall and saw something shiny glinting in the sunlight, reaching over, he picked it up.

"Oh, man. Mrs. Jelesnik," he said, holding it in his hand and examining the broken rhinestone eyeglass chain. A fractured, two inch piece of plastic tiger-striped earpiece was still attached to one end of the chain.

"I think I have the rest of it." A firefighter stood fifteen feet away from Jeff, holding the broken pair of tiger-striped glasses in his gloved hand. The rest of the rhinestone chain dangled from the other twisted earpiece.

Someone yelled from the other side of the triangle of rubble in the corner. "Over here! I've found her!"

The firefighter furiously threw pieces of concrete, cinder block and other debris over his shoulder as he dug into the heap of refuse. Jeff nearly jumped the whole pile in his effort to get to the other side.

A tiny hand poked out of the dusty pile of ruins as the man dug swiftly, but carefully. Jeff joined him, and two more firefighters arrived to assist. Jeff pinched a fingernail on the hand to check for capillary refill, a sign of blood flow, and found the refill time over five seconds. More than two seconds signals poor circulation.

"Hustle!" he shouted, realizing instantly what a stupid thing that was to say.

Of course they were hustling. They were all caught up in the same emotionally taxing situation of finding the child of one of their own in a desperate situation.

They all knew Missy from Scott showing her off whenever he got the chance, and they all loved and respected her proud father. Jeff was a close friend of Scott and Patty, dating back to junior high school. Being single, he spent a lot of time hanging out at their home. He convinced Scott to take the kids on fishing trips, teaching Casey and Scott how to tie their own flies. Next to Brian, Jeff was Scott's closest friend.

"Hang on, Missy," the usually-cool Jeff said over and over as he held onto the tiny hand. "I've got you. It's Uncle Jeff."

It took nearly thirty minutes to dig Missy out of the rubble, with the paramedics intubating her and starting IV lines before she was even completely freed. They put her on a ventilator and managed to get a sinus heart rhythm before transporting her and her mother to Children's Hospital. Once there, she was taken immediately into surgery, leaving Patty to sit in a waiting room.

* * *

The brownstone mansion was an imposing structure. Standing three stories high and surrounded by the tall oak trees, it looked to be the epitome of the American Dream.

As Scott and Leonard briskly walked the horse and wagon up the long driveway, they heard occasional gunfire.

"Is somebody shooting a gun? What's going on in there?"

"It's probably grandpa," Leonard said, pausing briefly. "The Bagley's are smart people, really, but the fire's got 'em crazy. Grandpa Bagley's been 'tetched' for a long time, but now the whole family's gone mad."

"What are they doing that's so crazy?"

"You'll see when you get inside. They're tearing the house apart, like they think we can move the whole thing in one little wagon. I gotta get 'em outta there before the fire comes along and burns 'em all up. That's why I asked for your help, so we can find a way to get 'em to go." Leonard stopped and looked at Scott. "Will you help me, sir, I'm pleadin' with you."

Scott smiled. "I'll do what I can, but I'm only one man, just like yourself. Let's go see what we can do."

They took a quick look back and saw the forward wall of the firestorm only a few short blocks away, moving toward them at a fairly good clip. The air thickened even more with smoke, and ashes were falling around them.

"We'd better get to hurryin', mister Scott." Leonard picked up his pace and tugged harder on the reins.

Scott smiled when he said mister Scott. "I hear that. We don't have any time to waste."

They reached the front porch and Leonard tied off the reins to the hitching post next to the steps. The two men ran onto the porch and started through the door, both stopping to take another look at the approaching conflagration.

"Y'know what, Leonard?" Scott said, motioning toward the fire. "I think we have a big problem here."

Leonard gave Scott a very strange look and charged on into the house. The place was in chaos. A late-forties man was standing on a chair, on top of a table, tugging on a huge chandelier. He saw Leonard come through the door and yelled to him.

"Leonard, give me a hand, here. We have to get these chandeliers down and loaded onto the wagon."

Leonard turned to Scott and whispered, "That's Mister Bagley." He looked back at Mr.

Bagley. "Do you really think that will be necessary, sir?"

"Yes. Get over here and help me."

Leonard took one step toward the table.

"Leonard!"

He turned toward the female voice just as a woman in a long dress with a towel wrapped around her hair ran in from another room and grabbed hold of his shirt sleeve.

"Leonard. I need your help in here."

"But—"

"No buts! Come on in here and help me move this china hutch out to the wagon."

Leonard turned to follow her, but was stopped by another voice.

"Leonard, I need you! Get a crowbar and help me get this railing off. We don't have much time." Leonard turned and looked at Scott, shrugging his shoulders, then put his finger up and twirled it around his ear in the universal crazy signal.

Hugging the wall, Scott moved slowly around the foyer, watching the action. Everyone in the house was busy trying to save something, none of it important enough to worry about. Clad in baggy slacks, the young man trying to remove the stairway bannister had already pulled the carpeting from the stairs and rolled it down, the two foot high carpet roll sitting against the bottom step. Mr. Bagley was flirting with disaster, standing on the chair and pulling on the crystal chandelier with all his might. Mrs. Bagley, who had hooked a big leather strap around the china hutch, was inside the loop, trying to drag it across the dining room.

It'll take six men and a horse to move that thing. Scott's thoughts were interrupted by a scream from upstairs. He jumped the roll of carpet and scrambled up the stairs. When he reached the top, he stopped and looked up and down a large hallway.

He called out. "Anybody here?"

The hallway floor was covered by carpet with a large floral pattern, the walls a pale yellow. A three foot oak wainscoting ran the length of the hall, with large paintings hanging every ten or so feet. No one was to be seen.

"Anybody here?"

"Help me down here." It was a male voice. Scott ran to his left, toward the sound of the voice, to where the main hall intersected another hallway.

"Here. Over here. Hurry!"

Scott looked down the hall and saw a boy, no older than sixteen, standing on an occasional table next to the wall. The pudgy boy with messy hair and a gap in his front teeth glanced at Scott and waved him over.

"Hurry, we haven't much time," he said. "We have to get all of them down and into the wagon."

He had a straight razor in his hand, and was cutting a painting out of its frame. When he finished cutting, he gently peeled the painting out of the frame and rolled it up, holding it out for Scott to take. Scott took it from him and watched him jump down from the table and scoot it down the hall to the next painting, then climb back up.

"You planning on cutting down all the paintings in the hallway?"

"In the house."

"Excuse me?"

"In the house. There are paintings throughout the house, so I've got to hurry," the teenage boy said while cutting carefully down the edge of the painting.

Scott put the rolled up artwork with the others and shook his head in disbelief. "The city's burning. This house is going to burn in just a few minutes."

"I know."

"You know? I don't think you understand, uh, what's your name?"

"James." He didn't look at Scott when he answered. He just kept cutting away.

"James? We have to get out of here. Finish that one and I'll help you carry all of them out to the wagon."

"But, there are so many more to be—"

"There's no time," Scott interrupted, gathering up an armload of rolled paintings. "Just hurry and get that done so we can boogie."

"Do what?"

"Hurry!"

"No, the other thing you said. Boogie? What is that?"

"It's ... there's no time to explain. We have to get out of here, so get it done."

The boy responded well to Scott's orders, cutting around the inside edge of the frame with the razor, then peeling it out slowly from the top. It was an original painting of fruit and flowers. A whole painting devoted to nothing but a few daisies and pansies, a pear, a bunch of grapes.

Scott was sickened. The colors were repulsive, reminding him of vomit.

James noticed him looking at it and held it up for a full view. "Do you like it? It's very valuable, you know." Scott grimaced and nodded. "Worth over ten thousand dollars."

Whoa, Scott thought. *Guess I just don't see it. Maybe I lack savoir-faire, or something, but I wouldn't hang that thing in my garage.*

"That's nice, James." He gathered up the last of the rolls and turned toward the other hallway. "I'll head on down with this load and you'll be right behind me, right?"

"I'll be there."

Scott hurried to the stairs and started down amid the sound of gunfire, screaming and yelling. He could even hear the roar of the fire as it feasted its way closer to the mansion. Descending the stairs, he heard someone yelling at the others, so he paused midway to listen.

"No! You will not take anything more! Mr. Bagley, sir, you can fire me, or horse whip me for that matter, I don't care. But I'm gonna get you folks outta here alive. All this stuff won't mean a darn if even one member of this here family gets burned up."

Leonard stood in the front doorway, holding Mrs. Bagley in a perfect fireman's carry. He ignored her feet kicking and fist pounding, while looking defiantly at Mr. Bagley, who stood silently on the same perch as before, hanging open-jawed on Leonard's every word. When Bagley didn't move quick enough, Leonard yelled some more.

"You gonna get movin' or do I have to come back in here and pack you out, too?"

"I'm coming, Leonard. I'm coming, just let me finish with this chandelier."

"No! Now!"

Bagley scrambled down from the chair and jumped from the table, dashing out the door past Leonard. Leonard hurried out and placed Mrs.

Bagley in the wagon's seat and ran back into the house, nearly running right over Scott, on his way outside with the paintings. Leonard looked at the paintings and shook his head in disbelief.

"Herbert! Get on outta here right now!"

The boy who'd been working on the stairs ran past Leonard and out the door just as James appeared at the top and started down. He carried the one painting, a handful of arrows and a holster for a pistol. No bow, no pistol, just arrows and a holster.

"Get on down here, boy," Leonard said to James.

Scott tossed the paintings into the back of the wagon and looked toward the south. The fire was less than two football fields away and bearing down on them, already creating enough heat to be very uncomfortable, the smoke and ash getting thicker by the second. Fire shot sixty feet into the air, roaring and popping, the Beast calling out its threat to its old nemesis Scott as he stood on the porch and watched his powerful enemy.

He smiled at the fire. *You old son of a bitch. You won't quit until you get me, will you? Maybe you will some day.* He heard Leonard screaming, cut his thoughts short, and headed back into the house, turning his head to yell out at his adversary. "But today ain't that day!"

He stepped through the door and saw Leonard shouting at James as he ran down the stairs.

"Get on outta here, Jimmy. And put your highfalootin little butt in that wagon." When James hesitated, Leonard barked at him again. "Move it!"

James reached the bottom and ran for the door, pausing to whisper something to Scott. "Leonard's the only person who's allowed to call me Jimmy, cause he powdered my bottom when I was a baby."

Scott nodded at him, thinking, *That's a whole lot more than I needed to know, James.* He turned to Leonard, who was stepping toward him, and started to say something. They heard the scream again, followed by more gunfire.

"Oh, no!" Leonard said tensely. "Grandpa's still up there shooting at the fire."

"Shooting at what?"

"The fire. He's in his room, shooting at the fire. Did I tell you he was 'tetched'?"

"You did," Scott nodded. "But you didn't say how much."

"Excuse my bad language, Mr. Scott, but old Grandpa Bagley is crazier'n a shithouse rat. He yelled down the stairs a while ago that he'd hold off the enemy until everyone gets away. Then the shooting started again and hasn't let up."

Someone screamed again.

"Who's screaming, Leonard?"

Leonard turned, looked up the stairs, whipped his head back around to Scott, his face filled with fear. "Grandma! Grandma's still in her bedroom!"

He bounced back and forth from one foot to the other, unable to comprehend how to handle the situation. Scott took Leonard by both shoulders and forced him to look into his eyes.

"Here's what we'll do. You tell me how to find Grandma's room and I'll get her out. You go and get Grandpa and we'll meet outside. Okay?"

Leonard nodded and grabbed Scott's sleeve, then both of them bolted up the stairs. Leonard pointed down the hallway to the left where Scott had been earlier.

"Go down the hall and turn right. Her room is at the end of that hall ... oh, and Mr. Scott?" Scott gave his full attention. "She can't walk. She's all crippled up."

"Okay," Scott said. "I'll see you on the outside."

"Good luck," Leonard said, shaking Scott's hand. "And thank you, Scott."

Scott smiled at him for finally leaving off the sir and mister. "Let's do it!"

The two men parted ways, each running his direction into the recesses of the stately mansion, while the fire continued its pursuit.

Chapter Seventeen

Patty sat in the waiting room in a state of emotional shock, oblivious to the pain and irritation from the injuries she'd received. None of them were serious enough to be life threatening, but a few of the small lacerations needed a stitch or two, and all of the abrasions needed to be cleaned up.

She stood and walked to the window, looking outside at what had started out to be a beautiful day, when a nurse tapped on the door and walked in.

"Mrs. McLean?"

Patty whirled around and faced her, scared to death of what she might have to say. "Yes? I'm Patty McLean. Is Missy okay? Can I see her?"

The nurse stepped over to her and took her by the hands, ushering her to a chair. She sat down on a coffee table covered with magazines, drawing Patty down into the chair facing her. As Patty stared blankly at the magazines on the table, she noticed one of them was a catalogue from Hunter Medical Supply Corporation. The good feeling that should have been generated was offset by her current situation, spawning the thought, *Yin and Yang are hard at work here, staring each other right in the eye.*

"I'm sorry, Patty, but your daughter is in surgery and will be for a while longer. I'll come and tell you just as soon as I know anything. Okay?" Patty nodded slowly. "My name is Jane. I'll help you with anything I can." Jane held Patty's hands up and inspected them, then made a quick visual inspection of the rest of her.

"You need some treatment for these injuries. Will you go down to Emergency with me to take care of them?"

Patty turned instantly defensive. "No! I'm not leaving my baby! I'll be fine."

She pulled away from Jane and stood back up, walking over to the window. Jane stood and looked at her for a moment, thinking the situation over.

"I understand. I wouldn't leave her either." Jane stepped around to Patty's side and sat back on the arm of a small, vinyl sofa. Touching Patty's arm, she said softly, "There's a small treatment room down the hall. It's actually closer to the O.R. than this room. Would you walk down there with me? I'll get one of the doctors to come in there to look at your injuries. There's a shower in it, too."

Patty turned and looked at the nurse with blank eyes. Jane smiled at her and took her by the hand, leading her toward the door.

"You can take a nice hot shower. It'll be better than just standing around in here, anyway."

Jane helped her get started in the shower and summoned a doctor to the room. After Patty showered, Jane assisted the doctor in sewing up the cuts. She handed her a small bottle of pain pills and suggested Patty take one. Patty refused to take any, and put the bottle on the back of the sink.

Patty started for the door. "Is it all right if I walk around for a little while?"

Just as she opened it, a doctor in surgical scrubs appeared in front of her. She stepped back into the room, allowing the doctor to move past her. After moving into the room, he turned to face her.

"Mrs. McLean? I'm Doctor Collingwood." He paused to collect his thoughts, then continued. "We've done everything possible for your daughter. I'm afraid the news isn't good."

* * *

Joellen and Brian arrived around two-thirty to find Patty walking through the hallway like a zombie. She fell into Jo's arms.

"They've taken her up to the PICU. Jo, my baby's on life support machines and the doctors don't think she's going to live. They're going to do some tests to see if her brain is still alive."

Patty couldn't say anymore. Foregoing the elevators and with Brian and Jo on each side supporting her, the three of them trudged up the stairs to the Pediatric Intensive Care Unit.

It was three-thirty when Patty sat down in the open-walled PICU room holding Missy's hand. Numb with shock and grief, Joellen sat in a chair beside Patty while Brian stood nearby.

Patty turned to her best friend. "When will Scott be back?"

Jo looked up at Brian with a question in her eyes.

He looked at his watch. "About two and a half hours. He's due back at six o'clock."

"Will you guys bring him here as soon as he gets back?"

"Of course," Jo said. "And we'll take care of Casey."

"Please," she said, staring from red eyes that were nearly swollen shut.

"It's no problem," Brian said. "Will you be all right here until we get back?"

Patty nodded.

"Bring him back as soon as he gets here. Will you promise me that?"

Joellen hugged her and patted her shoulder, then they left her sitting in the room with Missy.

* * *

"Here we go again," Scott said, running around the corner and heading toward the door at the end of the hallway. The big house was beginning to fill with smoke, Scott unaware that the eaves on the stately front porch had already caught fire. Just when he reached for the doorknob, he heard the scream again. He turned the knob, but the door wouldn't open.

"Locked up tight," he grunted to himself. "Guess I'll have to use the trusty old size eleven master key." He stepped back and slammed his foot into the door, splintering the casing, the door swinging open.

The elderly woman was lying on the floor in the middle of a very large bedroom. A massive canopy bed stood against one wall, with matching bureau and dresser on another. Large windows nearly filled a third wall, with heavy curtains hanging open.

"It's about time you got here," the woman cackled. "Where's your shining armor, sonny?"

Scott stopped short and grinned at her, then answered her question with his own, "I left it outside with my white horse?"

She laughed with the same cackling sound and reached one arm out to Scott. When he took her hand and kneeled down in front of her, she said, "I like the gesture, Prince Charming. But you can propose to me after we get out of this castle."

"I'd love to sit here and chat with you, ma'am," he said as he scooped her up in his arms. "But we have to get moving."

"Thank you, sonny. I can't walk, you know."

"I heard that about you."

Scott carried her through the broken doorway and into the hall. The smoke was much thicker and they could hear the fire's roar coming from another part of the house, but Scott wanted to try to make it through. Halfway down the hall, he saw flame licking out from the connecting hall, effectively cutting off their escape.

"What do you think?"

"Looks pretty bleak, sonny."

"Is there another way out?"

"Not unless you want to go down the dumbwaiter there isn't."

Scott turned and ran back into the bedroom, kicking the door shut and backing up against it. He saw the two big windows, but knew he'd have to bar the door shut before opening one. Even then, an open window might create enough of a draw to cause a flashover. If that happened, he and Grandma would be toast.

"Let me take a quick peek here," he said quickly, putting her on the bed and hurrying over to look out one window, then the other.

Both had a drop of at least twenty-five feet to the ground with no abutments to work with. He could tie a rope off to the bedpost and rappel down with the woman, but that would take some time to set up. Time he didn't have. He decided to let Grandma Bagley decide.

"The dumbwaiter goes clear down to the cellar, if the ropes haven't burned through," she said.

"You weren't joking about the dumbwaiter?"

"No, it's a big one."

"Big enough for us to ride in it?"

"Of course it is, Prince. We've used it to move furniture up and down for years, so I guess it would hold you and me."

Scott ran to the door and looked into the hall, seeing the entire end involved in flame. He ducked back into the room and pushed the door shut again.

The fire had already moved quickly through the house, from top to bottom, getting into the attic and spreading throughout in minutes. The only possible escape was out the windows or down the dumbwaiter.

"Where's the dumbwaiter, ma'am?"

"Right outside that door, in the hallway."

Scott picked her up and pulled the door open with his foot, then stepped into the doorway and over to the dumbwaiter. "I'll hold you here while you slide the door open."

She slid the door up, revealing a shaft with ropes hanging in it. "You have to pull on the ropes to get the car up here, Prince, so you better get to workin'."

He sat her on the floor and started pulling the car up to their level. Working furiously, it took several minutes to get it there. He fastened the available hook to the casing, picked Grandma up and placed her in the car. The heat from the fire was becoming unbearable when he climbed in and shut the door.

"Well, here goes nothin', Grandma."

With the door securely shut, he quickly took his leather gloves from his black duffel and put them on, then reached up and pulled slightly on the rope, lifting it an inch. He undid the hook and slid the rope through his gloved hands, letting the car descend toward the cellar.

Unbelievable, McLean, he thought. *This can't be happening again. Didn't you learn anything from the San Francisco fire, except how to get in trouble again?*

A loud whooshing sound from above jolted him from his thoughts. The fire had burned through the door on an upper floor and was shooting into the dumbwaiter shaft all around the ropes. He looked up and saw what had happened and let the rope slide through his hands faster, burning even through the gloves. Grandma Bagley sat silently, watching the excitement like it was a carnival ride.

"Hold onto your hat!" Scott yelled as they disappeared into the dark recesses of the mansion.

* * *

When Leonard reached Grandpa Bagley's door, he heard more gunfire in the room. Trying the doorknob, he found it locked, so he pounded on it and yelled to the old man.

"Open up, Grandpa!"

The shooting stopped and Grandpa yelled back. "Who's there?"

"It's me, Leonard. Open up the door!"

"Go away, son. I think I can hold 'em off."

"Open the door, Grandpa, or I'll break it down!"

"No! Go away!"

Leonard stepped back and then ran full force into the door with his shoulder, breaking it open. He fell headlong into the room, landing on the floor at the man's feet.

"Well, there you are, Sergeant. We've been waiting for reinforcements all day. Move your company over to the left side, it looks like they're trying to outflank us."

Leonard jumped up and stepped to the window beside the former Yankee Colonel and looked outside. The fire was spreading rapidly through the oak trees on the Bagley property. He put his hand on the Colonel's shoulder and attempted to nudge him away from the window.

"What are you doing, Sergeant? You have your orders." He pulled away from Leonard and fired another shot out the window.

"Hurry up and move those troops. We haven't much time."

Leonard stepped back and surveyed the situation. The fire was moving rapidly, threatening their lives. Grandpa Bagley had turned into a total nut case. The old man had a loaded rifle in his hands and wouldn't be afraid to use it on a cowardly sergeant that wanted to retreat. They both had to get out of the house quickly. Leonard went back to the doorway to think it over, then suddenly turned and walked back into the room, yelling at Grandpa.

"Colonel! Colonel, Sir!"

The Colonel turned and looked at him. "What do you want?"

"We have new orders, Sir. They're moving the front to another location and need you to command the troops there."

"Who sent the orders?"

"General Grant himself, Sir. General Grant sent the new orders, and we're to move out immediately."

Colonel Bagley fired one more shot at the fire, then turned around and stared at Leonard. Leonard thought he was going to open up on him, but he held his ground, standing at attention and staring right back at the crazy old man.

After a very long moment, the Colonel walked briskly toward Leonard and started barking orders. "Well? Why are you just standing there, Captain? Let's move out. Get those horses hooked up and move those cannon out of here. Put the regiment in formation and let's begin the march. We mustn't keep General Grant waiting."

The two men quick-stepped through the smoke filled hall and down the front stairs to the waiting wagon. The whole family was safe, except for Grandma Bagley and the stranger named Scott. When Leonard started back into the house to find them he watched the ceiling fall onto the big, front staircase. Fire filled the front of the house, blocking every entry and exit. Unable to do anything for Grandma and Scott, Leonard jumped onto the wagon and drove the family away to safety.

* * *

Scott sat on the floor of the car, watching curiously as the fire ate at the ropes above him. The dumbwaiter shaft seemed to be drawing the flames and smoke in like a chimney, but different. Smoke was drawing downward, rather than up.

What gives? Where I come from, smoke rises. It doesn't follow you down a shaft ... unless.

"See what the smoke's doing?"

"It looks like it's chasin' after us, Prince. They say smoke follows beauty, you know."

Scott looked through the darkness at her and smiled. "That must be it. For a minute there, I thought it was following me."

"Don't sell yourself short, sonny. You're the closest thing to a Greek God I've ever seen."

"Oh, Grandma," he said, blushing. "I'll bet you say that to all the men who drag you down elevator shafts."

She cackled. "You've gotta know just how doggone pretty you are. There's somethin' about you like I've never seen before."

"You're embarrassing me now."

They hit the bottom of the shaft with a bump. Scott reached out in the darkness to slide the door open, but there was no door. He poked his head out to look around, but the blackness of the cellar was all encompassing. He put one leg out and felt for the floor, then stepped into the basement.

"Well, here we are," he said as he reached in and picked her up in his arms. "Do you know your way around down here?"

"Haven't been down here in years, but I doubt it's changed much. I don't remember it being this dark, though."

Scott sat her on the edge of the car and took off his gloves, unzipped his duffel and tossed them in, then fished around inside the bag for his mag light. He found the flashlight and took it out, zipping the bag back up.

"Grandma Bagley. Do you have a name other than Grandma that I might call you?"

"Well, my name is Rosabelle, but you can call me Rosie if you'd like. Most everyone else does."

"Okay, Rosie. I'm Scott."

"That's a nice name, Scott. But I kinda like Prince."

"Then Prince it is," he grinned. "I have a lantern here that's like none you've ever seen. I can't tell you where I got it, but I'm going to have to use it anyway."

"Quit yer yackin' and let's have some light."

He twisted the mag light and produced the customary brilliant beam, then adjusted it to a floodlight effect.

"Oh, my." Rosie stared in disbelief. "I'm much too old to be surprised by many things. But that light ... it starts from such a small object and grows so large and bright. Is it of God or the devil?"

"It's a *good* thing, Rosie. Would that be from the devil?"

Before she could answer, a loud noise came from within the shaft. Scott picked Grandma from the platform just before the smoldering ropes crashed down from above. They were followed by pieces of burning debris, crashing down and exploding in a shower of sparks into the darkness of the cellar.

"Doesn't look good," Scott said grimly as he stepped back and shined his light around the cellar.

Moving it slowly around the room, he spotted two walls of shelves filled with jars of fruit. The third and fourth walls both had doorways leading to other rooms. He shined the light into one room. It was a coal bin.

"Is there a coal chute from the outside?"

"There's a chute, all right," she answered. "But it isn't big enough for a man to crawl through. One of the boys tried to put the dog down through it once and the poor thing had to be pushed out with a big stick. Nearly killed it."

They moved into the other doorway and found a storage room, lined around the walls with old furniture, some wooden crates and a big steamer trunk.

"Is there any way out of here, Rosie?"

"You can try the stairs, if you want. Other'n that, there's no windows or doors out of this dungeon."

Scott found an old wicker chair and placed Rosie in it. "I'll be right back. Now don't you run off."

"Funny boy," she cackled as he made his way for the stairs.

He climbed slowly up the wooden staircase, watching closely for hidden dangers. When he got almost to the top, Scott turned off the light and looked under the crack of the door. Smoke was pouring from the small opening and all he could see on the other side was a bright orange glow.

"This place is completely involved," he said with a whistle.

He could hear the ceiling falling and crashing to the floor and knew the wooden door wouldn't last long. Turning the mag back on, he scooted down the stairs into the storage room. He sat on the steamer trunk in front of Rosie, the mag light pointed up to illuminate the whole room.

"You seem a bit worried, Prince," she said.

"We have to find a way out of here soon. This whole house is going to end up right here in this cellar, and we don't want to be under it. Can you think of any other way out?"

Suddenly, a tremendous crash shattered their peaceful little hideout. A giant wooden beam smashed down through the floor above, showering splinters, sparks, and bringing the fire down with it.

"Damn!" Scott jumped and grabbed hold of a large dresser with a mirror on it and dragged it over in front of the doorway.

He stacked crates and suitcases on top in an attempt to seal the opening, then kneeled down beside Grandma. Using a straight beam, he shined the mag light at the blockade and waited.

"It looks like smoke is still getting in, Prince."

"Yeah, I don't think I'll be able to stop it. But it probably won't matter anyway, once the rest of the house comes down. From the sound of it, that won't be too long, either."

The ceiling above them burned through in places, opening jagged windows to the fire above.

"Look at that, Rosie. It's like looking straight into the bowels of hell."

All around them, burning embers fell, the blockade burned nearly away, jars exploded. The smoke was causing Scott to lose track of reality, and Rosie was fast fading into unconsciousness.

As Scott waited for the Beast to close in for the kill, he saw a rat run across the floor and on into the stacked furniture on the other wall. Another rat ran across, then another. They all ran into the same place and didn't come out.

"That's interesting," Scott mumbled aloud in his half conscious state. "The rats have an escape route while the people sit here and fry."

Rosie was nearly unconscious from the smoke and Scott wasn't far behind. The ceiling above them was burned through over nearly half the room. Flaming debris seemed to fall from everywhere.

Scott watched another rat scamper across the floor and disappear into the same spot. "Where are you guys all going? Maybe I'd better follow you and find out."

Stepping over to the rat's escape route, he started moving things out of the way. He dragged parts of a four poster bed, a chest of drawers, a bookcase. The last thing against the wall was the top of an oak dining table. It was pushed flat against the wall, but moved easily when Scott dragged it out into the middle of the room. After dropping the table top to the floor, he felt the hot smoke and air rush past him toward the wall.

"Holy cow, what was that?"

When he shined his light at the wall, he saw a two-by-three foot opening in the wall. Whatever was in there was drawing the air, and the rats, out of the cellar.

"Hot damn! Come on!"

He grabbed Rosie and laid her semi-conscious body by the opening, crawled through, then dragged her in with him. He dragged the steamer trunk in after them to block the opening. It barely fit into the hole, blocking the smoke.

The air was cool and fairly fresh inside the cavern, at least fresher and cooler than what they'd just left in the cellar. Scott turned his light on Rosie so he could assess her condition. She was semi-conscious, unresponsive to verbal stimuli, but breathing okay. Her heart rate was fast, but in the acceptable range and her color was pretty good. Considering she was quite old and had suffered a nasty dose of smoke inhalation, she was doing great.

There were a variety of noises in their new little haven, the rustle of tiny feet, along with squeaky, peeping sounds. The most noticeable noise, however, was the sound of running water.

"Water? Is there water down here, Rosie?"

She didn't answer. Scott turned and moved the light slowly around the small enclosure. The squeaking noises were just what he figured they'd be — rats. A lot of rats. They were sitting all around the walls on the floor, and up near the five foot ceiling on a small ledge. Scott didn't have any history of rat phobia, but then again, he'd never been confronted with a situation quite like this one.

"Oh, this is another fine mess you've gotten yourself into, Scotty," he grumbled to himself. "It looks like Willard, Ben and their extended family. That's nice." He noticed some movement along the ceiling and shined his light to see what it was. "Spiders, Rosie. Isn't this great? Rats and spiders. Maybe we can find a few snakes, or maybe a scorpion or two, just to make it complete. Now, I'm getting the willies. I think I'd rather face the fire than all these creepy-crawly things."

Rosie stirred some, pulling Scott from his creature trauma. He took a deep breath and exhaled slowly, hoping to relax a bit. It didn't help much.

"Okay. Let's figure this out now," he said, scanning the area with his flashlight. "I'm still trapped in a small, concrete cave with an unconscious, invalid golden-ager and a conflagration raging all around, trying its best to destroy us. We have a regiment of rats and a battalion of pretty nasty looking spiders sharing our crowded little sanctuary, and a fair amount of water is running somewhere nearby."

He glanced over at Rosie. "You know, it's probably going to flood us out any minute. Won't that be splendid? Just enough space to keep our heads above water while a thousand rats and a billion spiders fight for the right to use both our heads for life preservers."

Rosie groaned and tried to sit up. Scott helped her to sit, turning her so she could lean against the wall.

"How are you feeling?"

She brushed her silver hair back from her forehead. "I feel like I've been through a terrible fire, then dragged down a shaft and stuffed into a hole somewhere deep inside the earth. How about you?"

Scott laughed. "You're awfully sharp for someone who's been through all that. Wait'll you see what we've got now." He shined the light on the rats and spiders, then back on Rosie.

"I must admit, Prince, you really know how to woo a girl once you start sparkin' her. I don't remember ever havin' such an exciting time with a boy."

"I try hard." He paused briefly, then added, "There's running water somewhere here. Do you recall anything about running water?"

She thought about it for a moment. "I do. I remember the menfolk talking about a stream runnin' under the house. Or maybe it was a spring, I'm not sure. Anyway, I think that's where we pump our water from."

"Do you know where it goes? The stream, I mean."

"Nope. No idea, 'cept if it's a stream, I'd figure it eventually ends up in the river or the lake."

Scott twisted the mag light to get a solid, straight beam and turned on his knees. He shined the bright beam toward the sound of water, then crawled that direction. Rats moved slowly out of his path, the ones on the ledge staring right at him with their beady little black eyes. Every few seconds, spiders would drop in front of, or on him.

He brushed a big, skinny spider from the back of his left hand and thought, *I could have gone the rest of my life without this experience. When I get back, I think I'll destroy Brian's time machine.*

The beam of light suddenly stretched out in front of him, extending down into a chasm of some sort. He scrambled over and leaned down into it, shining the light onto a moving stream of water. The tunnel it traveled through was large enough to float a small boat, if he had one. If he had one, they could float out of there. His thoughts went into high gear, trying to figure out what to do. He scooted back up out of the chasm, thinking ... thinking.

The steamer trunk. The steamer trunk.

"The steamer trunk, Rosie!"

"What?"

"The steamer trunk. The stream. There's a tunnel."

"What are you trying to say, Prince?"

"We may have a way out of here. I think we can float out on the steamer trunk. Of course, I have no idea where we might float *to*, but that's beside the point."

He helped Rosie to slide across and hang her legs over the edge, dangling just above the water. When he pulled the trunk through the hole, the other end was on fire, so he swung it around and doused it in the stream. Fire and smoke belched through the opening and into their cave, nearly reaching clear across it.

"Wow, talk about the nick of time," Scott said.

"Excuse me?"

"Oh, sorry. Just talking to myself."

Scott leaned down and positioned the trunk under Rosie's legs, but found there was no way to lift her down and hold the trunk in place in the moving water. He jumped into the stream, the water rising over his waist. Grabbing Rosie's legs, he pulled her off the edge, landing her just right, straddling the trunk.

He tried pulling himself up on the ledge, but was chased back by the raging fire, blowing through the small cave like a blowtorch. He dropped into the water and grabbed onto the back of the steamer trunk.

"Hold on, Rosie, we're outta here."

"I like your style, Prince."

* * *

As Leonard guided the horse and wagon around the obstacles on the burning bridge, he told the Bagley family, "Hold on tight, everybody, we're almost there."

"Where are we going when we get to the other side, Leonard?" Mr. Bagley yelled to him.

"I figure we can go upriver a ways to an old fishin' spot of mine, sir. There's a good place to set up a camp and the fire probably won't get to us there."

"How do you know that?"

"I don't know, Mr. Bagley. But it's worth tryin' for."

Leonard guided the horse off the bridge onto a dirt trail along the river, finally pulling up in a clearing of trees.

"This is it," Leonard announced. "We should probably start setting up some cooking and sleeping quarters. After that, I'll teach you folks how to catch a mess of catfish."

Grandpa Bagley climbed down from the wagon and stood by the river, looking upstream.

James walked over and stood by him. "What are you looking for, Grandpa?"

"I'm expecting your grandma to come along any minute now."

"Grandpa," James said softly. "Grandma isn't coming. She didn't make it out of the house."

"Rosie's a trooper, son. There isn't an enemy alive that can keep her prisoner. I expect she'll find a way to escape."

James patted his grandfather on the shoulder and swallowed. "Okay Grandpa. You watch for her while we set up the new headquarters camp."

The Bagley family went about setting up a new residence on the east bank of the Chicago river while Grandpa stood his vigil like a sentry.

A little while later, Grandpa shattered the calm, yelling, "There she is! I knew she could do it!"

Everyone ran to the bank to see what craziness he was up to this time.

Pointing up the river, he said, "See that? She's even found a union soldier to help her out."

Leonard strained his eyes to see what was floating toward them on the river. When it got close enough, he jumped into the river and swam to it, grabbing on and pushing it to the shore.

"Grandma!" James yelled out.

Scott sat straddling the steamer trunk with Grandma Bagley slumped back against him, asleep. Leonard pushed the trunk against the shore and climbed out of the water, extending his hand to Scott.

"Mr. Scott ... how?" Leonard was at a loss for words.

Scott shrugged his shoulders. "It's a long story," Scott said while they lifted the old woman onto the bank.

They carried her up to the camp and sat her in the one chair they had saved from the fire.

Scott shook her. "How are you doing, Rosie?"

She looked up at him and reached out, tenderly touching his cheek. "I'm doing good, Prince. Thanks to you, I'm just fine."

She looked around at her family and her husband took her by the hand. He looked at Scott, appearing almost lucid, but quickly dispelled that thought.

"I'll see that you get a commendation for this, Corporal."

Scott smiled. "Thank you, Sir." He took out his watch and saw it was nearly three-thirty. "I have to get on my white horse and ride now, Rosie. It's been a lot of fun." He looked at Leonard and added, "Thanks for having me, Leonard. Good luck to you." Then he turned and headed downriver.

Rosie waved and called after him. "Thank you, Prince. I hope you complete your quest."

* * *

Scott walked along the bank of the Chicago river and saw a boy about fourteen shuttling people across the river in a small rowboat. The history books told of resourceful children performing services to make a few dollars during and after the fire. Scott stopped to watch, but the boy with a dirty face and hands called out to him.

"Hey mister, do you need a ride across the river?"

Scott looked over and saw the boy rowing toward him. He stood on the riverbank and waved him in.

"I could use one. What do you charge?"

"Nothin' for you," the boy said, showing a friendly smile.

"How come?"

"Everybody else is tryin' to get to this side, now. If you want to go across, hop in and help me row. I got payin' customers on the other side of the river."

Scott pulled the bow of the boat against the shore and put one foot in, then pushed off with the other, propelling the boat out into the river toward the west side.

"Here, I'll do that," he said as he sat down and took the oars from the boy and began to row the small boat. "Take a break for a few minutes."

As they crossed the river, Scott saw the riggings of many ships upriver. Some were smoldering and others burned brightly. He saw people running across a bridge that was burning freely. The boat neared the other shore and people crowded to be first in line to get into the small craft on its arrival.

"What do you charge for the ride across?"

"I been askin' a dollar a ride, but a couple of people paid more cuz they was grateful."

When the boat touched the other riverbank, a nattily dressed gentleman shoved some money into Scott's hand and climbed in around him, sitting down on a seat.

"Get me out of here!" the man growled. "That's a lot of money there, son." He was interrupted by the young boat owner.

"You crowded those other people outta the way, mister. That lady with the kids was next in line, so I'll take them next. You can go when it's your turn."

Scott unfolded the wadded up bill and examined it. "This is a hundred dollar bill," he said, holding it out to the boy.

"You're darn right that's a hundred," the man said smugly. "Now get this thing going before I have to row it myself!"

The boy looked carefully at the largest bill he had ever seen and responded in kind to the man's rudeness. "You'll get outta my boat and you'll get out now!" he ordered as he stuffed the hundred into the man's front jacket pocket. "I charge a dollar a head to the next in line and that mom and kids was next in line!"

The man pulled the bill out of his pocket and waved it at the boy. "Are you daft? Do you know how much money this is?"

"I may be daft, but I'm fair. Now get outta my boat!"

The man stood up in the boat and stared down menacingly at the boy, who stared right back. Then the man reached for the boy and Scott reached for him, causing the small boat to rock and throw the man headlong into the water of the Chicago river. The hundred dollar bill fluttered from his hand and Scott caught it in mid-air. He handed it to the boy as they watched the rude man float away. The crowd of people on the riverbank cheered as he was swept out into the middle of the river and deposited against the other shore, nearly a quarter mile downstream.

"Looks like you earned yourself a hundred bucks, my man," Scott said. "He wanted to get across and, well, see for yourself."

The boy looked down river at the man, then back at Scott. "I guess you're right. Thanks, mister."

Scott climbed out of the boat and helped the young mother and her three children in. Just before pushing the boat back out into the channel, he reached into his pocket and took out his Old Timer pocket knife. He tossed it to the boy. "Thanks kid. You're a good businessman."

The boy grinned widely and waved.

Scott left the river and ran all the way back to the McLean farm, stopping outside the barn to watch the colossal clouds of smoke continue to fill the sky above Chicago, happy to be there, yet happy to be going home soon. He missed his family.

Just before 1800 hours, he removed his black duffel from his shoulder and squeezed between the two barn doors, entering the stifling heat of the musty old barn. He climbed into the waiting ship, and with a brilliant flash, the time machine jumped into the space-time continuum from 1871 and traveled home.

* * *

Brian paced around the shop wringing his hands, ran them through his hair, then took off his John Lennon glasses. He cleaned the glasses on his shirt, put them back on and continued pacing. He'd been pacing in the shop for two hours, willing the clock to move faster. Jo opened the door from the kitchen and called him in to eat something, since her mother was feeding Casey anyway.

"I don't think I could eat, Jo. Not now."

She stepped down into the shop and went to her husband, putting her arms around him. "Okay, but isn't there something else we can do? Other than pacing the floor, I mean."

"I don't know what else to do. He's due back in fifteen minutes and we promised Patty we'd drive him to the hospital just as soon as he gets here."

"I'll wait with you then." Jo sat down on the doorstep. "You shouldn't be alone when you tell him—" Her voice broke as she started crying softly.

Brian sat down beside his wife and put his arm around her shoulders, pulling her gently to him. "Thanks," he whispered. "I think we can both use the moral support."

The couple sat together on the step and waited for the ship to return from Chicago. When the time arrived, a small, gray cloud appeared in the air above the empty shop area. It grew larger, flashed open a doughnut hole and deposited the time machine right where it was supposed to be. They heard the latch unlock and watched as a hand pushed the hatch open. When Scott stood up through the opening and saw his two friends standing near the ship, he knew immediately that something was terribly wrong.

"What's happened?" Scott said when he saw the ashen appearance of Jo and Brian. Climbing out of the ship, he stood facing them. "What is it?"

Brian tried to tell him, but hesitated and stopped, prompting Jo to take over.

"Scott," she said slowly. "There's been an accident. It's Missy. She's been hurt in an explosion at the cleaners. Patty's with her at the hospital."

Jo couldn't continue. She turned to Brian and buried her head against his chest. Scott stood and stared blankly, all the color draining from his face. Brian had to finish for her.

"Scott, it's serious. I told Patty I'd drive you to the hospital the minute you arrived, so let's go."

"I don't understand," Scott said. "Tell me what happened. Bri?" He looked at Jo. "Joellen?"

Brian took his arm and led him to the Volvo. "I'll tell you on the way, now get in the car."

He helped Scott into the back and got in to sit in the passenger seat, asking Jo to drive. Jo got in and eased the car out of the garage, then backed out of the driveway. They drove to Children's Hospital, leaving Casey at the house with Jo's mother. On the way, Brian turned around in the seat to talk to Scott, who was sitting in quiet shock, waiting for an explanation.

"Patty and Melissa were at the cleaners this morning when a boiler exploded. Missy was playing in the back. You know that place where she plays, back by the boilers. It took the firefighters about half an hour to dig her out of the pile of broken concrete and she hasn't regained consciousness since it happened."

Brian knew how bad it really was, but he didn't have the heart to be the one to tell Scott that his little girl was going to die.

"Broken concrete? An explosion buried my daughter in a pile of broken concrete?"

He put his hand to his forehead and held it there, gazing in anguish at Brian, the similitude too much to comprehend. He felt like he'd been kicked in the stomach, his heart bounding in his chest. He couldn't catch his breath as his mind jumped back and forth between the vivid memories of his father's death and the present.

"This can't possibly be happening," he moaned. "Not again. Not to my little girl, too."

Moments later, they arrived at Children's Hospital and Jo dropped them off right at the front doors. "I'll meet you upstairs," she called after them as she drove out to find a place to park the car.

Scott and Brian got off the elevator on the fifth floor and entered the Pediatric Intensive Care Unit. Across the unit, Patty sat next to the bed holding a tiny hand in hers. Scott could see only a small form with a lot of wires and tubes running to it. He walked numbly through the PICU to Patty's side and put his hand on her shoulder. She looked up at him from puffy, tear reddened eyes.

FIRES OF TIME * 445

Scott saw in those eyes that the situation was far more serious than he'd imagined. He knelt down and put his arms around his wife and looked at his little daughter. Her blackened, "raccoon's eyes" were swollen shut, a ventilator breathing for her. Scott began to cry as he laid his head in Patty's lap.

"I ... we'll ... be out in the waiting room," Brian said in a low voice as he turned and went back to wait for Jo, tears streaming down his face.

He and Jo were the godparents of the McLean children and loved those kids as if they were their own. They were present at the births of both Melissa and Casey and had shared in every part of their lives. Jo stepped into the lounge and ran to Brian, falling into his arms, mourning for the family in the other room.

Patty sat in the chair beside the bed holding onto her baby with her right hand, stroking her husband's singed and dirty hair with her left.

"Scott," she said matter-of-factly. "Missy's gone. They've got her on life support until they can talk to both of us together." Scott raised his head slowly and looked gravely at his wife. "They want to know if we'll allow Missy to be an organ donor," she added, her eyes blank.

Scott felt the ducts in his eyes break loose and unleash a blinding flood of tears down his cheeks to drip into his wife's lap. His throat was so thick he could hardly breathe and he started to say something, but his voice simply wouldn't work.

He looked again at his baby's little arms and imagined them around his neck, trying to squeeze the life out of him. Suddenly, clear as a bell, he heard her little voice say in his mind, *"I luzyou, Daddy."*

Still looking at her lifeless little body, he broke completely and sobbed into Patty's lap.

"Excuse me," a voice said from behind. "I'm sorry to bother you."

Scott turned and saw a man's legs standing just inside the room. When he looked up, the man spoke again.

"You must be Mr. McLean. I'm Dr. Collingwood. I've talked with your wife." Scott stood and shook the doctor's hand as he continued. "I know this is very difficult for you. Did your wife talk with you about organ donation? It seems cruel, I know, to come to you now, but time is of the essence. We must move quickly, if—"

Scott raised his hand to silence the doctor and turned to Patty with questioning eyes. They had discussed this subject in the past, but in connection with each other, not the children. They were in agreement about organ donation and fully aware that donating their own healthy organs could save the lives of many people. But the children's healthy organs? He managed to get a few words out.

"Do you feel the same?"

She nodded her head, saying very quietly, but resolutely, "Even more so if Missy can help another child."

Scott turned his tear streaked face to the doctor. "Yes, Doctor. Can we stay here with our daughter for a little while longer?"

"Take as long as you need." He turned to leave the room, then stopped and said, "We'll need you to sign some forms before you go."

Scott nodded to him as he turned back to his wife and daughter. The doctor added, "I'll leave the forms on the nurse's station desk. Thank you." He

FIRES OF TIME * 447

exited the room, leaving Scott and Patty to spend their last few moments with their baby.

* * *

Riding in the back seat of Jo Daniels' Volvo on the way home, Scott's grief was more than he could bear. He tried to formulate his thoughts into one steady pattern to think straight and clear for just a little while, but the thoughts kept swimming, merging in, out, around in his head like hundreds of cars on a freeway interchange.

If I'd only been here to watch her. Patty wouldn't have had to take her to the cleaners with her. No, no. She would have taken her anyway because she always takes her. Missy loves to go with her mommy and play in the big room with the boilers ... loved ... to go with her mommy.

Through tear filled eyes, he looked out the window at other people enjoying their late afternoon. The whole world looked dull and gray, like the way Russia always looks when shown on the news. He couldn't turn off the thoughts.

I remember when we put the old carpet back in that room. And the little television with the built in VCR. Missy's tellbishun. *She was so excited to be able to play in there and sit in her big girl recliner to watch her Pooh Bear videos. Why did she love Pooh Bear so much? He's a wimpy, geeky guy that doesn't even know how to spell honey. Tigger's pretty cool, though. We must have watched "The Blustery Day" fifty times. Owl's house blowing down and Eeyore finding him a new one ... that turns out to be Piglet's. And Piglet, what's up with him, or her — or what ever he is — a shrink could have a heyday with that bundle of insecurities. Missy never gets tired of watching those videos. Oh, man ... this can't be happening.*

Scott turned to look at Patty. She was staring back at him, going through the same thought processes. He put his arm around her and pulled her close, burying his face in her hair.

Holding onto his wife like a life preserver, Scott's thoughts started coming together and he began to hatch a plan. What he wasn't aware of, was that Patty had already hatched a pretty darn good plan of her own. She had a head start of several hours on Scott and, although her heart was breaking, her resolve was growing stronger by the minute.

* * *

As they got out of the Volvo in the Daniels' garage, Jo asked what they could do to help. In response, Patty asked if they would be willing to take Casey for the evening. Maybe take him to a movie or something to keep him occupied.

Brian answered for them. "Of course, we'll take him out to do anything he wants. It'll probably be good for us, too."

"Right," Joellen added. "We were going to take him out one day this week anyway, remember? For his birthday Saturday?"

Patty nodded slowly.

"Now, is there anything else we can help with?" Jo asked. "You know we're here for you."

Scott answered. "That goes without saying. Just knowing Casey's safe with you guys will take away a lot of worry."

"Casey will be just fine with us, okay? He fell asleep in front of the television earlier, so Brian carried him in and put him on the guest bed. My mom came over and fixed him a late lunch, and she's staying with him until we get back. He'll be fine."

"Thanks, you guys," Patty said as she and Scott walked slowly toward their home.

Inside the house, Patty and Scott separated, wandering aimlessly through their empty home. Scott went upstairs and Patty went to the laundry room to occupy herself by folding some clothes. The first thing she picked up was Missy's little Mickey Mouse shirt. It really had Minnie Mouse on the front, but Missy called all the mouse characters Mickey Mouse.

Patty couldn't continue folding the clothes. She put the shirt to her face and smelled it as she left the laundry room. When she walked into Missy's bedroom, Scott was already there, sitting on his knees on the floor holding one of Melissa's favorite books, *The Ear Book*. When he opened the jacket, tears streamed off of his chin and dripped all over the book.

Starting on the first page, he began to read, "TICK, TOCK, TICK, TOCK ... EARS, OUR EARS ... THEY HEAR A CLOCK." He looked up at Patty and said, "Pretty basic stuff, isn't it? I wonder why she likes this book so much."

Patty knelt down in front of him. "It isn't just the book. It's her daddy reading it to her that makes it so special."

"Don't you read it to her, too?"

"Not much. She has her mommy favorites that she has me read to her, and she has her daddy favorites. That's one of them ... that was one of them." They heard a door slam, then Casey yelled out that he was home.

"Has anyone talked with him yet?"

"He doesn't know a thing and I'd like to keep it that way for a little while. Do you mind?"

Scott shook his head. "No, it's a good idea."

They got up and went into their bathroom to wash their faces so Casey wouldn't see they'd been crying, then Patty went downstairs.

"Can I go with Brian and Jo, Mom? They want to take me out for my birthday." He was excited because he loved to go places with them.

"That's fine, Case," Patty said. "Have fun and be careful."

It took only a few minutes for him to get ready. He started out the back door, then stopped and called back. "Mom, why isn't Missy going?"

Patty swallowed the lump in her throat. "They just wanted to take you this time, Case. You know, for your birthday. See you later. Be careful."

"Bye."

After Casey left, Scott went down to the living room where Patty was on the sofa gazing out the front window. He sat beside her.

"Are you thinking what I'm thinking?"

"I hope so," she said. "If what you're thinking is to go for a ride in that machine of Brian's."

"That's it. Do you want to go along in the ship?"

"I have to, Scott."

Scott perked up slightly. "I know."

"I have some questions for you. Has Brian taught you how to do everything? I mean, to operate the ship. Everything that has to be done. Did that make any sense?"

"I understood what you meant, and yes, I know how to operate the ship. Well enough to get us where we need to go and back again."

"What do you think? Do we dare do it? Do you think it would be a waste of time?"

"Doing nothing would be a waste of time. I don't know if it'll work, but I'd try anything if I thought there was even a glimmer of hope."

"But remember what happened with the little boy? What he went through again. And then it still didn't work."

"I remember." He took her face in both hands and continued. "This is our little girl. Maybe it won't work. Maybe we'll regret it for the rest of our lives, but you said it already. We have to try, so let's get moving."

They put their heads together and started working out the plans for their trip back to the morning of that very day ... to embark on a seemingly futile rescue mission.

* * *

A little later, Patricia and Scott watched from their living room window as Brian and Joellen backed their silver Volvo out of the driveway with Casey strapped into the back seat. They watched until long after the car was out of sight, then turned and held each other for a while longer. Relaxing their hold and sitting slightly back, the two parents looked into one another's eyes with a common, fixed resolve.

"Are you ready?"

"As I'll ever be," Scott said. "Let's do it!"

Twenty minutes later, they left the house through the kitchen and stole over to the door in the rear of Brian's shop. After entering, they pulled the door tightly shut behind them. Inside the shop, Scott went directly to the base computer and Patty hurried to the time machine. She climbed up on the platform and opened the hatch, then reached inside and put Scott's duffel and the cell phone on one of the seats. Stepping back down, she went over to the computer and handed Scott a slip of paper containing times and addresses. Scott was just hanging up the phone from talking with a fire department dispatcher.

He explained. "That was dispatch. They said the time out was 0905 this morning, so I would suppose the explosion was within two or three minutes of that. About two minutes after nine?"

"Sounds fine. I looked up the address of the church behind the cleaners. It's on the paper."

"Okay," Scott said. "We set the ship down in the back of the church parking lot behind the fenced in dumpster. Most of the lot is surrounded by high shrubbery, so we should be pretty well hidden."

Scott pulled up the computer map and narrowed the coordinates down to the address Patty had written on the paper. He made a slight adjustment of a few seconds toward the rear, the same way he'd seen Brian do it.

"I hope that's the right amount of adjustment," he said.

"How do you pinpoint the location so closely?"

"Well, to be completely honest with you, I'm not exactly sure how it works. All I know is that the computer shows a lat and long reading." He pointed to the numbers that read so many degrees, minutes, and seconds to the north, with the same kind of numbers for the west. "Brian told me he picks exact spots by first choosing the location. He then moves one second per 100 yards in whatever direction he needs it to go. That's what I've done, and I really hope I've done it right or we could be in a world of hurt."

"You mean if we land in the middle of a busy street or somewhere like that?"

"Yeah, exactly. Or how 'bout right in front of the bay doors on '3's' which is just down from the church."

"Fire station three is that close?"

"Haven't you ever noticed that you can look out the rear window of the cleaners and see the back of the station?"

"I guess I never realized it was that close, since you've never been stationed there. How come? Why haven't you ever been stationed there?"

"It isn't a paramedic station, so I've only worked there a few times to fill in as engineer or firefighter." Turning back to the computer, Scott said, "How much time did we decide we were going to need?"

"Half an hour. Do you really think that'll be long enough?"

"It should be. We just need to be there long enough to make sure you get out of the building with Missy before the boiler blows. Then we have to get out of there before the fire department arrives and discovers us in our time machine." Scott paused briefly, then said, "I didn't hear anyone say if there were other injuries. Were there?"

With a somber frown, Patty nodded. "Two customers were injured, and Mrs. Jelesnik was killed."

Scott was taken aback. It took just a minute to catch his breath. "You'll need to warn those people out of the store, too. Okay?"

Patty nodded and agreed. "Good idea."

"What about Mel? Is he okay? Was he even there at the time?"

"I heard the firefighters talking about the old guy caught under his workbench in the back. One of them said he didn't have a scratch, but he was really pissed off about being trapped."

"Sounds like Mel. All right," Scott said briskly. "Five after nine was the dispatch time, so we need to leave there by nine o'clock straight up to be safe." He turned and looked at Patty. "Are you good with that?"

"I am. So do we want to get there at eight-thirty, then? To give us half an hour?"

Scott nodded. "Uh-huh. And we'll arrive back here in real time — thirty minutes."

After entering all of the times and coordinates, they studied the computer screen, double and triple checking all of the numbers for accuracy before entering them into the computer.

After entering the numbers, Scott turned to Patty, put his arms around her and kissed her. "All we do now is get in the ship and fly."

"I'm ready."

The McLeans climbed onto the platform, then one at a time and with Patty going first they entered the time machine and sat on the seats facing each other. They fastened their seat belts and Scott reached down and turned the keys.

Looking up at his wife before pushing the enter key, he said, "You ready?"

FIRES OF TIME * 455

She nodded and gave him a thumbs up, so he pushed the enter key on the onboard computer keyboard. The ship started up and went through the build-up sequence. Then, with its usual brilliant flash, it was gone.

* * *

The time machine settled down in the exact location Scott had planned, but something wasn't right. The sound it made just before landing was different than on any of the other trips he'd made. It sounded sluggish and lacked the crisp, high tech precision sound it usually made on arrival.

"Something's wrong."

"What do you mean?"

"I don't know. It just didn't sound right."

Patty's attention was drawn to the floor beneath Scott's seat. She pointed. "What are those flashing lights?"

Scott undid his seat belt and leaned down to get a close look at the computer. "I don't know. Brian never told me about any flashing lights." Looking closer, he saw two blinking red lights and the computer screen was flashing a message.

WARNING: LOW BATTERY — CHARGE BATTERY

A second message flashed right below the first.

WARNING: COMPRESSED AIR SUPPLY EMPTY — REFILL BOTTLE

"Oh, man!" Scott said, sitting back up in the seat. "Brian didn't get a chance to change the battery or the air bottle after I returned from the Chicago trip. How could I have been so stupid?"

"What does it mean?"

"It means we're stuck here if we don't get the battery changed and the air bottle filled." He thought for a minute. "I can change the battery with the spare from under your seat, but we don't have a spare air bottle." He reached up, unlocked and opened the hatch, then stood to take a look around. "Well, at least we landed in the right spot. Brian would be proud of my shot ... right up until he killed me." He sat back down and looked over at his wife. "I wonder what else I didn't think about before we left. We have to figure this out or we're gonna be caught here by the fire and police departments."

"Okay, just tell me what to do and I'll do it."

Scott leaned forward and extended his forearms with his palms facing down. "Okay, gotta think clearly here. Gotta figure this out."

After a pause, he jolted up straight. "Hold it! First things first! We have our little girl to save and that's the most important thing. We'll take care of that and then worry about the other problem. I can always call Brian for help if all else fails."

"But Brian's gone with Jo and Casey."

"Not until tonight, dear. This is this morning, remember?"

"It's all very confusing," she said, shaking her head. "But we still can't be caught here by anybody."

"Here's what we'll do." He glanced at the computer clock and checked his watch. "It is now 8:33, leaving us twenty-seven minutes. What time did you arrive at the store?"

"I should be getting there right about now."

And she was. As they looked on, Patty parked the Dodge Caravan in the parking lot next to the dry cleaning store and shut off the engine. She got out,

FIRES OF TIME * 457

went around to the sliding side door and opened it. Reaching in, she undid the belts on Melissa's car seat and allowed the little girl to climb out on her own. She picked up the new receipt books and the employee paychecks from the rear seat and closed the door on the minivan.

Missy was standing by the side door of the building reaching up to pull it open. When Patty opened the door and let Missy into the building, Mrs. Jelesnik was already there, having opened the business at seven o'clock.

"Hi, Mrs. Deewezik," Missy yelled as she ran to the elderly store manager.

"Missy," she said. "How's my favorite little girl in the whole wide world?" She picked Missy up and received a wonderful 3-year-old hug. "Are you going to play here with me today?"

"Uh-huh. I'm gonna watch Pooh Bear."

"Oh good, dear," she said as she put the child down. "I'm glad you're here."

"Good morning, Mrs. Jelesnik," Patty said as she set her armload of paper down on the counter. "I brought some new receipt books and the paychecks."

"Hi Patty," she said while she watched Missy run off to her playroom. "That's great, we were almost completely out of receipts. Are you staying for a while?"

Patty went back and checked on Missy, who was plugging a video into the VCR. When she returned she replied, "I wanted to go over last months paperwork, so I'll be here for a couple of hours, I guess."

"Oh, good." Mrs. Jelesnik smiled her grandmotherly smile. "I just love to watch that little girl play. She is the sweetest little thing I ever saw."

Patty smiled at her and glanced in at Missy. Looking back at Mrs. Jelesnik, she said proudly, "I think so, too."

A customer walked through the door and the manager went to help her, so Patty started taking items from a filing cabinet. Meanwhile, Missy was sitting on her little chair in front of her TV, fully engrossed in watching Tigger bounce around on his tail and sing his song about the wonderful thing about Tiggers.

* * *

Scott stood on the platform of the ship and leaned in so Patty could hand the motorcycle battery up to him.

"Grab my bag and come on out. I need the crescent wrench from it." He was lying on the ground under the ship when Patty handed him the wrench.

"Do you always carry wrenches in your fire department bag?" she said as she looked through the bag.

"No, I don't. I threw some extra things in there before we left because I had plans to maybe shut down the boiler while we were here. I guess there won't be time for that now. I should have thought it out better and suggested we come about an hour earlier. I just wasn't thinking clearly."

He put the old battery on the ground and grabbed the new one, then placed it in the tray and tightened it down. He put on the cables and tightened them, then undid the hose from the air tank. After scooting out from under the ship dragging the empty bottle, he sat up on the asphalt with his arms around his bent legs.

The quiet of the morning was suddenly shattered by the sound of air horns and sirens. They looked over across the vacant field and saw station three leaving on a call. Scott looked at his watch.

"Hmm, that's a full station response, engine, truck and EMT ambulance, but it's only 8:39. Did I miss something? Didn't station three respond on the explosion?"

"I don't know, Scott. I was frantic at the time, so I really don't remember who was here, other than Jeff and Tom." Patty stood and watched the emergency vehicles disappear into the distance.

"I've got it!" Scott yelled out, startling Patty. "Man, I'm just not thinking straight. This is a Survivair tank, the same as our SCBA tanks. I can just run over and trade it for an air bottle from the station."

He dropped his crescent wrench and the empty air bottle on the platform, and started to run through the gate to the vacant lot, but then stopped and came back.

"I'd better call you first. Where's the cell phone?"

Patty was already reaching for the phone down in the cockpit. She pulled herself back up from the hatch and handed the phone to Scott.

"What are you going to tell me?"

"Sorry about the lie, but it's for a good cause." He looked at his watch, seeing that he had eighteen minutes left, and dialed the number for the cleaners. Patty answered.

"Jelesnik Cleaners, Patty speaking, may I help you?"

"Hi, babe," he said, trying to sound cool. "Are you busy?"

"Scott? Is that you?"

"Yeah, I came back from the Chicago trip a little early and had to run to the station real quick. My truck broke down and I need a ride right away. Can you break free to come and get me?"

"Sure, I could probably leave Missy here with Mrs. Jelesnik for a few minutes. Where are you?"

"I'm at Sixtieth and Adams. And Patty?"

"Yes."

"Will you bring Missy? I've been missing her and I could sure use a hug from both of you."

"Okay. I could use one, too. Be right there."

"Thanks ... and please hurry."

Patty hung up and Scott punched the end button.

"Here, take this," he said, handing the phone to Patty. "I'm going for a bottle. You watch the building. If she isn't out of there in a reasonable time, call her back and tell her the truth."

"Her?"

"Yeah, her ... you ... both of you."

Scott broke on a dead run, out through the gate and across the field. Patty turned to say something, but he was long gone.

"What about the other people?" she quietly said to herself.

As Patty watched, she saw herself exit the cleaners with Missy and open the side door on the van. She watched herself strap the little girl in her car seat, then go around to the driver's side and climb in the minivan. The "other" Patty started the minivan, backed out and drove away. Patty turned to watch for Scott, but didn't see him. She started to worry because of the time.

Turning back to look at the cleaners, she again remembered the people inside. After a moment of hesitation, she glanced over her shoulder to see if Scott was anywhere in sight. To her relief, he was already running back across the field carrying another tank under his arm.

He ran up alongside the ship and dropped immediately to the ground to begin attaching the new tank. "It's 8:53," he said. "Did you get out of there?"

Patty punched the recall button on the cell phone to call the cleaners. "Yes, I did. But the others are still in there. I'm calling them right now." She pushed send and heard the phone ringing.

"Jelesnik Cleaners—"

Patty interrupted Mrs. Jelesnik. "Mrs. Jelesnik, this is Patty. Get out of the building."

"Do what, dear?"

Patty took a deep breath and continued calmly. "Listen. Don't ask any questions, there's no time. Get out of the building, now. And get everyone else out, too."

"Why, dear?"

Patty lost it. "Drop the phone and get out of the building! Now!" she shouted at the top of her voice.

She heard the phone drop and Mrs. Jelesnik yelling at some customers as she herded them from the business. They all ran out the front door of the building.

In all the excitement, neither Scott nor Patty noticed the silver-blue minivan had pulled back up to the side of the building. They also hadn't seen Patty get out and take Missy back inside.

Scott missed a few things, too. What he didn't know was the dispatcher who gave him the information about the dispatch time for the incident screwed up. The time of 0905 Scott was given wasn't the dispatch time. It was the arrival time. The actual dispatch time was 0900. The boiler blew at 0859. Scott scooted out from under the ship at 0856.

He jumped up on the platform and picked up the empty air bottle, dropping it into the cockpit. "Come on, let's go. I'll take the bottle back to the station later."

Patty jumped up on the platform and climbed into the cockpit with Scott right on her heels. In the ship, Scott checked his watch and the computer's clock. "We made it with a couple of minutes to spare."

"Can I take one more look?"

"Good idea, I'll join you."

They stood up together and looked toward the cleaners. What they saw was horrifying.

They caught a partial glimpse of Mrs. Jelesnik standing across the street from the store front, so she appeared to be safe. But around on the side of the building, Patty's Dodge Caravan was sitting by the door with the sliding door wide open. They saw the empty car seat and no sign of either mother or daughter.

They both yelled at once, but all they got out was, "Oh, my—"

A tremendous explosion rocked the entire neighborhood, launching debris high into the air. Fragments were hurled far enough to shower the ground around the time machine. The McLeans stood with mouths agape as something flew in their direction and hit the side of the ship. Their eyes were fixed on the object as it glanced off the side of the ship and tumbled across the asphalt.

Suddenly, a loud hissing noise filled the air, but it took a few seconds for Scott to realize that the time machine was taking off for its return trip. He numbly reached over, tapped Patty's shoulder and pointed down into the cockpit. She started to sit down with Scott, but they both hesitated long enough for the dust to clear and reveal the building. The laundromat dry cleaners was leveled, and Patty's minivan was destroyed.

The flying object, Missy's video of *The Blustery Day*, lay on the blacktop with the tape still spilling from the broken plastic case.

They ducked in and closed the hatch just as the ship jumped into the continuum. The image left burning in both their minds was of Patty running frantically around the demolished building screaming Missy's name.

Chapter Eighteen

The silver Volvo pulled into the driveway of the Daniels home and Brian turned off the ignition. Jo turned around in the passenger seat and spoke to Casey.

"Hurry back," she said as he jumped from the car and ran home.

They'd gone to Wendy's for dinner and had just sat down at their table when a man walking past them stumbled. His entire tray landed in Casey's lap, covering him with ketchup and two Biggie Frostys. The manager ran right over after it happened and had the mess immediately cleaned up. He took their receipt and told them they could go home to clean up and he'd replace their entire meal when they returned. He even gave the clumsy man some new food.

Brian and Jo took Casey and hurried back home, then waited outside in their driveway while he went in to change. They only had to wait a few minutes for him to run out of the house and dive into the back seat of the car.

"Seatbelt, Case," Brian said.

Casey fastened the belt as Brian backed the car out of the driveway and turned in the direction of Wendy's to return and finish the meal they'd started. Brian had no sooner depressed the accelerator and pulled away, when a gray cloud appeared in the garage and deposited the time machine in the usual spot.

A hand pushed the hatch to its fully opened position and Scott stood up in the opening, then reached back into the ship to help Patty out of the cockpit. She climbed down from the ship and waited for Scott to get out. After closing the hatch and stepping down from the platform, Scott noticed Patty was trembling, her lips quivering.

"We weren't able to save her!" Patty paused and stared at Scott. "We were able to save Mrs. Jelesnik, but not Missy." Patty's lips quivered even more as she shouted out her diatribe against the powers of fate and destiny. "Why? Why can one person be saved and not another? I want to know!"

Scott tried to comfort her, but she pulled away and paced around the floor, raging about the unfairness of it all.

"It isn't right, you know!" she hollered as she waved her arms and preached, ranting and railing at the world. "That was my baby, for crying out loud! Mrs. Jelesnik, I love her dearly. But let's face it. She's old. She's really, really old! Do you know how old she is? She's ... I don't know, but it's *really* old. She's lived her life already. Missy just got started."

She glared at Scott. He bit his lower lip, trying to hold his emotion in check.

"Twice! We made that sweet little treasure suffer and die a second time, and for what? So old

Mrs. Jelesnik can go on living while a bunch of vultures at the hospital harvest the organs from our baby? It's not right! It's not fair!"

Patty stopped as abruptly as she'd started. With her face contorted in agony, she dropped to her knees and buried her face in her hands.

"My God!" She continued sobbing. "What have we done? What have we done?" She began talking quietly, just above a whisper. "I had so many plans for Melissa. We'll never get to do the things I planned for us. There just never seems to be enough time to do the things we want to do." Her voice trailed off and she continued to sob unyieldingly.

Scott kneeled on the floor and buried his face between her shoulder and her neck. They stayed there on the cold concrete floor for a long time before pulling themselves together enough to leave the garage and go back over to their quiet and lonely house.

* * *

Sitting on the sofa in the family room a little later, Patty asked Scott about the memories. "Why don't I have any memories of the second explosion? I mean, except for what I remember seeing from the ship."

"I don't know. Some of them don't seem to come right away. I didn't learn about some of the memories from San Francisco for days after I returned, yet I remembered some of them as soon as I stepped from the ship."

"But I know Mrs. Jelesnik lived the second time and I don't remember a thing about Missy from the second time."

"You saw Mrs. Jelesnik outside the building. Do you want to call the hospital and see if they know anything? It's worth a try to see if the outcome was changed in any way."

Patty leaned her head on his shoulder and said resignedly, "That's grasping at straws. We should probably start facing reality because Casey is going to need us to be here for him, and he's all we have now."

Scott had a sudden flash of memory, sending a shiver through his body. He remembered Susan Caufield telling him that Kathy Morgan's son, Tim, was all she had left. He had felt such deep pity for her, and at the same time grateful that it wasn't him having to deal with such heartache. Fate had reared its ugly head and dealt him and Patty nearly the same heartbreaking hand. He swallowed the salty tears running down the back of his throat.

"You're right, do you want to call or do you want me to do it?"

She sat up on the sofa and studied his face. "You call."

Scott looked up the number of the children's hospital and made the call. A voice answered. "Children's Hospital, how may I direct your call?"

"I need some patient information, please."

"The patient's name?"

"Melissa McLean."

"MacLane?"

"McLean. M-C-L-E-A-N, but it's pronounced MacLane."

"One moment please." Long pause. "I show no Melissa McLean."

"Could she have been there earlier? Would you know that?"

"I show no Melissa McLean, sir."

"Would anyone else know?"

"Sir, the admitting and records department might know, but there won't be anyone in that office until tomorrow morning."

"I'm sorry, ma'am, but do your records show if a patient was there earlier and released? Or—Or if the patient died?"

"I'm sorry, my list only shows current hospital patients. You'll have to call back tomorrow and talk to admissions. I have other callers waiting. I'm sorry, sir."

The line went dead.

Scott painfully hung up the phone and turned back to Patty.

"I'm sorry, Scott."

"So am I."

"What are we going to do? Shouldn't we be contacting the rest of the family and making arrangements or something?"

"I suppose that would be the next thing to do." He hesitated then said softly, "I'm not experienced at this sort of thing — arranging funerals for my children."

He broke down again and Patty joined him.

They held tightly to one another on the saddest evening of both their lives.

Chapter Nineteen

Casey came home at just after ten o'clock, full of stories about the evening. He told Scott about the terrible Frosty accident and having to change clothes. Going to the video store and getting to choose a video game for his birthday gift. And about going to the batting cages and hitting ten times better than Brian, and how Jo hit better than Brian, too. He asked if they could look at the journal again after he got ready for bed.

"I don't even know where it is, son," Scott said.

"If I find it, can we read it tonight, Dad?" he pleaded.

"You go and take a shower and brush your teeth and we'll see," Scott answered.

Patty was just finishing her shower. "I'm through," she called from the bathroom. "You can have the shower now."

When Scott walked out to the bedroom after showering, Patty was sitting on their bed talking with

Casey about the journal. He wanted the whole family to read it again like they had the other night. Patty looked sadly at Scott and recalled the cute things Missy did when they looked at the journal the first time. She knew Scott was wrestling with the same thoughts.

"Mom said to ask you if we can read the journal now, Dad. Can we?"

Scott hesitated for a few seconds, looking solemnly at Patty.

He finally answered. "I guess, Case. If you can find it, bring it in here."

Patty smiled at Scott. *Bravo, Dad,* she thought, knowing full well how hard it would be.

"I know where it is, Dad," Casey said brightly. "It's in Missy's room. I'll go get it."

Scott felt the pressure welling up behind his eyes again and fought it back as he tried to swallow the fullness in his throat.

"Okay, son. Go get it."

Casey ran from the room as Scott looked helplessly at his wife. "How are we going to do this?"

She reached out and touched his arm. "I don't know, but that little boy is going to need us. And we're really going to need him right back. Maybe we should tell him now."

Scott nodded slowly.

Casey ran back into the room carrying the journal. "Here it is, Dad. I told you it was in Missy's room."

He jumped up on the bed with his parents and sat between them, then opened the book to the part about Packy's steamer company.

"See here, Case," Scott said, pointing to the only drawing on the page. "Later in Packy's life, he rarely drew pictures unless there was a good reason. He had just finished his academy training and been assigned to Engine Company 5, and I guess he just had to re-create the lithograph that was on his steamer. That's the company logo from Grandpa Packy's steamer. The Chicago."

"Cool," Casey said. "The Chicago."

Scott read from the journal:

> *Well, journal. Look at us now. Twenty years old and we made it at long last. I got my assignment today to Engine 5 and I couldn't be happier. It's one of the busiest in the city and I'll get a lot of good experience there. I've waited my whole life for this day, ever since the night of the great fire that destroyed most of the city.*
>
> *I never told you this, journal, but I was nearly killed that night. When I ran into the street, a steamer came around the corner and would have run right over me if it hadn't been for the man standing on the corner who grabbed my shirt and yanked me out of the way. The funny thing is, I never found out who he was, but I always felt like I knew him for some reason. Maybe, someday, I'll find out who he is and get the chance to thank him for saving me from certain death.*

Scott stopped abruptly and stared at the page.

"What's the matter, Dad?"

Scott didn't say anything, just stared at the page and re-read it over and over to himself.

I don't get it, he thought. *That was never in there before. Packy didn't ever write about feeling like he knew the man.* He read the page again and thought, *That's new. That's a new entry in a hundred year old journal.* With all the confusion since, Scott had forgotten about rescuing Packy in the street, so the entry in the journal was very puzzling to him.

Patty tugged on his arm to bring him out of his thoughts. "Are you all right?"

He turned toward her and nodded.

"Where'd you go, hon? Are you okay?"

Scott shook his head and rubbed his eyes. "Yeah, I'm fine. It's just ... it's just that when I read that page in the journal, I didn't recognize it. In fact, I still don't remember ever seeing that part."

Patty gave his arm a squeeze. "We're both having a hard time. I understand."

"A hard time with what, Mom?"

She looked at her son and started to cry.

"What's the matter, Mom? Why are you crying?"

"It's Missy, Case," Patty said, swallowing hard.

She looked at Scott, who was looking back through glassy eyes.

"What about her, Mom?"

Scott tried to explain. "Your little sister was—"

He couldn't continue either.

"She was what, Dad?"

Thinking about Missy, Patty had a sudden thought about her room. She remembered Casey saying the journal was in Missy's room, but didn't remember seeing the journal when they were in there earlier in the day.

Wiping her eyes with Scott's shirt sleeve, she stammered, "Where was the journal, Case?"

"In Missy's room."

"Right," she said futilely to her son. "But where was it exactly? Where did you just pick it up?"

"I told you, Mom, in Missy's room. It was on her bed, honest."

Scott looked at his son. "Just now? You found it in there just now?"

Casey gave his dad a pathetic look. "Yes, Dad. Just now."

"I didn't see it in there before, Scott," Patty said.

Scott stared into her eyes and tried to smile. "I think we're losing it here. What difference does it make where the journal was? It won't change anything."

"What are you guys talking about?" Casey said. "Can we get back to reading the—"

"Hi Mommy. Hi Daddy," a small voice said from the doorway.

Patty and Scott turned and gaped at the small figure in the doorway. They must have frightened the children with their bug-eyed expressions. Their mouths hanging open in shock, their bodies unable to handle the emotional overload their heads were sending. They just sat and gawked at the beautiful little apparition standing in the doorway.

While they stared, Missy ran across the room to them. Patty grabbed her and hugged her tightly, but Scott hadn't yet recovered from the shock. He watched as Patty squealed, then jumped up and stood on the bed, still holding Missy in her arms. Casey's eyes bugged out when his mom and Missy started jumping on the bed. Scott jumped up with her, and within seconds, all four McLeans were jumping up and down on Mom and Dad's bed.

"I remember, Scott," Patty said breathlessly. "I remember the second explosion, and guess what?" She burst out in tears. "Mrs. Jelesnik took her across the street with her. I didn't know that at first, so I ran around the building in a panic trying to find her. Missy's all right, honey. Missy's all right!"

They all fell on the bed and Scott and Patty put their arms around Missy and Casey, and each other, in a family group hug. The kids laughed hysterically and the parents cried every bit as much.

After hugging for a minute or so, Missy giggled infectiously and said, "We're a sabwish Casey. A Missy and Casey sabwish."

Scott squeezed tighter and kissed his daughter on the cheek. "And this is the best sabwish I've ever tasted."

Chapter Twenty

The kids turned back to the part in the journal about the great fire and were looking at the pictures. They had already quit trying to figure out what their weird parents were talking about as Patty told Scott of her sudden memory.

"This is really eerie. I remember both seeing myself at the cleaners and being inside." Scott nodded his head knowingly. "When I went to meet you where you said you were broken down, you weren't there. So I figured you'd gotten the truck started, and I drove back to the store. When Missy and I went in the side door, no one was there, so I walked up to the front to see if Mrs. Jelesnik had gone outside. When I walked outside, she ran over to me and asked why I'd just called and told her to get out of the building. It didn't make much sense until, for some strange reason, I recalled your saying you phoned the mother of the Caufield boy from the time machine. I don't know why I thought of that, but I'm grateful I did. Mrs. Jelesnik took Missy and ran straight across the street to wait, but I didn't see her do it. And then the boiler blew up."

She paused and caught her breath. Patty smiled to herself at the sight of Scott just listening in silence while holding both their children close. A moment later she went on.

"Do you know what it felt like? It felt like I was in one of the old Twilight Zone episodes. The one where the lady has the re-occurring dream about the nurse in the morgue that says, 'There's room for one more?' And then later, when she goes to get on a plane, the stewardess is the same person as the nurse in her dream, so she runs off the plane screaming and then the plane takes off and blows up. That's what it felt like. The only bad part was that I thought I'd left Missy inside."

Scott was so moved by her story that all he could say was, "Wow."

"Look, Dad," Casey said. "Look at the pictures in the journal."

Scott looked at the journal with the children. They were on the page that told about the steamer and the Great Fire. Missy counted the pictures in the margin, "Fowuh, fife, sis ... sebben. Sebben pishers, Daddy," she said proudly, looking up at him.

"There were only six the last time," Casey remarked.

"Whaddaya mean, only six, Case?"

"I mean only *six*, Dad. Missy counted them the same way last time and there were only six."

Patty leaned in to look at the pictures. "I remember her counting six pictures too, honey."

Pointing to one of them, Missy said, "What's that pisher, Daddy?"

Scott studied the picture closely. He'd looked at the journal hundreds of times since he was a small boy, but had never seen that one. "I'm not sure, babe. I've never noticed it before."

Patty looked strangely at Scott. "What do you mean, never noticed it? First, you said you hadn't read that other part before, and now you say you've never seen this picture? You've had this entire journal memorized for twenty-five years. What's up with that?"

Casey stirred briefly. "Look, Dad. It looks like a medal or something."

The whole McLean family studied the picture. It did look like a medal, or medallion of some sort. It looked like a medallion with a Maltese cross and a large number 5 on it. Looking closer, they could see the tiny letters Packy had drawn on the top bar of the number five. They were initials, JPM ... John Patrick McLean.

"It's a ring," Patty said.

And it was. It was a drawing of the ring Packy McLean wore when he was a member of Engine Company #5. The same ring that had been handed down through five generations. The same ring Scott was wearing on his right hand at that very moment.

Patty took Scott's right hand and held it beside the picture of the ring.

"It's a picture of your *ring*, Dad. How'd that happen?"

Patty locked eyes with Scott. "How *did* that happen? He didn't have that ring until he grew up and became a firefighter, did he?"

Scott's mind flashed on the image of the little boy staring at his hand as he held him by the front of his shirt after saving his life. He smiled a pure, knowing smile. The drawing confirmed the feelings that he had met his great, great grandfather, John Patrick McLean. If only for a brief moment in time.

Looking around at his family and smiling, Scott said, "I guess I have some fessin' up to do, don't I? But not tonight, it's just about bedtime."

"It's way past," Patty said as she gave the kids her go to bed look, and then broke into a smile. "But who cares about bedtime? We can stay up late because nobody's going to school, or work, tomorrow. It's a mom and dad holiday, and there are cookies to be made right now!"

The kids started jumping on the bed again, laughing and squealing. Then Casey asked if he could help Patty make the cookies.

"Come on, Case. Let's go make the cookies," Patty said. She looked at Scott and Missy. "How about you two?"

Missy stared at her dad. "Read a story, Daddy?"

Scott nodded. "There's nothing in this whole wide world I'd rather do. Go get any book you want."

Missy ran screaming from the room and Scott glanced toward Patty. "The Ear Book?"

"Not a chance," she said with a cheesy grin. "You told her any book, didn't you? I think you're in for trouble."

"No way."

"Way, big fella. Take a look."

She pointed at the door and burst out laughing when Missy ran back into the room carrying a book. "Maybe I should call for a wrecker." She started to leave the room, but Scott stopped her.

"Look at yourself, Patty, you're all healed up."

Patty held out her arms. "I know, hon. I'll have to remember that doctor ... what was his name? Brian something? Doctor Daniels? I'm not sure, but he does great work without even knowing it."

They both laughed and she left the room, but stood just outside the door to listen for a minute.

"Fos in Sos, Daddy," Missy said as she climbed on Scott's lap.

He looked at the book and thought, *I'll bet that Seuss guy wasn't any more a doctor than I am,* then opened the book to start reading.

Patty smiled and went down to the kitchen where Casey had already put most of the chocolate chip cookie ingredients out on the counter.

* * *

A little while later, after the first batch was finished, she took some steaming hot chocolate chip cookies up to Scott and Missy, but stopped outside the door again to listen. Scott was just finishing the storybook.

"THIS is what they call ... a tweedle beetle noodle poodle bottled paddled muddled duddled fuddled wuddled fox in socks, sir! Fox in socks, our game is done, sir. Thank you for a lot of fun, sir."

Missy squealed with delight as he read the last line. Scott closed the book and laid back on the bed. Missy climbed up, sat on his stomach and pulled on his mustache, causing him to let out a big groan.

Patty stepped into the room and held out her hand for Scott to give her the book. She glanced at the final page and grinned, then without looking up said, "Now, is your tongue numb?"

He sat up on the bed and winked at her. "No, nod a bid."

Missy put her little arms around his neck and squeezed the life out of him. "I luzyou, Daddy," she said sweetly.